THE PLEDGE

ROB KEAN

Warner Books

A Warner Communications
New York, NY 10020

Visit our Web site at
www.iplublishing.com

A Time Warner Company

Printed in the United States of America

Originally published in hardcover by Warner Books.
First Paperback Printing: July 2000

10 9 8 7 6 5 4 3 2 1

WARNER BOOKS

A Time Warner Company

WARNER BOOKS EDITION

Copyright © 1999 by Rob Kean
All rights reserved. No part of this book may be reproduced in any form or by any electronic or mechanical means, including information storage and retrieval systems, without permission in writing from the publisher, except by a reviewer who may quote brief passages in a review.

Cover art and design by George Cornell

Warner Books, Inc.
1271 Avenue of the Americas
New York, NY 10020

Visit our Web site at
www.twbookmark.com

 A Time Warner Company

Printed in the United States of America

Originally published in hardcover by Warner Books.
First Paperback Printing: July 2000

10 9 8 7 6 5 4 3 2 1

There were twelve of them.

They came from all directions but shared similar black attire, senior status, and a common disdain for the college administration. They glanced at one another proudly and silently, as they followed orders and moved toward the Rock.

Where their Leader was waiting. He wore the sacred black robe and held the lantern and the Sword. The newcomers gathered around the Leader and knelt reverently to the ground. Twenty-four dedicated eyes watched him and listened.

For a moment, all was powerfully silent.

Then the Leader raised the Sword high overhead and slammed it down on the Rock.

And the poetry began . . .

THE PLEDGE

"Full of surprises and suspense. . . . I could not put the book down, reading the entire thing in one weekend."

—*Roanoke Times*

"A very good story with a tautness worthy of a veteran . . . a lot of raw talent manifested in these pages."

—*Winston-Salem Journal*

"Chilling . . . compelling . . . absorbing and enjoyable literature. . . . Kean has hit a home run on his first try at bat. . . . Start this adventure as soon as possible."

—*Rockdale Citizen* (GA)

more . . .

"Fast paced."

—*Booklist*

"THE PLEDGE deserves to be a bestseller. It's a terrific read that sparkles with originality. The suspense is unremitting. It's hard to believe that someone so young has written a first novel this good."

—**Phillip Margolin, author of**
Gone But Not Forgotten

"A suspenseful, page-turning, Grisham-like whodunit . . . combines a compelling mystery, quirky original characters, and insight into the power of fraternities . . . well plotted [and] well written . . . a very enjoyable read."

—*Brunswick Times Record* **(ME)**

"This is a goodie. . . . Think of the mafia on a downsized scale. A grand read."

—**Broox Sledge, Book World**

"A surprisingly gripping first novel . . . [with] a fast pace and snappy dialogue. . . . Kean is a good storyteller."

—*Lexington Herald-Ledger*

"Rob Kean's got all the right moves—a relentless plot, breakneck pace, and a clean style laced with just enough in-your-face attitude."

—**F. Paul Wilson, author of** ***The Keep***

Acknowledgments

Only with the love and support of some remarkable people does this book exist as it does, and it's here that I give heartfelt thanks to:

Melissa and Charlotte Jerace, for pointing me down the right road, and helping me stay on it.

Melinda Jason, for reading it when I thought no one else would, and making things happen in a manner that still blows my mind.

Larry Kennar and Marti Blumenthal of Writers and Artists Agency, for literally waking me from a two A.M. nightmare and taking me back to my dream.

Lucas Foster and Cathy Konrad, for believing in what I'd come to doubt, and infecting me with your contagious enthusiasm.

My literary agent Eric Simonoff and the crew at Janklow & Nesbit Associates, for taking a chance on an accidental businessman, and voicing reason in an otherwise insane world.

My editor Rick Horgan, for being a fellow conspirator worthy of both trust and admiration, and lending me the sheer genius of your vision.

Jody Handley, Harvey-Jane Kowal, Maureen Egen, Jamie Raab, Tina Andreadis, Heather Fain, Larry Kirshbaum, and the rest of the great folks at Warner Books, for making me feel like part of the team.

Holly Pompeo and Jeremy Segal, for showing me the link between the idealism of college and the reality of business, and helping me grant truth to this fiction.

Adam Samarel and Andy Deeble, for providing their own brand of literary water along the way, and carrying me across the finish line.

Lina Foster, for selflessly listening to my silly fears, and quietly demonstrating a true hero's courage.

The consummate professionals at Deloitte & Touche, LLP, for nurturing a misfit, and making him feel blessed and lucky on his way out the door. I'll never forget you guys.

The rest of my friends who dream by land, sea, and air, the best of whose character is showcased within these pages, and without whom I'd be nothing. You know who you are.

Betsy, for putting the apple in your big brother's eye.

Dad, for patching my wounds and sending me back on the field, no matter what the score.

And most of all, Mom, for being my harshest critic, my biggest fan, and the prevailing gust in my ever-grateful sail. This one's for you.

THE PLEDGE

BOOK I
The Players

CHAPTER ONE

The 200th Year
Sunday, February 22

6:44 A.M.

They'd killed him hours before, but he still had a few minutes to suffer.

He lay young and naked, his pale, poisoned body a wisp on the damp carpet. Midnight torture had flattened him, but now, as the morning sun shone through a bay window and off his bare ass, he stirred from his nightlong coma. He knew something was terribly wrong the moment he opened his eyes.

I'm blind, he thought, too far gone to panic.

He sorted his tangled limbs and sat up with great effort. He felt the blindfold, stiff with dried toxins and his own varied secretions.

Then, as his world spun, he remembered.

The race. The rematch. The countless fists, beating him senseless. The pitiless feet, beating him a little more.

And the timeless poetry, raining rhymes from above.

Pain and pride are inseparable twins

This is where lifelong love begins . . .

Pride, buried beneath the pain. Lifelong love, nowhere to be found. A candlelit world of knuckles and shadows and boots and confusion.

And orders.

You are the weak, and we are the strong
So march while we maim you, and sing us the song . . .

His legs and lips, marching and mumbling. His throat, gagging on a song and something wicked. His belly, throwing it all up.

You've failed us again, but you'll fail us no more.
Go hands, knees, and mouth-mop, and clean the damn floor . . .

His hands and knees set sloppy in a hideous scum.

His tongue, cleaning the damn floor.

Now, he struggled to his feet and listened to a distant voice—his, but not his—singing vague and pathetic bits of a jumbled rhyme he could normally sing in his sleep.

"Hell . . . yell . . . obey . . . no way . . . weakness . . ." Trailing off breathlessly, he flopped back to the floor. The cold sogginess of the rug reminded him he was naked.

And why.

Back on your feet, boys, it's not over yet
There's one bad-ass brother you still haven't met . . .

His fingers groped for something, anything stable, and found a smooth rung on the balcony rail that overlooked the first floor of the fraternity house. Hauling himself to his feet once again, he let his broken hand linger on the rail for balance, and with his good hand he battled the blindfold. He wrestled weakly with the knot itself, then clawed at the fabric, somehow forcing the cloth down his face until it hung loose around his neck.

Pausing a moment to catch his breath, he heard a subtle noise behind him, a sound of movement that, on mornings of reasonable clarity, might have registered as human and covert. On this morning, however, he was his own, polluted world. It didn't occur to him to gauge the proximity and aim of another.

Slowly, very slowly, he opened his eyes.

Sunlight slammed his eyeballs and knocked him backward into the leather chair beneath the hanging portrait of some famous guy. The leather was gummy and soaked— with what, he didn't know and, at this point, certainly didn't care. He'd swallowed enough of just about everything the night before; a topical dose of the unknown on his legs wouldn't kill him.

Something else would.

But like most who die suddenly and violently, he was oblivious to forthcoming disaster. He merely knew during these, the final moments of his conscious life, that the puddle in which he sat was stinging the shit out of his rug-burned thighs.

And that someday soon, it would all be worth it.

For someday soon, he'd be a brother.

But first, he'd be sick.

He leapt to his feet.

Way too quickly.

His sight blurred, then filled with strange colors, and as he vomited, he lurched against the railing. The varnished wood tackled him at thigh level, and without feeling the hands on his back, or knowing their intention, he toppled forward into space.

I'm flying, he thought, as the bottom dropped out of his world.

Fifteen feet later, he landed headfirst.

As he lay there very still, strangely pain-free and fearless, his world slowly stopped spinning, soon to stop altogether.

7:14 A.M.

Penny Ward pulled her battered Chevy into the ice-capped parking lot of the Sigma Delta Phi fraternity house and skidded on bald tires into her usual parking spot between the rear kitchen entrance and the big blue Dumpster. She applied the parking brake, gently put the engine out of its misery, then held on for dear life as it convulsed, sputtered, and died with a sigh. Exhaling a sigh of her own, she squinted at the chapel clock in the distance.

Seven fifteen. Fifteen minutes late, she observed without worry. On a Sunday morning in February, the brothers of Sigma wouldn't be awake for another three hours, at least. Until then, they'd be sleeping off the previous night's sins.

And she'd be cooking for them.

Penny was the breakfast chef; nine bucks an hour commanded her to make sure the Sigma brothers got their fill of omelettes and waffles, five mornings a week.

Sunday was one of her mornings.

She sighed again and leaned across the ripped vinyl seat to grab her handbag. As she did, she couldn't help stealing a quick glance in the cracked rearview mirror. The sight made her cringe. She needed a haircut and a dye job, big time. She also needed the body of a twenty-year-old who'd not yet borne children, but she knew better than to ask for miracles.

She was fifty, gray and a little heavy, but in one piece. She supposed she could live with that.

She looped a finger through the handle of her bag, threw her shoulder into the driver-side door, and freed herself from the car.

Her first step toward the fraternity house found nothing but sheer ice, and down she went, hard, smacking the palm of her hand against the rusted bumper as she fell.

"*Shit!*" she yelled, and immediately felt guilty. It was the Sabbath, after all.

Lying flat on her back, she examined her wound and noted that it was bleeding all over the sleeve of the white leather jacket that had cost her a full month's pay.

"*Shit again!*" This time she meant it.

Once inside, she hurled her purse onto the cutting board, then headed for the first-aid kit in the first-floor bathroom. She stomped through the spacious dining room, thumbing her wound and wishing she had weekends off like the rest of the world.

As she entered the living room, a light, jingling sound caught her attention, and she knew what it was even before she'd looked up from her gash. Dog tags. Sure enough, from behind one of the sofas jutted the black, beefy hindquarters of Geronimo, the slobbery mutt owned by one of the juniors who lived on the second floor. Penny generally liked dogs, but she had no place in her heart for this one; she spent a good deal of her daily time and energy shooing his voracious appetite from the kitchen. Judging from the dog's posture, Penny guessed that the beast was, as usual, licking something off the floor.

Something was obstructed from Penny's view.

Something undoubtedly disgusting.

Whatever it was, she had no desire to look.

But as she hustled past, something made her glance down and to the left, and when she did, she gasped.

On the floor, beneath the second-floor balcony, lay a naked, twisted body. It took Penny a moment to place the face, then a moment more to attach a name to the carnage. It was a pledge—Chad something-or-other; she knew that much. She also knew that this was far more than just a standard, drunken pass-out, and her heart began to pound. The pledge's body was bent unnaturally, and his skin was covered with some sort of black writing. A pool of blood encircled his head, and it was this puddle that Geronimo was lapping.

Penny backpedaled on weak feet that barely felt the floor beneath them. Her own wound forgotten, she wheeled and fled back toward the kitchen. She picked up the kitchen phone, whispered something Catholic, and tried to remember the number for 911.

CHAPTER TWO

The 200th Year
Sunday, February 22

7:54 A.M.

A steady diet of power and sex kept Anson J. Templeton feeling young and tyrannical, and his job as dean of Simsbury College kept him well supplied with both commodities. He was, in his own eyes, the academic world's first self-styled prick. He drank only European-blend coffee and insisted that faculty and staff refer to him as "Dean" or "Sir." Only Linda Regis, the health professor, was permitted to call him anything different. She could call him "Anson" over the phone and "Stallion" in bed; Templeton preferred the latter.

This morning, as he stood before his bathroom mirror and arranged his vanishing blond hair, he was tremendously pleased with himself, for today had all the makings of a personal holy day. He was exactly one day into his forty-eighth year, and to celebrate he'd planned a relaxing weekend excursion with Linda up to Boothbay Harbor, where a waterfront romper room had been reserved in his name. The thought of Linda's body against his own made him momentarily shiver. He loved American women. They were so fit. They were so vulgar.

He leaned over the sink and snipped some nose hairs.

A sharp knock on the bathroom door startled him, and he jammed the scissors into the freshly shaved skin between his nose and upper lip. He cursed, made a face at the mirror, then hung his head with exasperation.

"Anson? Are you *in* there?"

It was Judith, his wife. She was awake, and undoubtedly fatter than she'd been the day before.

"Anson?"

"What," snapped Templeton, as he dabbed his fresh wound with a tissue.

"Telephone."

He frowned and glanced at his Rolex: 7:57 on a Sunday morning. It couldn't be Linda; she wouldn't dare.

He tossed the tissue in the toilet and flushed it down with the ball of his bare foot. "I'm coming."

He slithered into his bathrobe, tore himself a waxy strip of dental floss, and padded to the bedroom.

The cordless phone lay on his nightstand, faceup and blinking for help; Judith had once again forgotten to return it to the charging stand the night before. He would have scolded her, but she'd already rolled over and gone back to sleep. He'd let her lie dormant, for she had a tendency to wake up horny.

Not for the first time, he considered the irony: He loved money and sex, but hated his rich, horny wife.

He carried the phone back into the bathroom and shut the door.

"Hello?"

"D-Dean Templeton?" A deep voice, thick with the Yankee inflection of a lifelong local.

"Yes?"

"G-George Bianco."

"Who?"

"C-Campus Secur-urity."

Templeton remembered now; Bianco was the hulking, stuttering, mildly retarded Simsbury security guard, who, as a pious gesture had been hired fifteen years ago and had prospered simply because Simsbury had little need for locks on its doors, let alone security.

"What can I do for you on a Sunday morning, Mr. Bianco? Some drunken troublemaker pull that pesky fire alarm again? Feel free to make a citizen's arrest when you catch the rascal."

Silence. "Um, n-no . . . We . . . w-we've had an in-incident here at the Sigma House."

"What's the trouble, George?" asked Templeton, playing casual as he fiddled with the floss. "Did they run out of their beloved Budweiser?"

Silence.

"Earth to George." He shook the floss off his finger and into the trash, picked up the comb, and once again ran it across his scalp.

"W-we've . . . w-we've . . ."

"Spit it out. You sound like a rap album."

"W-we've got a situa-ation here, Dean T-Templeton."

"I gather," said Templeton, growing impatient.

"I th-think y-you should get down here."

"George," said Templeton, as if addressing a small child. "I'm not going *anywhere* until you tell me what's going on."

A brief pause. "Th-there's b-been an accident."

Templeton froze, his senses suddenly acute. "What sort of accident?" he asked slowly.

"A b-bloody one."

The sun crept higher, highlighting the postcard polish of Simsbury College: Wintry light glinting off unruffled snowbanks. Clumps of white skewered on green pine. Ice glazed on vines of ivy. Clock towers and steeples. Statues and walkways.

And the red, rotating flash of ambulance lights, sprinkling all the spearmint splendor with a little bit of blood.

8:15 A.M.

Seated behind the lambskin wheel of his weekend car, Templeton lifted his gaze from the road to the sky as the great, white Sigma Delta Phi mansion loomed into view. He swore softly as his eyes fell back to earth. Parked on the huge, snow-covered lawn was an ambulance, its red lights spinning and blazing like obscene disco balls. Next to the ambulance squatted a Cumberland County police cruiser, its driver-side door open, revealing the heavy outline of a uniformed officer dictating the situation into a handheld radio.

Not good, thought Templeton, as he pulled into the parking lot.

It was time for some damage control.

It was time for him to earn his keep.

And play a little God.

The scene inside the Sigma House, a classically designed infrastructure that generally buzzed with boisterous bravado, was absolutely silent. Roughly two dozen bleary-eyed and bed-headed Sigma brothers lined the living room and stairwell. Most wore sleeping attire, boxer shorts and muscle tees. All eyes were fixed on the floor beneath the balcony where two emergency medical technicians and security guard George Bianco knelt over a motionless body.

Templeton made his entrance slowly, with practiced drama. He sensed the eyes of the brothers shift his way, and felt a surge of pride as some attempted a subtle retreat back up the stairs.

Power, he thought warmly, coldly. *I scare the living shit out of them.*

He knelt beside Bianco and nodded a cheerless hello, and the security guard returned the greeting with a grim head-bob. The EMTs, busy securing some mechanical doodad to the body, didn't acknowledge his arrival.

He removed his glasses and carefully clipped them to the neck of his sweater. Tilting his head analytically, he began to study the body, personally assessing the damage.

The young man's eyes were shut, his lashes peaceful. The rest of him was a violent mess.

Blood from a head gash matted the boy's hair into disheveled clumps and streaked his forehead and cheekbones, staining light blond facial hair that had not yet evolved from the peach-fuzz stage.

"How old is this lad?" Templeton murmured to no one in particular.

"He's a freshman," came the nervous reply from a voice halfway up the stairwell. "A pledge."

Templeton shook his head and continued moving his eyes down the pledge's body.

He didn't make it far.

The pledge's neck was broken. *No, not just broken. Bent.* Later, Templeton would recall that the neck of Chad Francis Ewing had looked like the sprung torso of a jack-in-the-box. He shook his head again, marveling at the degree of force necessary to shatter a human neck like that. Peering up at the balcony, fifteen feet above the living-room floor, he put the pieces together quickly and drew the only conclusion that made sense.

The pledge had fallen and landed directly on his head.

He raised his eyebrows, breathed deeply, and returned his attention to the body.

A sharp bone had pierced the skin of the left shoulder, and the wound now oozed a thin river of blood. The entire torso was smothered with plasma and grime.

Templeton leaned closer. *No, not grime. Ink.*

The pledge had been written on.

The pledge had been *vandalized.*

Phrases scrawled with Magic Marker covered a good portion of the pledge's naked skin, but Templeton had been too focused on the carnage to notice the scriptures that lay beneath the gore. Seeing them now, more every second, he held his eyeglasses to his face and read, tilting his head back and forth.

And as he read, he began to see a pattern.

Across the hairless chest:
Not yet a man, but ready to try.
Stick it all the way up and I'll try not to cry.

Across the concave stomach:
Body by breast milk, courage by Tyco.
Beat me some more, and make me a psycho.

Down one skinny leg:
Call me a weakling. Call me a dud.
But give me some credit for spilling my blood.

Poetry, thought Templeton, as he processed the markings. *Interesting.*

Several more couplets marred the pledge's flesh, each in some way touching on the themes of graphic violence and sex. And the pledge's penis had been . . . *deleted* was the only word that came to mind. Colored black from base to tip.

The cost of inclusion, guessed Templeton.

Or the mark of exclusion.

Or something darker and richer.

The EMTs finished strapping and buckling the pledge to the stretcher and prepared to lift it. Templeton turned to the nearest EMT, a brawny man with Latin features who was scribbling furiously on a clipboard. His official name tag read "De Lasa."

"Is he dead?" asked Templeton.

"Not yet," answered De Lasa, without looking up.

"What are his chances?"

"Not good."

Templeton nodded pensively. "I hope that attitude isn't a reflection on the skill with which he was treated."

De Lasa halted his pen in mid-scribble, and looked up slowly. "Who the fuck are you?"

"Th-this," sputtered Bianco, blinking wildly, "th-this is D-Dean of the C-College Anson T-Templeton."

De Lasa glared at Templeton, unimpressed by the introduction. "Look, Mr. *Dean.* This kid has a broken neck and severe head injuries. He'll be *lucky* if he dies."

Templeton nodded, stood, and pulled Bianco through the mystical streams of light emanating from three Greek letters etched on a stained-glass window, and into one of the room's many morning shadows. Placing a hand on each of the security guard's meaty arms, he took a moment to appreciate Bianco's height and width, then swallowed a sardonic grin as he was reminded of a judgment he'd formed early in life: the bigger the man, the smaller the brain.

"You can leave now, George," he whispered, looking up into vacant brown eyes. "I'll take it from here."

"Huh?"

"Go away."

"Oh. O-okay." Clumsily, Bianco turned to leave.

"Oh, George?" said Templeton, suddenly remembering.

Bianco jerked around eagerly. "Y-yes?"

"Don't misunderstand what you saw here this morning."

A look of total blankness overcame Bianco's face. "Uh, e-excuse me?"

"I said, don't *misunderstand* what you saw here this morning."

"O-okay."

"That will be all."

He gently rubbed the back of his neck as he watched Bianco lumber out the front door. *All men,* he thought with relief, *are not created equal.* Now the lone Simsbury authority figure in the Sigma House, Templeton sat on the bottom step of the stairwell and oversaw the remainder of the proceedings from an impassive distance.

While meaning and money played catch in his mind.

The Sigma brothers watched solemnly as the pledge was carried out the heavy front door, and listened with heads bowed to the retreating blare of the siren as the ambulance sped toward St. Elizabeth's Hospital.

When the sounds of crisis could no longer be heard, Dean Templeton's voice broke the silence.

"Everyone into the dining room, and shut the door. Now."

The brothers of Sigma Delta Phi filed dutifully into the dining room. Templeton locked the front and side doors and followed them in.

9:00 A.M.

During the time that Dean Templeton measured feet from floor to balcony and calculated fiscal consequences, a nationwide force slept.

And in a quiet Boston suburb a two-billion-dollar trust earned interest by the second.

CHAPTER THREE

The 200th Year
Sunday, February 22

9:45 A.M.

The heat was off in the Administration Building, so Templeton kept the collar of his thousand-dollar Italian leather jacket wrapped snugly around his neck as he sat in his office and sipped a cappuccino. Chad Ewing's personnel file lay open in front of him, the pages scattered randomly, but Templeton was done reviewing it. He now studied the ceiling, playing on the one certainty that stood clear in his mind on this dizzy morning.

Chad Ewing was going to die.

And when he did, all hell would threaten to break loose. Bad publicity. Lawsuits. Maybe even criminal charges. At the same time, Templeton knew that not *all* of the consequences from the incident had to be negative.

Not if he played the game properly.

He saw his job as a means to an end. The pay was good, the benefits excellent. The position afforded him flexible working hours, summers off, a clamshell sink in his office bathroom, and the power to make or break the young lives of which he was custodian.

He was dean of the world-renowned Simsbury College.

Enough said.

And the job was basically painless, for Simsbury's squeaky-clean students, among the brightest young men and women in the nation, according to the annual *U.S.News & World Report* survey, rarely caused trouble. Oh sure, occasionally the more liberal factions of the student body would freak out and organize a peaceful protest in support of small, furry animals, or gays and lesbians, or a woman's right to choose, or whatever else was politically correct in these hypersensitive times. Saturday-night brawls were not uncommon, and more than once Templeton had been awakened from a sound slumber to authorize an alcohol-induced stomach-pumping. A couple of years ago there'd been that Angela McSheffrey incident . . .

But most of the time, Anson Templeton's job was fret-free: in the office well after sunup, out before sundown. Extended lunches of the foodless variety with Linda. A steadily growing bank account. The best parts of the job were missing from the job description.

Templeton had married for money, for his undergraduate years at Oxford University had taught him that the most surefire way to make money was to *inherit* it. Oxford had been filled with the silver-spoon ilk, and he would have given his envious soul to wear their shoes. They walked the campus without a care in the world, knowing that after graduation they'd be set for life—job or no job. As the fourth son of a glassblower's apprentice and a blue-collar loser who had married for love and then lived in squalor, Templeton had been afforded no such comfort, which was why his number-one goal upon graduation was to wed a rich girl with a sick daddy.

He selected as his victim Judith Gilmartin. She was the lonely, lumpy daughter of Byron Gilmartin, a richer-than-Midas London entrepreneur pushing sixty. At the time, Templeton conservatively estimated that Byron—he of the tobacco-beaten lungs and double-bypassed heart—had no more than ten years left. His timely passing would leave Templeton relatively young and filthy rich.

Templeton married Judith on a resplendent spring day, then watched in horror as his father-in-law lived another eighteen years.

Worse still, during that time Byron insisted that his educated son-in-law work for a living. As an active member of Oxford University's Board of Directors, Byron created an administrative position at the college, and that was the beginning of Anson J. Templeton's career in education.

With Byron's help, he climbed the ladder swiftly. His brief stint as dean of student life led to a short foray as dean of admissions. Ten years after beginning this unwanted career, right about the time he'd expected his father-in-law to drop dead and leave behind a gold mine, Templeton was named dean of the college.

It was then that he uncovered a gold mine on his own.

Until that point, he'd viewed Oxford as an excessively hyped monument to boring books, tedious lectures, musty dormitories, undercooked food, and overrated women. He'd never bought into the glory of Oxford, never been awed by the name, nor the prestige, nor the gardener-groomed ivy. In fact, he himself had only attended the school because he'd been accepted, and his weary mother had forced him to enroll.

As the new dean of the college, however, he discovered a new and secret side to Oxford.

A side dominated by money.

Big money.

He took an immediate liking to this side. Reputation, he quickly learned, had a surprisingly lofty price tag, and the business of keeping Oxford's reputation clean proved to be easy and profitable. A British Parliament member's freshman son, not quite ready for the rigors of college, had failed out? Dean Templeton would graciously grant readmittance one semester later, in exchange for a quiet, five-figure contribution from the boy's father. The new professor, a free-spirited young woman, had been arrested for naked table-dancing at a disreputable pub? Dean Templeton would forgive, forget, and kill the story, in exchange for a weekend of wine, pheasant, and fellatio in a rural cottage.

He reinvented himself as an aloof disciplinarian, a small-framed man with big-time power. He consorted with royalty and attended polo matches. He filled his closet with designer suits, and his black book with the phone numbers of loose women who needed favors. He played chess against men of equally superior intellect, and as he played he imagined himself the wealthy, white king, sending out worthless pawns and knights to protect himself against the black forces.

And all the while, he waited for his father-in-law to die.

The miracle occurred in the form of a plane crash—a sudden, suspicious, to-this-day-unexplained explosion that ripped Byron's private plane and its fourteen passengers to pieces. Byron's remains were found scattered across a Scottish potato field. More important, his will was found hidden in the back of his desk drawer. The sound-mind wishes of the testament were blessedly straightforward:

One-half of Byron's estate would be left to his darling daughter, Judith, and her beloved husband, Anson.

The next day, Templeton retired from Oxford, effective immediately, citing profound grief as his reason. He then seized solitary control of Judith's share of the inheritance, fully intent on doubling it, then tripling it, then leaving her with nothing but divorce papers, a stack of forged account documents, and a few bags of her high-calorie macadamia nuts.

He sank the majority of the money into risky investment opportunities, all of which failed. The rest he gambled away. Within two years of Byron's death, Templeton found himself on the verge of bankruptcy, with sizable debts owed to men with guns. Finally, with nowhere left to turn, he escaped to America, his cumbersome wife in tow. He'd been tempted to leave her behind in London, but had reconsidered. Judith's mother was still alive, and her will was almost as bountiful as Byron's had been.

Besides, someone had to pay for his plane ticket.

The Templetons settled first in Boston, then moved to cheaper accommodations in tax-free New Hampshire. Virtually broke, Templeton saw no alternative but to find a job, and he figured his best bet was to search for re-employment in the "education business." He also guessed that finding a job would be easy.

After all, he had Oxford University on his résumé.

He'd no sooner thrown his hat into the ring than Simsbury College, the small, liberal arts college in Georgeville, Maine, came calling. Simsbury's previous dean had been killed in a freak skiing accident (bunny slope, bright sunshine, broken neck), leaving the Board of Directors in a mad scramble for a replacement. Their desperation translated into an attractive job offer for Templeton. He accepted on the spot.

The world of Simsbury delighted in his hiring. A born-and-bred Oxford man was taking the reins of the fourth-oldest college in America! How deserved! How fitting! The Board of Directors publicly proclaimed the coupling of Templeton and Simsbury College as a "match made in heaven." The tragic death of Dean Ackerly notwithstanding, it was a joyous time to be a Simsbury Cardinal, and a heady time to be Templeton, who spent his first three weeks as dean shaking the firm hands of admiring students, faculty, and alumni.

Except, that is, for the hours he spent alone in his office, staring at the wall, cursing his luck, and remembering the thickly abundant, papery feel of all the money he'd pissed away.

In the five years since, he'd eased back into the comfortable lifestyle he'd enjoyed during his Oxford years, aided by annual raises and profitable connections. His offshore retirement plan had doubled, then quadrupled, then required a second account. His three-car garage now housed six different autos, and he was currently making room for a motorcycle (speed was one of Linda's many aphrodisiacs). His closet had also replenished itself.

There'd never been much for him to fear at Simsbury College. Not-so-confidential medical problems rendered college president Edison Carlisle an administrative nonfactor. For the most part, the Board of Directors allowed Templeton solitary reign. The college, in the sleepy outskirts of Cumberland County, remained relatively stain-free for years at a time.

This, however, was a fresh new day. There was suddenly *much* to fear. The imminent death of Chad Ewing would suck some of the purity from Simsbury College. The newspapers would have a minor field day. The lawyers would stand at the ready. The students would whisper, point fingers, and pass judgment. The relatives of the dead would demand some answers. The Board of Directors would have a collective heart attack.

Despite all this, he also knew that Chad Ewing's passing offered a potential financial windfall.

As long as it was ruled an accident.

10:31 A.M.

The Freshman returned to his dorm room in an exhausted trance, not knowing that it would be almost a month before he slept again. He opened the door, stumbled past his boxered, baffled roommate, and dropped to his knees in front of his dresser.

Later, the full enormity of what had occurred over the last twelve hours would hit him. But right now, in the clutches of the most terrifying hangover of his young life, he desperately needed something comforting.

He raised his glassy gaze to the top of his dresser.

Until now, the rosary beads that dangled from his lamp had been for show, to pacify his Catholic mother on her monthly visits. But now, having seen what he'd just seen, and knowing what he knew, he decided it would be a good time to invite God back into his life.

He closed his eyes, clasped his hands together, and prayed.

10:44 A.M.

Police officer Obediah Ames was just three years shy of mandatory retirement, and although he'd been passed over numerous times for promotion, he still took a measure of pride in his work. In the last five years he hadn't missed a day due to illness, and he never failed to get his reports done accurately and on time. This morning, as he banged the knuckles of his right hand on the wire-windowed door to police chief Martin Sullivan's office, he used his left hand to clutch both the written accounts of his morning call and a half-drained Styrofoam coffee cup.

Sullivan glanced up from his sports page, and waved for Ames to enter.

"Morning, Sully," Ames said as he tossed the report on Sullivan's desk.

"What's so good about it?" mumbled Sullivan. "Celtics rot, and I stayed up late to watch them prove it to me." He tossed the sports page in the nonrecyclable bucket, and reached for the report. "Is this the accident up at the school?"

"Some accident," snorted Ames.

Sullivan convulsed with a one-breath laugh, then shook

his head and began to read, his face contorting and grimacing as he skimmed the well-documented but grisly facts surrounding the headfirst fall of a Simsbury freshman named Chad Ewing. When he was finished, he raised his eyebrows, shook his head, and put the report in his in-box.

"Is he gonna die?" he asked Ames.

"Without a doubt."

"Hmm."

"It's a shame," said Ames as he pointed to the report. "You want me to file that for you?"

Sullivan shook his head slowly, frowning, then leaned back in his chair. "Which frat house was this?"

"I forget the name, but it's right there in the report."

"The big white one?"

"The big white what?"

"The big white fraternity house."

"They're all big and white."

"The *really* big and white one."

"Yeah. The huge one. The one on the corner of College and Maine."

Sullivan smirked tightly and nodded, then leaned forward and busied himself with some loose papers. Ames waited, thinking that maybe the chief was searching for materials pertinent to the morning's "accident." But after a long minute of nothing, it was clear that the chief was done talking and had turned his attention to something else entirely.

"Uh, Chief," began Ames, awkwardly. "You, uh, want me to file that report?"

Sullivan looked up, appearing almost surprised to see Ames still standing there. "No."

Ames blinked. "What are you going to do with it?"

Sullivan returned to his shuffling. "Nothing, until I hear from the coroner."

Knowing the coroner, knowing him well, in fact, Ames smiled. "And when that doesn't happen?"

Sullivan picked something from his nose, examined it, and flicked it toward the recycling bucket. "When that doesn't happen, I'll do a little dance while I wait for a phone call."

He looked up again with suddenly hard eyes and pointed to the report. "Because then I'll know that report is worth a fucking fortune."

11:16 A.M.

Templeton had spent the last forty minutes with his head stuck to the telephone, relaying the morning's misfortune. His first call had been to Linda, to explain the situation and regretfully inform her that they probably wouldn't be seeing each other that day. She had, at first, expressed deep concern for the impending loss of a student. Then she'd steered the conversation toward the upcoming tenure announcements (she was up for tenure this year and displaying the same sort of competitive drive as she exhibited in other, more sultry endeavors) before pulling a complete one-eighty and talking him into a quick round of phone sex.

Templeton had hung up feeling far less tense.

His next call hadn't been quite as sexy. It had begun with a somber "Good morning, Mrs. Ewing" and had included phrases like "unfortunate accident," "terribly sorry," and "the college will pay for your airfare." It had been a one-way dialogue, a conveying of bad news and trite apologies, and Templeton had actually been tremendously relieved when Chad Ewing's mother wailed her fourth "Oh God!" into the phone and hung up.

He knew he'd have to call the Ewings back and solidify some details. For the moment, though, he'd been content to let the parents of the dying boy take out some of their shock on each other, a thousand miles away.

Next he'd called the local lunatic, President Edison Carlisle, and had given him only the basics of the accident. Carlisle had gasped, stammered incoherent sentence fragments for a moment or two, then proposed an 8:00 P.M. "all-hands meeting" at the Sigma House. Wisely, Templeton had volunteered to organize it.

Now, finally off the phone, he exhaled deeply. He sat very still for a while, deep in strategic thought.

He viewed the current situation as being analogous to a tough spot in a chess match. Chad Ewing was a pawn, and essentially off the board already. The police were pawns, too, but slightly more dangerous in that they were, for now, still *on* the board. Carlisle was a knight who'd seen his best days and was wandering a confused, twilight path nowhere near the action. The Ewings and the Board of Directors stood as bishops and rooks in the second row, more mobile, more dangerous, but not yet involved. And their involvement would be as limited as possible, because Templeton was the king's appendage, and he moved the pieces.

And he had an extra piece up his sleeve.

Mark Jessy.

The thought of Mark Jessy reminded him he still had one more call to make before calling the Ewings back. He picked up the phone and began to dial.

CHAPTER FOUR

The 200th Year
Sunday, February 22

12:31 P.M.

As Dr. Charles F. K. Marston worked dutifully to save Chad Ewing's life, a familiar voice nagged him.

Let him go.

The voice wasn't sinister; it never was. Rather, it was peaceful and reasonable, echoing the conscience of the good Doc Marston, who knew from experience that victims of severe head and neck injuries never fully recovered but, rather, spent the rest of their lives bedridden and inert.

The truth was, in his twenty-seven years as chief of staff at St. Elizabeth's, he'd never seen a more mangled head and neck than that of this patient. Chad Ewing had no business being alive. Of course, he wasn't *really* alive; a space-age machine was *keeping* him alive.

The list of injuries was long: Broken neck. Shattered skull. Apparent spinal cord trauma to the cervical region. (Translation: quadriplegia.) Compound fracture of the collarbone. Completely smashed right hand. Some broken ribs. Probable lung damage. Dehydration from inebriation. Significant blood loss.

Merciful God, thought Marston. *When I go, let me go in my sleep.*

He raked a sleeve across his face, checked a vital reading, and remained the one decisive barrier between his patient and the hereafter.

Via the phone, Chad Ewing's tearful father had given Marston permission to perform whatever procedures were necessary to save or prolong his son's life. The Ewings were flying out from Chicago and would be there that night.

Marston had promised to do his best.

Unfortunately, his best wouldn't be enough. Mr. Ewing would never again see the son he'd known. He'd never see that bright, boyish smile. He'd never see that way of walking he had. He'd never see his gloved hand catch a ball, and his bare hand throw it back. (*Do fathers and sons still play catch?* Marston wondered briefly, strangely.) At best, Mr. Ewing would see a small photograph in a tasteful frame atop a closed casket, and he'd live with the memory of what his son had been, not what he'd become.

Although Marston had kept his word to Mr. Ewing, at this extremely unstable point there was nothing to do but wait, so while rookie nurses Dennis Bradley and Janine Hammond kept careful watch over the cardiograph and the ventilator, and tended to the many tubes that snaked their way into the victim's skin, Marston watched in silence.

He leaned against a workstation and, removing his gloves, ran powdery fingers through his hair. With a heavy sigh, he expunged all medical thoughts from his head and tried to make sense of the situation from a purely logical perspective.

In his forty medical years, he'd never attended a case that troubled his good sense as much as this one. Chad Ewing had been rushed in shortly before 9:00 A.M., stark naked and reeking of whiskey and vomit, with vulgar poems written all over his body. The EMTs had told Marston they weren't sure what had happened, but the boy seemed to have fallen approximately fifteen feet, headfirst, from the balcony of a frat house over at Simsbury. Granted, this wasn't an everyday accident scenario, but it wasn't the nudity of the boy, nor the poetry, that confused Dr. Marston. Nor was it the whiskey smell of the vomitus, nor the inconsistent injuries (how could someone fall smack on his head and end up with broken ribs and a crushed hand?). There was something else—something he couldn't quite put a finger on.

Suddenly, he realized what it was. He'd been so focused on what *was* there that he hadn't noticed what *wasn't* there. There was something missing; something so obvious that it now screamed for recognition.

Visitors.

There was no one in the waiting room weeping for Chad Ewing.

Not a soul. And there hadn't been all morning.

A policeman had been there briefly, but had left after the formalities, taking the EMTs with him. Other than that, no one concerned with the life and livelihood of Chad Ewing had paced the small waiting room outside the ER. No friends. No classmates. No dean. No president. No press.

No one.

Marston had treated plenty of fistfight victims from the college. He'd set many a broken nose, while a dozen of the pugilist's concerned friends waited anxiously, some even going so far as to take their prayers to the hospital chapel.

A broken nose.

He looked at Chad Ewing. *Broken everything.*

His musings were sharply interrupted by the piercing, high-pitched tone that meant his patient's heart had stopped.

"*Code nine-nine!*" shouted both nurses in unison.

Forgetting his confusion, Marston sprang into action. While the nurses ran in circles, he grabbed the hypodermic he'd prepared and stepped to the gurney. He stood over the patient's chest and looked down, past the rhymes, through the pungent haze of 151-proof and body vapors. He probed the breastplate, determined the point of entry, and poised to insert the needle.

But the needle's point stopped in midair and never punctured skin. Instead, the hypodermic was laid carefully, peacefully, onto the cold metal gurney.

Let him go, Dr. Marston's voice had protested.

And this time he listened.

He backed slowly away from the body, eyes glued to the dying face of Chad Ewing. Bradley and Hammond halted their chaotic scramble, and they, too, took up a somber, silent deathwatch.

The flat-line alarm choked, sputtered, then ceased.

Chad Ewing had beaten the machines.

Chad Ewing was dead.

Marston lifted his weary eyes to the ceiling. *Thank God*, he whispered. *Thank merciful God.*

The breeze wafted over the pine trees and steeples, slipped under the heavy door of the fraternity house, and whisked past the young brothers, bringing tears to eyes and fears to bellies.

The breeze died quickly, though, and for a moment, all was noiseless and still.

And then steely resolve rose to the surface of the strongest and flowed to the will of the merely strong. Orders were barked. Fingers pointed. Buckets and mops and brooms materialized, and the whole damn mess was swept under the rug and scrubbed into oblivion.

CHAPTER FIVE

The 200th Year
Sunday, February 22

7:55 P.M.

The Sigma Delta Phi fraternity house featured two beautifully designed libraries; one for ghosts, and the other for sex.

That the house contained more than one library wasn't shocking (there was space enough for six, money enough for dozens). It frustrated the alumni, though, that neither was used for its original purpose. The older of the two libraries, located on the first floor, had been built during the construction of the present house, completed a century-and-a-half ago, after the *first* Sigma House—a shack by comparison—burned to the ground. The "upstairs libes" was an interior decorator's fantasy, with antique sofas, leather thrones, and a magnificent fireplace that roared when lit. The only drawbacks were the archaic lighting system (wall-hung lanterns) and north-facing windows, tandem problems that ensured that the upstairs libes was never bathed in sufficient light. Depending on one's tolerance for cold, the room was conducive to either napping or freezing; what it *wasn't* conducive to was studying. Hence, it now sat like a sealed-off, silent testament to the way things used to be, a barren parlor reserved for special occasions, ancient photographs, and the rich and famous ghosts of Sigma past.

Cognizant of the upstairs library's disuse, the Sigma Alumni Corporation had voted to convert one of the basement storage rooms into a more modern, practical library, though one that still oozed of appropriate lavishness. This "downstairs libes," now just five years old, had been furnished with long, luxurious sofas, solid oak conference tables, and several bright reading lamps that seemed to shout, "Come, young brothers, read and bask in my light! Get super grades, get super jobs, then give tons of money back to the brotherhood so the alumni can build more superrooms!"

There was just one problem. Located in the basement, the downstairs libes was subject to the intense noise and air pollution generated by the nearby, nightly bellowing barroom. This discovery had been made only after the library's completion, and the alumni had declared the whole project a sad waste of money.

After all, they reasoned, *what can the undergrad brothers possibly do in a library that neighbors a barroom?*

Have sex! the undergrad brothers cried, when they were sure no alumni were listening.

For although the downstairs libes was poorly located for studying purposes, it was perfectly situated for drunken seductions. Collegiate mating calls, begun in the barroom, could be consummated right next door, in a room romantic for three simple reasons: The couches were velvet soft, the doors actually *locked,* and most important, there was a hole, roughly half the circumference of a baseball, in the wall separating the downstairs libes from the boiler room. The presence and meaning of this hole were kept as secret as possible, but those in the know knew this: Every Sunday night, at the conclusion of Sigma's weekly meeting, the social chairman awarded a prize to the brother who'd put on the best live sex show over the weekend.

Because the downstairs libes was such a hotbed of sexual activity, the floor and couches were often littered with used condoms and semen stains. It was the pledges' duty to keep the library clean, but on this day of death, upkeep of the room had been neglected. Fortunately, one of the juniors had noticed this after dinner and strongly suggested that the meeting take place in the upstairs libes.

And that's where the six men met, to discuss the first-ever sudden death of a student at Simsbury, the elite liberal arts college in Georgeville, Maine.

And to await the arrival of the victim's parents.

As the men settled into those kingly leather chairs and sofas, Templeton noted that this was indeed a diverse gathering of power. Steve Hughes, Sigma alumni chairman, was a slim, athletic-looking investment banker, a polite millionaire who probably had very few enemies. Sigma House attorney Jeff Edelstein, on the other hand, was an obese, pit-stained Wall Street lawyer, an obnoxious millionaire who probably had very few friends. Both were Sigma alums of the mouthpiece variety, two decades beyond graduation, well on their way to early retirement.

Sigma undergrad president Dave Fairchild, a senior, was the show horse of Simsbury, sufficiently handsome to make Templeton jealous, were he the type to compare himself to twenty-two-year-olds. Fairchild was a six-foot-two mixture of blond, blue, and build, tethered to earth only by a tiny chip in one of his front teeth. And this dental blemish did little to take away from his appearance; if anything, it authenticated him, giving him the aura of a humble young guy who could be trusted with the strictest daddy's daughter.

In every other way, Fairchild was flawless, a man worthy of his many fans. He was a scholar, a chemistry and international law double major headed for graduation with national honors. He was a leader, perhaps the only one in his class truly qualified to make such a claim on med-school applications and résumés. Not that he'd have to fill out either, of course, for on top of all his comely, collegiate accomplishments, he was also a projected early-round pick in the upcoming National Hockey League entry draft.

The faculty and administration called him "the best of what we strive for here at Simsbury."

The girls called him a babe.

Templeton called him a useful tool, especially in delicate situations like this.

In contrast to Fairchild, Sigma resident tough-guy A. J. Dominic was the bronco of Simsbury, the sort of menace whose destructive capabilities were compounded by his massive size. The senior was the epitome of brawn, with light, nearly ivory hair bristled close to the scalp and icy eyes that bulged maniacally when caged behind a football face mask. He'd been in Templeton's office twice for fighting, most recently for nearly beating to death a guy from the Brunswick Naval Base.

Though Dominic had certainly earned his reputation as an intimidator, Templeton knew that his *real* boss saw the senior powerhouse as a young man with neither physical nor mental weaknesses. Admirable traits indeed, in the world of Sigma. Dominic would be a most important brother in the days to come.

Despite his lofty title, Simsbury president Edison Carlisle was the least influential man at the meeting. Mr. President was sixty-eight years old, and of as much administrative worth to Simsbury College as the Queen was to England. He was, in Templeton's opinion, a paper doll cut from fossilized pulp. His wavery voice spoke nothing logical, and his mind seemed to retain nothing at all. Templeton had heard from a reliable source that Carlisle had been diagnosed over Christmas break with initial-stage Alzheimer's disease. Based on some of the feeble-minded things Carlisle had done and said over the past five years, Templeton believed this diagnosis to be long overdue.

Still, with fancy degrees hanging all over his office, Carlisle was the number-one darling of the Board of Directors, which made Templeton, at best, number two. For that reason, Templeton knew he had to be wary of the man.

Especially in delicate situations like this.

Templeton eyed his watch. "I expect them any minute. Their flight got in at seven fifteen."

"That's assuming it was on schedule," said Edelstein.

"My flight from New York was delayed a whole god-damned hour."

Carlisle looked around like a lost dope. "New York? I thought you said the Ewings were from Cheyenne."

Templeton stared at Carlisle. "Uh, no, they're from Chicago."

"Chicago?"

"Chicago. Illinois. Home of the Bulls."

"Oh."

Gone, thought Templeton. *The man is completely gone.*

He opened his mouth to say something to Hughes, but was interrupted by the sound of the giant library door sliding open like a vault. He and the others turned to the doorway.

In walked the Ewings, led by a somber-faced lad with a Sigma pledge pin fastened over his heart. Carla Ewing had the makings of a rather stunning woman, her shoulder-length brown hair framing high cheekbones and a strong jawline. Roy Ewing stood broad-shouldered and handsome, his hair a shock of dark pepper waves. On other days, the Ewings might have made a striking couple. Tonight, however, puffy-faced and drained, they looked every bit like parents who'd just lost their only son.

The pledge made a hasty escape, leaving the Ewings standing stiffly in the doorway. Templeton jumped to his feet, hand outstretched. "Anson Templeton, dean of the college. We spoke on the phone."

The Ewings just stared at Templeton for a long moment, then Carla Ewing whispered, "I want to know what happened to my baby."

She collapsed against her husband's chest and began to sob.

8:16 P.M.

With fumbling fingers the Freshman locked himself inside his dorm room, then backed away from the door, staring obsessively at the doorknob, willing the lock to be even stronger than the manufacturer had intended.

He sat on the edge of his bed in the darkness, haunted by the silence that continued to scream at him.

He told himself he was crazy. They weren't coming for him. They had no reason to. It had been an accident. But even as he lied to himself, he remembered the beatings and the blindness and the burning and the all-over violation.

And he remembered other things too.

He looked at the clock beside his bed and took careful note. Before the clock struck midnight he was due back in the hell he himself had chosen, and the thought made him twitch with fear.

He set his alarm clock for 11:00 P.M., then lay down slowly. He wrapped his arms tightly around himself, and as shock shivers racked his body, he searched for sleep but never found it.

8:54 P.M.

The meeting with the Ewings, as Templeton would later explain to his *real* boss, had gone smoothly. Sure, there'd been some weeping, moaning, and carrying on, but that had been expected. On three separate occasions, the horror of it all had reduced Carla Ewing to kneeling, shrieking sobs, the most dramatic fit occurring when she threw herself on the now spotless patch of hardwood that had broken her son's fall and smashed the life out of him. And, at one point, Roy Ewing had commented through tight lips that the railing over which his son had fallen felt low and unstable. Counselor Edelstein, ever on the watch for potential lawsuits, had waddled forth and countered this charge by asserting that every aspect, *every aspect,* of the Sigma Delta Phi fraternity house was well within the guidelines set forth by the Maine Housing Authority.

Apart from these few tense scenes, the meeting had passed with as much grace as could fit the situation. Toward the meeting's end, Fairchild, that useful tool, had sweetly commented that the Ewings' son would be missed, and that the brothers would be planting a tree on the lawn in his honor, just as soon as the soil permitted it. The gathering had concluded with Templeton giving Roy Ewing directions to the finest hotel in Cumberland County; the college, he made sure to add, would be picking up the tab.

With nothing more to say or do but cry, the Ewings had then dragged their grief out the front door, into the long night. President Carlisle had muttered something about the good grace of God and followed them out.

Now the remaining men sat readjusting, once again back in the shadows of the upstairs libes.

Hughes turned to Fairchild and Dominic. "I'm sorry you boys had to see that."

Dominic barked a short, tough laugh. "Are you kidding me, man? I've seen Arabs with their fucking *heads* blown off. Don't apologize to me because some people can't handle death."

Hughes nodded vaguely, unable or unwilling to fathom Dominic's response, then turned to Templeton. "I guess that could've gone better."

Templeton shrugged. "It could've gone worse."

"I don't see how. Roy Ewing's going to sue."

"Oh please."

"He won't sue," agreed Edelstein. "And if he does, he'll lose. That railing's as high and hard as a well-hung cock."

"There'll be no lawsuit," Templeton said with finality. "At least not yet."

Silence.

"What about the police?" asked Hughes.

Templeton nodded toward Edelstein. "What's your guess?"

"Tough to say. It depends on whether they found anything suspicious here this morning."

Templeton looked at Fairchild and Dominic. The two seniors exchanged looks, then Dominic guffawed scornfully. "Are you *shitting* me? Hey, man, this kid *fell,* plain and simple. It was *his* fault, not ours."

"Easy, A. J."

Edelstein mopped his brow with a handkerchief then stuffed it back in his shirt pocket. "The, uh, police tend to stay out of our business, but then again, we've never had a death here. Worst-case scenario, we face charges of serving alcohol to minors. We'll plead guilty and pay a fine. We piss the kind of money they'll be looking for." He glanced at Hughes quickly, then looked at the floor. Templeton noted the body language and concluded that which he'd already known: The police, or any local law authorities, wouldn't pose the slightest threat to Sigma.

Having seen and heard enough from the Sigma side, Templeton stood and assumed command of the discussion. "I've been around colleges for a long time, gentlemen, and I'm well aware of what happens in the secret alcoves of fraternities. I know about the oaths, the rituals, the traditions. I know what lifelong brotherhood means to young men, and I know about the horrible things they'll inflict and endure to achieve it. I also know *hazing* when I see it, and I sure as hell saw it this morning. That boy was naked. He looked like a billboard. He smelled like a distillery. The whole thing sort of walks and talks like a duck, if you ask me."

He stopped pacing and looked up. "Chad Ewing was hazed, gentlemen, and now he's dead."

He continued pacing. "Now, if the Ewings or our Board of Directors discover this, your ancient brotherhood will be dead, too. Your precious mansion here will be turned into a dormitory, and your doting alumni will be facing a multimillion-dollar lawsuit." Templeton stopped abruptly and pointed at Fairchild. "This is *your* mess, Dave Fairchild. *You* guys got yourself into it, and *you* guys better be ready to get yourselves out of it. If heads start rolling, they'll be *yours,* not mine."

Fairchild nodded respectfully.

"Dean Templeton," probed Hughes, "what sort of disciplinary actions do you anticipate the college will take?"

Templeton pretended to be thoughtful for a moment. "That depends largely on how much the Board finds out. And as of right now, I don't know what Carlisle is thinking, if anything."

"Could you speculate?"

"It's not my job to speculate," answered Templeton, though he'd done nothing *but* all day.

"For Christ's sake," Edelstein griped. "I'll pay you myself."

You already are, Templeton was tempted to say. "In all probability, the Board will want a Disciplinary Squad investigation. Punishments will hinge on the D-Squad's findings."

With that, Edelstein shared a smile with Dominic, and Templeton knew instantly what they were thinking, for he himself had already thought it. A student-led D-Squad inquiry would create the illusion of a full-scale investigation, but everyone in the room knew that it could be controlled, especially given the Mark Jessy factor.

"Are you sure about that?" asked Hughes. "I mean, we're not talking about a sexual assault case here. We're talking about a *fatality*."

"An *accidental* fatality," Edelstein pointed out.

Hughes swallowed hard and nodded. "Right. Regardless, it seems to me this goes beyond the scope of a student disciplinary committee. What makes you so sure that the Board, hateful as they are toward fraternities *to begin with,* isn't going to just step in and shut us down? I find it hard to believe they're going to sit back and let a bunch of kids argue the rights and wrongs of a death."

Templeton again feigned situational analysis, then shook his head. "The Board members are a stubborn bunch of Yankees. They don't like to shake things up.

Their decisions and actions are driven by tradition." He smiled knowingly at Hughes. "Kind of like yours."

"What's that supposed to mean?"

"It means that the Board goes by the book. And the book says that in the absence of local or federal intervention, the D-Squad will be given adult responsibilities and placed in charge of all on-campus investigations." Templeton began to pace again. "In the morning, I suspect the Ewings will pay a visit to the morgue. After that, I'd like to meet with them again. I expect they'll be here most of the week." He looked at Fairchild, then at Dominic. "And while they're here, it would behoove you guys to forego the normal Sigma behavior."

Fairchild blinked and shook his head. "How do you mean?"

Templeton smirked. "That's a catchy poker face, but I think you know exactly what I mean. I watch you guys every day. You Sigmas rove the campus in tight, inseparable wolf packs, slapping hands and showing off for your gaggle of groupies. You're the big men on campus, and I think the entire student body will be looking your way to see—"

"This isn't high school anymore, Dean Templeton," said Fairchild. "We left our prom king crowns back home."

"Oh, I'm well aware this isn't high school," Templeton replied, "because if it were, Chad Ewing would've slept last night in a twin bed, across the hall from his loving parents." He moved closer to the two Sigma undergrads. "But instead he's in a morgue, and his parents are living out their worst nightmare."

He looked hard at Fairchild, then at Dominic. "And

until they've taken their nightmare back to Chicago, I
want you guys to look devastated."

"We *are* devastated," insisted Fairchild.

Templeton nodded slowly and smiled. "I'm sure."

All across the country, Sigma alums took to their cell
phones. An investment banker in Portland called a tax attorney in Boston. A stockbroker in New York called an
insurance executive in Hartford. An oil mogul in Houston
called a ship manufacturer in Miami. A corporate raider
in Philadelphia called an airline president in Los Angeles.
An advertising chairman in Cleveland called a sports
agent in Chicago, and he called an NFL team owner va-
cationing in Honolulu.

The conversations were brief, and though the exact
content varied due to time and source, there was one underlying theme to all the troubling talk: Something had
gone wrong. Something had gone terribly wrong, and
now two centuries of unflinching tradition paced uneasy
circles around the gurney of a dead young man.

CHAPTER SIX

The 200th Year
Sunday, February 22

9:28 P.M.

Templeton was no stranger to the sudden death of a student. In fact, he knew it quite well. One misty Oxford morning, upon returning to his cross-campus apartment after an all-night sojourn with two academically struggling coeds who weren't above trading sexual experimentation for disciplinary immunity, he'd come upon the body of one Alexander Fortuin, a rugby player who'd passed out drunk in one of the campus's many substantial rain puddles and drowned. Very unfortunate. Even worse, though, was the British equivalent of a civil suit filed against Oxford by the grieving Fortuins, who claimed that "improper upkeep of the property and faulty drainage facilities" had caused their son's death. The case had been categorically giggled out of court, but not before providing front-page fodder for the tabloids. The Oxford Board of Directors had talked themselves into a mild panic, and they'd turned their distress on Templeton.

Now, sitting at his office desk—the second time on a

Sunday; unheard of—he compared the years-ago death of
Alexander Fortuin to the hours-ago death of Chad Ewing.
Both casualties, he noted, were spectacular in their own
gruesome way. Both featured the obvious presence of
liquor consumed on college property. Given these similarities, and that Ewing's corpse carried with it some suspicious baggage, Templeton knew he had every reason to
expect that at *least* Sigma, and perhaps Simsbury, would
be named a defendant in a blockbuster civil suit.

Inexplicably, he now feared no such implications. Yes,
he'd witnessed the morning carnage, and yes, he'd heard
clearly Roy Ewing's hinted allegations. However, instinct
told him that neither of the Ewings was cut out for the degree of mudslinging necessary to win a civil suit. The
Ewings, he predicted, would sob and moan and curse the
fates for the next few days, and then they'd fly home to
sob and moan and curse the fates some more.

Unless, of course, they were permitted to ask too many
questions, in which case the "accidental fatality" of Chad
Ewing, regardless of the Mark Jessy factor, would become a very ugly affair. *Very ugly indeed,* concluded
Templeton, as he subconsciously fingered his wallet.

He switched on his computer, selected his e-mail option, and began to type:

*T-Bone. Met with Ewings, Hughes, Fat Man,
Carlisle, and two of your soldiers. Smooth. Regarding your earlier e-mail, it seems whoever does your
research is quick and brilliant (but then, I already
knew that, didn't I?). Clearly, the biggest asset is the
coroner, and the biggest potential liability is Dr.
Marston. I have an idea about how to circumvent the*

latter, but it sounds like you're well on your way to doing so, as it is. As for the former, it tentatively looks as though Wednesday will be our window of opportunity for a memorial. First things first, though. Parents to view body tomorrow, and I've arranged for a guide (don't worry, she's safe). Shouldn't we do something about the flesh rhymes?

And don't you just love these small, ignorant towns?

Templeton gave the message a Greater Boston address, marked it urgent and private, and clicked the "send" icon. The hard drive hummed a moment, the busy cursor evolving from an apple into a red, running bull that let fly a snort of steam before changing in flashy stages back to an arrow. The "message-sent" window splashed itself across the screen.

Templeton snorted like the bull, smiled at his humor, turned off the computer, and rose from his desk. Fetching his trench coat and gloves, he glanced at the clock on the wall. Nine forty-one. Time enough for a quickie with Linda, given her disdain for foreplay. He grinned at the prospect and began to get an erection.

11:55 P.M.

The Tradition of the Triumvirate was the oldest and strictest of the many old and strict traditions that had survived the first one hundred ninety-nine and one-half years of the brotherhood.

And certainly the most intimidating.

A single candle flickered atop a marble slab in the center of a long antique table in the Sigma Delta Phi Brotherhood Room, located at the secret end of the third-floor hallway in the most beautiful by far of the many beautiful structures on Simsbury's famous campus. At the table sat three seniors, the Triumvirate members, each of whom wore ghostly black robes (to honor the Sigma ghosts in their presence) and black hooded masks. The candle cast their shimmering shadows onto the wall behind them.

On either side of the three men, against the surrounding walls, stood roughly three dozen additional brothers, all dressed in similar black attire, all backed by equally large shadows. One held a battle-ax; another, the Sword of Tradition. The rest stood ramrod straight, like oversized toy soldiers, arms fixed at their sides.

In front of the table, in two rows, knelt the sixteen remaining pledges. Now that Chad Ewing was dead, the pledges fit neatly into two even lines, eight per row. Each pledge wore a black blindfold, which was just fine with them, because although it left them sightless, it also masked the terror in their eyes. Each knew by now, after three weeks of hell they hadn't in their worst nightmares foreseen, that the brothers feasted on fear.

"Pledges," commanded the Triumvirate Leader, in a voice that seemed to descend from somewhere beyond the ceiling, "remove your blindfolds."

The pledges hastily obeyed the order, and as their eyes adjusted to the deep-water dimness of the Brotherhood Room, what they saw didn't surprise them, but only added to their horror.

The Triumvirate.

Rhymes.

Orders.

Thirty-two hands trembled as one, as thirty-two ears waited for a tongue-lashing.

Or worse.

The Triumvirate Leader began to rhyme:

I rhyme of tradition and centuried years.
I rhyme of alumni and hierarchical tiers.

I rhyme of survival through fire and war.
I rhyme of history and written-down lore.

I rhyme facts familiar,
And then rhyme of more.

I rhyme of a weakling, of a dead, stupid pledge.
I rhyme of death's consequence and search-for-blame's dredge.

I rhyme of the law, both collegiate and common.
I rhyme of sweet silence and evading the lawmen.

I rhyme unbending orders and forbid disobedience.
I rhyme of a cover-up and detail the ingredients.

Keep quiet, young pledges, and you'll someday be brothers,
Or Chad will be joined by unfaithful others.

"Is that understood?" asked the Leader, his rhymes done for now.

And the pledges shouted their answer, together, the way they'd been taught:

We'd no sooner stray, than burn deep in hell,
Say we with a bad-ass and brotherly yell.

The rhymes you command, we pledge to obey.
Weakness invites us, but we say no way!

The Leader seemed to regard this response for a moment, as if he'd never heard it before. Then he nodded. "Good boys. Now put your blindfolds back on and get the fuck out of here."

The pledges quickly replaced their blindfolds, got down on their hands and knees, and got the fuck out of there.

12:13 A.M.

When they were sure the Pledgemaster had properly booted the pledges out of the house, the twelve senior Sigmas reassembled in the Brotherhood Room. They locked the door, relit the candle, and assumed the Greek identities given to them by the seldom-seen man who gave the orders and represented all they aimed to protect.

The man with the big boat.

The man they called Alpha.

They spoke in hushed tones for several minutes. Then they exchanged secret handshakes, extinguished the candle, and left the room.

But the ghosts remained, and they whispered rhymes to one another in the darkness.

CHAPTER SEVEN

*The 200th Year
Monday, February 23*

6:05 A.M.

A hopeful sun began its rise over Georgeville, Maine, but the air remained savagely cold, and the entrance to the St. Elizabeth's morgue remained hidden in dark shadows.

He emerged from these shadows alone, wearing black clothes and a navy blue baseball hat, and carrying a bag. The bag held a drill, a flashlight, and a stun gun, just in case he ran into a janitor who didn't appreciate his unlawful entrance. The bag also contained chemicals, the names of which he couldn't pronounce.

His instructions had been simple. *Clean the body.*

Ten grand said he could follow that order.

He went straight to work.

The drill made quick work of the simple lock, and within seconds he was inside the morgue, at the top of the stairs that led down to the bodies.

He put the drill back in his bag and pulled out the flashlight. He descended the stairs swiftly but silently, searching for the mutilated body of one Chad Ewing.

8:22 A.M.

Two hours later, Roy and Carla Ewing arrived at the hospital to identify their dead son.

They were hustled inside by the hospital administrator, an elderly, talkative, gnome of a woman named Meredith Lacroix, who shook their hands lamely and announced that Dean Templeton had personally asked her to greet them this morning. She gently took their arms, and as she led them toward the stairway that led to the basement, she spewed forth the same meaningless words of sympathy the Ewings had been hearing for the past nineteen and a half hours.

This time, however, Roy and Carla Ewing didn't listen. Carla was busy remembering a breathtakingly beautiful blue-eyed baby boy, smooth skin and little hands and a milk belly. She was busy remembering the kitchen wall's pencil notches that monitored growth spurts, homemade Christmas ornaments, and the little hands traced onto red construction paper, cut out and Scotch-taped to the refrigerator. She was busy remembering her baby's first date, her baby's first love, and her baby's first heartbreak.

And Roy Ewing was busy remembering young legs churning viciously and comically on a too-big bike, and poison-ivied arms gamely swinging a too-big baseball bat. *"Watch the ball all the way, Chad. Watch it hit the bat before you start to run!"* He was busy remembering a summertime camping trip to a place where moose were an awesome sight to eight-year-old eyes . . . the simple-but-meaningful jingle of car keys as they dropped from his hand into the hand of his only son . . . and later, an acceptance letter from Simsbury, and a shared, celebratory six-pack of bottled beer.

And now the grieving parents were busy watching the memories consolidate, lose color, and shrink to the size and form of a lifeless outline beneath a white hospital sheet. The past, once a parental joy, now wore a too-tight toe tag that signified their only son was now a number, dead one month shy of his nineteenth birthday.

Meredith Lacroix shut up long enough to pull back the sheet, and there he was. His head was swollen and mis-shapen, his face badly bruised. His neck was bent, thick, warped, and puffy, and his skin gleamed a sick, pasty white.

But it was Chad, *their* Chad, his breathtakingly beauti-ful blue eyes closed forever. Roy and Carla Ewing col-lapsed into each other, and the sobbing began once more.

What they didn't notice was Meredith Lacroix, who was staring slightly baffled at the body, and deciding that she must have been mixed up concerning an earlier story she'd heard about "ink" and "poetry," for the body of Chad Ewing was spotless.

Absolutely spotless.

During the hour that death rose from a gurney and broke the connected heart of a dead son's parents, the young men and women of Simsbury rose as well. They rose from college cots and couches, from library cubbies and gymnasium sweat contraptions. They rose from the honey and petals of weekend romance, and the ashes of weekend heartbreak.

Most rose with no knowledge of death.

Or how it would be taught to them.

Meanwhile, scattered across Cumberland County, a significant few rose as well, with no knowledge of the parts they'd play in the education.

And the many men of a nationwide force rose when they were goddamned good and ready, for they were in complete control of their namesakes, their fortunes, and every single game they played.

CHAPTER EIGHT

The 200th Year
Monday, February 23

NOON

The majority of people entitled to an opinion believed that Simsbury College was ruled by a check-and-balance combination of the Board of Directors, alumni, professors, and the ever-nebulous "Institution of Education." In a perfectly ignorant world, this would perhaps be the case. The truth of the matter, however—a truth known only by current students, and seemingly forgotten somewhere during the transition to alumni status—was that Old Madame Rumor, the Goddess of Gossip, dominated the daily *whos* and *whats* of Simsbury College.

The Madame, as she was called, lived a constant stream of short, hectic lives, but She was truly immortal. She enjoyed continual rebirth, usually on Mondays, often at breakfast. She started as a sleepy whisper on the early breeze, yawned from shared bed covers and corner closets, and Her swift evolution could be tracked by campus clock. Monday mornings found Her groggy and uncertain, but filled with potential energy.

With whom did she make flippy-flop?

The entire men's basketball team, two at a time. I say we call her Double-Dribble.

And She usually took it from there.

The Madame gathered strength through mention. She begged to be heard, and loved to be carried. She traveled in packs and alone, on tongues and in book bags. She went to class and checked mail, played pool and made phone calls. And through it all, Her gospel spread exponentially.

By lunchtime, She would have introduced herself to every student with a social pulse and a receptive handshake. By now She was a heated electron, random but purposeful, bouncing freely about campus, often appearing to students in two or three different forms like a talented witch, and leaving it to the individual to decide which of Her to believe and pass along.

By nightfall, the Madame was mature, tired, and ready for bed. The real facts would be out by now, there for the students to mull over and compare with what the cagey old Madame had told them. The reality usually held less graphic appeal, so most clung to the Madame like remoras to a shark.

The Madame could do more to shape a student's four years at Simsbury than any professor could; She decided which girls were sluts and which girls were prudes, which guys were harmless and which guys were players. The campus reveled with Her, partied with Her, slept with Her. They feared her, too, but as long as they stayed on Her good side, She was a load of fun.

The Madame that greeted the campus on this very cold morning was at the top of Her game, for no news was ever bigger. A Sigma pledge—Chad Ewing was his name, wasn't it?—had fallen to his death early Sunday morning. The Madame was so outrageous today that some students actually refused to believe Her, choosing instead to focus on more credible tales, like the one that claimed the captain of the women's soccer team was a practicing bisexual.

But sure enough, when the students checked their mailboxes at lunch, each had received a folded white notice from the dean of the college, confirming a weekend tragedy.

TO: All students
FROM: A. Templeton, Dean of the College
RE: Chad Ewing

It is with great sorrow that I report the passing of a fellow student. Chad Ewing, who came to us this year from Glen Ellyn, Illinois, died suddenly on Sunday morning. A freshman, Chad rowed crew last fall, and recently pledged Sigma Delta Phi. He will be missed.

While funeral arrangements are not yet final, Sigma is planning a brief memorial service for Chad on Wednesday @ 1:00 P.M. in the Merriweather Chapel. The Gregory Health Center will be providing twenty-four-hour counseling for those in need.

So it was true! Now only one question teased the collective student curiosity, one that sought to probe beneath the surface of the dean's vanilla memo.

What *really* happened?

By early afternoon, the Madame was reporting that Chad Ewing had been sacrificed during a pledge activity. One version claimed he'd been thrown off the Sigma roof. Another reported that he'd been somehow kicked out of the fraternity and had been so distraught that he jumped off a second-floor balcony. Still another maintained that he'd passed out at the top of the stairway to the second floor and rolled down the stairs to his death.

Whatever the cause of death, the campus was on fire. Although most students didn't have a clue who Chad Ewing was, by day's end he was the biggest man on campus.

"He was one of my best friends." This from a sophomore woman who'd lived two doors down from him, but had never spoken to him.

"He was on my pre-orientation trip." This from a freshman guy who'd never been on a pre-orientation trip.

"He was in my Anthro class." This from a senior woman who wouldn't have been able to identify Chad Ewing if he'd fallen off a balcony and landed on her head.

And so it went, on the cold, snowy campus of Simsbury College. Finally, something to wake the students out of the dreary drudgery that was winter in Georgeville, Maine.

The Madame was back.

12:30 P.M.

Templeton looked around the table and thought, *Two senile bastards, a token, a cocksucker, and a bitch*.

The emergency Board of Directors meeting hadn't

been *his* idea. In fact, he'd considered it completely unnecessary and a waste of college funds. As far as he was
concerned, he had things well under control (and all the
most dangerous chess pieces right where he wanted
them). However, the chairman of the Board, Henry Davenport, obviously didn't feel the same way, which he'd
made clear to Templeton during a panicked 9:00 A.M.
phone call.

"Anson," he boomed, "I just heard the news. When
were you planning on calling us?"

"I was just about to, Hank," Templeton lied. "I've been
busy all morning with the Ewings."

This had lowered Davenport's blood pressure only
slightly. "The Ewings don't sign your paycheck, Anson.
It's important that you let us know when students start
dropping dead, got it? I think we should meet for lunch.
Today."

So now they sat—Templeton, President Carlisle, and
four of the twelve Board members—around the long, oak
table in the Administration Building conference room,
eating lobster rolls and Cape Cod potato chips, and casually discussing the current state of the annual alumni
fund-raising campaign. Important stuff, indeed.

Templeton finished his roll with a tidy bite, wiped his
hands on a paper napkin, and turned to Carlisle. The president was turning his untouched roll around and around,
apparently not sure which of the identical ends looked
more appetizing. He finally just shoved the roll into his
mouth. When he bit down, a shredded, pasty mass of lobster and a tomato chunk fell from the hot dog bun and
landed on the table with a gooey plop. This went unno-
ticed by everyone, including Carlisle, who sat happily

chewing, mayo and tomato seeds smeared all over his chin.

When the lunch dishes had been cleared and the coffee had been served, Davenport cleared his throat. "Should we read the minutes from the last meeting?" he asked, his eyes scanning the table over smudgeless, gold-rimmed reading glasses.

No, thought Templeton, knowing that a minute's recap by five senior citizens could take close to an hour. *Please, no.*

Roosevelt "Rosie" Jefferson, the only black member of the Board, leaned forward in his chair. "Let's vote."

"On what?" asked Gerald W. Estabrook, loud enough for his own hearing aid to perceive.

"On whether to read the minutes."

Now it was Lillian Farrington's turn. Lillian was the only female member of the Board, and the only member who'd never attended Simsbury. She'd somehow inherited the position when her husband Samuel passed away from emphysema, two years prior. Evidently, she hadn't learned any lessons from his passing, since she now puffed madly on a thin, brown cigarette that emitted blue smoke and a nauseating stench, and was in blatant disregard of the No Smoking signs plastered all over campus. With no emotional ties to Simsbury, and Sam Farrington's paper-mill fortune earning more interest than could ever be spent, her apathy was legendary. That she'd made this meeting at all shocked Templeton.

"I don't think we need to hear the minutes," she wheezed. "*Or* vote. I'm not getting any younger sitting here, you know."

"Neither am I, Lillian," agreed Templeton. "Let's skip

the minutes." He looked to Carlisle for support. Mr. President stared cross-eyed at the table, picking his teeth with a flattened coffee straw.

Davenport nodded. "Okay. Since this isn't a regularly scheduled meeting, we'll bypass some of the formalities." He put away the minutes from the last meeting, took off his glasses, and squinted. "Dean Templeton, I'd like you to explain to the Board what on Christ's throne happened this weekend, and what the current situation is. We've only heard rumors from fellow alumni. I, for one, would like to get the facts straight."

Templeton nodded, cleared his throat, and proceeded to give the watered-down version of Chad Ewing's fall. "Understand that the majority of my facts are based merely on what I've been told. But so far, here's what we know: Saturday night there was a small house party at Sigma. According to Dave Fairchild, Sigma's president, all brothers and pledges were in attendance. There was some beer on the premises, and Chad Ewing showed signs of inebriation by eleven o'clock.

"One of the Sigma brothers, a senior named Chris Killian, helped Chad upstairs and tried to put him to bed, but Chad responded belligerently, as he was known to do. Mr. Killian was finally able to convince Chad to lie down on a couch located in the second-floor hallway. According to Fairchild, Chad was safely asleep by midnight."

He sipped his water. "Now, bear in mind, what happened between midnight and about seven A.M. is speculative, as there were no witnesses. As best can be figured, Chad awoke sometime early on Sunday morning. Disoriented—and probably still quite drunk—he wandered too close to the edge of the balcony, lost his balance, and fell over the railing to the first floor below."

Templeton paused and shrugged, as though to suggest that the hand of fate is sometimes inexplicably cruel. "His body was discovered by the breakfast chef, who contacted the appropriate authorities. By the time I arrived, the EMTs were administering lifesaving procedures.

"He was pronounced dead early yesterday afternoon. An autopsy's pending."

Davenport digested the recap, nodding slowly. "What about the family of the deceased?"

"They arrived last night, from Chicago. They're upset, understandably, but—"

"Where are the Irvings now?" Farrington asked.

"Ewings. They're over at Sigma, planning the memorial service, which is set for Wednesday."

"This boy was a pledge?" asked Jefferson.

"That's right."

Heavy silence. Jefferson looked knowingly at Davenport. "I'd like to know who gave him the liquor. It's my understanding the pledge process is dry these days."

"It *is* dry," lied Templeton. "The Sigmas had a party on Saturday night, completely independent of any pledge activity. And as I said, there was beer on the premises. It would've been easy for Mr. Ewing to get his hands—"

"Have we considered the possibility that the older boys *made* him drink?" asked Davenport.

"Peer pressure," added Jefferson. "That's what I was just wondering."

Templeton shook his head. "From what I've heard, Chad was a frequent abuser of liquor."

"Peer pressure," Jefferson repeated, as though he'd coined the term. "Isn't it possible that the brothers used the element of peer pressure to encourage Mr. Ewing's reckless behavior? To encourage him to *binge drink*?"

"Kids drink these days," explained Templeton. "They drink a lot. They don't need any encouragement." He looked around the table. The Board members didn't look persuaded by his argument. He'd expected this and was ready. Out of the corner of his eye, he saw Carlisle gawking out the window. The coast was clear.

"And we haven't ruled out suicide."

Davenport's expression changed from disapproval to surprise. "Suicide?"

"Afraid so, Hank. With kids this age, in this high-pressured setting, it's always a possibility. I took the liberty of examining Ewing's personnel file. Three pink slips this semester already. He was failing two of his four classes. The guys at Sigma told me his girlfriend from home had just jilted him for some other guy. They also told me he was drinking a lot, even on weeknights, and always to the point of blackout. Based on what I've heard, I'd say he was exhibiting classic signs of depression."

He paused to let this new, bullshit theory register with the Board members. "Anyway, although this *is* a rather unusual suicide scenario, it's a possibility we plan to investigate."

No one said anything for several seconds. Farrington puffed away. Jefferson tapped his mug handle with a spoon. Carlisle wrestled with a coffee creamer.

"Are the police involved?" yelled Estabrook.

"No."

"Good God," muttered Jefferson.

"*Thank* God," added Davenport.

"Why not?" asked Farrington.

"They've ruled it an accident," said Templeton, hoping that no one would bother corroborating this. "And I've spoken with an attorney, who asserts that because the accident took place in an independently owned house, the school's potential liability is nil." The bullshit was flowing freely now.

"Well," Davenport said haughtily, "I've spoken to *our* attorney, and he doesn't share the same optimism. That independently owned house sits smack dab in the middle of college-owned property."

"What does Sigma's attorney say?" asked Jefferson.

"They're looking at a possible fine," Templeton replied. "That's, uh, assuming . . ." Templeton fumbled for some assortment of official-sounding legal jargon, "that's assuming the state attorney general files some sort of motion, which is doubtful in the, uh, absence of criminal charges. It should be noted, however, that Sigma's alumni are ready to accept all fiscal consequences stemming from this accident."

"What about a civil suit?" barked Estabrook, a former ambulance-chaser himself.

"Doubtful, though it's too soon to tell."

There was a stuffy silence as the Board members did rough, legal calculations. Then Davenport turned to Templeton. "What about the college, Anson? Where do we, as the *U.S. News and World Report*'s sixth most prestigious college in America, go from here."

"Well," said Templeton, carefully weighing his words, "I suggest we conduct the appropriate ceremonies, say the appropriate words, and then get back to doing what we do best: educating bright men and women. The Ewings would no doubt prefer we let the whole thing die down."

Jefferson nodded skeptically. "I see. Is that how Oxford would handle the situation?"

Templeton paused before answering. "Yes, I think Oxford would definitely handle the situation this way."

Jefferson nodded again, even more slowly, then said, "I find this unacceptable." He turned to Davenport. "Hank?"

"Absolutely," agreed Davenport, though Templeton thought he noted a slight hesitation in the chairman's voice. "Absolutely. Dean Templeton, do you remember the task force we reorganized last April?"

Templeton nodded. He remembered. Six years ago, under pressure from a politically correct educational environment, the Board had assembled a faculty-led task force, whose objective was to critically examine the role of single-sex fraternities and sororities on campus. The initiative had been dealt a setback, however, by the unexpected death of Templeton's predecessor, Dean Ackerly. The Board had recommissioned the task force roughly a year ago, renaming it the Ackerly Task Force. Convinced the task force's underlying objective was to shut down all fraternities, Templeton's *real* boss had gone ballistic. Templeton, for some reason, hadn't been overly alarmed.

Until now.

"Indications are," continued Davenport, "that the Ackerly Task Force will recommend the gradual phasing out of Greek organizations."

"Why?" asked Templeton, trying to sound nonchalant.

"Several reasons," Jefferson answered. "The most obvious being the destructive sort of rabble-rousing that tends to take place at these houses. Also, the task force has determined that the legal environment is now quite harsh on archaic, sexually segregated institutions."

"Alumni of these archaic, sexually segregated institutions donate roughly eighty-five percent of the twenty-million-dollar annual endowment," Templeton pointed out. "And sixty percent of that comes from Sigmas."

A moment of speechlessness followed this disclosure. Then Estabrook hollered, "That can't be true." He turned to Davenport. "Is that true, Hank?"

Looking somewhat awed by the numbers that had just been thrown at him, as well as a bit sheepish for not having had a clear handle on these figures coming into the meeting, Davenport replied with a weak shrug.

"That's close to twelve million a year from Sigma alone, if I'm not mistaken," added Templeton.

"Anson," Jefferson said, his tone both fatherly and unimpressed, "some things are more important than money."

Horseshit, thought Templeton.

"Anyway," Davenport continued, with a cautious sideways glance at Jefferson, "if the task force recommends a gradual phase-out, we'll, uh, implement it. At the end of this year, we'll start entertaining bids from educational consultants who specialize in this sort of delicate transition."

Jefferson leaned forward. "The point is this. At a time when we've chosen to critically examine fraternities, it wouldn't make sense for us to overlook this incident. This *death.*"

He looked at Farrington, who nodded through a plume of smoke.

Davenport straightened and peered down his nose. "Dean Templeton, I've always been quite proud of our in-house judicial system. It's right in line with the thinking of our founders. I suggest we initiate a full Disciplinary Squad investigation into the death of Chad Ewing. If it's uncovered that Sigma contributed to this death, they'll be suitably punished."

"They'll be shut *down*," said Jefferson, his lips quivering with indignation. "And if it turns out they're guilty of anything more than lack of decent judgment, I'll call the police myself and tell them to get their butts back here and make some arrests."

Settle down, Rosie, thought Templeton.

"Settle down, Rosie," said Davenport.

"I'll *not* do that," countered Jefferson. "Frankly, I've heard bad things about that fraternity before. Weren't they involved in that . . . *sexual mess* a couple years back?"

He deferred to Davenport, who suddenly appeared downright uncomfortable. *He's out of his element,* thought Templeton. *Jefferson's stealing his thunder.*

When no one addressed Jefferson's question, he answered it himself. "It was them, all right. And now it's them again. It's time we take a good, hard look at Sigma Delta Phi."

"Will you accept the findings of the D-Squad?" asked Templeton.

"We always have," cut in Davenport, while the other three Board members nodded. "It's a system in which we have great faith. You just make sure it's done quickly and cleanly."

More nods. A motion to vote was carried, and the proposal unanimously passed. The death of Chad Ewing would be investigated by the Simsbury College Disciplinary Squad.

Templeton sat back in his chair, suppressing a smile. For the fourth time in two days, he thought specifically of Mark Jessy.

CHAPTER NINE

The 200th Year
Monday, February 23

2:36 P.M.

It was on days like this, with the February wind roaring relentlessly across the snow-swept campus, that Mark Jessy wondered just what the hell he was doing at Simsbury College. He'd been offered full or partial scholarships to six warm-weather schools, each blessed with constant sunshine and tanned beauties. So just how did he end up here, in collegiate Siberia? It was a question he pondered frequently, yet was never able to answer.

He moved quickly on this cold afternoon, desperate to get to class before frostbite set in. One bare, gelid hand curled around a tattered notebook, the other cupped the rapidly fading warmth of a roast beef melt. He bobbed and swore and dreamt of spring break as he carefully maneuvered his frame—six feet and one hundred seventy pounds, according to this year's lacrosse roster—over the frozen tundra.

He wore the standard Simsbury College uniform, an intentionally unintentional outfit, one designed to cast him as a humble pauper amid towering buildings donated by millionaire alums. Of course, he really *was* a pauper, so *his* disguise came naturally. It really *was* fish blood and diesel oil on his brown, beaten hiking boots. His loose, abused Levi's had been slashed not by carefully aimed scissors, but by slips of the fillet knife and the passage of time. The untucked state of his gray thermal and red flannel wasn't intended to adhere to any look-at-me-I-don't-give-a-shit fashion trend but to cover a gigantic rip in the butt of his jeans, one that gave free passage to every nasty tailwind. And he'd actually worn his heavy hunting jacket on a bona fide hunting trip.

Completing Mark's casual look was the baseball hat pulled low over his father's black hair and his mother's green eyes. The cap, once white, now the smutty color of bluefish gore, featured the faded green outline of a cartoon naked lady. She displayed an exceptional body— "I'd do her," Mark's friends liked to joke, as if two-dimensional cap designs could be seduced—but the breast and crotch area were concealed by the words "Debaitable Babe." Piercing one oversized red lip was a fishhook, attached to a neon yellow fishing line that swirled and looped its way into the following motto: "Catch some fish, catch a buzz, but don't catch the clap!" The hat came from the charter boat on which he worked during the summer.

Right now, however, the glow and good times of summer seemed light-years away. The air was colder than the underbelly of a winter flounder, and the entire campus seemed consumed by the death of a Sigma pledge named Chad Ewing.

Mark had heard all the outrageous stories and had dismissed the majority of them. He himself had been front-and-center at the Sigma party that preceded the death, and it hadn't seemed any more out of control than usual. *Then again,* he admitted to himself, *what would I know? I was drunk out of my mind.*

He figured he'd find out soon enough what had happened. He was a former Sigma brother himself, and still had many close friends in the fraternity. Three of them—seniors Dave Fairchild, Ran Robinson, and A. J. Dominic—were in his next class. They'd give him the details.

"Excuse me," called a forceful feminine voice from behind him. He stopped and turned. Three women—one short and round, two tall and skinny—approached him with unmistakable determination.

"Hi," said Mark, trying to place their names, concluding he'd never met them.

They stopped a measurable distance from him, the chunky one sandwiched between her lanky comrades. The two taller women carried bland-colored backpacks, each blaring bumper-stickered messages: *"Keep Your Laws off My Body," "Dead Men Don't Rape."* All three stood arms-crossed and hips-cocked, a trio of she-soldiers flashing a bodily sneer.

"We don't like your hat," the short one said.

Mark made a surprised face, then smiled. "Really?"

"Yes, *really.*"

"Okay . . ." Mark replied hesitantly.

The short one, obviously the general of this small but aggressive militia, took a step forward. "The logo suggests that attractive women are to be lured, baited, and caught as prizes. We find it extremely offensive." She punctuated her sentence with an emphatic nod.

He stared at the three women for a moment. "Wait a minute. Let me get this straight. You guys followed me, and stopped me, on a cold day like this, just to tell me you don't like my *hat*?"

"That's right."

Mark laughed. "I think you guys need a hobby."

"This is no joke," said one of the tall women, stepping forward. "What you're wearing is a direct threat to women. What's more, the logo makes light of sexually transmitted diseases."

"It's a *hat*!" Mark almost shouted.

"On you, it's a *message*."

Mark nodded deliberately, then took a giant bite of his sandwich. "I'll bet you guys are vegetarians too, right?" he mumbled loudly through slabs of dead cow.

"You're a pig," spat the general. "But we already knew that, didn't we girls?" The girls nodded. "You're Mark Jessy, aren't you?"

Mark shifted, swallowed, cocked his head, and squinted. "I get it," he said slowly. "You guys are members of the SWA."

"That's the Simsbury *Women's* Association to you."

"Right. I should've guessed by your sunny dispositions."

The women just stared at him, their faces small and hateful.

Mark sighed. "Look. It's just a hat. I didn't mean to offend anybody by wearing it. If it bothers you that much, I'll take it off, and I'll never wear it again." He took off the hat and stuffed it in his back pocket. "See? No hard feelings."

"Tell it to the judge, you animal," the general hissed.

"Marcia. Caitlin. Let's go." She began to walk away, and her sidekicks followed. A few strides into her angry retreat, however, she turned and spat one last warning.

"We're watching you, Mark Jessy. We're always watching you. Remember that."

He watched from his ice patch as the three women stormed off in the direction of some other battle. Then, shaking his head, he turned and continued to class.

2:48 P.M.

In keeping with tradition, Board members Davenport and Jefferson had stopped at their favorite Freeport restaurant for martinis and shrimp cocktail on their way back to Boston. They'd spent the first martini spouting grandchildren anecdotes to the accommodating bartender while he peeled and shucked shrimp and arranged them precisely on a frilly glass plate. They now sat sipping the second round, chewing deliberately, and trading thoughts on the death of Chad Ewing.

"I feared it would come to this," Davenport lamented as he finished martini number two, without a cautious thought as to how he was going to drive another two hours to his home in Weston. "Kids these days are just so damned reckless."

Jefferson, having spent himself during his climactic tirade at the Board meeting, stared into his martini glass and said nothing.

"And I'll tell you something," added Davenport, "this couldn't have come at a worse time. Our fund-raising drive is in full swing, and high school seniors are about to decide where to spend their next four years. Not to mention the obvious legal consequences. This death has *explosive* potential."

He shook his head. "Thank *God* the police aren't investigating. And thank *God* we have Templeton right on top of it."

Jefferson squinted hard and licked his gums. "You think he can handle it?"

Davenport turned to Jefferson. "He's a born-and-bred Oxford man. Of course he can handle it."

2:58 P.M.

Mark arrived at the Palmer Building mere seconds, he imagined, before the skin on his face froze and fell off. His altercation with the SWA women had prolonged his outdoor stay, and he now felt the cold in every extremity. He welcomed the indoor warmth as he scuffed his ragged boots up the stairs to the second floor.

The auditorium was nearly empty. He was early for a change—so early he was tempted to turn around and head back down to the Palmer lounge or maybe just skip class altogether. The thought of retreating back to his apartment and taking a long winter's nap with Casey stretched warmly across his legs was compelling. He pondered the decision while he nibbled at his sandwich.

No, he'd stay. To hike back to his apartment would take a supreme effort on a day like today, and he'd only have to venture back to campus for the Disciplinary Squad meeting set for five. Besides, his three o'clock class on Monday and Wednesday was his favorite. Introduction to Health Science, with Professor Linda Regis. The class was known as a "gut," meaning it could be frequently skipped, but easily aced. These sort of classes were rare at such a fine and challenging academic institution as Simsbury, but eagerly sought, especially by male athletes drawn to multiple-choice exams. The high testosterone level in this particular class, however, was not due solely to the light workload. The main attraction of Intro to Health was Professor Linda Regis, and all her wonderful physical attributes.

And today, noted Mark, his admiration somewhat tempered by having been called both a pig and an animal in the past half hour, Professor Regis was looking quite good as she toiled about the lectern, her figure not a mystery beneath black stretch pants and a tight green sweater. As Ran Robinson would say, Professor Regis wasn't ugly.

Committing himself for the duration, Mark found a seat in the back row, finished his sandwich, and placidly grooved to the heat radiating from the physical plant's high-powered heaters and the silky movements of Professor Regis. He watched her pace this way and that, shuffling papers and arranging overheads. At one point she stood over a lit projector, and Mark made out a happy little smirk on her face and a flush to her cheeks that defied even the pale beam of the bulb. He wondered, offhand, if she was in love. Then he wondered who the lucky guy was.

"What are you looking at, Indian boy?"

For a millisecond Mark stiffened at the reference to his American Indian heritage, then he relaxed as he caught sight of Dave Fairchild, grinning slyly past his chipped tooth and sliding into the seat next to him. Next to Fairchild was Ran Robinson, who was also smirking.

"We caught you, Jessy. Pervert."

Mark smiled broadly to cover the twinge of embarrassment. "Hey guys. Just enjoying the local scenery."

Ran craned his neck to better his view. "And what fine scenery it is. She's not ugly."

Ran and Fairchild were Mark's best friends, holdovers from his Sigma days. They'd pledged together as freshmen and lived together as sophomores. Owing to the Angela McSheffrey ordeal they'd been forced to live apart, but they'd drunk many toasts to lifelong friendship and all that jazz.

They hadn't seen much of one another lately; the two Sigmas were consumed with whipping the pledges into shape, while Mark was busy captaining the lacrosse team. They'd partied like rock stars on Saturday, however, and it had been just like old times.

Like Mark, Fairchild was a senior athlete, but the similarities between the two ended right there. Fairchild was also a brilliant student who scored so well on exams that he threw off the scale for muddlers like Mark. He never missed class, never missed practice, never failed to live up to his own lofty expectations, and never missed the opportunity to make the world a better place to live. He was the kind of guy who made everyone else look bad. That he seemed to be totally unaware of his many gifts made him tolerable. That he seemed to take pride in his few faults—the chip in his tooth, his complete lack of dancing ability—made him lovable.

It was widely believed that Fairchild could have any woman on campus. It was also widely believed that Fairchild was demented, for he rarely engaged in flirtation with his female fans, let alone sexual intercourse. On occasion he'd walk a woman home, and for the next two

weeks the lucky girl would float about campus in a mesmerized trance. (*Dave Fairchild had kissed her! Dave
Fairchild had gently and respectfully groped her! Dave
Fairchild had actually called her the next day and even
taken her downtown for yogurt and conversation, and
when would he call again!*) Fairchild was careful not to
become emotionally involved, though, and although
some cynics privately hypothesized that Fairchild was
afraid of women, and maybe even a virgin, Mark was of
the mind that Sigma's number-one superstar simply held
himself to a higher overall code of ethics and conduct
than other twenty-two-year-old men, having neither the
time nor the conscience for a bedroom relationship that
would end on graduation day.

Since Michael "Ran" Robinson was Sigma's only non-
varsity athlete, there certainly was no reasonable foundation for the childhood nickname he'd brought with him to
Simsbury. *Drinking* games were his specialty, and he in-
vented and mastered them nightly. He was about five-ten
and slightly overweight, with spindly legs that somehow
supported a barrel-shaped torso. He had immovably thick
brown hair and a boyish face, and his smile produced two
of the greatest dimples this side of brown eyes. He was
polite, sympathetic, and slightly naive, but had a mischie-
vous sense of humor. He was the epicenter of most party
spectacles.

Into the seat next to Ran, A. J. Dominic now lowered
his considerable mass. Mark nodded a greeting to A. J.,
and the linebacker returned it gruffly.

Mark referred to Dominic as a close friend, but in reality the two had a strained relationship. Ever since the Angela McSheffrey fiasco, Dominic had been distant toward

Mark. This didn't break Mark's heart, but it troubled him, for Dominic was good to his friends and painful to his enemies. Mark wasn't sure which category he fell into.

Dominic had a reputation for being a classroom knucklehead, but those who knew him knew better. What he lacked in natural intelligence, he made up for with a demonic work ethic. He was a consistent dean's list scholar, no small feat at Simsbury. He was also the lone bright spot on a pitiful football team, and had once played a whole game with a bone sticking out of his finger.

Mark guessed that Dominic's discipline and drive were the product of the four post–high school years he'd spent as a Marine, an affiliation that had thrust him into several Middle East "peacekeeping missions." His tour of duty had delayed his enrollment at Simsbury, and now no one was quite sure how old he was; it was assumed he was somewhere in his mid-twenties. Regardless, he'd allegedly killed an enemy soldier—"a fucking Arab towelhead," as he liked to put it—which meant the world of Simsbury viewed the Marine-turned-student with a three-part mixture of scorn, awe, and fear.

Although Dominic's opportunities for battle were currently confined to Sigma's barroom and local watering holes, the hulking upperclassman had still managed to wage bloody war on two different enemies since September. One had been a modern-day hippie who'd lit a cigarette a little too close to an in-season linebacker, the other had been a local Navy pilot who'd unceremoniously crashed a Sigma party and pissed off the wrong Marine. Each had received a complete reworking of his facial configuration, compliments of Anthony James Dominic, a liberal arts student who'd been trained to kill with his bare hands.

Despite the numerous punishments he'd handed out, however, he'd never once been punished himself. Mark often wondered just who in the Administration Building was looking out for Dominic, and often wished he had the same guardian angel; it might have saved him some trouble.

Now, as Dominic examined his own enormous biceps with approving eyes, Mark turned to Fairchild and asked the day's most prevalent question. "Hey. What happened?"

"When?"

Mark knew that Dave Fairchild, Phi Beta Kappa candidate and future King of the World, was smarter than this. "What do you mean 'when'? Yesterday morning, that's when."

Dominic tore his attention from his own godly physique to answer the question. "Kid fell," he grunted, then leaned back in his seat.

Before Mark could ask how or why, Professor Regis moved into the preliminaries of her lecture on dietary supplements. The details of Chad Ewing's historic plunge would have to wait.

Mark, Fairchild, Ran, and Dominic settled into their seats, and for the next ninety minutes watched Professor Regis's ass as it wiggled back and forth across the room.

4:15 P.M.

Templeton thumbed quickly through his mail, filing the important pieces and throwing the rest in the garbage. Then, pressing his intercom button, he informed his secretary that he wouldn't be taking any calls for the rest of the afternoon, and could she please just forward them to voice mail.

He pushed his chair back from his desk, swiveled, and peered through venetian blinds at the darkening campus. He watched for a moment as students forged eager trajectories across the quadrangle, and he felt a powerful burst of self-importance, for he knew that he controlled their blossoming existences.

He twisted the blind shut and turned back around. Leaning back in his chair, he thought back to the meeting with the Board.

He couldn't believe that they were actually serious about the Ackerly Task Force. The "gradual phasing-out" of fraternities and sororities would be an act of monumental idiocy; the Board would be foolish to alienate such a bountiful money source, not to mention anger an alumni contingent that reacted dangerously to opposition.

On a more personal level, he couldn't care less *how* long Greek organizations lasted at Simsbury, so long as they lasted long enough for him to get where he needed to be.

Or until Judith's mother died and her will was read, whichever came first.

The thought of money reminded him he still had some work to do today. He fished a notebook from his desk drawer and ripped off a page. Across the top of the page he wrote the names of three students. Under two of the names, he jotted some notes and recollections about what he knew of them.

Under the third name, however, he wrote nothing at all,

for everything he needed to know about the student was vaulted in an offshore savings account, earning interest.

4:39 P.M.

After class, Mark and the three Sigmas headed back across the darkening campus together. A light, dusty snow had begun to fall, adding a new and tricky element to the cross-campus trek. The terrain slickened as flakes met icy ground, and Mark, Fairchild, and Ran giggled as they fought to stay balanced. Dominic, of course, was above giggling, so he marched slightly ahead of the other three.

They veered onto one of the many winding, concrete paths that traversed the campus, fanning out across the walk, completely consuming its width. They strutted, knowing that no one could pass them and that no one would even try.

Mark glanced at the giant clock on the steeple of the Merriweather Chapel. Not one to carry a watch, he lived and died by that clock. Four fifty. The Disciplinary Squad meeting began in ten minutes. He was willing to bet two bills he could guess what the topic of discussion would be.

"So," he began casually, with Chad Ewing in mind. "Big weekend, yeah?"

Fairchild grunted and nodded. Ran said nothing. Dominic kept his gaze planted firmly on the whitening pavement in front of him.

And that was that.

Mark wondered whether he should tell them about his upcoming D-Squad meeting; he was willing to bet *three* bills they'd be interested. He decided instead to focus on spring break, the two-week party rapidly approaching. They'd all planned a trip to South Padre Island, off the coast of Texas, and the countdown to takeoff had already begun.

South Padre was a better topic on this bitter day, and the four seniors spent the next fifteen minutes standing in the cold Maine air, talking about the warm Texas sun.

5:05 P.M.

The Freshman stood in the swirling snow, watching as the senior parted from his three friends and began to jog across campus.

And as he watched, his mind flirted with an idea, one so preposterous that he closed his eyes, and tried to force it out of his head.

But couldn't.

He opened his eyes slowly, and when he could no longer see the older student's hiking boots kicking up snow, he turned and hurried, almost against his will, to the library.

Where he confirmed the truth of something he'd recently overheard.

And learned so much more.

CHAPTER TEN

The 200th Year
Monday, February 23

5:12 P.M.

Inside the Administration Building, Mark climbed the three flights of stairs with the indifferent swagger of a twenty-two-year-old athlete who'd rather be someplace else. He whistled the tune that had awakened him that morning, rubbed loose knuckles across his latest lacrosse injury, and, thinking about the Angela McSheffrey incident two years before, briefly remembered how it had felt to admit to charges he could barely fathom, in a setting he could barely stomach.

A setting in which he was now an involuntary prop.

By the time he arrived in the conference room, the other three were already seated at the long oak table. The dean looked up as he walked in. "Well, Mr. Jessy," he sneered, one eye on his shiny Rolex. "Only ten minutes late this time. You're getting prompt in your old age."

"Sorry I'm late," Mark offered, as if he meant it.

"I'll just bet you are."

"No, really. Tardiness is a peeve of mine."

"Yes, I'm sure. Sit down."

Mark shed his jacket and sat. As he made himself comfortable, he noticed Simon Schwitters staring at him as though he'd just shouted a racial slur at a rally for diversity. A year ago, such a look might have caused him to wonder if he'd somehow wronged the junior swimmer, but he'd learned by now that expressions of total disapproval from Schwitters were par for the course.

Like most students who'd ridden the prep-school pipeline to Simsbury, Schwitters took himself not just seriously, but severely. This was most evident in his everyday appearance, which could best be described as casual Wall Street. Today, for example, he wore a white button-down under a tweed blazer that matched, in color, the leather-bound legal pad that lay before him. His pointy nose supported designer eyeglasses, and a scalpy-white part pushed the majority of his brown hair in the direction of his conservative political beliefs.

As always, Schwitters's intense posture suggested he was in the midst of a strictly diagrammed, lifelong career, as opposed to a brief, four-year sojourn at a fun, pretty little school in northern New England. As always, he proudly displayed a Zeta Rho pin on the lapel of his jacket. And as always, his sneer for Mark lasted about twice as long as his sneer for others.

There was definitely something personal going on here.

Once, during an uncharacteristic fit of arrogance, Mark had told himself it was jealousy, and then nearly cracked up in hysterics at the thought, for why would anyone be jealous of *his* situation (then again, who really knew the full truth of his situation)? But in time, he'd settled on the envy theory, for aside from just inherent dislike, no other explanation made sense. Maybe Schwitters begrudged Mark his far cooler friends, or was indignant that Mark played a sport that centered around an actual ball, that had an actual scoreboard and fan following. Or maybe he was pissed because he'd had to lobby tooth and nail for a spot on the Disciplinary Squad, while Mark had simply been handed the position. Whatever the case, Mark's best guess was that he had something Schwitters wanted, and for that reason Simon Schwitters wasn't a Mark Jessy fan.

And the feeling was mutual.

Mark smiled, winked at Schwitters's sour puss, and turned to his right.

Halfway between Mark and the dean sat senior Shawn Jakes. Shawn was one of a handful of genuine blondes on campus, with eyes that rang blue even in black-and-white newspaper pictures and a five-eight figure that belonged on the cover of the swimsuit magazines she so vehemently despised. She was, quite simply, the finest looking Simsbury female. And today she was looking better than ever to Mark, perhaps because he knew he was in her doghouse. She hadn't yet acknowledged his arrival, and probably wouldn't. There would be no exchange of winks.

He guessed that Shawn's presence at this meeting would make things more interesting. A staunch opponent of fraternities, Sigma in particular, she undoubtedly had a few opinions about the death of a pledge.

The dean's pompous, British twang broke the momentary silence. The first official D-Squad meeting of the academic year was under way.

"I'm sure you've heard all sorts of tabloid tales regarding what happened this weekend," the dean began, "but you're probably not sure where to separate fact from fiction, so I'll do it for you." He took off his glasses and laid them carefully on the table. "Sunday morning, a Sigma pledge named Chad Ewing fell from the second-floor balcony of Sigma. He died a short time later at St. Elizabeth's Hospital.

"Although no one witnessed the accident, sources say he'd been quite drunk the night before. More than likely, this inebriated condition contributed to the fall."

The dean sipped a steamy mug of something before continuing. "I met with the Board of Directors this afternoon. Obviously, they're saddened by the accident, and feel the college would best be served if we"—he made a circular, inclusive motion with his arm—"conducted a formal investigation."

Finished, he looked around the table, searching for feedback.

"What will our focus be?" asked Schwitters, looking and sounding like the lawyer he considered himself to already be.

"Essentially," answered the dean, "whether Sigma had anything to do with it."

"What's the likelihood of this?"

The dean shook his head, the look on his face indicating that this possibility was out of the question. "Slim. Initial reports are that Ewing was an abuser of alcohol. My gut reaction is that Sigma's only fault lies in their failure to better monitor the poor lad's beer consumption."

"Was there a pledge activity the night before?" asked Shawn, apparently not sharing the same gut reaction.

The dean shook his head quickly. "No. According to Sigma president Dave Fairchild, there was a small house party on Saturday. Nothing more."

"He's telling the truth," said Mark. "I was there."

"Shocker," muttered Shawn.

Mark looked at Shawn and raised his eyebrows, and she gave him a mocking look in return.

"I think we can rule out hazing," concluded the dean, ignoring the typical Mark–Shawn exchange. "As I've said, I think our focus should be more toward Sigma's inability to monitor the alcohol consumption of its members. Perhaps Sigma should be forced to organize a seminar on the dangers of alcohol abuse."

"Oh *please,*" said Shawn.

"What about an autopsy?" Schwitters asked professionally. "Do we know what his BAC was?"

"*What?!*" Mark nearly hollered.

Schwitters turned to Mark with a condescending look. "Blood alcohol content," he explained, as if interpreting a foreign language.

"Don't worry, Simon," Shawn said. "If anyone knows what that phrase means, it's Mark."

"Funny," retorted Mark. Then, turning to the dean, he said, "Can we have a reality check here? We're not talking about some Self-Paced Calculus cheating scandal. We're talking about a *dead student.*" He nodded toward Schwitters. "Are you gonna let this poodle start performing autopsies?"

"The autopsy's under way," said the dean, "and under the care of a licensed medical examiner, so we'll know more in a couple of days. But frankly, I agree with Mark. I don't think we should be concerned with autopsy results. The young man fell from a height and landed on his head. Cause of death is obvious."

"Maybe to you."

The dean shot a warning glance in Shawn's direction.

"Anything else?" asked Schwitters. "Anything suspicious?"

The dean turned to Schwitters and smiled faintly. "Like what? Miss Scarlet in the pantry with a butcher knife? This is an elite college, not Scotland Yard. I think you'd best prepare yourself for the disappointment—the relief, I daresay—of this being no more than an unfortunate accident, as opposed to some sort of sacrificial slaying."

Schwitters nodded agreeably. "What I meant was, is there anything else we should know about the deceased? For instance, did he regularly engage in self-destructive behavior? Anything like that?" He turned his palms upward and raised his eyebrows suggestively.

"The lad was a binge drinker," offered the dean. "He drank frequently and excessively."

"Binge drinker," Shawn said wryly. "Is that the politically correct way of saying he was an alcoholic?"

"If you want to call it that."

"If that's your definition," said Shawn, looking right at Mark, "then everyone at this school is a clinical drunk."

Ignore her, thought Mark, knowing, of course, he could never.

"My point exactly," said the dean, pointing a finger at Shawn. "This terrible tragedy might be an opportune time to initiate some sort of introspective drug and alcohol seminar, as I've suggested before. It's obvious we need to address some potentially deadly habits."

"Come on, Dean," pressed Shawn. "Aren't you just a *little* skeptical? I mean, a *pledge* falls off a balcony and dies. Sounds a little sketchy to me."

"As I've stated before—"

"I know what you've been *told.* I want to know how you *feel.*"

"Don't start throwing dime-store psychobabble at me. I'm the dean of the college."

"I'm aware of that, but in this capacity you're the D-Squad advisor. I'm merely asking your opinion."

"I don't like your tone of voice."

Shawn sighed. "Okay. I'm sorry. Dean Templeton, in your *vast wisdom,* do you think maybe it's *possible* that Chad Ewing's death was the result of a brutal hazing episode at dear old Sigma House?"

"Don't mock me, Miss Jakes."

"Kiss it, Dean Templeton."

For a moment the two locked eyes, then the dean averted his in order to smooth, with his hands, the nonexistent wrinkles in his apparel. When he spoke again, his tone was softer, almost secretive. "There might be more to this than I've let on," he confided, looking down at the personnel file in front of him. "Frankly, some are questioning whether this might be a suicide."

Mark, who'd strategically tuned out after his "poodle" comment, now returned his attention to the discussion. "Really?"

The dean nodded ruefully. "There are some classic signs. Gradewise, he was doing poorly. Socially, not much better. Mrs. Ewing allowed that her son had seemed depressed lately. Disturbed, almost."

"Do you have a picture of this kid?" Mark asked. "I'm not sure I know who he is . . . I mean, who he *was*."

Shawn fired Mark a look of distaste.

The dean shuffled through the personnel file in front of him, pulled out a photo, and slid it across the table. Mark squinted at the tiny picture that had been trimmed neatly to fit the small box at the top corner of Chad Ewing's successful application, and concluded he didn't have a clue who the kid was. The photo, presumably from high school, depicted a boy who looked no older than sixteen, a boy with light brown hair, cut in a disjointed style Mark recognized from the Cape Cod surfing ranks. His smooth baby face hinted at a complexion that didn't need a regular shave.

Mark could tell by the relative width of Chad's neck that the kid hadn't carried much bulk around, and he compared the underlying physique he saw in his mind to that of behemoths like Dominic. Having made the comparison, he now made a snap observation.

Chad Ewing didn't look like Sigma material.

A fleeting breeze of pity drafted through Mark, but was quickly deflected by the sudden and self-serving acknowledgment that he himself *was* Sigma material, with two annual composite pictures of proud, brotherly faces to prove it. Why this selfish thought occurred to him now, he didn't know, but it did provoke a twinge of guilt.

In an instant, though, he'd shackled that emotion as well. He was entitled to a little leeway, having already seen death up-close and personal—having carried it with him for thirteen years. Death slept in his desk drawer, on top of his dresser, and beneath a pile of linty sweaters in the corner of his bedroom. Death paced like a hidden animal in his mind, and though he felt sympathy for Chad Ewing's family, he couldn't help but also feel relief, for this time he stood on the *lesser* of death's two evil sides.

The distant side.

He forced the tragic memories back into a dark corner and passed the photo to Shawn.

She glanced at it quickly, having probably already committed the dead student's illustrated life story to memory, and forwarded it to the dean, who slipped it back amid the letter-sized sheets of varying color before closing the manila folder around them. "So," he began conclusively, "given the rather bleak time of year, the age and emotional state of the student, and the physical circumstances surrounding the death, suicide seems as likely a scenario as any right now."

A typical D-Squad silence followed this summary remark. Schwitters furrowed his brow and scribbled thoughts beneath the personalized letterhead on his legal pad. Shawn twisted her face into an intelligent scowl and wrestled with something. Mark stared at the hands of her slowly ticking, made-from-recycled-materials watch, and absently planned the rest of his evening.

He was still eyeing the watch when it shot suddenly into the air. Acknowledging her raised hand, the dean motioned for her to speak.

"If I were going to kill myself," she began, "that's not the way I'd do it."

The dean blinked. "I . . . I beg your pardon."

"And you know what? I'll bet if I polled the rest of the

student body, not a single student would list drinking oneself into a stupor and throwing oneself headfirst from a marginally high, indoor balcony as the preferred form of bidding the cruel world good-bye." She paused to consider options, then nodded almost sheepishly. "Call me a coward, but I think I'd opt for a glass of chardonnay and a bottle of sleeping pills."

The dean looked down at the personnel file and fussed with it. "Unfortunately, we can't speak for Chad Ewing, now can we?"

"*You* can, apparently."

The dean looked up. "What?"

"You're trying to cram Chad's death into this neat little suicide box, but it won't fit."

The dean pointed the personnel file at Shawn. "You're *way* out of line."

Shawn gave a sarcastic little smile and looked away. The dean continued glaring at her over the elevated file. Schwitters tapped his engraved pen lightly on the table. Mark just sat and waited for the next round.

"So," Schwitters said, pocketing his pen, "when do we start?"

"Soon," answered the dean, the personnel file still hovering before his face, his eyes still glued on Shawn. "I want this handled quickly."

"What's our time frame?"

"One week."

"What if we decide a trial's necessary?"

The dean chuckled and shook his head. "We'll cross that bridge when we come to it, but I'm sure it won't be necessary."

"I'm so glad," said Shawn, "that you've already exonerated Sigma. Why are we even bothering with the investigation at all?"

"Because the Board has ordered us to. The D-Squad's *their* long arm of the law, Shawn, not yours."

"This whole thing stinks already."

"No, Shawn. That's bullshit you smell, and it's coming right from your mouth."

"What a classy thing to say."

The dean shrugged. "Hey, I'm sorry if I offended you, but if you continually latch on to far-fetched theories, then I'm afraid—"

"*Far-fetched?*" Shawn's eyes grew wide, then narrowed critically as she dispatched all sarcasm. "Dean Templeton, I have a friend who slept at Sigma on Saturday night. That means she was there on Sunday morning. She said that when they found Chad, he was stark naked, with obscene poetry written all over his body."

The dean smiled. "Right. A *friend*. Just who is this *friend*?"

"Does it matter?"

"No," answered the dean, losing his smile, "because it's a lie."

"My friends don't lie."

"That, Miss Jakes, is something you can attempt to prove during the next week."

"I intend to."

The dean looked at Schwitters and shook his head, and the swimmer responded dutifully with a minor eye-roll. Turning to Shawn again, the dean spoke. "As usual, you appear primed to promote one of your many causes, at the expense of the grieving student body."

"I'm concerned that a fellow student's dead. I want to

know why." Suddenly, she turned on Mark. "And *you*! I can't believe one-third of this investigation rests in the arms of a guy who's spent half his college career in Sigma's barroom!"

Mark smiled. "Perhaps I should start spending more of my time with *you*."

"Perhaps you should shut up."

The dean stood quickly and tucked the file under his arm. "That's all for today."

"Should we start conducting depositions?" Schwitters asked hopefully.

"No. Not until Thursday."

"Why not?" demanded Shawn.

"You know the procedure. Before we conduct depositions, we have a preliminary hearing. And before we do that, we allow all parties involved some time to prepare, and in this case, grieve. The memorial service is set for Wednesday. Therefore, our investigation starts Thursday." The dean gulped the last of his coffee, wiped his mouth with a primly monogrammed handkerchief, and continued, "Besides, I'll be tied up with this whole mess until Thursday, anyway. I won't have any time to supervise you guys."

He looked hard at Shawn. "And believe me, young lady, I want to be there when you start asking questions."

6:06 P.M.

Though the student members of the D-Squad had already left, Templeton remained seated in the conference room. His hands were folded calmly on the table in front of him, but his mind spun in a frantic rotation.

Who the fuck is Shawn's anonymous friend?

And who the fuck does this D-Squad distaff think she is?

Closing his eyes, he recalled Sunday morning, revisiting a scene in the Sigma living room he'd hoped would never be made public. He saw many masculine faces. He saw the crumpled, bloody body again—how could he forget that. But he saw no woman, no *girl*, no sneaky little bitch.

Opening his eyes, he finally settled on the only logical explanation: Shawn had probably heard some campus rumor and, being the world-saving, militant bitch she was, had decided to believe it.

He hoped he was right.

Still, he'd play it safe.

He strode down the hall to his office and shut the door carefully behind him. Sitting at his desk, he reached for the phone, quickly punched the eleven numbers of a private line, and waited for an answer.

A familiar voice of power picked up on the sixth ring.

"T-Bone. It's Templeton. Someone's got a big mouth."

CHAPTER ELEVEN

The 200th Year
Monday, February 23

6:09 P.M.

Mark jogged up alongside Shawn and fell into step beside her, but she paid no notice. She neatly avoided his attempts at eye contact and kept her focused pace dead ahead as her ragged hiking boots carried her steadily toward the senior apartments at the south end of campus.

He turned, backpedaled, and turned on the charm. "Can I carry your books?"

"No."

"Aw, come on. Why not?"

"You haven't carried a book all year. You couldn't possibly remember how."

"How hard could it be?" He took the backpack from her shoulder, and though she sighed in protest, she let him have it.

"I missed you yesterday," he offered.

"You needed some time to dry out."

"I didn't need all day."

"Oh yes you did."

"Okay," said Mark, not wanting to fight. He bit his lip a moment, then ducked, backpack and all, into her range of vision and began to play facial games, searching for an adorable mask that would soften her and perhaps make her forget why she was mad at him.

She looked at him seriously, unfazed by his contrived display. "I told you never to come to my room when you're drunk. I meant it."

"*Me?* I wasn't drunk."

"You were *sloshed*."

"So was ninety percent of the student body—"

"Like Chad Ewing? Don't try that 'everyone else is doing it' argument with me. It belittles both of us."

"I know," Mark admitted quickly, perhaps too quickly. "I'm sorry, and when we get to your apartment, I'll make it up to you—"

"Hold it," said Shawn, stopping and turning with a game smile. "Just what makes you think I'm going to let you in? I don't recall inviting—"

"I'll cook you dinner."

She resumed walking. "Oh, now there's a treat. Bagels and beer. I can't wait."

"No beer. I've got practice tonight."

"Then no sex either. It'll weaken your legs."

"Actually, I happen to be one of those rare athletes who can—"

"You know what, Mark? I'm *completely* uninterested in your cocky banter this evening."

Mark clamped his lips firmly shut and looked down at the frosted walkway. He kicked a jagged block of ice for several paces and waited for Shawn to bring up the topic that was *really* eating her.

He didn't have to wait long.

"Sometimes Dean Templeton makes me want to resort to violence," she muttered.

Mark kicked the ice block one final time, watched it spin off the path and into snow, and said, "Clearly."

"He's so pompous. He's so condescending."

"He's all that," agreed Mark, "but Shawn"—he approached the topic delicately—"you made it sound as though he's at the center of some deep murder conspiracy. I mean, I'm just as bummed as the next guy that a student's dead, but there's no such thing as *murder* at Simsbury. This death was an accident, or, at worst, a suicide."

Shawn stopped in her tracks and gave him that familiar look, the one that indicated he wasn't living up to her intellectual expectations. "You're gorgeous to look at, Mark, but sometimes you really are stupid. Do you honestly believe a kid would drink himself into a stupor, take off all his clothes, write dirty limericks all over his skin, then dive off the balcony?" She continued walking. "It's almost comical. The only thing missing is a rubber chicken tied around his ankle."

Mark had to admit, she had a valid point. Still, he was quick to defend Sigma and knew he always would be; as a former brother, he guessed it was an ingrained instinct. "I think someone fed you a tall tale."

"My source is reliable."

"Who is it?" The question was borderline rhetorical; Shawn could really keep a secret.

Predictably, she ignored the question. "*You* know what

goes on during pledging. You told me yourself. That stupid vegetable race you guys used to do?" She shuddered at the recollection of the war stories he'd told her, and he regretted his big mouth. Unlike Shawn, he didn't keep secrets very well, even pledge secrets, considered the most sacred of all.

She stopped abruptly. "Think of everything you know, everything you've seen. Then look me in the eye and tell me you don't think your Sigma buddies had something to do with this."

"It was an accident."

"No. This was no accident. Slipping on a banana peel, *that's* an accident. Spilling milk, *that's* an accident. Being found without a stitch of clothing, but with all sorts of injuries, smelling like a bottle of whatever, rhymes written all over the skin, that's *no* accident. That's torture." She threw up her arms. "For God's sake, it's murder!"

"Jesus, Shawn. These are my friends you're talking about. I think I know them pretty well. They don't run around killing people."

"Maybe not intentionally. But during a pledge activity gone bad? Based on what you've told me, anything goes during pledging. And if that's the case, I'm surprised someone hasn't died before."

"This from a girl who has *never,* not *once,* set foot inside Sigma."

"That's right. And if I'm lucky, that streak of nonvisitation will stay intact through graduation day. That house is nothing more than a pretty cave, filled with pretty cavemen who walk around with pretty girls flung over their shoulders and clubs in their hands, which they use to bludgeon the pledges."

"It's just a frat house."

"You know better than that. Deep down, you know what happened to Chad Ewing. It's so obvious."

"Maybe to you."

"Oh, I'm not alone on this one. My source said this kid looked like he'd been sacrificed. She said the amount of blood was mind-blowing."

I'll bet I've seen more, thought Mark, shuddering within. "Who was it, Shawn?" he asked again. "Was it Jocelyn?"

Shawn pressed her lips together and quickened her pace.

"It was Jocelyn, wasn't it? Your reliable source is a pathological anorexic who would have oral sex with another woman if she thought it would please her boyfriend."

"That's disgusting."

"Sorry, but if I know Jocelyn, she's lying."

"My friends don't lie."

"Yeah? Well my friends don't kill."

"As far as you know."

"What's that supposed to mean?"

"It means I think some of your friends are sick in the head."

"You insult my friends, you insult me."

"Get over it. Or better yet, leave."

Mark was tempted to turn and walk away, but he fought the urge for two reasons. First, he really wasn't that mad. He was well aware of Shawn's sentiments toward Sigma, and he'd long since grown numb to her occasional tirades. Second, and more important, it had been several days since they'd spent any time together. He'd missed her more than he'd ever dare let on.

"The bottom line," Shawn said with finality, "is that Chad Ewing's dead, and I want an explanation."

"You didn't even know him," Mark said, immediately wishing he hadn't.

"Mark Jessy, I'm not even going to dignify that statement with a response."

They walked in silence the rest of the way to her apartment.

6:30 P.M.

Night had officially fallen on Simsbury, and while its students dodged the slick spots on the walking paths, their conversation bubbled with the events of the day.

Chad Ewing's name was still on everyone's lips, but it was mixed in with other important words and phrases—like "job interview," "keg party," "midterm," and "spring break."

The snow fell moderately now, steady and pure, drawing a white blanket over all and covering the dark corners where the dark secrets lay.

6:59 P.M.

They lay naked in her bed, bodies in motion now bodies at rest. Her perfect curves filled his empty spaces, her skin moist and hot. Her head rested on his chest, and though he couldn't see her face, he could feel her soft breath, rhythmic and thoughtful, and he imagined her blue eyes staring into candlelit space.

"I can just see it now," Shawn murmured. "Chad

Ewing's death will be yet another example of the dean sweeping an issue under the rug. Just like always."

Mark rolled his eyes. "Like when?"

"Like with *you.*"

"Ha! I hardly call that sweeping it under the rug."

She looked up at him, her eyes wide and challenging. "Oh yeah? What *would* you call it?"

Mark was in no mood to discuss his sordid Simsbury past; the topic tended to back him into a vulnerable corner, not to mention chuck him down a childhood lane of painful memories. Shawn, however, seemed fond of the subject—in fairness, she had no idea where it brought him—and she referred to it often. She knew that most students believed that on a cold night in March, two years earlier, Mark Jessy had gotten away with murder.

And now she was just dying to do battle. The D-Squad meeting had left her riled, and the sex had left her spirited. Her face wore an argumentative look, her jaw clenched, her turquoise eyes swimming with battle hopes.

Mark slid a hand down her bare rib cage, found what little loose flesh hung from her hard body, and tweaked it sharply.

She yelped and convulsed. "Hey!"

While she squirmed to free herself, he continued to dart his fingers here and there, randomly assaulting her naked body, until her squeals of indignant protest were reduced to exasperated giggles.

She swung herself on top of him and sat up. The sheets fell away from her shoulders, revealing a body that roughly fifty percent of the campus longed to hold, and the other fifty longed to resemble.

Mark stared up at his girlfriend, reminded himself how

lucky he was, and struggled to keep from saying those three words he'd last said to a woman who was now dead.

"So," she drawled. "You think you can seduce me out of my bad mood?"

"I believe I already have."

"Oh, you *do,* do you? Am I that shallow?" She began to stroke him.

He reflexively clutched the side of the bed and groaned something unintelligible.

She smiled. "Twice in one night? What about your legs?"

"Just practice tonight," he managed to say. "No game."

She threw back her head and laughed. "Oh, Mark," she sang. "You're *so* disciplined." She lowered herself on top of him and looked into his eyes. "What am I going to do with you, you apathetic little meathead?"

"Pretty much whatever you want."

She groaned and wrapped her arms around his neck. "You feel *so* good."

"You bring out the best in me."

She giggled softly and began to walk her lips down his chest. "Prove it."

CHAPTER TWELVE

Simsbury College had successfully fought off coeducation until the year of its bicentennial celebration when, under pressure from various women's groups, lawyers, and changing times, the Board of Directors had finally seen no other alternative but to start enrolling women.

The men of the Old Guard had been the toughest to convince, and since they donated the majority of money, the Board had handled them delicately. The most compelling argument had gone something like this: *"Think of it this way, Senator Davidson. Roughly half the young people in America are women, and some of them have some very rich daddies."*

The issue had been hard fought, but in the end, modern thinking prevailed.

Still, some men of the Old Guard viewed the whole transition as a travesty. *No offense,* they liked to say, to any woman that would listen, *but this darned school has gone downhill since coeducation. No offense,* was the standard female reply, *but since coeducation, women's athletic teams have won twenty-four New England Championships and six national titles. What have the men won?* This sort of exchange merely prolonged the battle, and there was more than one cranky alumnus who donated money to be used only for men's athletics.

The upside was that, since coeducation's inception, sexual intercourse between men and women at Simsbury had increased dramatically. One-night stands were the norm, but many of these random couplings had escalated into full-fledged relationships. And now, every year, the Merriweather Chapel hosted several Simsbury weddings.

Of course, with only fourteen hundred students, and only a quarter mile of secluded campus area, there was no such thing as a stranger at Simsbury. Each student had his or her own inescapable identity (generally christened by the Madame), which was why the relationship between Mark Jessy and Shawn Jakes was one of the most peculiar in the romantic annals of Simsbury College.

But then, Shawn Jakes *was* a walking contradiction on her own, just as likely to toss out a flippant "kiss it" as to deliver an inspired soliloquy on one of the many topics that roused her dander. She was gracious, yet would sooner eat shit than concede defeat—or so said those who'd watched her garner All-America skiing honors in each of her first three years at Simsbury. She had high standards, yet had once allowed a homeless woman to live with her for the entire spring semester. Natural selection had blessed her with flawless genetics, yet she championed sick, weak underdogs.

She was rich, the second of three daughters born to one of Aspen's most affluent families, but she dressed like a peasant. She wore blue jeans and balled-up sweaters, and wouldn't be caught dead wearing jewelry other than the occasional pair of modest hoop earrings made from recycled materials. Her hiking boots, once an array of snazzy swooshes and colors, looked as if they'd endured years of combat. She owned a souped-up Jeep CJ, but only drove it when she had to. She preferred to walk.

She was friendly, though in an aloof sort of way, and while she had friends, she seemed to spend a lot of time by herself. Her roommates, other than that slut she'd been paired with freshman year, tended to be studious types. Her suitemate this year was a lesbian.

She was from the Rocky Mountains, but loved the ocean, and though she was a biology major, she apparently had no interest in being a doctor. Her senior thesis centered on saving the commercial fishing industry, of all things, and her research frequently coaxed her to Portland, where she had been known to spend entire Sunday afternoons on the wharf in the Old Port, watching rusted, cankered fishing boats unload their haul. She had her sights set on a career in environmental consulting, where she hoped to stop corporate czars like her father from plucking every green tree from the earth. She was Daddy's girl now, but would one day be Daddy's worst nightmare.

She held lawyers in great contempt—except those who performed pro-bono work for the outmatched environment—and her college essay ridiculing the farcical state of the American justice system had been published as a writing example in a best-selling book that instructed high-schoolers how to earn acceptance to the college of their dreams. Nevertheless, she was currently serving her third term as the strongest fiber in Simsbury's legal arm, the D-Squad, and was reportedly the sharpest litigious thorn in Dean Templeton's bony side.

She had a passion for justice. And although various elements on campus saw her differently—based mostly on whether she chose to shine the bright light of her personality on them—on one point everyone agreed.

She knew the difference between right and wrong.

Which made it all the more baffling that she seemed nearly in love with a guy like Mark Jessy. Sure, he was good looking and fun to hang out with, and he was a magician on the lacrosse field, but that kind of stuff had never impressed her before. What's more, he appeared to be exceedingly confident, bordering on cocky. He was a known troublemaker who missed his share of classes. And the thugs he ran with—except Dave Fairchild, of course—seemed to think their athletic skills gave them license to commit any breach of etiquette. Mark, it seemed, stood for nothing Shawn stood for. Which begged the following question from the student body: *What on earth does she see in him?*

The answer, had they figured it out, would have knocked their disk drives into silly mode.

Shawn Jakes and Mark Jessy were together due to the unlikely combination of a misthrown Frisbee, a commercial fishing boat, and a coin flip, and despite Mark's once having been convicted of sexual assault and attempted rape.

CHAPTER THIRTEEN

On the misty morning that Mark left the seaside village of Wellfleet, Massachusetts, for the high-pressure academia of Simsbury College, his Uncle Kiko gave him some advice.

"Mark," said Kiko, as he put a razor's edge on the last of six pointed harpoon lilies, "never tell people more than they need to know, 'specially at a fancy little school like that. It's like paying for a gumball with a hundred-dollar bill. The gum'll lose its flavor quick as a tuna tail, and then you're stuck carrying around all that change."

Normally, such an attempt at wisdom from his uncle would have left Mark in a state of amused confusion. However, on this day of transition—ten years after a day of tragedy—he understood the surface of the man's message and vowed to heed it at Simsbury. He'd keep his secret buried, for it was nobody's business but his own—and bad business at that.

And so, later that day, when Mark's assigned roommate, Elliot, asked the whereabouts of "Mr. and Mrs. Jessy," Mark curtly replied that both were dead. Elliot stammered an awkward apology, Mark graciously accepted it, and they both quickly changed the subject.

There was *more* to Mark's story, of course, but that night, over a six-pack of Elliot's expensive bottled beer, Mark told only a few small scraps of it. He told about moving to Wellfleet from upstate New York when he was nine. He told about growing up a townie in a tourist town, and about never taking his studies too seriously, because on Cape Cod, better to be brilliant with baited trawls and booby traps and boat transmissions. He talked about Uncle Kiko, a beaten-down commercial fisherman who lived alone, deep in the woods of Wellfleet, in a homemade shack that barely repelled the elements.

But he didn't tell about the nightmares, or about the photo he looked at only when he had to. He said nothing of the horse ranch in Cazenovia, New York, or the full-blooded Native American father who'd made him a wooden lacrosse stick, and taught him to play the Mohawk way, or the fair-haired Swedish-American mother who'd strung together the string of neck beads he always wore, and taught him to treat people fairly. The tragic events at Cherry Plain, the hounding by the FBI—these were his secrets to keep.

But he told enough, and somewhere between his story's finish and autumn's dying beginning, Old Madame Rumor took flight.

Poor Mark Jessy has no parents, she exulted, *and hasn't since childhood. How inspirational that he's made it this far!*

This was the sort of hardship story to which Simsbury's students were unaccustomed, though, to be sure,
they lent a charitable ear. They all came from nuclear,
country-club families, and the thought of a real-life Orphan Andy walking among them kindled warm, fuzzy
feelings.

Initially, Mark allowed himself to be an inspiration, almost welcoming the fifteen minutes of fame his tragic
past lent him. He was, after all, a freshman, one of three
hundred and fifty-nine high school superstars now wandering young and scared across a famous campus, seeking an identity. By the third week of classes, however,
he'd grown rather ashamed of his status as a walking
feel-good story.

His was no story to feel good about.

After Mark finished telling half of his life story on that
first freshman night, Elliot suggested they drain their
bottles and head on over to Sigma Delta Phi, just to see
what this whole fraternity thing was all about. He'd
heard that Sigma was having a party, a *fifteen-keg* party,
and didn't that sound like a neat way to kick off a college
career?

Mark shrugged, threw on some crappy shoes, and followed Elliot across campus, more to humor his new
roommate than anything else. But as they rounded the
last turn in the winding, branching path that connected
the ivy-veined dorms and buildings to each other, he was
met with a sight he'd somehow missed during his campus tour the previous April, a sight that stopped him
cold.

Although he'd lived the years since his childhood

tragedy in what could accurately be described as a ramshackle hut, he'd seen his share of impressive sights—sixty-ton humpbacks, rogue waves, and a hurricane's destruction among them.

But he'd never seen a sight quite like the Sigma Delta Phi fraternity house.

He hailed from a mansionless world, where man-made items tended to be impromptu rigs of the duct-taped variety, not gigantic houses that towered richly above all else. The only comparison his nautical mind could draw was that the Sigma House resembled, in size, color, and aura, the iceberg he and Kiko had spotted during a northern water excursion a few winters back. Of course, he'd experienced the iceberg from a far greater distance than he now stood from Sigma, and the iceberg hadn't been fitted with ivory siding, symmetrical windows, and two-story Greek columns.

It hadn't rumbled like this either.

Actually, Sigma House wasn't just rumbling. It was shaking, literally, as if in the midst of its own self-induced earthquake. Had Mark not been able to make out the mob of silhouettes flailing within, he might have believed that something decidedly inhuman and violent was going on inside. But as he moved toward the house he could see the movements, could see that they were young and human and flailing to the bass rumblings of music.

Elliot opened the door to the thunder of college life, squawked something unintelligible over his shoulder, and was immediately swallowed up by the crowd.

Mark stood in the front doorway for a long moment, taking in the unbelievable sights and sounds.

Wall-to-wall students, limb-tangled and loud, most either holding or chugging plastic cups of cheap beer . . . A derailed drunk sitting on an expensive-looking sofa, his tongue jammed in the mouth of the woman who straddled him . . . A pigtailed drunk wearing green sunglasses, her new pelvic tattoo on display for a convention of drooling dudes . . . Future doctors and lawyers and teachers and brokers randomly mingling, nine to forty-five months away from the real world.

Mark watched dumbstruck. His liberal arts education had begun.

Freshman year flew by like the hazy hours that connect Saturday to Sunday, and the majority of Mark's recollections would consist of dim sensory snatches. The chilly onset of autumn, and the basement heat of fraternity parties. The foul odor of Theta Kappa Rho's barroom, and the sweet smell of sorority girls who wanted to do more than just kiss. The terror of pending academic probation, and the relief of three C's and a D.

The more he enjoyed of the social scene, the more he realized that he'd been born to be a brother of Sigma Delta Phi, whose spectacular house he'd visited that first night. Sigmas dominated the rosters of all the varsity teams and traveled the campus with attitude, in muscular, multibrother hordes. They threw the craziest parties and, despite their lecherous reputations, bagged the pickiest women. They refused to compromise and rejected anyone or anything that wasn't the best.

And so, on the last Saturday in January, Mark and twelve other freshman athletes pledged their lifelong devotion to Sigma, thus beginning a six-week stretch that amused, confused, and abused Mark and his fellow pledges. Each pledge kept his own drunken impressions of pledging; Mark found only the rhymes, those candlelit Triumvirate poems—unique to Sigma, or so it was said— impressive, especially since they slid from the mouths of jocks. And although he found some of the commands and messages within the rhymes slightly warped, he figured they were mainly for show, so he listened with a straight face and kept his thoughts to himself.

Pledge Mark Jessy, if given your druthers,
would you kill and die for men you called brothers?

Sure. Now give me my pin and let me move in.

The pledges swapped blood (actually, in this the age of AIDS they simply slashed their forearms and dripped blood on a stained-glass etching of Sigma Delta Phi's Greek letters) on the second Friday in March of that year, and the subsequent party spilled so much alcohol into Mark's system that he overslept lacrosse practice the following morning. A strict disciplinarian, Coach Capofina first threatened to revoke Mark's scholarship, then saw that he ran nothing but wind sprints for a week. By the end of his sentence, Mark was ten pounds lighter and two lines lower on the depth chart. The bench became his friend. Mark Jessy, former New England High School Lacrosse Player of the Year, spent the bulk of his freshman season as mop-up man on a college powerhouse, scoring meaningless goals in games that had already been decided.

Though the experience was degrading, his Sigma brothers kept him upbeat and focused. Athletes themselves, they reminded him he was just a freshman, and his time on the playing fields would come. Their encouragement gave him his first glimpse into the best qualities of fraternity life, qualities that had nothing to do with the physical beauty of both the house and the women that hung out there, qualities that had been missing from his life since he was nine.

Family qualities.

And because the fraternity operated in strict, hierarchical fashion, he figured his life in the Sigma family could only get better. Freshmen were merely expected to clean the barroom, drink as much beer as they could stomach, and carry themselves confidently and belligerently in true Sigma style. Sophomores lived in triples on the second floor of the house and recruited new members. Juniors lived in doubles on the same floor and planned all the parties.

But it was the seniors who ran the show; they had, after all, shed blood as freshmen, recruited freshmen as sophomores, and thrown wild parties as juniors. By the time senior year rolled around, a Sigma knew everything there was to know about the rich, unbending tradition of the brotherhood and had earned the right to hold an executive position and live in a cushy single suite on the third floor.

And to think up new and creative rhymes.

Mark had heard in-house rumors that, prior to the beginning of each academic year, incoming seniors would be carted off in a fancy yacht by some billionaire alumnus, where they'd be handed the symbolic reins of the brotherhood. The alumnus, acting on behalf of alumni everywhere, would give the seniors secret Greek nicknames and instructions for the upcoming year. Mark knew the seniors often held private meetings in the Brotherhood Room during the school year, and he guessed it was during these meetings that the seniors made decisions regarding the brotherhood, based on funneled input from the hundreds of alumni who gave truckloads of money to the one-of-its-kind, too-special-for-national-affiliation fraternity they still held dear to their hearts.

The knowledge of these private meetings gave Mark a warm feeling, for it told him that Sigma brotherhood was forever.

He'd never be alone again.

Mark's improbable journey into Shawn's arms began the moment she bloodied his lips.

And intensified the moment she threatened to do it again.

On the spring semester's final Friday, the early May sun finally banished winter from the green earth of the quad and beckoned restless students outside. By noon, footballs and final-exam chatter battled each other for airspace above the huge lawn, as a good chunk of Simsbury's stressed scholars worked out some anxiety and reacquainted themselves with their old friend, grass.

Mark was out there, too, on the pretense of studying for his upcoming Environmental Philosophy final. Fresh off his first all-night cram, however, he was there to sleep as much as anything else. Sweatshirt under his head, sunglasses over his eyes, he reclined while spring's warmth soothed his frazzled state.

He'd just closed his eyes when a smash to his face opened them, and he sat up so quickly his shades fell off. The obvious culprit was the Frisbee on the ground next to him. Running his tongue over his lips, he tasted blood.

Angrily, he lifted his head.

Then gaped.

Above him, blocking out the sun and the pine and everything else, stood the most gorgeous creature he'd ever laid eyes on. Cascades of blond hair framed a stunning, worried face. Caribbean eyes looked down with deep concern. He had the overwhelming urge to pull the whole hovering figure down on top of him.

"Oh my God!" she said as she bent down on her knee and tucked strands of gold behind her ear. "Are you okay?" As she leaned forward to examine his face, her outfit contracted, and he couldn't help but notice the tanned thigh that emerged from her denim cutoffs and the white lace that whispered one of Victoria's secrets over the droop in her cotton tee shirt.

"I'm *so* sorry. Here, let me see . . ." She touched a light fingertip to his lower lip.

"Is the sky falling?" he asked, puckering cooperatively.

She giggled. "No. Just my toys."

"I might have to sue you."

She laughed, then stood and tossed the Frisbee to her playmate. Deciding it was time to introduce himself, Mark stood slowly and dramatically, trying to appear as tall and broad and impressive as possible.

"Well, then," she said, unmoved by what she saw before her, "I guess I'd better get a lawyer."

"I'd be willing to settle for a date."

"A date? At this school?" She scratched her head in

mock confusion. "I've never heard of such a thing. Don't you mean you'd be willing to settle for a *fuck*?"

"Okay," said Mark, playing along, "but we'll have to skip the foreplay. My lip's a little tender, thanks to you."

She smiled coolly and tossed all the gold over her shoulders. "Okay, Mr. Gland. What's your name?"

"Mark Jessy. And you are?"

She opened her eyes and mouth wide, then clapped her hands together. "Mark Jessy! I believe you know my roommate, Dara Devasto."

Like scads of other guys on campus, Mark knew Dara Devasto intimately, but while beer and time had fuzzed the details of the quasi-romantic nights he'd spent in Watson 14's bottom bunk, he was sure he would've remembered at least a vague physical description of the top bunk's dweller, had one existed, especially one who looked like *this*.

And then he remembered.

"Dara lives in a single," he said, proud of his recollective abilities, if not his choice of first-semester bedmates. "Her roommate went home for October break and never came back."

"And since mine's still celebrating Christmas, the dean of student life decided to consolidate." Her smile adjusted slyly. "As a result, I've been privy to a sexual scouting report on half the jocks on campus."

Mark nodded and swallowed. "Yeah," he said casually, back on his game. "Dara and I go way back. We were in the same church group as youths."

She grinned. "Then I guess that means there are *two* reasons why I can't go to bed with you."

Mark crossed his arms and grinned. "The first being?"

"I only fuck agnostics."

He chuckled and rocked on his heels. "And the second?"

"Dara told me you suck in bed."

With that, she turned and walked away, without looking back, without even the slightest indication that she'd just had contact with another human being.

His face in flames, Mark watched her go, then gathered his unread books and diminished self-esteem and retreated to his room. He pulled out the freshmen facebook—a.k.a. The Menu—an annual publication that grouped photos of new freshmen with their campus and home addresses. He flipped through the pages, scanning the rows, searching for the face of the girl who'd just shot him down, a face he eventually found smiling at the world from a retouched high school picture, three alphabetic squares to the left of his own.

Shawn Cara Jakes. Aspen, Colorado. Watson Hall.

He began his conquest that night at Sigma. He got creamed in a few games of foozball, made up some lame excuses for his preppy outfit of white Polo and pressed Dockers, and offered a few cheers for a group of celebrating seniors who were splintering a few of the more fragile pieces of furniture. (As a pledge, Mark had almost felt unworthy in the presence of Sigma's fancy decor and had even been afraid to touch some of the antiques for fear he'd break something. But the upperclassmen had since reassured him that being a Sigma undergrad was sometimes all about "breaking shit," just as being a Sigma alumnus was sometimes all about paying to repair the damage.) He watched the wooden slaughter burn itself out, then rekindle with Remy Slickering's shouted suggestion that they head on up to the third floor and throw his damn refrigerator out the Brotherhood Room window! The attendant brothers stormed on destructive legs to the third floor, and Mark bolted on spotless Docksiders out the side door of the barroom.

He set a course for Watson Hall, in search of Shawn Cara Jakes, from Aspen, Colorado.

Five minutes later he was standing outside a familiar door, one through which he'd passed many times during the fall, creeping to and from a squeaky bunk. He knocked twice, hoping the muted footsteps on the other side of the door weren't Dara's. He figured they weren't, for it was Friday night; Dara's footsteps were probably engaged in a crude, campuswide party prowl, stalking men in a dirty mood.

The door swung open.

It wasn't Dara.

She wore baggy jeans, an even baggier sweater, and a sleek ponytail that pulled back all that wonderful blond hair and revealed every inch of that wonderful face. "Well, well," Shawn said brightly, "good evening, Mr. Gland. To what do I owe this pleasure? Beer, I suppose."

Mark the Conqueror smiled and shook his head, then stepped past her.

"By all means," she said, leaving the door open. "Come in and make yourself at home." She walked across the room and hushed the classical music a few notches. "I'm sorry, but I forgot your name."

"Yeah, right."

"Yeah *really*. Believe it or not, you aren't the only cow-boy to put a saddle on Dara's bed. You're one of *many*, sport."

Mark kept his grin and strolled around the living area. Spying an open book on the coffee table, he picked it up. "*Crime and Punishment*. Sounds boring."

"Actually," she said as she collapsed on her couch and smiled, "it makes a pretty wild statement on conscience. Of course, a dumb, cocky jock like you would find it boring. No pictures."

"Speaking of pictureless books," he segued (*Too quickly?* he wondered, as he began to sling it), "we've got two libraries *full* of them over at Sigma. Why don't you come on over and peruse the selection? And if you find nothing to your liking, it just so happens we're having a party that you might—"

Shawn jumped to her feet and gasped. "A *frat party*! With real *frat* brothers? Why didn't you say so?" She held up a hand. "Wait here. I'll go fetch my condoms." She disappeared into her bedroom, and moments later Mark heard her opening and slamming dresser drawers.

"Don't worry," he called. "I've got some in my room."

"I prefer mine," she shouted back. "They're ribbed, for *my* pleasure."

Mark laughed out loud. This was fun!

She returned condomless, her ponytail now fed neatly through the back of a baseball hat. She folded her arms, leaned against the wall, and looked wearily at her suitor. "What's your plan, Mr. Gland?"

"My plan?"

"What are you doing here?"

"Oh," said Mark. "I came to ask you a question."

"Humor me."

He hesitated a moment, letting the drama build. "If I kissed you, would you kiss me back?"

She stared at him, eyebrows raised, former grin on the midtransitional road to somewhere uncertain. Misreading both her silence and her expression, he took a conquering step forward. "You're the most beautiful—"

"You kiss me and I'll bite your lips off," she said evenly, her eyes suddenly plated with a dark blue armor that stopped Mark in mid-conquer.

"That's not a very friendly thing to say," he said.

She sighed, uncrossed her arms, and gently rubbed her forehead. "Look, Mark—"

"Aha!" he said, clinging to one last thread of flirtatious combativeness. "You *do* remember my name."

"Yeah, whatever. Look," she began while toeing the carpet, "though I enjoy being kissed, I'm not interested in being kissed by you. Unlike the rest of the girls on campus, I don't get hot and sweaty over lacrosse players. Not even cute ones."

Mark dipped his head and stared at the floor, as the skin-searing realization registered: She'd shot him down *again*, and set a land-speed record in the process.

"I'm flattered that you'd make the effort," she continued. "However, I'm afraid you'll go back to Sigma empty-handed. Dara and I share shampoo, but that's pretty much it. Her sketchy habits are hers alone."

Mark the Conqueror nodded, said something like, "Oh well, nice meeting you," then turned to flee.

But stopped at the threshold of escape.

One of his two remaining ounces of pride told him to run, to get away from Shawn Cara Jakes while there were still ounces of pride to be counted within his blushing flesh. The other ounce, however, pointed out that his face couldn't get any redder and that, as usual, he really had nothing to lose.

So he turned in the doorway, cocked his head pensively, looked her right in the eye, and said, " '*Can her convictions not be mine now? Her feelings, her aspirations at least . . .* '"

She just stared at him, expression unchanged, apparently not getting it.

He nodded toward the coffee table. "It's a quote from the last page of *Crime and Punishment.*" Then, as an almost fearful look slowly descended over her face, he shrugged and said, "You probably haven't gotten that far yet."

He turned away, but used a hand on the archway to twist toward her one last time. "Then again, it's possible I got the quote wrong." He grinned. "Because I haven't read the book since high school."

As the two remaining ounces of pride initiated a reproductive orgy within his cooling flesh, Mark left.

He made a pit stop at his dorm and traded in his white Polo and pressed Dockers for a ripped Gap tee and ripped Gap jeans. He kicked off his spotless Docksiders for ancient canvas hikers stained with fish guts and beer. He returned to Sigma empty-handed but in one piece, and joined a rousing game of Boot Tag, a collegiate contest that required loving brothers to vomit on one another.

Meanwhile, back in Watson, Shawn did everything in her power to keep from skipping to the last page of *Crime and Punishment.* She returned Tchaikovsky to his appropriate volume and hummed along. She poured a glass of red wine, swirled it, and watched the legs run down the curve of the glass. She removed her baseball hat and shook free her ponytail. She examined prints that had graced her walls since September and thumbed through Dara's collection of "mood music."

She picked up *Crime and Punishment* and turned to the last page.

Although the quote jumped out at her immediately from the surrounding jungle of prose, she ignored it initially, pretending instead to be reading the final page out of mere curiosity to see where this boring story was heading. She started with the first complete sentence and began to read methodically, and as she did, she slowly brought the wineglass to her lips. The merlot was just reaching her tongue when the first of the thirteen words reached her widening eyes, and by the time she'd swallowed a modest mouthful, that which she'd almost feared had proven true.

Somehow, Mark Jessy had pulled a Dostoevsky quote out of his ass.

And recited it word-for-word.

She closed the book, placed it gently on the table, and eyed the Mickey Mouse clock on Dara's desk. It was 11:11. Time to make a wish. She replaced the pleasantry of Tchaikovsky with the passion of Sarah McLachlan, stretched out on the couch with her wine, and wished against her will for Mark to come back.

CHAPTER FOURTEEN

Had someone told Mark at any point during the first six months of his sophomore year that he was aimed like a bullet toward trouble, he would never have believed it. His childhood had taught him that trouble began with costumes and ended with chaos. Trouble had nothing to do with his status as a happy, live-in Sigma brother. Trouble had nothing to do with nightly parties with new best friends.

Trouble had nothing to do with sex.

Until the night of March third.

Ironically, the night had been a blast initially, with the kickoff of the first annual "Seniors Serve the Sophomores" party. A new tradition! The party theme, oddly enough, had been the brainchild of the seniors. Given what he knew of house hierarchy, Mark had originally thought this a little out of character; it was the responsibility of the *juniors* to plan parties, and whoever heard of *seniors* serving *sophomores*? He didn't give it much thought, though, after house president Scott Patterson served him his first of many toxic margaritas. Mark and the rest of the sophomores spent a good portion of the night sitting on makeshift thrones in the barroom, toasting one another while the seniors responded to their beck and call.

The liquor flowed freely, and good judgment left Mark, as Kiko might say, like the steady ebb of a moon tide. Every time he looked up, a different senior was handing him a cocktail of some sort. The plastic cups gathered like used artillery shells at his feet, and a haze of giddy, inescapable uncertainty descended over him. He sat dumbly sipping, growing ever drunker, watching the night unfold.

He watched Ran Robinson invent and master yet another drinking game . . . A. J. Dominic take and beat all comers in yet another push-up contest . . . Tommy Lange snort a condom up his nose and pull it out his mouth . . . and Brendan Coe stretch the same condom over his own head and face.

He looked on as six party-hunting Phi Omega men arrived in the barroom uninvited, and he dimly registered Dominic and seven seniors pounding them senseless. The Phi Omegas fled for their lives, their blood forming shallow pools of dirty red on the floor.

The line between what was real and what wasn't grew even less distinct as three big-haired, flat-tummied girls entered the barroom like strippers at a bachelor party, their walks seductive, their miniskirts and halter tops concealing just about nothing. Mark watched his brothers stare. Then he watched the cement floor rise up to smack his face as he tumbled from his throne.

"I'm okay!" he shouted, more to the floor than to anyone else. But he really *wasn't* okay. He wasn't okay at *all*. The floor had him by the hands and knees, and his mind and belly joined hands somewhere in his throat, threatening to erupt.

He was drunk.

So drunk he was terrified.

Two hands helped him to his feet, two others guided him to the corner of the barroom, where adjoining walls could better support him. He half-crouched, hands on knees like a smashed center fielder, his eyes closed, his inner babble telling him to seek help.

When he opened his eyes he found Billy Lynnroy's big, comical face inches from his own.

"Mark, you stud," mouthed Billy devilishly. "One of those girls likes you, man."

"Huh?"

"She *likes* you." He turned and pointed somewhere. "*That* one. She thinks you're cute."

"Leave me alone, Billy." Mark pushed him away, nearly falling over. He crouched lower, lending more reliance to the wall. "Somebody help me," he whispered. "Somebody help . . ."

A thin-fingered hand attached to a jeweled wrist appeared before his face, and he looked up. The tallest of the three girls was standing over him, her face cute, her hair auburn, her halter-topped, skimpy-skirted body nice, her smile friendly. "Here," she offered, wiggling her fingers. "Take my hand."

Mark took her hand, and she pulled him up. The quick ascension stunned his already warped sense of balance, and he fell against her. She caught him, held him for a moment, then gently pushed him away. She propped him against the wall, cupped his cheek with a cool hand, and bubbled some dialogue at him. Mark tried to focus, tried to listen, tried to ask her to take him to the infirmary, to the hospital, to the bathroom. However, he could do none of these things. So he just stood there, waiting to die.

Smiling, she leaned forward, her lips brushing his ear. "Come with me," she whispered above the din.

She took his hands in hers and led him across the barroom. He was distantly aware of brotherly hands patting him on the back, brotherly voices hooting rhymes that barely rhymed, brotherly bodies making sexual gestures. Amid the carnival of brotherly clamor, he allowed himself to be guided out of the barroom and into the brief hallway that led to the boiler room and the downstairs libes. The girl turned, facing him as she floated backward, and encouraged him to "keep coming, boy." The last thing Mark would truly remember was how blue the girl's eyes were, beneath the dark red strands of teased bangs.

Then the force of all those drinks overcame him completely, and the night became a dreamlike sequence of alien snapshots and recordings.

An unlocked door, squeaking open. A silent encasement of books and walls. The click of a lock. A mutual grin. Lips meeting, parting, then meeting again. Whispers exchanged in dim lamplight. Fingers groping, finding breasts and asses and zippers. Bodies exposed. Skin touching skin. Hands grabbing, pulling, and pushing.

A punch, repeating its smacking echo on skin.

A welling of anger.

A final lunge.

A body beneath him.

A scream.

He awoke to the daybreak thunder of a rare winter rainstorm teamed with a titanic hangover. His shirtless torso was draped across the seat cushions of the downstairs libes sofa, his legs arced behind him like the lower half of a twisted, two-pronged boomerang.

He forced his muscles to roll him completely to the floor. Itchy carpet wetness on his ass told him that his pants weren't all the way up.

Suddenly he remembered the girl.

He sat up, surveying the library with one working eye. Where was she?

Nowhere.

He sighed, groaned, and as he fixed his gaze on his naked waist and thighs, he struggled to remember the previous night. Had he had sex? Had he worn a condom?

Where was she?

Who was she?

He had no answers, only an odd feeling, as if he'd survived a brush with something that had just about killed him.

He stood, carefully, and began the long, agonized climb to his room.

CHAPTER FIFTEEN

When Mark checked his mailbox the following Monday he found a single envelope depicting the official college seal, addressed to Mark Morningstar Jessy. He sat on the sofa in the student lounge and opened the letter.

Dear Mark,

Angela McSheffrey, a resident of Georgeville, has filed a formal complaint with the school, charging that on Saturday night, March 3, you sexually assaulted and attempted to rape her during a party at the Sigma Delta Phi fraternity house.

Ms. McSheffrey has indicated that she would like this matter handled by the college, and she wishes to keep the local and state authorities out of the matter. I, for one, am encouraged by her attitude, as it bespeaks her willingness to cooperate. Consistent with the Simsbury College Charter, the case will be turned over to

*the in-house Disciplinary Squad. You are requested to
be present at the preliminary hearing, this Thursday,
March 8, at 4:00 P.M.*

*Sincerely,
Anson J. Templeton
Dean of the College*

What?
Mark read the letter again, and again after that.
And again.
What?!
His first thought was that the whole thing was a joke.
The guys, he figured, were having a little fun with him.
He looked around the student lounge, then over to the
glass windows, where he half-expected to spy any num-
ber of his fraternity brothers laughing as they watched his
reaction to the fabrication he held in his hand.

However, he didn't know a soul in the game room, and
deep down, his instincts told him the letter was for real.

As the twice-creased piece of college stationery fell
from his limp hand to the floor of the donated room, his
thoughts turned to his parents.

And it was all he could do to keep from crying.

He spent most of the day incarcerated in his room,
slogging through a welter of emotions that ranged from
incredulity to anger to self-loathing.

Over the course of the day, virtually every Sigma
brother stopped by to pat his back and tousle his hair and
declare that they were behind him all the way. The last to
pay a visit was Sigma president Scott Patterson.

"Hey, buddy," he said while lowering his all-conference frame onto the couch. "How's it going?"

"I feel great," replied Mark dully, "for a rapist."

"*Attempted* rapist," Patterson pointed out. "And besides, don't talk like that." He leaned over the arm of the couch and silenced the softly whining CD player. "Listen, I gotta pick up Sheila at the Cage, so I won't drone, but I just met with the dean and the Sigma Alumni Corporation, and I figured you'd want to know what was said.

"Here's the deal. Angela McSheffrey called the dean early this morning and gave him a fairly detailed account of Saturday night. According to her, you lured her into the downstairs library and tried to rape her, and her two friends witnessed the whole thing. Remember her two friends?"

"No. Barely."

"Well, no matter. Here's the thing. Political Correctness rules these days, and the Simsbury Women's Association has this school by the balls. If you ask me, they're a bunch of angry lesbians. If you ask the faculty and administration, though, the SWA is an organization vital to this dear little liberal arts college. Anyway, the SWA got wind of what's going on, and they've requested to have a representative at your hearing."

"Great."

"Needless to say, the SWA isn't on your side. They represent the interests of *women*. *All* women. You're a man, and you tried to rape one of their own, and they want someone at the hearing to make sure you don't get away with it."

Mark nodded mindlessly.

"Templeton said he'd consider it, which I'm assuming means he'll allow it. Christ, if he doesn't, every self-righteous bitch on campus will start burning bras left and right." Patterson took a deep breath and put his hand on Mark's shoulder. "Mark, the Sigma alumni are concerned. They're with you all the way, of course, but they also want to make sure that the fraternity itself is not disciplined. Steve Hughes thinks the Board of Directors has turned unfriendly toward frats and that they'd love to make an example of us. In the past, I might've suggested we all band together and rise up . . ." he trailed with a sigh, "but this time, I think it might be best if you took one for the team."

"Don't worry," Mark muttered. "This was my fault alone. I'll make sure the D-Squad knows that."

Patterson nodded, clapped him on the back, and said, "I think the alumni would appreciate that." Standing, he began to pace the room. "Go in there, admit you were wrong, and just let the chips fall where they may. Rape *is* a gray area, and it's bound to be your word against Angela's.

"Still," he continued, "the environment being what it is, I recommend you limit *your* words to those of the apologetic variety." Stopping, he crouched, clenched a fist, and shook it. "*Think,* Mark. *Think* back to Saturday night. I know you were drunk—Christ, part of me blames us brothers for letting you get that way—but is there *anything* you remember? Anything that might poke holes in her story?"

Once again, Mark thought back to Saturday night. What *did* he remember? The taste of cocktails. A game. A fight. A girl. A fall. A slow, winding walk. Silence. Lips. A nipple. Confusion.

Violence?

"I remember nothing," he said finally.

Patterson shook his head commiseratingly. "Then wave the white flag, Mark, to borrow a phrase from your ancestors. Wave it *high*, man, for the whole world to see. The time is right to nail a jock's dick to the wall, and that'll happen for *sure* if you don't surrender. Don't let your pride get you kicked out of college, man."

"Maybe I should call this girl," Mark said softly. "Maybe if I apologize—"

"I wouldn't advise that. I'm no expert on the psyche of rape victims, but I'm guessing you've cut her *deep*. You'll only make things worse by calling her, and you'll probably end up with a restraining order slapped against you. Then you'll have the police involved. Trust me, you don't want that."

No, Mark definitely didn't want that.

"Just leave her alone," advised Patterson. "Leave her alone, take it like a man, and pray with the rest of us that the D-Squad believes in second chances."

CHAPTER SIXTEEN

The foundation of the Disciplinary Squad rested in the original Simsbury College Charter, drafted when rooms were lit by lanterns and men were men of honor. In theory, the D-Squad provided the school with an internal mechanism to handle allegations of wrongdoing. Formation of the D-Squad was based on the haughty belief that gifted Simsbury students could do a better job of policing the situation than the State of Maine, or even federal authorities, ever could. The founders felt that a "judicious, disciplinary committee of peers" would allow faculty and students to settle disputes themselves, in a mature manner. Conceptually, the D-Squad was a revolutionary idea—a model for other staid, stuffy New England colleges and universities to copy.

In practice, however, it wasn't as applauseworthy. The D-Squad rarely convened (about once a year, to hear an open-and-shut plagiarism case), and it wasn't much of a squad, its members consisting of the dean and three students seeking impressive credentials to trumpet on applications to Harvard Law. Nevertheless, the faculty, administration, and Board of Directors were deeply in love with the D-Squad, and through the years it remained a revered institution.

The sexual assault/attempted rape case of Mark Jessy was historic, the first of its kind, and Mark knew going in that the charge was much more serious than any previously heard by the D-Squad. The severity of the situation had left his stomach knotted and rumbling, and as he waited outside the Administrative Building conference room on Thursday afternoon, he fought several urges to throw up the banana nut muffin he'd forced down his throat that morning.

Trying to improve on his limited wardrobe, he'd borrowed a jacket from Fairchild and a tie from Ran. (He'd considered wearing his blue Sigma blazer, but had nixed that as too provocative. He had, however, opted to bring the small, stainless steel blue eagle—the Sigma mascot—that had been ceremoniously presented to him the night before as a symbol of brotherly support.) The borrowed articles felt alien, adding to his discomfort. Still, he supposed he looked respectable enough. He'd taken the time to actually part his hair, and he'd cleaned his fingernails for the first time in weeks. As he squirmed in one of the waiting room's leather chairs, he rubbed the blue eagle between his fingers and tried—without success—not to look guilty.

Shortly after four, the dean opened the door of the conference room and motioned for Mark to enter. Mark stood, put the blue eagle in his pocket, smoothed his hair and clothing, and followed the dean inside.

Following gestured instructions, he took a lonely seat

on one side of a long oak table. Then he looked around
the room.

Directly across from him sat the plaintiff, a drunken
memory resurrected. Gone was the halter top. Unteased
was the auburn hair. Angela McSheffrey wore a turtleneck sweater beneath a navy blazer and a look of total hatred, which she aimed like a dart right between Mark's
eyes.

He bit his lip and looked away.

At the head of the table sat the dean, looking every
bit like the pompous snob he was rumored to be. Behind him, on an elevated platform bench that resembled
a church pew, sat two guys Mark didn't know. He took
in their black robes and impartial expressions and
guessed they were two of the D-Squad student members. He wondered who and where the third member
was.

Against the wall, spilling out of a leather chair, sat a
portly woman with short hair that looked as if it had been
chopped by unprofessional hands. She was androgynous,
brutal to look at, and she stared at Mark with eyes so ven-
omous that he flinched and turned away.

The dean stood and maneuvered to the center of the
room. "Mr. Jessy, I am Anson Templeton, dean of the college. In that capacity, I also serve as advisor to the Disciplinary Squad." He turned and motioned toward the two
students seated on the platform. "This is Brad Perry and
Jeff Grandell, two members of the Disciplinary Squad."

He then pointed to the heavy, wall-set woman. "This is
Marily Greenledger, president of the Simsbury Women's
Association. She's asked permission to sit in on today's
proceedings."

Marily Greenledger gave Mark another evil look, and he swallowed hard.

He was doomed.

The dean motioned to his left. "This is Angela Mc-Sheffrey. She has requested this hearing, and will be considered the plaintiff. While we're waiting for our third—"

Just then the door flew open, and a striking whorl of blond and blue and fleece and denim bustled in, negating the dean's need to finish his sentence and answering Mark's question regarding the identity of the third member of the D-Squad.

The third member was none other than Shawn Cara Jakes.

"Sorry I'm late," she apologized breathlessly. "I got hung up in lab."

Mark closed his eyes and dropped his head.

Now he was *really* doomed.

"This is Shawn Jakes," announced the dean. "The third member of the squad."

Mortified, Mark made eye contact with her and nodded. She returned the nod pleasantly as if she'd never met him before, as if she'd never threatened to bite off his lips. "Hello, Mark."

The dean sipped from a steaming mug, patted his lips with a napkin, and explained how the process would work. Today's session would be purely informational, to satisfy the Q's and A's. After the D-Squad members had finished questioning, they would adjourn to decide one of two things: a unanimous punishment, should the defendant concede guilt, or an investigative scope, should the defendant deny charges. Continued investigations would span an additional week or so, at the end of which the D-Squad members would declare their intention to either dismiss the charges or prosecute on behalf of the college. Should the D-Squad, or any faction thereof, choose to prosecute, it would perform duties similar to those performed by any district attorney's office. The dean would act as impartial judge in an actual trial. The Board of Directors would serve as the jury. The defendant would have the option of seeking student legal representation. The conference room would be transformed into a courtroom, and the case would be heard in conjunction with procedural bylaws set forth in the Simsbury College Charter.

Finished, the dean turned to the plaintiff. "All right, then. Angela, why don't you give us your version of Saturday night."

The dean took out a notepad, and the three student members followed his lead. Angela cleared her throat and began to speak.

"Saturday night," she said in a thick down-East accent, her tone painfully vulnerable, "me and my two friends, Tanya and Becky, went to the Hayloft for a few drinks, then decided to head on over here to see if maybe we could hang out at one of the frats. We'd done that before, although this was our first time at Sigma House. I guess we got there around midnight.

"We drank a few beers and talked with some brothers. I noticed *this* guy"—she jerked her thumb in Mark's direction—"sitting on the floor in the corner of the room. He looked wicked drunk, and I was like, 'Maybe he needs help.' So I went over, helped him up, and said, 'Do you want to go sit down somewhere quiet?' "

She paused, swallowing, eyeballs darting.

"I took him out of the barroom, into this . . . this hall-way, I guess. . . . He was stumbling, so I was holding his hands, like this"—she held her hands in front of her, above the table—"to steady him, you know? I took him into the downstairs library, turned on a light, then tried to get him to sit on the couch. He told me to lock the door. so I did. . . . I guess that was a stupid thing to do."

She trailed off and hung her head for a second, then looked to Greenledger, who nodded. Gathering strength, she continued.

"When . . . when he kissed me the first time, I was like, 'Whatever, kissing's pretty harmless,' . . . so . . . you know . . . we kissed a little."

She shifted nervously. "He kissed me harder and I told him to go easy. Then he kissed me *harder*, and I told him to stop. He . . . he grabbed my halter top and pulled it down." Her voice dropped a unit in intensity, muffled by memory. "He . . . he felt my breast . . . pinched my nip-ple . . . I was like . . . 'No.'"

A single tear squeezed from her eye and rolled down her cheek. "He put his hand on my . . . behind . . . and put *my* hand on *his* behind. . . . I pushed him away."

Another tear. "He . . . he came back at me again . . . harder. He grabbed my breast again . . . squeezed it . . . squeezed it hard . . . I could . . . hear him . . . working on his zipper . . . I pushed him . . . away . . . '*No,*' I said . . . but he pulled me with him."

The tears streamed. "I punched him in the chest . . . then I punched him again. But I think it just made him angry. He . . . he pulled his . . . his pants down to his

knees . . . '*No*,' I yelled. . . . '*Stop*,' I yelled. . . . But he
was like . . . he took out his penis . . . and *lunged* at me."

She was weeping now, her voice cracking and fluttery.
"He forced himself on me. He pushed himself under
my . . . my skirt. . . . He tried to put himself . . . his
penis . . . inside me. . . . I screamed."

Greenledger labored to her feet, lumbered to Angela's
side, and placed a supportive hand on her heaving shoulder.

"He pushed harder . . . I could feel . . . his . . . him . . .
I screamed again. . . . My friends were *pounding* on the
door . . . they were like, 'Angela, what's going on in
there? Are you okay?'

"Then I felt his body go totally limp, as if he was
passed out . . . like he was *dead* . . . I rolled him off
me . . . I ran to the door and opened it . . . my friends
pulled me outside."

She breathed deeply several times, composing herself.
"We took off in Becky's car, and Tanya was like, 'We saw
him attack you.' I guess they'd gone looking for me. They
checked the bathroom, and then the boiler room . . . and
that's when they heard me scream. They looked through
a hole in the wall . . . and saw him on top of me . . . *pushing*. . . . Becky was saying, 'He tried to rape you, Angela.
He tried to rape you.'"

Oh my God, thought Mark. *The hole in the wall.*

"That . . . later that night . . . I had a nightmare . . . he
was raping me . . . over and over . . . I woke up screaming . . ."

Nightmares, thought Mark, without really thinking.
Screaming.

"Same thing Sunday night," continued Angela. "So . . . so Monday morning I called the dean."

She pointed at Mark, her face that of a cold attacker, a victim no more. "Because, bottom line," she stated with newfound authority, "he had no right to do that to me. I said no with both my voice and my actions. He *ignored* me, *attacked* me, and tried to *rape* me, and my friends will vouch for that, if they have to."

There was a scratchy, two-minute silence, as the members of the D-Squad scribbled in their notepads. The dean fingered his cuff link. Greenledger remained standing, rubbing and patting and making everything okay. Mark just sat there, growing sicker by the second.

When the D-Squad members had finished taking notes, the dean looked up at Mark. "Mr. Jessy?"

Mark sat there a long moment, staring directly into the nothingness he'd been staring into since the beginning of her testimony. *Now's the time to tell them, Mark. Tell them why you never could've done this. Tell them about the lessons your mom drilled into you, tell them about that Long Island tourist who came to Wellfleet and date-raped Jennifer Wyatt. Tell them how long you looked for the guy.*

Then he remembered Scott Patterson's words: "*Don't let your pride get you kicked out of college.*"

"I never," he began, "meant to hurt you, Angela. I acted alone, and take full responsibility for my actions. I am sorrier than you'll ever know."

He sat.

Another long silence.

"Thank you, Mark," said the dean.

"*Thank you?!*" screeched Greenledger. "Why are you

thanking him? He just admitted to *attempted rape.* You shouldn't be *thanking* him. You should be *castrating* him."

"Easy, Marily—"

"Don't even! Angela told him to *go easy,* and he still came at her with all his hard, male oppression." Greenledger's eyes narrowed like small knife wounds, and she turned to Mark. "It's payback time, you bastard."

Silence again.

"Very well," said the dean, turning to the D-Squad. "Do the student members have any questions they wish to ask?"

Brad Perry raised a pencil. "Yes." He looked at Angela. "Miss McSheffrey—"

"Mizz McSheffrey."

Perry nodded deferentially to Greenledger. *"Mizz Mc-Sheffrey,* I gathered from your testimony that you wore a miniskirt and a halter top to a *fraternity* party. Don't you think that's a fairly risqué outfit to be wearing—"

"Oh my God! Objection!"

"Ms. Greenledger," said the dean, "you're not a lawyer."

"I don't give a shit!" screamed Greenledger. "Ms. McSheffrey is *not* the one on trial here." She pointed at Mark. *"That* pig is! And for the record, women have a right to walk around dressed however they please, even in Simsbury's beloved *frat* houses. I can walk *naked* into Sigma if I want to. I'd be guilty of indecent exposure, but I wouldn't deserve to be raped."

The D-Squad members looked at one another and nodded. Then Shawn raised a finger. "I have a question. Angela, what did you think you'd accomplish by taking an extremely drunk young man into a secluded room and locking the door? Did you expect some sort of political discussion—"

"*Hold* it," barked Greenledger. "Again, I can see where *this* one's going, and I don't like it. A woman has the right to sit *naked* with a man who's on every drug imaginable, with the words '*fuck me*' written across her forehead, and she still retains the right to say no."

"Ms. Greenledger," pleaded the dean, "bear in mind, this is the first sexual offense hearing at Simsbury—"

"Which means it's a landmark case. The precedents will be set today, and on behalf of the SWA I'm here to make sure these precedents are satisfactory. So far, they haven't been."

The D-Squad members searched one another's faces for additional questions. Finding none, they looked at the dean.

"Okay," the dean said. "I guess that pretty much covers it. Angela, thank you for your bravery. Mark, thank you for your cooperation. Marily, thank you for your input."

The dean then launched into a concluding speech regarding technicalities and time lines, but Mark heard nothing, for his mind was spiraling downward, dredging up images of the past: his mother in traditional tribal dress, a tumult of voices, the crackle of gunfire.

"*Mark!*"

He blinked, snapped to, and discovered every disdainful, pitying eye beaded his way. In his tortured musings, he'd obviously missed something.

"I'm sorry," he said, his voice barely his own, "could you say that again?"

"I *said*," repeated the dean, "that we'll be in touch."

"Oh. Okay." And with that he stood, turned, and walked dazedly out of the room.

The next day Mark found himself seated across from the dean in an office that smelled of extravagance.

"Mark," the dean began, "thanks again for your cooperation at the hearing yesterday. You did the right thing by not fighting this."

"Oh. You're welcome."

The dean slurped his coffee. "In fact, your graphic remorse made this a very difficult decision for the D-Squad. Remember, while the D-Squad's first priority is to protect Simsbury's integrity, its second aim is to judge fairly, with an eye for moral development. What good would a punishment do if it didn't help you grow as a person, and continue on a track to manhood?"

He rubbed his nose and sighed regretfully. "Unfortunately, however, the D-Squad members found your crime so grave that normal dictates no longer applied. They felt behooved to hand down a punishment as equally severe as your transgression.

"They voted, two-to-one, to expel you from Simsbury College."

Even though Mark had half-expected it, the sound of his punishment was enough to suck the breath out of him and replace it with panic. He sat there, mouth working but not speaking, mind scrambling for some desperate argument that would earn a reprieve. *I'm so sorry, I didn't mean it, it'll never happen again, don't make me leave, where will I go, what school will have me now, I can't chase fish with Kiko for the rest of my life . . .*

"The vote was two-to-one to expel," the dean repeated, as Mark continued his unspoken, rambling plea for forgiveness, "and then I cast *my* vote."

Mark's internal reel of sob stories whirred to a halt. Refocusing, he noticed an almost heroic smile on the dean's face. "I . . . what did you say?"

"I said, '*And then I cast my vote.*'"

Mark blinked. "What vote?"

"The vote I'm ultimately entitled to in the event the student members reach a split decision on punishment following a preliminary hearing where the defendant admits guilt. The vote that carries the most weight."

Mark just stared at him.

The dean leaned forward. "Would you like to know how I voted?"

Mark hesitated a moment, then nodded.

The dean slapped the table enthusiastically, reached into his desk drawer, and pulled out a single sheet of paper, which he handed to Mark. "Read."

Mark took the paper tentatively, eyed the dean once more, and began to read.

To: Files
From: A. Templeton
Re: Mark Jessy's Disciplinary Sanctions

After careful consideration, I am vetoing the D-Squad's split punitive finding for permanent expulsion in the case of <u>Angela McSheffrey v. Mark Jessy</u>.

Mr. Jessy displayed obvious remorse for his offense, in a manner that suggested he is already punishing himself for what he has done. In addition, I feel that the college would be best served by his continuing education; he is well liked by his peers and is now in the position to help heighten sensitivities to the dangers of improper sexual conduct. I believe Mr. Jessy will embrace this cause.

Therefore, I outline his amended punishment as follows:

1. *Mr. Jessy must immediately disaffiliate from Sigma Delta Phi. Though he is welcome to attend future Sigma social functions, he may not remain a dues-paying brother, nor may he continue living in the Sigma fraternity house.*
2. *Mr. Jessy must organize at least one "awareness seminar" between now and the period ending one year from the date of this memo. Form and content of this seminar must meet prior approval from the Simsbury Women's Association.*
3. *Mr. Jessy must fill one of the two D-Squad positions that will be vacated after the current academic year. He must serve on the D-Squad until he graduates.*

Failure to comply with any of these sanctions will result in Mr. Jessy's immediate dismissal from the college.

This decision does not come easily, and by no means does it bespeak a lack of faith in the student members of the Disciplinary Squad, nor a lack of respect for Ms. McSheffrey. I am, however, compelled to act in the best interests of the college as a whole. I believe this modified penalty goes the furthest to accomplish that end.

Mark read the memo again, then looked up at the dean. "Is this for real?"

Templeton smiled and nodded. "How do you feel about it?"

Mark eyed the memo again, placed it on the dean's desk, then leaned back in his chair to process what he'd just read. He supposed he was relieved and grateful for the second chance, but the details of the dean's proposal hit him hard. The prospect of organizing an "awareness seminar" didn't bother him; how hard could it be? Stipulations #1 and #3, however, were a kick to the gut, and he wondered if the benefits that accompanied a Simsbury diploma would outweigh the mental damage that would come from their satisfaction.

For the truth was, stipulations #1 and #3 echoed the two central themes of Cherry Plain, and the tragedy that had befallen his parents there. The first element he'd learned to loathe. The second, he'd forever crave.

The law.

And family.

"Are those penalties open to any sort of discussion?" he asked.

"No," answered the dean. "It's either this or immediate

expulsion. As it is, I'm going to have a hell of a time sell-ing this compromise to the D-Squad and the SWA."

Mark nodded absently, and continued to think. He fig-ured he could serve on the D-Squad for two years; really, how hard could *that* be? It wasn't as if the squad heard very many cases; in his nearly two years at Simsbury, he'd heard of only two D-Squad hearings, one bagging a freshman stress-case who'd freaked and stupidly plagia-rized a published article written by one of the professors, the other nailing a sophomore from Mississippi who'd in-sisted on hanging a Dixie flag in a dormitory window that faced the Simsbury African-American Society House. To Mark's knowledge, neither case had gone to trial, and neither had involved anyone even remotely cool. It was highly unlikely that he'd ever have to sit in judgment of friends.

And even if that day came, no one could force him to cooperate.

So the biggest remaining sticking point was the lan-guage about Sigma. He couldn't fathom disaffiliating from the fraternity, any more than he could fathom disaf-filiating from his arms and legs. He suspected he could live without the meetings, the secrets, the traditions, and the passwords, but he couldn't imagine being severed, once again, from people he loved, and who loved him back.

Severed, once again, from family.

But then, would he really *be* severed? Certainly not in the way he'd been severed from his parents. He could still spend his free time at Sigma. He could still sit behind the bar with best friends for life, spit beer at the freshmen, and watch Saturdays turn into Sundays. Although this

punishment would take the official brotherhood pin from
the cloth over his heart, it couldn't take anything else.

For the Sigmas would always be his brothers.

No matter what.

"Okay," he found himself saying to the dean. "You've
got a deal."

The dean smiled. "Smart lad," he said, standing and
extending a hand. "And don't worry about this being on
your transcript. As long as you fulfill your requirements,
I'll make sure your record stays clean."

"Wow," Mark said as he shook on it. "Thanks."

"Don't mention it. You just stay out of trouble for the
rest of the year. The next time I want to see you is at the
annual fall meeting of the D-Squad, next September. Got
it?"

"Got it."

"Good."

Mark hesitated a moment, then turned to leave. Before
opening the door, however, he was struck by a warm urge,
so he stopped and turned. "Dean Templeton," he said sincerely, "I'm in kind of a daze right now, so it's hard to
know what to think. But I want you to know how much I
appreciate your going to bat for me like this. I feel like
you've saved my life." He shifted awkwardly. "So . . .
thanks, you know?"

"You're quite welcome, Mark," said the dean with a
smile. "It's my distinct pleasure."

On scathing tongues of spiteful brothers, the news
spread quickly through Sigma's sacred halls: Mark Jessy
had been forced to drop out of the house because of some
cock-teasing townie bitch.

By dinnertime the brothers had decided that a going-away party was in order. After all, it was Thursday, so they'd be partying anyway. But now they had a reason. The seniors ordered the juniors to plan a bash, and the juniors ordered the sophomores to go pick up seven beer kegs from Dicky Bass's Discount Liquor Store. The stage was set.

And what a party it was.

The brothers sang, chanted, rhymed, and broke shit. They toasted Mark's bravery. They toasted his loyalty. They toasted his penis. They vomited in his honor. At midnight, Ran and Fairchild dragged Mark up to the third floor and out onto the roof. And there they sat, three good friends, Ran and Fairchild sipping slowly from a shared bottle of Jim Beam, Mark just staring out across the campus.

Fairchild put his arm around Mark and patted his friend's heart. "Hey," he said. "You okay?"

Mark nodded.

Ran, too, threw his arm over Mark's shoulders. "You're a true brother, man. There are Mark Jessy rhymes just waiting to be written."

Mark leaned back on his elbows. "You guys promise we'll always be brothers?"

Fairchild nodded exuberantly, and in his eagerness would have rolled off the roof were it not for Ran's saving grab.

"*Hell* yes!" Fairchild bellowed, righting himself. "*Given* we'll always be brothers!"

"Hey," breathed Ran, leaning closer, "in five years, none of this shit will matter. And every Homecoming, we'll meet *right here*. This is *our* spot. I'll bring the beer, you'll bring yourself, and we'll party like rock stars. We'll remember it all, man. Just you and me."

"And me," added Fairchild. "Don't forget me."

"And Dave."

Fairchild crawled back to the window. "It's cold up here. I'm going back downstairs." He looked over his shoulder. "You boys coming?"

"Yeah. All over your face." Ran laughed and kissed Mark sloppily on the cheek, then heaved his own inebriated frame through the open window and landed on the floor with a thud. He scraped himself from the floor and called out, "Hey, Mark. You coming or what?"

"Or what. I'll be down in a few."

Mark heard another crash and guessed Ran would be spending the night on the floor. Now alone, Mark stared out into the night, listening to the faint but familiar sounds rising from the barroom on wings of a blue eagle. And despite his earlier self-assurances, he couldn't help but dwell on the one devastating notion he thought he'd cast from his mind.

He'd lost his family again.

And this time, it was all his fault.

Hugging his knees to his chest, he began to rock like a child, and for the first time since that awful day on the soft meadow grass of Cherry Plain, he felt the tears begin their blurry advance.

He buried his head between his knees, immersing the beads that hung from his neck in shadows, and cried for a long time.

While Mark cried rooftop, Shawn sat strapped to her desk, putting the finishing touches on a thirty-two-page term paper on fossil fuel depletion. Digging a bottle of whiteout from the drawer, she dabbed and blew until the paper was as perfect as it would ever be. She then placed the paper neatly in her backpack and stretched out on the couch.

Her thoughts turned in gradual, midnight manner from energy conservation to Simsbury's newest outlaw. Boy, Mark Jessy had really done it this time. And yet there was something about his case that bothered her. True, he fit the classic mold of a spoiled-athlete-turned-sex-offender. True, he'd admitted to heinous charges. True, the dean's "compromise" was a slap on the wrist that would justifiably piss off the majority of women on campus.

Still, there had been something intangible about Angela McSheffrey's testimony that Shawn just didn't buy. And this skepticism bugged her, because it meant that she, like juries around the country, was disbelieving the words of a female victim. Nevertheless, the mistrust was there, and it now mildly captivated her not-yet-whipped mind.

She reached for her phone and dialed a four-digit extension.

"Hello?"

"Hey, Dara, it's Shawn."

"Shawn!" gushed Dara Devasto. "Hello, my erstwhile roomie! How goes the struggle for a clean environment?"

"Fine. How goes the fight for philosophical fame?"

"Fine, although it's rapidly occurring to me that to succeed as a philosopher I'll need to do many heavy drugs. What can I do for you at this late hour?"

Shawn glanced at her clock and noted it was now the

next day. "Ooh, sorry. Listen, Dara, I have some personal questions to ask you."

"Yippee. Let's talk dirty."

"It's about Mark Jessy."

"Sweet. He's one of my favorite topics."

Shawn scrunched her brow, closed her eyes, and asked, "You really did sleep with him, right?"

"What! Of course! When I bring guys home with me, I fuck them."

Shawn grimaced, though in truth she'd expected such a blunt, raunchy response. One of Simsbury's worst-kept secrets was that Dara Devasto had serious postgraduate designs on writing soft porn or working as a phone-sex girl for a few years before pursuing a masters in philosophy. "Thank you for your candor."

"My pleasure."

"Was he, uh, ever drunk when he came over?"

"We met at a Sigma party. That answer your question?"

"On those nights he was drunk," probed Shawn, "did he act overly aggressive? Did he ever *force* you to have sex? Was he rough?"

"Wait a minute . . . am I a material witness?"

Shawn laughed lightly, as if to suggest the question was absurd, but it came out as a forced grunt. "No. Of course not."

"Because I heard all about his little rape trial yesterday. Seems he found himself a bit of trouble with a local slut, huh?"

"Well—"

"The answer to your question, Shawn, is *yes*. Hey, I have another call. Can you hold?"

While Shawn held, an easing sort of comfort descended on her, as if her former roommate was a doctor who'd just communicated the happy results of a blood test. She told herself this was simply because Dara's affirmative disclosure supported Angela McSheffrey's claims, which was a *good* thing. But deep down, she knew Dara's disclosure actually supported what she *wanted* to believe, that Mark was exactly what he appeared to be on the surface, a dumb, cocky jock, one who might get lucky once in his life and fish a cute little *Crime and Punishment* quote from his ass, but one whose luck would eventually run out when faced with brave opposition that didn't care how handsome or athletic or slightly charming he was. Shawn now felt a swell of pride, knowing she'd helped a blue-collar girl like Angela stick it to a rich kid who'd probably been handed every break in life. That was the beauty of the D-Squad, the last pristine institution of justice on earth. Money and power and contrived wild cards couldn't buy guilt, nor could they buy acquittal. O. J. Simpson should've been so unlucky—

"I'm back," said Dara. "That was my mom. She's such a dodo bird. She keeps forgetting it's three hours earlier in Santa Monica. She says hi."

"Hi."

"Yeah. So anyway, *yes,* Mark was rough with me."

"Well, then I'd say he had this coming—"

"Once."

Shawn hesitated. "Excuse me?"

"He was rough with me *once.* Because I told him to be."

"I . . ."

"You sound shocked," said Dara with a laugh. "That's okay, so was he. He didn't like the idea one bit. I had to literally take his hand and whack it against my butt, and even then he didn't seem too comfortable about the whole thing. And to tell you the truth, it wasn't all that thrilling for me either. If you ask me, the whole pain-fetish thing is overrated, and I'm sure glad I figured that out before I went out and bought a whip or something—"

"Okay, I get the picture."

"Yeah . . ." said Dara absently.

Shawn eyed her watch and, concluding this conversation was going nowhere, decided to wrap it up. "So, you're basically saying—"

"I'm basically saying that Mark's sort of a mama's boy," finished Dara. "Only thing is, his mother's dead, but my brother-in-law's mother is too, and he actually reminds me a lot of Mark—"

"Wait a minute," said Shawn, suddenly digesting what she'd just heard. "Mark's mother is *dead*?"

There was a pause. "Jesus, Shawn, what secluded palace have you been living in? Yes, she's *dead*."

"Wow . . ."

"*Both* his parents are."

"What!?"

"Please tell me you knew this and just forgot—"

"No, I never *knew* this," spat Shawn, not certain whether her sudden annoyance was directed at Dara's snideness, or her own incorrect assumption that Mark was just another rich kid who'd been handed every break in life. "What . . . how did they die?"

"Beats me," said Dara. "The subject never came up.

But whenever I hear two parents dead at a relatively young age, I automatically assume car accident."

"God. How awful."

"I'd put money on a drunk-driving wreck. Mark's half American Indian, and you know what lushes *they* are."

Speechless, Shawn just shook her head slowly. Normally, she might've combated Dara's ignorant generalization, but on this night, after Mark Jessy had once again roughed up the grain of her *own* stereotypes, she felt too small and hypocritical to argue.

"Anyway," Dara said, "that was the last time we hooked up. He started avoiding me at parties, and I started fucking J. C. Miller."

"So," Shawn concluded, hoping to steer clear from any J. C. Miller yarns. "It's not like Mark ever *raped* you."

"What! There's no such thing in my bed."

Now there's a dangerous attitude, thought Shawn.

"No," continued Dara, "I'm telling you, Shawn, the boy's a kitten."

"Interesting."

"Hey, do you want me to testify?"

"Oh no," Shawn said quickly. "For you to testify would mean you'd have to give intimate details of your time with Mark. What's more—"

"And that would bother me *how*? This is the future 'Dirty Dara' you're talking to. Besides, do you think I'd be embarrassed to admit I had sex with Mark Jessy? I can name twenty girls who'd give their tit in a tote bag to say the same thing."

Shawn rolled her eyes, shook her head, and managed a smile. "Thanks, Dara. You've been helpful."

"Are you sure you don't want me to testify?"

"I'm sure. Your opinion on his *potential* for rape would have little bearing on what he actually *did*."

"Oh well."

"Besides," Shawn added softly, "it's too late now. Mark's trial is over."

CHAPTER SEVENTEEN

Mark took the decision of whether or not to return to Simsbury for his junior year to the place he'd taken all the other quandaries of his life.

The ocean.

And so the penultimate day of summer vacation found him sitting on his surfboard, floating aimlessly over the swells, his left hand dangling in the Atlantic, his right hand clutching a coin. Heads, he decided, and he'd show Simsbury he was worthy of an identity other than that of a convicted sex offender. He'd declare environmental studies as a major and study for a change. He'd hang out at Sigma, but party a little less. He'd get in shape for lacrosse and maybe kick some ass.

Tails, he'd transfer to Boston College and start over.

He wiped the salt from his face, flipped the coin, and inspected it carefully. Swearing out loud, he tossed the coin into the sea and watched it sink into the depths. Then he lay down on his board and paddled for shore.

That night, he packed his bags for Simsbury.

* * *

As had been the case the previous two years, the autumn and winter months of junior year passed like sound-buffed picture slides through Mark's internal projector. This time, however, each frame meant more, for each had a history.

The ignominy of living once again in a dormitory. The first few impersonal dinners in the independent dining hall. The subsequent meals alone in his dorm room. The evil stares cast by heavy women who wore combat boots and no makeup. The weight of an invisible scarlet letter R, for rapist.

The library, three nights a week. The gym, every single day. The simultaneous blossom of mind and muscle. The conservative return to the social scene. The weekend nights at Sigma, with best friends he still called brothers. The thankful knowledge he was still welcome there, twenty-four and seven.

The girl in the laundry room with the great face and body. The first joke. The first giggle. The first date, later that night, with Jessica LaChance, a freshman who liked vanilla frozen yogurt and wanted to be a veterinarian when she grew up.

The second date. The third, fourth, and fifth. The cautious move to the bedroom. The naked uncertainty. The tentative touching. The asking. The permission. The fumble for a condom.

The consenting sex between two young adults.

And that was when the specter of Angela McSheffrey began to dissipate like a watered-down wicked witch. On the morning he awoke naked and rested next to Jessica, he could finally put out of his mind, for an hour at least, the label that had been attached to him.

The pity party had ended.

Of course, not everyone was ready to let him forget what he'd done on a drunken night in a basement library. The SWA members had their own special glare they saved exclusively for him. An editorial in the school newspaper publicly asked, without naming names, why the administration continued to give "pathetic, paper-doll punishments to athletes, members of a certain fraternity in particular." A letter to the editor, in the very next issue, demanded to know how a convicted sex offender (still no names mentioned) could be allowed to sit on the D-Squad.

Conversely, a few sick guys considered Mark a hero for having nearly put the uninvited root to a local girl. One imbecile called him a "hard-hogged inspiration to men," and Mark punched him in the face. And there were some girls who let Mark know, in whispering ways, that they found his dangerous reputation sexy. One lash-batting freshman told him she'd gladly let him play rough with *her*; he told her to seek counseling.

By spring break, though, Mark's crime was more or less old news, and the majority of students seemed willing to let him achieve all but one of the goals he'd set while sitting on a surfboard. Besides, there were more worldly issues dividing the campus. Entire countries were raping each other. U.S. troops were policing foreign lands, and big brothers and friends from high school toed international lines, ready to trade their blood for democracy and oil and money and freedom. Notable figures were contracting HIV, victims of either bad luck or an irresponsible lifestyle. As always, the rights of the unborn fetus and abortion issues continued to straddle Bible and body.

With the world gone mad, there seemed no point in belaboring the sophomoric sin committed by Mark Jessy.

It was over.

On Easter Sunday, spring launched an all-out attack on winter's annual reign of terror, and by the time Simsbury's semiannual Christians had risen from their own temporary graves, Good had triumphed over Evil. While victorious steeple bongs rang ripples through the earth's slushy wounds, dazed civilians filed toward the cast-iron doors of Merriweather Chapel to celebrate resurrection and merit the monthly offerings wired by more religious parents. Mohawk Mark Jessy watched the parade with curiosity as mild as the air, then celebrated his *own* rebirth in the only fashion accessible to an orphan with precisely ninety-eight dollars to his name: He stole Jessica's Honda and set a sunroofed, CD'ed course for Portland, where suds could be sipped for a nickel a glass, and the sea could be sniffed for free.

Seven Jimmy Buffet songs later, he stepped from the cramped confines of the car to the wide open pavement of the nearly empty parking lot at the base of the Old Port town pier. A windy rush of brine zipped his jacket as he started down the wharf, which was deserted save for a few scurrying deckhands and one lone figure at the far end. He took his time wandering its length, pausing to look down on and admire barnacled boats and bask in the windy rays of low-tide, seaside sun. This was *his* place of worship, and its natural congregation sang salty psalms, each making a promise that the most well-deserved Cape Cod summer of Mark's life was less than two months away.

As he approached the end of the wharf, he spied the pre-looped lines of a dragger straining against iron cleats, so he strolled closer to check their source. The Wellfleet crews often fished Maine's early spring waters, and wouldn't it be wild if he bumped into someone he knew at the tip of a fish pier, hundreds of nautical miles from home. He hopped atop a railroad tie and studied the ship deck below. He didn't recognize any of the crew, and the vessel name, *Mary C,* rang familiar only in that, like all boats, it was named after a woman.

He turned away from the boat, and it was then that he saw her.

Her crossed legs relied on a vertical railroad tie. Her nylon sweats luffed like sails in the breeze. Her hands hid somewhere in the recesses of a blue barn jacket. Her hair rode the whipping wind forward, concealing her face beneath blond chaos, but Mark had no doubt who it was.

Shawn Jakes.

His first instinct was to run, for though she'd captained the front row of several of his environmental studies classes, they hadn't spoken in any way since his hearing. And if she'd responded with threats of violence to his freshman antics, he could only imagine what sort of wrath she'd rain down on him *now*.

He turned to flee.

But, for the second time in three years, stopped at the threshold of escape.

For he was a junior now, new-and-improved and nearly a man, with near–dean's list credentials, an All-America nomination for lacrosse, and positive school newspaper reviews for the "awareness seminar" he'd co-ordinated: "Personal Fouls: The Disturbing Culture of Sex and Violence Among Athletes." Back from depths far lower than had accompanied a dorm room rejection, he told himself he was too tough for even Shawn's lip-gnashing teeth.

Taking a deep breath, he braved the few rotted planks that separated them, struck a neat pose, and relayed the first piece of wit that popped into his mind.

"Looking for a summer job?"

They watched the sun drown through the wharfside windows of a small seafood restaurant, the crudely painted name of which Mark would never remember. He'd remember everything else, though. The spirited discussions about the commercial fishing industry, on which Shawn seemed to be a stunning expert. The passionate glow to her cheeks, as she alternated her conversational glance between Mark and the deep blue, darkening harbor. The gawking stares of the local salts, who probably wished their wives looked and glowed a little bit like Shawn.

They searched domestic beers and oysters (don't get any fresh ideas, Mr. Gland), for pearls of wit and white. She poked fun at the way he flared his nostrils every time he made his late entrance to Fisheries Management class. Like an animal's defense mechanism, she noted. Yes, he agreed, sort of like a freshman threatening to bite another freshman's lips off.

They traded digs all night, but managed to avoid any references to his sophomore sex crime. And by night's end, he had to admit it was the best time he'd ever had with a woman.

At midnight they again found the coolness of the Old Port air, made more shivery by the tingle of a mutual attraction neither had fully yet acknowledged. He escorted her to her Jeep, told her he'd had a very nice time, and invited her to come watch a lacrosse game. She smiled and said she'd had a very nice time, too, and that it was too bad a D-Squad case hadn't arisen over the course of the year, because she'd been looking forward to hearing his *own* views on crime and punishment.

Mark smiled and said good night. Then he drove back to campus, thinking all the while that Shawn was some kind of woman and wondering if he should've kissed her.

Shawn recovered from her odd disappointment at Mark not kissing her, in time to finish all her take-home exams a week before they were due. She packed her trunk for Aspen, then decided to hang out a few days on campus to unwind before the first leg of her ridiculously long drive home. One day, while lounging on the quad, she noticed clumps of students parading toward the athletic fields. She spotted a friend amid the many and asked what was up.

"Lacrosse tourney game," said the friend, looking amazed at her ignorance. "Us versus Princeton."

Impulsively, she fell in stride with the throng, and

though her first brief thought was of Mark Jessy, she quickly forced his harborside image from her mind. She wasn't going just to watch *him.* She was obviously going because it was a big game. Everyone else was going; why shouldn't she go, too?

By the time they arrived at the field the game was raging. Students and relatives and local lacrosse fans filled the aluminum bleachers, lined the mucky sidelines, and huddled around kegs of beer. The brothers of Theta Kappa Rho ran shirtless and painted throughout, leading drunken cheers that mixed athletic themes with sexual ones. Security guards did their by-the-hour-best to ignore the peripheral anarchy, their sunglassed eyes directed firmly on the modern-day warfare playing out between refereed lines.

Shawn had never seen a Simsbury lacrosse game; in fact, as she stood among the masses, she couldn't recall having ever attended *any* Simsbury sporting events, save for the ones she herself had participated in. She guessed this was due to her natural aversion to watching other people perform, an activity that usually made her fidgety.

Her friend had stolen a program, and when she was done listing whom among the twenty-four rostered players she'd kissed, she gave it to Shawn. A bold heading announced the significance of the contest: "Simsbury vs. Princeton, First Round, NCAA Tournament." It was the informational blurb on the inside cover, however, that piqued Shawn's curiosity, a sensation that intensified as she read.

Welcome to today's match, featuring the fourth-seeded Cardinals (14–2) playing host to the fifth-seeded Tigers of Princeton (13–2). The home team is led by AP All-American Mark Jessy, who finished third in the nation in scoring (55g, 44a, 99p) and was recently hailed by *Sports Illustrated* as "the best kept secret in college lacrosse . . ."

Shawn trailed off the page and focused hard on the patch of soppy ground visible between the bottom edge of the program's recycled paper and her sandals; she was doing everything in her power to keep from seeking out the leader of the home team.

After two minutes of staring intently at the mud, however, she finally convinced herself she was being childish, and since she was here, she might as well watch the damn game. If Mark lived up to his notices . . . well, good for him. In fact, she almost hoped he *was* as good as advertised, for then he'd fit neatly into a one-dimensional niche she could handle. She *wanted* to think of him as the stereotypical villain of his own contrived "awareness seminar," not as a sharp wit who could cite both Russian classics and the recent history of Georges Bank fishing regulations.

She consulted the program and noted he was number ten. Then she stuffed the pages in her pocket, and began watching twenty-two helmeted men chase, pass, and cradle a hard rubber ball while they whacked each other with sticks of varying length.

Just before halftime, the ball rolled toward her side of the field, and she jumped back as a player from each team converged on the ball and collided with shattering force. The Simsbury player clearly got the better of the exchange, driving the Princeton player violently to the turf.

While the student body hollered with delight and did the tomahawk chop, Shawn glimpsed the Simsbury player's wild green eyes as he scooped up the ball and sped away. Then she targeted the red number ten etched on his white shirt.

Mark Jessy.

I'm telling you, Shawn, the boy's a kitten . . .

Mesmerized, she watched the kitten tear gracefully and relentlessly up and down the field, eluding and killing people. And despite the weak inner voice pointing out that Mark was *better* than advertised, and thus fit *more* neatly into the one-dimensional niche, she simply couldn't tear her eyes off him, and she was disgusted with herself.

As the game progressed, however, she couldn't help but become caught up in the action, a true fan and Simsbury socialite at last. She hugged her friend and sang the fight song after every goal for the good guys. She booed every call for the bad guys. She took part in a thousand-fan chant that labeled the Princeton goalie a "sieve." She participated in a wave that circled the field at least six times. She even swung her make-believe tomahawk every time Mark Jessy humiliated an opponent. Mostly, though, she just screamed, supportively and belligerently.

With less than a minute to go, Simsbury led by one, but Princeton threatened with a man-advantage. Suddenly, the ball squirted free from its fluid run of pass-and-catch and rolled toward midfield. While twenty-one players and two thousand fans moved and shrieked in slow motion, Mark raced in from nowhere, scooped up the ball, and tore down the field.

Only Princeton's three long-sticks remained in position to defend Mark's attack. The Simsbury star made fools of the first two and went one-on-one with the remaining man, who managed to clobber him to the outside with slashes that went unpenalized only because the time remaining now measured seconds. About twenty yards from the goal, however, he spun in a dramatic three-sixty, humiliating the one final opponent whose forward momentum carried him harmlessly out of bounds and into the throng of semi-naked, heavily inebriated Theta Kappa Rhos. Having left his net to challenge, Princeton's goalie lowered his shoulder and lanced his stick and met Mark with a mauling hit that thundered above the storm of the crowd but failed to prevent one last weak-but-effective shot from bouncing into the untended net.

The aluminum bleachers and mucky sidelines exploded, spewing students and relatives and local lacrosse fans around and atop the twenty-four Cardinals who'd fallen in a heap on Mark Jessy. Caught up in the riotous mob, Shawn ran in circles and screamed like an insane woman.

And as she watched the pile of people on top of Mark grow, and wished with all her will to be on the bottom with him, she admitted with an almost euphoric sense of relief that she didn't care *what* stereotypical niche Mark fit into.

For the first time in her life, Shawn had a crush.

And it felt great.

That evening, Mark sentenced himself to his room to study for his last exam. He sat at his desk like a good soldier, ice pack perched atop his shirtless shoulder, open text angled toward his face. The game, however, had left him achy and antsy, and the words and terms that needed to be memorized bounced off his eyes. So he poked the stereo on, fiddled with the knob, and as Don Henley sang of summer boys, he limped to his window and looked out on the mid-spring world.

Branches of dense pine filtered the sun's last light, cutting shadows in next year's sophomores, juniors, and seniors as they hauled trunks and sacks across the dimming quad toward the blinking hazards of the waiting airport shuttle. The departing image reminded him of home, and he reflexively reached for the phone. Kiko couldn't drive, afford interstate bus fare, or even read very well, which meant he relied on phone calls to learn each game's outcome.

Mark had just started dialing when he heard a knock on his door. Expecting a farewell visit from Jessica, he traded the phone for the funny good-bye card he'd bought and hobbled across the room.

He opened the door.

It wasn't Jessica.

She wore beachcombing pants loosely cuffed over flip-flops, and a peach sweater that contrasted breathtakingly with the blue-eyed face that had clearly spent the day in the sun.

"Hi," Shawn Jakes said. "Are you busy?"

"Not at all," lied Mark as he dropped Jessica's card on the floor. "Come in."

She slid past him and glided to the middle of his scrambled room. "Oh," she said, noticing the open books on his desk. "You're studying. I can come back—"

"No, not at all. I *was* studying . . . but . . . you know, my shoulder . . ."

"Yeah," she said, eyeing the ice on his bare shoulder, then eyeing his bare chest, thankfully avoiding any questions regarding the source of the tight black beads that encircled his bare neck. "What happened?"

"Princeton's goalie hits like a truck," he said with a smile.

"Ouch."

"I'll live."

"I hope so. You're . . . an amazing player."

"Thanks."

Silence, awkward and long.

"Here," blurted Mark, sweeping clear a spot on the couch. "Have a seat. I think I have something"—he crouched in front of his miniature refrigerator—"cold in here."

"Oh, that's okay," she answered from behind him, "I just came to say good-bye."

"Oh?" Mark said, straightening.

"Yeah. And to pay you back for the other night." She fished through her pockets. "That was an expensive tab you picked up."

"Nonsense," Mark said, although the bill had left him with barely enough to cover his bus ride home. "It was on me."

Now she smiled. "You mean, it was like a *date*?"

"Something like that, I guess."

Silence again. Mark rubbed his shoulder. Shawn rocked on her heels and examined the walls.

Say something, Mark thought to himself. *Don't just stand there like an id—*

"Hey, by the way," she gushed suddenly, her eyes wide, "I just found out I'll be back East this summer." She glanced at the carpet. "And I was wondering . . . do you think I could meet your uncle? Maybe spend the day with him on his boat?"

"Sure," said Mark, trying not to sound as if a summer-time visit from Shawn Cara Jakes would make his entire life. "Kiko's always looking for an extra deckhand."

"Great," she said, then grinned. "I mean, I'll stay out of your way. I realize you've probably got a whole list of hearts to break this summer."

"No problem. I'll show you the Cape."

"I've seen the Cape."

"Not *my* way, you haven't."

She opened her mouth to respond, then hesitated. "Sounds like fun," she said finally, with a hint of what Mark would've sworn was suggestion, had this been any-one other than the woman who'd sat in judgment of him at his rape trial. She started for the door. "I guess I'll see you when the sun is hot."

"Wait a minute," said Mark. "Don't you want my phone number or something?"

She turned with a smirk. "Nah. I'll get it from Dara. I'm assuming she's got it written across her inner thigh."

And then she was gone, her exit leaving behind a faint, lovely smell.

Mark watched the creaking door for a moment, then collapsed on the couch.

And began counting the days.

Sixty-seven days later, looking like a late-afternoon model for Coppertone, Oakleys, and ponytails, she bounced down the bumpy pine path, her topless, doorless Jeep absorbing every shock along the way before parking its four Rocky Mountain wheels between a tangled mass of netting and a pile of buoys. She hugged Mark, shook Kiko's hand, then set to preparing a tasty meal of chicken and wild, western mushrooms that they devoured amid the buzz of wild, eastern mosquitoes. She listened politely to Kiko's suppertime fish tales and graciously accepted his invitation to star in two of her own the next day.

She dragged the ocean's commercial floor with Kiko from dawn till noon, returning in time to angle the ocean's recreational surface on *De-baitable Babe*'s afternoon charter. She screeched with delight as five hundred pounds of bluefish flew over the gunwale, and with help she gaffed a couple of the bigger ones. She sunbathed in white bikini and bloodied denim on the sportfishing vessel's lucky bow and damn near caused a riot among the six paying customers, the drunkest of whom gave her a fifty-buck tip at the trip's conclusion and asked her to (hiccup) marry him. She thanked him for the offer and announced that she would be taking the first mate out to dinner.

She gave Mark the Jeep keys and let him whisk her to Provincetown's Lobster Pot, where she ordered white wine and lobster tails for two sandwiched around a half-dozen oysters, three of which she pushed in his direction without any warnings against big, glandular ideas. Afterward, while walking the wharf, she agreed with him that though yachts *were* fun to look at, she too would prefer a more practical vessel. She sat beside him at the end of the pier and smiled at the seagulls calling incessantly to one another in the advancing darkness. She closed her eyes as the harbor breeze seemed to delight something deep within her. She slipped a warm hand into his and put her head on his shoulder.

In the morning she flipped pancakes and laughed while Kiko recounted between breakfast bites how she'd given his crew a "collective pulpit" the day before. When apprised that "pulpit" was shipspeak for "erection," she said, with a wink thrown Mark's mortified way, that she'd figured that much, and anything for the boys.

She clapped excitedly as Mark piled two fly rods and two surfboards into the Jeep, and two instructional hours later squealed with glee upon catching and actually riding her first wave. She flexed, spat water, and hummed the *Jaws* theme every time her board capsized fin-up. She cackled, splashed about like a dolphin, and awed the regular surfers, who on this day could do nothing more than lie on their bellies and just plain *stare* at the sensational-looking woman on a ten-foot longboard.

After the tide arrived, she drank beer and ate animal crackers (his lucky fishing snack, he'd explained earlier) and cast home-tied flies into the surf. She equaled her date's haul of "schoolie" striped bass, and kissed each one on the lips before returning it gently to the wash so it could grow up big and strong and breed like a rabbit to strengthen its species' numbers.

And when the fish had moved on, and the sun had gone down, she pulled him close and led him in a tuneless, timeless, ocean dance.

She locked eyes with his and explained in a soft voice that there *were* no old friends from summer camp, that she'd really driven two thousand miles to amend her answer to a past question.

"If you kissed me," she whispered above the beach strains, "I would kiss you back."

She then took a step back, stripped naked, and walked toward the water.

Mark watched her join the gentle sea's embrace, then shed his clothes and followed her.

He spent the first night of senior year at Chewnocker's— the local tavern co-owned by a wookie-like mountain man and the only resident orthopedic surgeon in Georgeville— surrounded by Ran Robinson, A. J. Dominic, Pete Thresher, and several pitchers of beer. The general topic of conversation was, of course, who'd gotten laid by whom over the summer. Mark waited until the others had finished touting their own sexual exploits before dropping his own bomb.

He was seeing Shawn Jakes, and things were getting pretty fucking serious.

Incredulous cries greeted this announcement, but he convinced them it was true, and even claimed his bachelor days were over.

"A player like you?" Ran reasoned, then shook his head. "First time you do something stupid, you'll be out on your ass. I give it two weeks, *max*."

Ran's prediction was way off. It was a full month before Shawn first locked Mark out of her room, after Madame Rumor spotted Mark Jessy and J. C. Miller streaking after a Sigma party one night. Her rationale was, as always, clearheaded.

"With all the trouble you've had, Mark, one would

think that you'd be a little more hesitant to whip out your penis!"

"Come on, Shawn. We're all born naked. What's wrong with getting back to nature every once in a while?"

"Oh right. The Sigma boys are *so* earthy! The closest they come to nature is when they stumble outside to puke in the bushes."

The fight resolved nothing, and there'd be several more just like it in the months to come, interspersed with the occasional deeper discussion of Mark's staunch refusal to talk about his parents and the huge, unattractive wall he erected every time the topic came up (Shawn finally gave up her search for the truth in December, when candlelit questions summoned nothing but more disappointing guardedness; ultimately, she could trust only that his reasons for family secrecy were good ones, and all in due time).

Despite their on-again, off-again friction, the relationship managed to intensify. Mark knew how to humor her, though her chuckles were often accompanied by slaps to the back of his head. And Shawn knew how to broaden his intellectual horizons, though he sometimes snored during the campus plays she dragged him to.

Regardless, they had fun together. Of course, in college, what else is there?

BOOK II
The Field

CHAPTER EIGHTEEN

The 200th Year
Monday, February 23

8:20 P.M.

The fun was gone from Sigma Delta Phi, and it would stay gone until the twelve senior brothers could weave their wonderful magic and save the brotherhood.

As always, they met in the Brotherhood Room, their athletic frames filling the fancy leather chairs. As always, they met under the guise of their Greek nicknames.

As always, Beta kicked things off.

"I just talked to Alpha."

"You *did*?" asked Kappa, the worship evident in his voice.

"I did."

"Really? In person?"

"Well, no," admitted Beta. "I talked to the alum who runs Alpha's southwest something-or-other division, but it's the message, not the messenger." Then, seeing the clear disappointment in Kappa's expression, he said, "For God's sake, Kappa, Alpha's not going to take time out from making billions to call the undergrads when he can just as easily have one of the other alums do it."

"Obviously," barked Gamma. "What did he say?"

"The D-Squad met today."

"And?" prompted Gamma, his muscles visibly tensing.

Beta sipped from a water bottle. "Shawn Jakes is on the warpath."

"*Bitch!*" spat Epsilon.

"I never did like that girl," Iota commented.

"And speaking of Shawn," Beta continued, "it looks like we have a problem."

"Oh, like we didn't already?"

"Shut up, Rho," warned Gamma, leaning forward and twitching his neck. "What is it, Beta?"

Beta turned to Kappa. "Did Jocelyn sleep here on Saturday night?"

Kappa thought, then shrugged. "Shit, I don't know."

"Think."

Kappa squinted momentarily, then spat on the floor. "Yeah, she did."

Beta nodded slowly. "I knew it."

"Why? What's wrong?"

"Supposedly, Shawn has some *anonymous source* who claims that pledge Ewing was found naked, with vulgar poetry written all over his body."

"So? What's that have to do with Jocelyn?"

Beta looked at him seriously. "Is she still friendly with Shawn?"

"Of course. So what?"

Beta nodded again and looked around the room. The rest of the brothers got the picture.

"You *idiot!*" screamed Theta. "Kappa, what the hell was she doing downstairs?"

"Fuck you!" Kappa shouted, his body curled defensively. "I didn't invite her down, but she's got legs!"

"Dammit man, you gotta keep that bitch on a leash."

Kappa punched the arm of his chair and gritted his teeth. "I kind of had other things on my mind, peckerhead! You know, the little matter of a dying pledge!"

"He was already dead," said Omega. "Your mind should've been focused on protecting the brotherhood."

"That's the number-one priority," added Epsilon.

"All right, already!" Kappa waved his arms in front of him, as if to silence an orchestra, then slumped back in his chair and put his hand over his eyes. "I'll take care of it."

"Good. The sooner the better."

Without looking up, Kappa flashed his middle finger in Gamma's general direction.

"That's enough," Beta said, finishing his water. "Other than that, the meeting went well. Templeton delayed the preliminary hearing until Thursday. Until then, I suggest—"

"Wait a minute," interrupted Zeta. "*What* hearing?"

Beta stared at him. "The preliminary hearing into the death of Sigma pledge Chad Francis Ewing." He looked around the room. "C'mon guys! I *expected* this. One of our pledges is *dead*. He fell off the *balcony*. You *know* how the Board of Directors feels about fraternities. They want an investigation, and the D-Squad is going to give them one."

"And," Gamma added gravely, "if they find out what *really* happened, we'll be closed down before we get a chance to pack our bags. Shit, someone might even have to go to jail."

He threw up his devastating arms. "I mean, do you guys realize how *fucked* we could be?"

9:03 P.M.

Now sipping a homemade martini, chairman Henry Davenport sat in his gold-buttoned suit at his gold-trimmed desk, holding a gold-plated pen while he thumbed slowly through the gold-embroidered Annual Alumni Gift Ledger. Next to the ledger lay a pad of personalized stationery, the exposed page of which was divided into two columns. As he flipped through the ledger, he kept careful score on the pad, pausing every few minutes or so to wet his lips with martini and shake some life into the cranky pen.

Minutes passed, pages flipped, and the glass emptied, and when he reached the back cover of the ledger, Davenport attacked his calculator, jotted down some figures, then leaned back in his chair and frowned.

Templeton had been wrong: Eighty-five percent of the annual endowment did *not* come from alumni with Greek affiliation, and sixty of that did *not* come from Sigma.

It was more like ninety and seventy, respectively.

10:45 P.M.

Jocelyn Patricola opened the oven door and, squinting through the onrush of heat, noted with satisfaction that the nachos were bubbling and browning and just about done. She closed the oven door and glanced at her watch. Ten forty-five. Pete had said he'd be there by 10:30. She shrugged, accepting that Pete was always late, and that she loved him too much to care.

She bounced into the bathroom for one final hair check and saw that her brown hair fell soft and shiny, as her new shampoo had promised it would. She splashed a dab of perfume on her wrists, freed another button on her see-through blouse, spun a Sade CD, and poured a glass of chardonnay. She sipped her wine, checked the nachos every few seconds, and smiled when she heard the back door open and close quickly.

"I'm in here, honey," she sang as she wriggled into a pot holder and opened the oven door. She quickly extracted the tray of nachos and dropped it on the stove with a clang. Over the hiss of hot cheese, she heard boots scuff into the kitchen behind her.

"These look done," she said, then whipped off the pot holder and turned to greet her boyfriend.

She was met with a blow to the head, followed by a series of quick, sharp jabs to the chest and arms. She screamed as she slammed into the refrigerator and covered her head with her arms as she crashed to the floor.

Her first terrifying thought—that there was a killer in her apartment—led to a reassuring one: If she could survive until Pete got there, he'd pummel whoever loomed above her. But even as both these notions played off each other inside her dazed head, she heard the voice she loved spit down at her.

"You stupid bitch!"

She separated her arms from her face and stole a cowering upward glance. Pete's face glowed with the raw heat of winter and rage.

She sat up slowly, her trembling hand cupping the side

of her head as she begged herself not to cry. "What . . ." she moaned softly, "what was that for?"

He circled like a boxer, his boots clomping loudly on the linoleum. "Tell me something," he said, his voice low and full of malice. "Do you enjoy coming over to Sigma with me? Do you and your bitchy friends like drinking the beer *we* pay for?"

She shook her head and whimpered.

He knelt beside her. "No?"

"O-of course," she stammered finally. "I *love* going to Sigma with you."

He nodded, his face incredibly void. "I thought so. That's why I was surprised to hear how you've been chatting with Shawn about Chad Ewing."

Quick, deny it! "I don't know what you're talking about."

"Don't fuck with me, Jocelyn. You told Shawn he was naked and that he had rhymes written all over him, didn't you? And now that cunt is going to organize a fucking peace rally, or something."

He knew. There was no point in denying it now; she still had the scar from the last time she'd lied to her boyfriend.

She sniffed hard. "Well . . . yeah . . . that's what I saw."

Pete stuck his finger in her mouth, hooked her cheek, and twisted. He yanked her head down and toward him, and the pain was unreal. "*No!*" he bellowed. "You didn't see a fucking *thing*, because you were upstairs *sleeping*. The next time you see Shawn you'll tell her you made a mistake. Understand?"

Through the humiliation and agony, she nodded.

Satisfied by her wordless obedience, he released her

mouth and rose calmly to his feet, as if the whole altercation had never taken place. He grabbed a handful of nachos and stomped toward the living room, and though several retaliatory urges scorched through her, Jocelyn just sat there in pain while Pete replaced Sade with the screaming type of music that made him feel romantic.

CHAPTER NINETEEN

The 200th Year
Tuesday, February 24

10:49 A.M.

Several years back, right about the time Simsbury's decision makers deemed the men's lacrosse and hockey teams worthy of Division I competition, one of the many bored-but-wealthy alums, named Theodore Lipshit, donated twelve million dollars expressly for the construction of a new, space-age athletic facility. Students and alumni alike were overjoyed at the prospect. Unfortunately, Lipshit was as egomaniacal as he was rich, and to everyone's dismay he insisted the new facility bear his name. Hence, upon completion, this eighth wonder of the Simsbury world was baptized the Lipshit Field House. Athletic rivals giggled.

Thankfully, over time the field house came to be known by a more rugged moniker: the Cage. Although this, too, was not exactly what Cardinals young and old had in mind, *anything* was better than Lipshit.

Despite its grungy nickname, the Cage was a truly awesome structure, twice as big as the Janis Performing Arts Center (previously the largest building on campus), and four times the size of the library (a fact that frosted the asses of intellectual types). The Cage housed an Olympic-sized swimming pool, a basketball court, and a climate-controlled hockey rink. A glass aerobics room overlooked the track oval, which circled three clay tennis courts and a six-on-six indoor soccer field. The cushy men's and women's locker rooms were separated by a state-of-the-art trainer's room. The weight room contained the best equipment money could buy.

To avoid the afternoon masses, Mark lifted in the morning whenever he could find the time; he'd been turned on to the idea by Fairchild, who'd been turned on to the idea by Dominic. Occasionally, they were able to recruit Ran for comic relief. Today, all four happened to have open mornings, so they'd met at half-past nine. They were now done with their workout, and had just exited the sixty-eight-degree mildness of the Cage for the arctic conditions outdoors. They zipped their collars over the lower halves of their faces, then turned down the flaps so they could engage in macho talk while they made their way to Sigma for lunch.

Dominic promised to bring death upon some asshole who'd looked at him funny in the mailroom. Fairchild stopped several times to dry-heave into the snow and sarcastically thank Dominic for the brutal mass-gaining workout he'd designed. With each delay, of course, Ran threatened to puke for real if he didn't get some food in his belly soon.

But there still was no talk of either Chad Ewing's death or the pending D-Squad investigation. Mark knew that his presence blocked discussion, and this knowledge drove from him the camaraderie he normally felt after working out with his Sigma buddies. His friends didn't trust the party he represented, perhaps didn't trust *him*, and it hurt. He was dying to tell them he was on their side, that his goal was to make a mockery of the investigation, but he didn't know how to broach the subject. For the first time, he felt awkward around his former Sigma brothers.

And for the thousandth time he wished he'd never laid drunken eyes on a girl named Angela McSheffrey.

4:14 P.M.

As crippled sunlight crawled through the windows of the stuffy dorm room, Roy and Carla Ewing prepared to pack what was left of their only son's life into suitcases and cardboard boxes. That it had been only six months since they completed the joyous reverse of this exercise only added to the current cruelty; both felt as if they'd literally kill for it to be September again.

Now it would be winter forever.

Chad's side of the room appeared as though he'd just stepped out and would be returning momentarily. His bed was unmade. A letter from a high school friend lay open on his desk. A laundry basket filled with clean darks sat on the floor next to his dresser. The undisturbed state reminded the Ewings that their oldest child had been alive not long ago. The room was evidence of existence, yet proof of demise.

They examined even the tiniest items with mournful adoration. His Chicago Bulls banner. His Snoopy piggy bank. His Simsbury baseball hat. Carla closed her eyes and sniffed a bottle of cologne until she thought her lungs might collapse. What she'd give to wrap her arms around that smell. It was all she could do to place the bottle in the laundry sack, where it would sit in their dusty attic with the rest of the shattered dreams.

On his hands and knees, Roy collected sacred items from beneath Chad's bed. Underwear. A deflated football. A few shoe boxes. As he started to stand, he noticed a small bundle of trash against the back wall that he was inclined to ignore. However, not even crumbs would be ignored today, if they'd once touched Chad's lips. He'd gather every piece of his son, including this pile of apparent rubble.

He jammed his armpit against the hard metal bed frame and strained his fingers beyond hurt. His hand finally closed on the dirty bundle, and he struggled to his feet.

The balled-up mass of fabric was bound so tightly that it was a moment before he realized there were several pieces to the wad. He shook the clump and the particles reluctantly separated. Into his left hand fell three rags, while into his right fell just one.

And that's when the smell hit him.

Beer.

He wrinkled his nose as he examined the damp tatters with eyes that didn't understand. The three in his left hand were actually bandannas, and for a lip-quivering instant he recalled the sugar-and-spice hair kerchiefs Carla had insisted on wearing during her second pregnancy, as if to petition God (successfully) for a child they could name Julie. Not clear on the bandannas' meaning, he turned his attention to the sticky cloth he held in his right hand.

What he saw made him drop the rag in horror.

Blood.

Lots and lots of blood.

8:16 P.M.

Though growing tired of this late-night office activity, Templeton knew he'd be handsomely compensated for his troubles. And on this night, he knew his stay would be brief.

He flicked on his desk lamp, then added his computer to the working pieces of technology in the room. He moused his way to the e-mail screen and began to hunt and peck:

> *T-Bone. Just came from dinner with the Ewings. A few more tears, but that's to be expected. I gently persuaded them to retrieve the body on Thursday morning, and to fly out around midday. Looks like we're on for tomorrow with the coroner. I assume your man is ready to play dress-up.*
>
> *I like your idea for Doc Marston.*
>
> *Don't you just love these small, ignorant towns?*

He addressed the message and sent it urgent and private. Two minutes later, all technology had been shut down for the night, and Templeton was gone.

CHAPTER TWENTY

The 200th Year
Wednesday, February 25

1:03 P.M.

The day had dawned gray and gusty, and by noon a heavy snow had begun to fall. It was perfect weather to honor the dead.

Out of respect for the friends and family of the deceased, President Carlisle had canceled all Wednesday classes, a rare and noble gesture that struck a moral chord in the blossoming souls of Simsbury's elite students, many of whom grappled with the ensuing dilemma. Did they dare bolt for the day, maybe go skiing or head on over to the nearby Bowdoin College library to track down that elusive periodical crucial to midterm papers? Or would the Gods of Decency strike them dead, or at least make them bomb their next job interview, if they skipped the memorial service of a fellow student?

No formal opinion poll was necessary to determine that collective moral conscience had prevailed. Merriweather Chapel was mobbed.

Mark had been one of the many wafflers, but for different reasons. The truth was that he'd been scared to go to the memorial. He'd already been to one in his life.

And one had been enough.

Through the prayers and eulogies the service passed without incident, save for the appearance of a rude photographer bent on recording the Ewings' grief as they walked down the aisle after the final hymn. The photographer managed a couple of flashy rounds before Simsbury security and a few Sigmas politely tossed him. The incident sparked more tears from the Ewings, murmurs of disapproval, and, for Mark, a horrifying flashback that borrowed him briefly from the distant side of death.

For just a moment he was nine years old, dressed up and perplexed in the front row of a tiny cathedral in Cazenovia, less than a mile from Cherry Plain. For just a moment strobes of light, in *his* direction, showering him with questions he'd never understand. And then strong arms carried him past the cameras and chaos to the safety of Cape Cod . . .

The sudden moan of organ music saved him from his memories, and reality found him staring at the shoes of classmates as they shuffled past. He blinked, stood, and obediently followed Shawn and the entire congregation outside to the quad, for what the minister termed "a very special conclusion to our service."

The student body formed a huge ring around the Sigma brothers, Mr. and Mrs. Ewing, and Chad's younger sister, Julie, around whom the snow spiraled as she separated herself from her parents, walked to the middle of the circle, and held up a single, white helium balloon.

On the balloon was simply written, *"Chad."*

She kissed it once and let it go.

All eyes watched the balloon float upward, through the driving snow and over the dead trees, until, like Chad Ewing, it was gone forever.

1:34 P.M.

He pulled the rented Toyota into the parking lot of the Cumberland County Coroner's Office, killed the engine, and looked at his watch.

Perfect. Right now, Roy Ewing would be attending the memorial service for his son, which meant there was absolutely no chance of him showing up now. They'd planned this well.

He ran down his mental checklist. *Wavy hairpiece?* He reached up and centered it on his head. *Dark sunglasses?* He looked out at the sky, which spewed forth snow at an increasing rate. Would sunglasses look suspicious? He reached into the glove compartment and pulled out the cheesy shades he'd bought for two bucks in Old Orchard Beach. He put them on his face and checked his reflection.

He looked like a mourner.

Woe was he.

The glasses would stay.

He was all set to leave the car when he remembered that he still needed to make one further adjustment. He grabbed the bottle of lemon juice from the paper bag on the passenger seat, took off his glasses, and squeezed a drop in each eye. He teared instantly, but since the sting was certainly worth the money, he forced his lids to stay open until he could literally feel red veins web the whites of his eyes.

He exited the car and moved toward the Coroner's Office, practicing his mourner's walk and altering his state of mind.

I am Roy Ewing, he told himself. *My son is dead, and I am devastated.*

This would be easy.

Dick Finnerty, Cumberland County coroner, had been born in a converted chicken coop a mile down the road. He'd been delivered by a midwife. He'd seen the outside of Maine only once, during a moose-hunting trip to Canada thirty-two years ago. He'd spent the rest of his sixty-four years entrenching himself in the community he now served, which was why he considered himself the foremost authority on the wishes of his hardworking, God-fearing constituents, at least when it came to death and decency.

The people of Cumberland County had eyes for the Bible, not tabloid rags. They didn't want to know that Marion Leverone, mother of four, wife of Bob, had died of complications due to syphilis contracted during a fling. They wanted to know that she'd died of complications due to *pneumonia,* and that her last words had been words of love. And they didn't want to know that Peter Wallace, son of Reverend Wallace, had died of a heroin overdose at age twenty-four and that traces of semen had been found in his anus. They wanted to know that Peter Wallace had died of a rare, pre-existing heart condition and that he'd loved his pretty high school sweetheart until the day God claimed his soul.

The issue was not *how* or *why* a member of the com-

munity had died. Rather, the issue was simply that someone was dead.

And had left loved ones behind.

His big-city colleagues just didn't understand this, but
he did, which was why, for the past thirty-nine years, he'd
lent his sense of decency to a field inundated with ring-
masters fostering a circus atmosphere. Others poked their
scalpels here, their noses there, and even held press conferences. Finnerty held *family* conferences and kept his
nose halfway between fact and compassion.

He was the last of a dying breed.

Now, this last-of-a-dying-breed sat at his desk, sipping
his beloved coffee, and waiting for the father of Chad
Francis Ewing, a Simsbury student who'd died on Sunday and now lay downstairs.

As he reviewed his notes yet again, Finnerty noted that
this was another one of those cases that raised the issue of
fact versus compassion. This time, however, the deceased
hadn't been a local resident. Therefore, Finnerty felt no
inherent loyalty toward the Ewing family, no sense of
duty to protect the dead boy's reputation.

And given what Finnerty had discovered, Chad
Ewing's reputation at Simsbury, whatever it had been before, would be unavoidably smeared.

Should, that is, he choose to throw out compassion and
divulge the facts.

The intercom on his phone beeped twice. Finnerty
frowned, pressed the "talk" button, and said, "What is it,
Dorothy."

Dorothy Rucker's voice screeched over the speakerphone, "Roy Ewing here to see you."

"Send him in."

Moments later, Dorothy opened the door, and in walked a striking figure, tall and seemingly composed. The removal of his dark glasses, however, revealed crimson, disconsolate eyes, the type of eyes Finnerty dealt with daily.

Happiness was Disney's business. Finnerty's, at this moment, was head trauma and a broken neck, and the presence of a substance he'd heard a lot about lately, but hadn't actually seen in quite some time.

His was the delicate handling of a dead boy's father.

His was the death of Chad Ewing, and the moral decisions that went along with the unfortunate truth.

1:59 P.M.

Alone on the quad, the Freshman watched the individual snowflakes gather on the grizzled stump of a lifeless bush. The crowd of mourners had already dispersed, but for some reason he found himself unable to move from this spot, and as he kept his stare fixed downward, he felt the first sting of tears.

He was sure he'd cry again, in the forthcoming days and years, for a whole host of psychological reasons that could be deeply tweaked and analyzed. But now, minutes after watching a white balloon float toward Heaven, he simply cried because he was alive and Chad was dead, and the difference had been nothing more than dumb luck.

2:03 P.M.

Finnerty supposed he'd made up his mind the moment he'd laid eyes on the man. There was a definite likability to Roy Ewing, an aura that made a decent man like

Finnerty believe that Ewing was a decent man as well. That so, Finnerty now settled on a solution upon which his gut had already decided:

The truth about Chad Ewing would be buried alongside the battered boy's body.

Finnerty took a breath filled with solace and began to speak. "I understand all too well, Roy, that sometimes young folks make . . . ," he paused, working his mouth around slippery words of sympathy, "ill-advised decisions. And whether these . . . *decisions* are driven by chemical addiction or the desire to have a good time or the need to impress in order to fit in is . . . usually irrelevant. What's done is done," he offered with a slight fatalistic shrug. Then, leaning forward, he said, "Basically, I'm saying that I agree with you. The Lord decided it was your boy's time, and that's all the world needs to know."

Roy Ewing nodded, closed his eyes, and began to cry tears that seemed to reflect relief more than sadness.

Finnerty reached for a tissue and handed it to Ewing, who accepted it with whispered thanks. "I'll make sure your boy's memory is a Christian one, Roy. We all make mistakes, and I'd sooner be damned to hell than let the police or some college judicial branch make merry out of this one."

Ewing opened his eyes and sniffed. "I . . . I can't ever repay you for this . . ."

"You'll never need to. My job is to help God pave the road between life and the hereafter. It's neither my place, nor anyone else's, to use your son's death as some . . . political tool.

"Mind you, there are *some* things I'll have to leave in

the report, for consistency's sake. For example, the alcohol content. It's doubtful that both the police *and* Doc Marston missed the fact that your boy had been drinking. Liquor leaves external clues, like odor, evidence of nausea, stuff like that.

"But as for the other . . . *stuff* . . . you can rest assured that there'll be no mention of it. As far as I'm concerned, your son died of head trauma, due to an accidental, alcohol-related fall."

"May he rest in peace," Ewing whispered.

"Amen," said Finnerty, while silently thanking God that his own son was alive and well and living nearby.

Ewing stood slowly, like a man who had just absorbed an enormous beating; Finnerty stood and extended his hand. "My deepest sympathies," he said as he shook, then turned to the calendar on the wall. "When will you and the missus be heading back to Chicago?"

"Tomorrow. Late morning."

"Have you . . . arranged for transportation of your son?"

Ewing nodded grimly.

"Today's my only full day here," said Finnerty. "Usually I'm only here in the afternoons. My apprentice Rick will be here tomorrow when you come to . . . sign for the body. I suggest you come early, so you have time to fill out all the paperwork and still catch your plane."

Ewing nodded, then leaned closer to Finnerty. "Mr. Finnerty, if you don't mind," he began in a confidential tone, "I'd appreciate if your apprentice didn't mention this conversation to my wife when I bring her here tomorrow. As it is, she can barely function. I think to heap the truth on top of all that's happened . . . well, you know.

It's bad enough her son is gone. I don't think she could handle the real reason why."

"I understand. I'll speak to Rick and let him know."

Ewing sighed and almost managed a smile. "Thank you, Mr. Finnerty. Thank you."

"You're wel—" A movement over Ewing's shoulder stopped Finnerty mid-word. Squinting, he spotted Betsy Kimball, the intern, standing awkwardly in the doorway.

"What is it, Betsy?" demanded Finnerty, slightly annoyed at the lack of manners displayed by today's youth.

Betsy looked mortified. "I'm sorry to interrupt, Dr. Finnerty, but your wife is on the phone downstairs. Shall I tell her that you'll call back?"

"Of course you should."

"Oh no," said Ewing quickly, turning from Betsy to Finnerty. "Please, take the call. If there's one thing I've learned, it's never to keep the good woman waiting." Again, he almost fashioned a smile.

"Isn't that the God-blessed truth. Betsy, tell her I'll be right there."

Betsy nodded and left.

Ewing grabbed his coat. "I'll see myself out."

"Are you sure?"

"Yes. And thanks again. For everything."

Finnerty watched Ewing make his way out of the room and toward the front door of the office, then he himself turned and made his way downstairs, stopping long enough to throw his report on Chad Ewing in the wastebasket.

He'd write a new one later.

*   *   *

The stranger waited until he'd pulled out of the coroner's parking lot and was halfway down Maine Street before he yanked the rug off his head. He scratched his scalp aggressively, then whipped off the sunglasses and tossed them on the seat next to him. He reached for his baseball hat, pulled it low over his wigless head of short brown, and allowed a huge smile to crack the armor of his Roy Ewing facade.

It had been easy.

It had been very easy.

CHAPTER TWENTY-ONE

The 200th Year
Wednesday, February 25

8:01 P.M.

Templeton lay naked on the satin sheets and waited for Professor Linda Regis to finish undressing. As the pile of apparel grew on the floor of her Popham Beach studio, he realized how much he'd been looking forward to this. The memorial service had left him mildly stressed, and the pending preliminary D-Squad hearing aggravated his condition, so he'd phoned Judith and told her that he'd be exercising in the Cage after work and could she leave a little supper on the stove?

Linda shed the last of her clothes and grinned slyly as she began stalking the bed, her predatory footsteps keeping deliberate time with the mystical purr of the CD player. Templeton savored the head-to-toe sight, his admiration roving from the sleek, short hair to the equally jet eyes, then down the sinewy curves of Greek flesh that bronzed a body built for sex.

She was truly a magnificent woman.

One who didn't put much stock in foreplay.

She pounced suddenly like a beautiful bobcat, straddled Templeton with thighs that could crush, and shoved him inside her. She moaned once, swept one claw swiftly down his torso, then pinned his hands to the bed and began to rock. He struggled once for show, then surrendered.

She moved her hips in a circular fashion, her short grunts deepening into prolonged groans, her head rolling from side to side. Every fiber in her body stood on alert, in the manner that always suggested to him that she viewed intercourse not as an act of sex, but as a sporting event. For her, pleasure was a dangerously competitive contest, and she never lost.

She wrapped one hand around his throat and began to apply pressure as she quickened her thrusting pace. Then, with teeth shining white amid olive, she added a second hand to the fray, doubling the pressure on his windpipe, cutting off his air altogether.

Now he struggled for real. He clawed at her flexed forearms, but she just shook her head. He wiggled and flopped, but she pounded him into submission. As the fog of orgasmic anoxia overcame him, he gave in to climactic unconsciousness, and his last sensation was of Linda's battering ram of a body slamming repetitively into his own, severing him at the hips.

He blacked out.

He came to almost immediately, as he always did, feeling a little disoriented, but otherwise fine. Linda now lay peacefully on top of him, as if she'd just enjoyed a tender coupling, and Templeton wondered, not for the first time, if his mistress was mentally all there.

She peered into his eyes, an amused expression on her face. "You okay, sport?"

He nodded breathlessly, reflexively rubbing his throat. "You're going to . . . kill me . . . someday . . . doing that."

She smirked and kissed him on the nose. "Maybe," she said. "But what a way to go."

9:44 P.M.

In a plush hotel room, Roy and Carla Ewing sat on separate beds and stared at separate walls, neither sure how to go on living.

The minutes passed in strangled silence.

But then, from the room's darkened corner, a vulnerable gasp arose, soft at first, but repeating and intensifying. The sound dragged the parents from their listless grief and reminded them they were still parents of Julie, who was still alive, and who needed them now, more than ever.

10:15 P.M.

With the memorial service over, the preliminary D-Squad hearing was just eighteen hours away, which meant the Chad Ewing mess was far from over, perhaps just beginning. Uneasiness drove the twelve seniors to the Brotherhood Room to discuss strategy before the pledge activity set for eleven.

"The service was in good taste," Beta said.

"I'm just glad it's over," commented Kappa. "And I'll be even happier when the Ewings leave. Them being here all the time gives me the creeps."

"Hey," cautioned Beta. "We owe them our hospitality, at the very least."

"*Not*. Their fucking son took the easy road out, and now *we* have to clean up *his* shit."

"That's way out of line, Gamma," Mu said softly.

"No it's not."

"Yes it is," said Beta. "Show some respect."

"What happens tomorrow?" Epsilon asked, wisely intervening before Gamma lost his temper.

"We make our case before the D-Squad," answered Beta. "I'm told they may ask a few questions."

"Who's going to answer them?"

"That," Beta said, "is something we need to decide right now."

"You should do it," said Mu. "You're great at this sort of thing."

"Personally," Delta joked, "I'd rather be great in bed."

"There's no chance of that," said Rho, and most of the others chuckled.

"I agree with Mu," said Theta, who didn't laugh. "Beta should be our representative. The whole school wants to have sex with him, including the dean and all the members of the Board." He looked at Beta and grinned. "You're everyone's fucking hero."

"I'll do it," said Beta. "But not alone. I don't want to look like the official spokesperson. There's strength in numbers."

"What about Gamma? For intimidation?"

The brothers exchanged looks and nods.

"I want Kappa there, too," Gamma said. "If his bitch ever decides to yap again, I want him there for damage control."

"I don't think any witnesses will be called tomorrow," said Beta.

"I still want him there."

"I'll go," said Kappa. "But for the record, you won't

have to worry about Jocelyn opening her mouth. She'll keep quiet."

"She'd better."

"She will."

"So it's the three of us," concluded Beta. "Let's meet after the Triumvirate so we can figure out what we're going to say."

Brothers Gamma and Kappa nodded.

Epsilon turned to Beta. "Any messages from Alpha?"

"Not really, but I *did* just get off the phone with his contact guy."

"And?"

"On behalf of alumni everywhere, he wished us luck at the hearing."

At this, the other eleven exchanged affirming nods and buoyant looks of pride. The alumni were behind them.

"We got to talking," continued Beta, "about the specifics of the hearing, and he brought up an interesting point."

He paused, and twenty-two ears waited.

"Mark Jessy's on the D-Squad," he said finally. "He's also our friend. We should make every effort to ensure that he stays on our side."

"Of *course* he'll stay on our side," said Delta, sounding almost offended. "He's one of *us*, for Christ's sake!"

"No he's not," Gamma clarified. "He's not one of us."

"C'mon, Gamma," countered Beta. "He's one of us, and you know it."

"He may be one of *you*, but he'll never be one of *me*."

Beta dismissed Gamma with a wave of his arm. "I'm not going to argue with you." He looked around the room. "Although Mark's our friend, we have to remember that technically he's against us right now. He's in a tough spot—us on one side, his girlfriend on the other."

"*Shawn*. That girl needs to be hate-fucked."

"You can masturbate after the meeting, Upsilon. Anyway, it's been suggested that we take Mark out to a bar this weekend. Maybe start a scrap with some townies and put ourselves in a position to go to battle *with* Mark."

"A fight?" Gamma smiled. "Why, Beta, that doesn't sound like you."

"Hey, it's my job to relay alumni orders. Personally, I'd rather buy Mark a few drinks and just spend some time—"

"Screw that. I'm not buying his loyalty."

"Then don't come," said Beta to Kappa. Then, turning to the general gathering, he said, "Personally, *I'm* up for it. Mark's a friend. A *good* friend. I think we should show him he's still our buddy."

"I agree," said Mu.

"Friday night?" Omega asked.

Beta nodded.

"I'll go. Jessy's a good man."

"Yes," Beta said, looking at Gamma in particular. "He is."

11:00 P.M.

The conference call spanned thousands of miles and four time zones, and, through the wonders of modern technology, involved eight Sigma alums. They touched briefly on the Chad Ewing crisis and traded thoughts on what they knew, what they'd heard.

Yes, they'd heard the memorial service had gone off without a hitch. Yes, it sounded like the county coroner had been neatly suckered. Yes, it appeared as if that crooked Templeton had a handle on the situation.

No, there wasn't a thing on earth money couldn't buy.

They chortled at this last unanimous agreement, then turned their talk to business.

CHAPTER TWENTY-TWO

*The 200th Year
Thursday, February 26*

7:34 A.M.

His baseball hat pulled low, his turtleneck stretched high, and his nerves shot to hell, the Freshman trudged across the deserted quad. As he walked, he thought of a thousand reasons why he should just turn back, not the least of which was his own love of life.

But on he marched, his heavy lids warding off morning's glinting reflection, his trembling fingers wrapped around something small and huge in his jacket pocket.

He hoped this simple act would clear his conscience. Having endured one hundred straight hours of sleepless demons, he hoped this would be the end.

But deep down, he knew it would be just the beginning.

10:17 A.M.

Richard O. Mashassit, apprentice to Richard K. Finnerty, sat across from the parents of Chad Ewing and read them the layman's details behind their son's death, as summarized in report form by the coroner himself. Head trauma. Broken neck. BAC of .28. Terribly sorry. Terribly, terribly sorry.

The parents of Chad Ewing sat stone-faced while he spoke at them. Ninety-six hours of indescribable heartache had hardened them. They were, in certain ways, dead like their son. Neither felt pain, just a despicable numbness.

Done reading, Mashassit handed them a thin stack of papers. Release forms, he explained. The parents of Chad Ewing signed without reading, both realizing with horrendous bitterness that their only son had been reduced to paperwork.

And then the meeting was over, which was just as well, because the parents of Chad Ewing couldn't wait to get out of there. They couldn't wait to get home, to get on with the rest of their incomplete lives. They were sick of Georgeville, Simsbury in particular. They were understanding people, but it seemed incomprehensibly unfair that all the other students were alive, except their son.

They watched two uniformed men load their son's box into an airport courier van.

Then the parents of Chad Ewing loaded themselves into their strawberry-scented, rented Toyota and headed for the airport.

12:17 P.M.

A fishy, chippy smell dominated the dining hall, where Mark waited, agitated and starving. Shawn was uncharacteristically late, and he'd characteristically missed breakfast. Satisfaction of his hunger, he knew, was merely a lunch line away. Relief would take far more than his girlfriend's arrival, though, for even as he watched the hallway for the first sign of blond he realized he wasn't so much mildly perturbed as deeply disturbed, and it had nothing to do with his girlfriend's tardiness.

And everything to do with the D-Squad.

They'd met first thing, to rehearse the questions Shawn and Schwitters planned to fire at Sigma's representatives during the upcoming preliminary hearing. Though Mark had contributed nothing, the squad's plans had planted in his belly a weedy seed of unease he wished he could cough onto the floor and kick beneath the salad bar.

He craved the end of the Chad Ewing investigation, for despite the apathy he'd thus far displayed, he could feel himself being yanked in two directions. And since conclusion of the matter seemed distant, he knew he'd have to maintain his air of aloofness and maybe step it up a bit. He figured he had more to lose by attacking his Sigma friends than by mildly pissing off the D-Squad members.

Besides, he was sure the brothers of Sigma Delta Phi were innocent.

Strong arms seized him from behind and wrapped him in a headlock. Spinning from the hold, he found himself facing Fairchild.

"Hey! What's up, friend?"

"Not much. What about you?"

"Just waiting for Shawn," said Mark, trying to sound as though he couldn't believe he was waiting around for a *girl*.

"Oh, stop. You love her, and I know it." Fairchild snagged a carrot stick from the tray of a freshman hockey player and attacked it. "Listen," he said to Mark between crunches, "I've got class in ten minutes, so I can't chat. What are you doing tomorrow night?"

Mark thought for a moment. "Nothing. I was going to take Shawn to Carmello's, but she's got some worthy cause to promote somewhere, so I'm on my own."

"Not anymore. You're coming to Chewnocker's with us."

"I am?"

"You are."

Mark considered the invitation for only a second. "Okay, but no fights. I can't afford another broken rib this spring."

Fairchild regarded him a moment, then said, "No fights. Just a night of billiards and beer with the boys."

"I don't know," said Mark. "A. J.'s looking pretty tense these days. His engine tends to overheat when he's stressed."

"That's why we're going. It's been a shitty week, if you ask me, and I think it's time we all got back to the business of being seniors." Fairchild smiled. "Plus, we have to get ourselves mentally ready for South Padre."

"I was ready a month ago." Mark noticed Shawn weaving her way toward them. "Here comes my lunch date."

Fairchild looked over his shoulder. "So she does," he said. "Looking better than us two put together, I might add." He turned back to Mark and poked his chest with what was left of the carrot. "Tomorrow. Nine o'clock." Popping the carrot in his mouth, he winked and turned away. "Hey, Shawn," he said as he headed for the door.

"Hey, yourself, Dave." Shawn shed her backpack and

sighed apologetically for Mark's benefit. "Sorry. I was on the phone with my sister."

"And how is Jana?" asked Mark as they joined the lunch line.

"Pregnant."

"No shit!"

"Nice mouth."

"Sorry. You don't seem very excited."

"I'm not," Shawn said, as she grabbed a tray and shook off the excess water.

"Why not?" said Mark, shaking his tray as well. "You're going to be an auntie!"

"I'd rather be the sister of a pediatrician. She just *started* med school, and now Bobby wants her to drop out and have the baby."

"Well, she can always go back."

"Why does *she* have to quit? Why can't her husband, the ambulance-chaser, stay home with the baby?"

"I guess there are a lot of ambulances to chase."

Shawn ignored the comment and filled her tray with healthful foods. Mark filled his with similar grub, but added a two-pack of Ring-Dings, one of which he'd eat, the other of which he'd save, to use as a makeshift hockey puck with his Sigma friends at some later, goofy date.

While Mark discussed weekends and wombs with Fairchild and Shawn, a nationwide deal was signed: a multibrother contract that called for the incorporation of a bank, the construction of a factory, and the swapping of forty million dollars.

Business, as always, was very good.

CHAPTER TWENTY-THREE

The 200th Year
Thursday, February 26

4:22 P.M.

Templeton reached into his private desk drawer and fumbled about until he found the half-empty bottle of scotch, which he pulled from its hiding place, freed from its cap, and swigged. He sipped twice more, then let out a labored sigh that was hot with the fumes of booze.

The preliminary hearing into the death of Chad Ewing had adjourned twenty minutes earlier, and the D-Squad advisor was rattled. The liquor, he hoped, would help him see things in a calmer light.

His hand trembled as he lifted the bottle to his mouth again.

The hearing had been, in ten politically correct words or less, more confrontational than he'd hoped it would be. Sigma had been represented by Dave Fairchild, A. J. Dominic, and Pete Thresher. The college, of course, had been represented by Shawn Jakes, Simon Schwitters, and that nonfactor, Mark Jessy. Fairchild, that useful tool, had masterfully recapped everything he knew about the accident and Chad Ewing's "suicidal" disposition, his chipped tooth adding just the right amount of vulnerability. A sense of victory had welled within Templeton throughout Fairchild's testimony, and he'd fought several urges to clap out loud.

Until, that is, Shawn followed Fairchild's account with a single question, one that delivered a coup de grâce to an exchange Templeton wouldn't soon forget.

Fairchild: "One of the brothers took Chad upstairs and urged him to sleep off his inebriation. You see, freshmen often don't know their limits when it comes to alcohol. And, as brothers, we look out for the pledges, the way we look out for each other."

Shawn: "Mr. Fairchild, do you normally '*look out for your pledges*' by getting them tanked, stripping them naked, and writing sick little poems all over their bodies?"

A long, stiff silence had followed, broken when Templeton finally found his tongue and reprimanded Shawn for "turning a respectable institution into a talk show."

The hearing had culminated thirty minutes later, with Dominic hissing to Shawn that she was treading on dangerous ground and Shawn promising to bring down Sigma "brick by dirty brick."

So, thought Templeton now, between soothing sips, the death of Chad Ewing wasn't going to simply disappear. Shawn was indeed on the warpath, with some pretty pointed questions. And honed by Schwitters' legal expertise, these questions could cut ugly slashes in the hide of something hidden.

Soon, Templeton would have no choice but to deploy

his most dangerous chess piece, that nonfactor, Mark Jessy.

Unless, of course, that particular piece began to deploy on its own.

4:41 P.M.

By the time Mark returned to his apartment from an afternoon of listening to professors extol the UN's latest global deforestation ban, watching his girlfriend accuse his best friends of murder, and checking mail, the sun had dipped beneath the evergreens, pulling with it an evening shade of auburn that dripped dusk on a world of otherwise white. On a normal day he would never have made it to practice. Luckily, practice didn't start until eight; evening practice was Coach Capofina's noble-yet-fruitless attempt to curb, or at least delay, his players' Thursday-night beer consumption.

Mark welcomed the warmth and solitude of his minimally lit single mod—one of twelve that bordered the lacrosse field—and flipped on the overheads in time to catch Casey. A fourteen-week-old, eighteen-pound golden retriever, she reacted to his entrance by seizing the cuff of his jeans and snarling with joy.

"Hi, girl!" Mark cooed. "Were you good today?" The stench in the air, and the half-eaten pillow on the living-room floor, told him she *hadn't* been, but his knowledge that she'd been left alone for ten hours guilted him into forgiving her.

Puppy still latched to his ankle, he struggled to the kitchen, snagged a slice of pizza from the fridge, and chewed it ferociously. Noticing her master's snack, Casey forgot her denim prey and began drooling freely.

Not one to tease, Mark dropped the crust, which she proudly took to her favorite laundry pile to lord over and eventually consume.

Mark had originally intended to nap before dinner. The hearing, however, had played games with his head; sleep, he figured, would be virtually impossible, so he opted instead to take Casey outside for an educational romp. His goal was to turn her into one of those studly, Frisbee-catching dogs. However, she'd yet to graduate from the tennis-ball stage.

Twilight domed the snow-covered lacrosse field, but the rays of the sinking sun still glinted on the wind-blown drifts, and Mark knew the safety bulbs that lined the nearby Cage parking lot would, within the hour, begin their nightly shift. He led his puppy over thirty yards of difficult tundra, then knelt.

"See this, Casey?" He shook the ball provocatively. "See it?"

She saw it, but didn't seem to care.

He tossed the ball over her head. It landed no more than six feet away, disappearing into the snow. Somewhat enthralled, she bounded to where she'd seen it last, sniffed the ground once, then immediately lost interest as her nose led her toward a thin row of baby pines just off the end line. For a puppy still exploring this strange world, quarry better than a round hunk of rubber and fuzz undoubtedly lay within the saplings.

Mark retrieved the ball himself and, as he watched Casey dig for nothing, allowed his mind to drift back to the hearing.

He'd sat there like a black-robed idiot. Countless times he'd tried to make eye contact with Fairchild, Dominic, and Thresher, desperate to convey his apathy, his belief in their innocence. They hadn't glanced his way, though, and by meeting's confrontational end he'd sunk to the lowest depths possible on a raised bench, convinced the Sigmas saw him as nothing more than Shawn's pussy-whipped ally.

Shawn and Sigma.

Two huge parts of Mark's life had collided.

And, on impact, had once again left him very much alone.

4:56 P.M.

His morning mission now in the hands of college employees, the Freshman stood before Sigma House, pledge manual beneath his arm, pledge pin over his heart. *Don't go in there,* he told himself. *It's just dinner. They won't miss you. Go back to your room and try to nap. Go back to your room and pray. Go back to your dorm and pack your bags and call your dad and run for your life . . .*

He walked slowly toward the fraternity house.

5:05 P.M.

Mark was halfway to his apartment with Casey when he noticed the Ford Explorer cruising slowly through the Cage parking lot, keeping four-wheeled time with his two-legged pace.

He stopped. So did the Explorer. He set Casey down, told her to stay, and made his way toward the parking lot. The driver-side door of the Bronco opened, and out stepped a tall man wearing a Gore-Tex parka and L.L. Bean boots. *Subtle,* thought Mark. *What a day I'm hav-*

ing. He fingered his neck beads and stepped over one final snowbank onto the frozen slush of the pavement.

"Hello, Mark," said the man, holding up the star-shaped badge that hung from his own neck. "Deputy Trevor Mawn of the FBI's U.S. Marshal Serv—"

"I remember who you are," Mark replied.

Mawn hesitated, then tucked the badge into his jacket. "I have some questions—"

"Let's see if I can guess," Mark said sarcastically. "Have I seen him? Have I heard from him? Do I know where he is? Same three questions you asked three years ago." He shook his head. "Boy, you guys are predictable. Say, it's after five o'clock. I thought the best thing about government jobs was the hours."

"As they say, Mark, justice never sleeps. Neither do I."

"How stirring."

"My men and I work long days," said Mawn, shrugging. "Someday you will too."

"Not for a company that kills innocent—"

"Look, Mark, have you got three answers for me or not?"

"Same three as before. No, no, and no. And even if I did know where he was, I'd *never* tell you."

"Then you'd be guilty of aiding and abetting a fugitive."

"Ha! I'd consider it an *honor* to go to jail for this particular cause."

"Still got that nasty chip on your shoulder, I see."

"Growing up without parents does that to a guy."

Mawn paused, searching for a better strategy. "You know," he said finally, "we could tap your phones."

"Oh, good idea," Mark gushed. "But don't stop there.

Give a headset to one of your finest, and let him waste tax dollars listening to me talk to my buddies, my girlfriend, and Monty's Pizza." He shook his head scornfully. "No wonder you Washington dingbats can't balance your checkbooks."

"He's still on our list of the Ten Most Wanted. It's worth a few dollars of the taxpayers' money to bring him to justice."

"Oh please."

Mawn looked down at the wind-scalloped snow. "Mark, I realize he's your father, and there's a bond there, but he killed a federal agent."

"And in the process became an American icon," added Mark, biting back his fury. "Ironic, huh? Your *outlaw*, everyone else's *hero*." He nodded toward the center of campus, where the library stood as a temple to facts and opinions. "If you don't believe that, go read the editorials on microfiche. Look under C."

Mawn shook his head. "You don't get it. By law, deadly force can be used by a law enforcement officer—"

"—*only* when confronted by immediate danger of death or serious bodily harm."

Mawn started to respond, then paused as Mark's citation of standard FBI policy seemed to register. "She *was* armed."

Mark gasped in genuine horror. "We *all* were! But unlike yours, *our* weapons were props. *Props!* Like the feathers and moccasins we were wearing. Like the tacky tourist uniform you're wearing right now."

"You're oversimplifying."

"Bullshit. You oppressive bastards are the ones who oversimplified." Mark pointed at Mawn, wishing for a brief, uncontrollable instant that his finger was loaded. "In your eyes, a weapon's a weapon, even if the woman holding it is sitting Indian-style and singing, even if she spends her days braiding horse tails and her nights ushering bugs outside rather than killing them."

Mawn raised his eyebrows and shifted his shoulders, as if to physically negotiate with history. "It was an unfortunate misunderstanding, a tragic accident, but—"

"No! Spilling milk, *that's* an accident. When a trained sniper takes aim—"

"*Enough*, Mark. I'm not here to trade analogies or get in a pissing match over who fired the first shots."

"The *only* shots."

"The *accidental* shots. And now my job is to find the man who retaliated with premeditated hands."

"*Bare* hands."

"*Guilty* hands, ones stained with blood when we caught him."

Mark barked a laugh of disdain. "Was that before or after he turned himself in? And if you want to see bloodstains, I've got something in my apartment that I think will interest—"

"*Enough!*" Mawn shouted.

This time the word thundered like a gunshot across the empty winter field. As the deputy's face seethed with anger, he ran a frustrated hand through his hair.

"He's making a fool out of you, isn't he?" Mark said.

Mawn said nothing.

"He was the perfect patsy. The savage, primitive redskin who killed a lily-white government agent, then fled when he found out Uncle Sam wouldn't accept a self-defense or temporary-insanity plea. He fit the perfect stereotype of an outlaw, and you could justify a hyped-up, nationwide search to draw attention away from the fact that *your* department's responsible for this whole fucking mess to begin with."

Mark stepped forward, fists now clenched in a mixture of hatred and pride. "Only problem is, the savage, primitive redskin is outsmarting you. You guys thought you'd have your man within a week or so, and here you are, thirteen years later, and you don't have a fucking clue where he is."

"On the contrary," said Mawn. "We're close. We're *very* close."

Mark allowed this information to sink in, then shrugged and actually smiled. "Then it looks like you're wasting your time here." He motioned toward the horizon. "Go do whatever tricky little thing you have to do to get even closer, then cry in your beer when you finally realize you're chasing a shadow. Meanwhile, we have enough to deal with here at Simsbury without visits from bullies waving top-ten lists."

"I know," said Mawn, nodding. "I read about that frat boy in the paper." He shook his head. "Death seems to follow you, doesn't it, Mark?"

"It sure does," said Mark recklessly. "Maybe I should put that on my résumé."

Mawn grinned slyly and shook his head. "I wouldn't." Turning, he got back in the Explorer and started the engine. Then he leaned out the window and gave Mark a disappointed look. "I was hoping three years of top-notch education had matured you into a man, Mark. I was hoping, by now, that you'd see what your father did was wrong. Obviously, I was mistaken." His expression turned hard. "But mark my words, we *will* find him."

"You'll find him," said Mark coolly, "the day O. J. Simpson finds the real killer."

Mawn pointed at Mark. "You just keep believing that. Just keep believing that one man can elude the best-trained criminal investigators in the world, because one day soon, my cocky friend, you're going to find yourself in court, watching the prosecution of a crime that was committed right in front of you. You can *count* on it."

Despite the hate churning in his gut, Mark managed to smile broadly and waggle his fingers tauntingly. "Goodbye, Deputy. See you in another three years."

He turned, plucked Casey from a boot print in the snow, and fingered his neck beads as he continued toward his apartment.

10:32 P.M.

It had been several days since the brothers had been able to dish out a proper beating. And now, with the Ewings gone and the hearing over, it was time to get back to business as usual.

The business of following orders.

And giving them.

The forty-one undergrads met briefly in the Brotherhood Room, then summoned the pledges.

It would be a night of tradition, brotherhood, and violence.

CHAPTER TWENTY-FOUR

The 200th Year
Friday, February 27

6:22 A.M.

The gunshot awoke Mark from his nightmare, and he sat up with a strangled gasp just before all the blood in the world could spill onto soft meadow grass.

He sat there a moment, sweating coldly as the dream's screams faded into the early-morning silence. He blinked at the gloom, and at the foot of his mattress made out a heaving bundle of knocked-out puppy. The sight calmed him somewhat.

He stood and wobbled sleepily to his desk, flicked on the lamp, and opened the top drawer. He groped with knowing fingers, found what he was looking for, and pulled it from its hiding place.

He held the photo under the light and studied it, then closed his eyes and saw the scene imprinted in his mind. A man and a woman, smiling beside a horse corral. A small boy atop broad shoulders. A blond ponytail to clutch for balance.

Recommitted to memory, the familial image once again chased the animal back to its pen.

He put death back in its drawer, turned off the lamp, and returned to his mattress. He turned the pillow over, punched it once, and settled back into sleep mode.

Minutes later, he was asleep again. And this time, he dreamt about lacrosse and, later, sex.

One by one, in various dorm rooms, the pledges of Sigma Delta Phi awoke to a glorious new day.

They took stock of their injuries, then carefully dressed in clothes that would mask the physical damage. Long sleeves covered bruises. Baseball hats shaded facial cuts.

They were impervious to physical pain. They were linebackers and free safeties and midfielders. They'd endured broken ribs and arms and ankles before. They'd had body parts surgically repaired. What they had now were merely flesh wounds.

Flesh wounds that nonetheless needed to be hidden.

For it was the duty of the pledges to protect the brotherhood.

They walked slowly to class, in groups of two or three. Arrogant struts disguised limps. Macho sneers masked shattered egos.

They were Sigmas, dammit, and quickly learning that pain and pride were not so inseparable.

One was temporary.

One was forever.

12:15 P.M.

The dean had drawn on the college expense account to purchase Mexican food from Rosita's, and the spread of seasoned chicken and beef, hard and soft tortilla shells, sizzling vegetables, and various cheeses and sauces was delicious. The dean, Shawn, and Schwitters sat dining and strategizing at one end of the table, while Mark sat clear at the other end, eating as much and as fast as his belly would allow.

When only greasy stains remained on paper plates, the dean wiped his mouth with a napkin and leaned back in his chair. "We need to determine a direction."

Shawn and Schwitters exchanged looks. "We discussed it last night," said Schwitters. "And we've still got some questions."

Mark looked up briefly, unaware that there'd been a meeting the night before, but silently pleased he hadn't been included.

"What questions are those?" the dean asked, expressing mild surprise.

Schwitters pulled out a piece of paper and eyed it. "For starters, we'd like to speak with the cook who found the body."

"Excuse me," said Mark, seizing this moment to begin his campaign of legal sabotage. "Could you not refer to your own little fantasies as 'we.' 'We' includes 'me,' and I think 'we' should drop this case.'

Schwitters crossed his arms and made a petty face. "Oh really, jock? Have you even given it a moment of thought?"

"I don't need to, jock-wanna-be. It was an accident."

"You're a fool, Mark," said Shawn.

The dean stroked his chin. "Actually, Shawn, I'm inclined to agree with him. Tell me, exactly why do you feel the need to question the cook?"

"It might corroborate the story Shawn heard," said Schwitters. "You know, that Chad was naked, and that he had . . . what"—he glanced Shawn's way—"*poems* all over his skin."

The dean turned to Shawn. "If you've got such a reliable source, why don't you call her in for testimony?"

"I'm working on that."

"Of course, you're forgetting *I* was there that morning, too. I assure you, Chad was wearing boxers and a tee shirt, and there wasn't a Magic Marker within—"

"Who said anything about a Magic Marker?" cut in Shawn, her tone opportunistic and accusing. "In all our conversations to date, I don't recall ever having talked about a Magic Marker."

"Shawn, if we're talking ink dark enough to read, we have to be talking—"

"We don't *have* to be talking about anything." Shawn reached across the table, grabbed Schwitters's ballpoint pen from his shirt pocket, and held it up. "See this? It uses ink, too. And I'll bet it writes on skin. I'm no poet, but I'll bet I could write a knock-knock joke on my arm right now."

The dean sighed deeply and shook his head. "You're reaching, Shawn. There was no ink of *any* kind, *anywhere* on the body."

Shawn stared at the dean a moment. "You didn't get there until well after the body was first discovered. Someone could've cleaned him up a little."

"Doubtful." Dismissing Shawn, the dean turned to Schwitters. "What else have you got?"

Schwitters put a finger on the paper. "We should talk to Chad's roommate, and the doctor at St. Elizabeth's. We'd also like to leave open the possibility of speaking to the coroner."

The dean shook his head incredulously. "Simon, *think* about what you're saying. You're *not* an attorney. You're an appointed student whose job is to do what's best for Simsbury."

"Isn't that what we're doing?" asked Shawn.

"I don't think it's appropriate to start dragging in medical examiners and physicians." The dean sipped his Coke. "You're college students. Try to stay within your bounds."

"We're trying to get at the truth."

"How inspirational. Don't forget justice and the American Way."

"Kiss it, Dean Templeton."

"We'd like to start investigating on Monday," Schwitters said. "We promise to be thorough, tasteful, and quick."

The dean sighed again and studied Shawn and Schwitters with alternating glances. "You'd better be all of those things," he said finally, "because if this turns into an all-out circus, I'm calling it off." He looked around the room. "I mean it."

"Don't worry. It'll go smoothly."

"It had better."

2:33 P.M.

Unlike most Generation X-ers earning liberal arts degrees, Betsy Kimball would need no postgraduate backpack jaunt through Europe to find herself, nor a soul-enriching stint in the Peace Corps to justify future inclusion in the white-collar establishment. On the contrary, she'd known what noble career she'd eventually pursue since she was eight, when her cocker spaniel Natasha dropped dead for no apparent reason. When her hysteria had subsided, she'd demanded explanations first from her parents (both Portland neurosurgeons), then from God, and when this trinity had failed to provide logical answers anger had set in, and she'd taken matters into her own hands. She exhumed Natasha from her backyard grave, and was about to probe the dead dog's innards with a Swiss Army knife when her mother ran screaming out the back door and halted the autopsy before it began. Feeling cheated out of the truth, Betsy decided right then and there what she'd one day be.

A medical examiner.

In time, she got over the Natasha heartbreak, but her brief obsession with a pet's death mutated into a longer-lasting fascination with the hows and whys of mortality. She could say now with professional conviction that dead bodies intrigued her, for to her they held last-day clues that could be read like mystery novels. Corpses were perfect, eternal snapshots.

Her favorite TV show, of course, was *Quincy*, the syndicated series of afternoon reruns featuring a mythical medical examiner with a knack for solving murders in his spare time. She owned a rare collection of videos, consisting of every episode ever aired, which she watched and rewatched, putting herself in Quincy's shoes, dreaming of the day she too could solve crimes that had stumped a city's finest men in blue.

Upon enrolling at Bowdoin College, she'd signed on to intern at the Cumberland County Coroner's Office. She'd discovered right away, however, that Cumberland County wasn't exactly a hotbed of suspicious deaths. What's more, Coroner Finnerty rarely let his pupil near any of the bodies. Only twice had he let Betsy assist him, each time on decrepit, century-old women. Still, she'd taken full advantage of these opportunities by carefully combing every rash and wrinkle, searching for signs of foul play.

Though she wasn't in it for the money, the nine bucks an hour was a nice bonus. She'd forgotten to pick up her paycheck on Wednesday, and she wanted the extra cash for the weekend. As she hurried into the coroner's building, she glanced at her watch and reminded herself she was due back on campus by three to finish her lab assignment.

She shouted a hello to Rick Mashassit, whom she could hear working downstairs, then made her way to the unattended receptionist's desk. She saw an envelope with her name on it, lying atop an open newspaper. She grabbed her check and turned to leave, but then noticed the newsprint.

What was that?

She doubled back and lowered herself into Dorothy Rucker's battered vinyl chair, eyes glued to the newspaper. She leaned close, examining the picture that consumed a quarter of the page.

The photo depicted a man, a woman, and a teenage girl, all joyless. They appeared to be leading a train of people—specifically, a horde of young men dressed in dark suits.

The headline "A Time to Mourn" floated like a bold, black cloud above the photo, and a captioned river ran beneath the sad scene.

*Family and friends of Chad Ewing lead the student
body of Simsbury College out to the quad for the
conclusion of the Memorial Service honoring the
freshman, who died early Sunday morning. Story,
page 31.*

Betsy wasn't interested in the story; she already knew
what had happened. There was something about the
photo, however, that nagged her.

Something wasn't right.

She closed her eyes, called up her memory, and analyzed the images that ran through her head. She saw
them, studied them, and compared them.

Two men.

Two *different* men.

That's it!

Her pulse now racing at the potential magnitude of her
discovery, she tore out the photo and stuffed it in the back
pocket of her jeans, then reassembled the newspaper and
consulted her watch. She had twenty minutes to make it
back to lab, which would run for an additional two hours
and couldn't end quickly enough.

She couldn't wait to focus on what was shaping up to
be the biggest break of her young, medical-examining
life.

She couldn't wait to play Quincy.

3:14 P.M.

The conference call connected Chairman Davenport
with two of the Board members who'd missed Monday's
briefing with Templeton.

"Two weeks from today," bellowed Donald Adickes III

into the phone from his mansion in New Jersey. "Two weeks from today that *U.S.News and World Report* survey is released. We damn well better be back in the top five schools in the country. If we're not, you can bet this death will be to blame."

"I wouldn't worry about it, Don," replied Christian Geagan from his retirement cottage on Cape Cod. "*U.S.News* is a national publication. I doubt they've picked up on what happened at our quiet little school in Georgeville."

"Don't be too sure about that," countered Adickes. "I'm looking at yesterday's *Portland Press Herald* and today's *Boston Globe*. Seems both of *these* papers have picked up on what happened at our quiet little school in Georgeville."

"What do the articles say?" said Davenport.

"Here's a quote from the *Herald*: 'The ivied walls of Simsbury College have been sullied by the stain of sudden death.' There's a picture too."

"It's only the *Herald*. It's not like anybody important reads it."

"Yeah? Well, the *Globe* story is UPI."

"Oh."

"Goddammit," barked Davenport. "Fax me both articles, and a copy of the photograph. I want some ammo when I call Templeton."

"Speaking of," segued Geagan, "what's the status of the D-Squad investigation?"

"It's under way, as far as I know."

"Let's push for a resolution by spring break," suggested Adickes. "Prospective Student Weekend is barely more than a month off. We've got the children of some real big pissers interested in Simsbury, and it would be a

shame if some high school senior and his CEO father
were to visit in the middle of a student-led murder investigation. Not exactly the kind of atmosphere we'd like to
portray."

"I agree," said Davenport. "And I'll tell you something, I'm not so sure I *want* the D-Squad to find anything. I don't think we're ready to deal with the
headaches involved with shutting down the most promi-
nent fraternity on campus."

"What sort of headaches are you referring to?"

"Financial ones. Do you guys realize that virtually all
our endowment comes from Greek alumni? And most of
that comes from Sigma?"

"I've been saying that from day one!" shouted
Adickes. "Why do you think I was so against the formation of that damned Ackerly Task Force? Some of these
fraternities and sororities have been around for two hundred years. They're institutions, for Christ's sake! Shutting them down is going to cost us *millions* in support."

"That shouldn't be an issue," offered Geagan. "This is
Simsbury College, not Philip Morris. The task force was
organized in the best interests of our educational—"

"Oh balls!"

"Let me finish, Don. If the D-Squad finds Sigma responsible for this death, then we'll shut 'em down. And
at the end of the semester, if the task force tells us that
Simsbury will be a better place without frats and sororities, we'll shut 'em *all* down. I don't care *what* the cost
is."

"Spoken like a man who spent his life mired in the
poverty of public education," said Adickes.

"Hey, at least I sleep at night," Geagan replied. "What about you?"

"I sleep fine," retorted Adickes, "in my waterbed, next to my twenty-eight-year-old girlfriend with fake tits who waits on me hand and foot. Believe me, pal, money talks."

"That's enough, gentlemen," Davenport interrupted. "Let's wait and see what the D-Squad finds. And as far as the task force is concerned, that decision is still a ways off."

"Hey, Hank," said Geagan, "pass this message along to Templeton. 'A student is dead. I want to know why.'"

"And pass this one along, too," added Adickes. "'A student is dead. And I want the world to forget him.'"

3:32 P.M.

Templeton quickly proofread the e-mail text that splashed gold across the blue outbox of his computer screen.

> *T-Bone. Met with my little detectives today. They have a few "questions" which need answering. Possible subjects: Marston, Finnerty, Penny Ward, Jason Lyle. I understand Finnerty and Marston are done deals, but can I do anything to mitigate these other two risks?*
>
> *And don't you just love these small, ignorant towns?*
>
> *P.S. Thanks for the deposit.*

He transmitted, then sat back in his chair and exhaled a farewell to a tricky week. He'd earned the weekend that lay before him and the fantastic prize that came with it. He'd told Judith that he'd be attending an administrative conference in Portland. She'd been too bored or fat to press him for details, and for that he was glad.

He wasn't ready for a divorce.

Yet.

He picked up the phone and punched a number pleasing to dial. The connection rang twice before a woman answered.

"Hello, love."

"Hello yourself."

"Are you ready?"

"I'm packed and waiting by the door, like a good little girl."

"I hope you don't plan on staying good all weekend."

"Oh, I stashed a little naughtiness in my overnight bag."

"That's my girl. I'll be there in ten."

Templeton hung up and closed down his office. As he pulled the door shut behind him, he popped a vitamin E tablet in his mouth and smiled. He had a feeling Linda Regis might get tenure after all.

5:05 P.M.

The sun sank, and young spirits soared. Books and résumés were put safely away, and beer kegs tapped. Stereo speakers on windowsills called to one another, and with a primal scream from the quad, Simsbury began its first full weekend without Chad Ewing.

CHAPTER TWENTY-FIVE

The 200th Year
Saturday, February 28

7:04 A.M.

Carla Ewing tiptoed as she neared the closed door of her late son's bedroom—as though her creaking steps would summon him gurgling and crying from a toddler's slumber. Of course, she knew this was ridiculous, for her son was now beginning his first full day in a mahogany box, six feet beneath the frozen ground in Parkview Cemetery. Still, some habits—the motherly ones—were more ingrained than others.

She opened the door slowly, allowing her eyes to pan deliberately across the carpeted floor, up the postered walls, over the empty bed. She took in the sights and smells that screamed Chad's name, and was torn by the urge to both enshrine and burn the room.

As she stood in the doorway, tears welling once again in her eyes, she was reminded of a song from her youth. As the notes and lyrics complained in her head, she experienced the angry confusion she'd felt when she first heard the song, and it amazed her that it had

been written about a stupid war, not the death of her
only son.

8:34 A.M.

Georgeville didn't need a chief of police, police chief
Martin Sullivan liked to joke, but rather a full-time camp
counselor; someone to chaperone the two-step contests,
clean the roadkill, and warn the civilians when the black
flies were swarming and droving. In his fourteen years as
chief, he'd investigated one possible homicide. One. And
that had turned out to be nothing more than a bizarre
hunting accident. It had resulted when eighty-two-year-
old John Barnes mistook his kindling-gathering wife, Eu-
nice, for a six-point buck and fired a bullet through her
chest. Barnes had been so distraught that Sullivan quickly
ruled out foul play.

Sullivan enjoyed the lack of action (aided by a coroner
who simply refused to meddle). Why shouldn't he? In
Vietnam he'd seen enough chaos to last four lifetimes. In
fact, there was really only one aspect of Georgeville that
Sullivan disliked, one party unworthy of the Georgeville
Police Department's code of ethics.

Those Simsbury assholes.

His grudge dated back to the sixties, when real men
were going off to war. Not the Simsbury boys, though.
Oh no. They'd been too busy jacking off to visions of
Wall Street and Wharton to be bothered by duty's call.
And as if draft dodging hadn't been contemptible
enough, they'd actually marched in *protest.* They'd *spit*
on returning soldiers like him—soldiers who'd spent
years overseas, fighting for freedom and wondering

which day would be their last while the precious little Simsbury boys rode their polo ponies.

This morning, Sullivan's attitude toward Simsbury was particularly foul. The night before, he'd responded to a "four-twelve in progress, at Chewnocker's." Arriving on the scene, he'd found six severely beaten locals in the parking lot, all of whom vaguely remembered getting jumped by at least a dozen "college assholes." Sullivan hadn't been surprised to hear the odds. Cowardice was a streak that ran deep in the Simsbury character.

So now he was exacting a little revenge, the sort that had him behind the wheel of an unmarked cruiser for the first time since October.

The call he'd been waiting for had actually come on Tuesday, from a number his phone's Caller ID unit hadn't been able to trace. Not that he'd needed to know the caller's identity; the content of the conversation was all that mattered, enough to confirm that he was speaking to a wealthy Simsbury alum.

One with ties to the big white fraternity house on the corner of College and Maine.

One hoping to curtail any criminal investigation into the recent death of Chad Ewing.

Knowing this, knowing that the coroner hadn't called, and knowing as a result that the "accident" report Officer Ames had prepared indeed represented a fortune, Sullivan had done his little dance and then played hardball. He'd hemmed and hawed and yanked the caller around, before finally agreeing to meet one of his "representatives" on Saturday—"say, sometime between eight and

nine," in the rear parking lot of what had once been Paul
& Dory's Neighborhood Market.

So here it was, Saturday morning, closer to nine than
eight.

And here he was, easing bald cruiser radials over the
snow-filled pavement cavities of an unkempt delivery
access that led to the rear lot of the former Paul &
Dory's.

P&D's had been one of three mom-and-pop establish-
ments to go under when Super Stop & Shop came to
town, a community tragedy that had surprised Sullivan in
that the residents had not only voted to let it happen but
had allowed it to smother some of their civic pride. Not
one of the three failed shells had been reacquired (actually, one had very briefly been Kelly's Gym). Instead, the
abandoned buildings had been left to dilapidate on their
own, while the surrounding acres served as alternative
rubbish dumps for those neighboring diners and hair sa-
lons whose proprietors were too cheap or lazy to get commercial waste disposal licenses.

As Sullivan idled toward the black BMW parked beside P&D's own trashy headstone, it occurred to him that
Simsbury alums were prototypical corporate franchisers.
The forthcoming transaction, he decided, wouldn't just
avenge and symbolically compensate those comrades
who'd spilled blood in 'Nam and Chewnocker's parking
lot but also Paul and Dory Bunker, who'd been forced to
liquidate and retire to the hills of Tennessee rather than
the beaches of Florida.

He parked an intentional distance from the BMW, exited the town's cream-colored Buick, and made his way
toward money.

The Beamer's door opened, and from it emerged a good-sized man wearing Saturday garb and a Yankees baseball cap. (*A New Yorker,* thought Sullivan, briefly conjuring images of Bucky Dent's Fenway dagger and the throngs of pushy jerks who invaded Maine's beaches every July. *All the more reason to hate what this rich prick represents.*)

"Good morning," said the rich prick.

"That remains to be seen," Sullivan replied.

The rich prick smirked, then turned to watch two sea-gulls battle for possession of a chicken bone. When the victor had taken flight with its booty, and the loser had squawked all its bitter protests and returned to the rubbish pile, the rich prick turned back to Sullivan and nodded at the possibilities. "How much will it take?"

Whoa, thought Sullivan. *That didn't take long.* "How much will *what* take to do *what*?" he countered, thinking he might earn more monetary dividends and personal satisfaction by toying.

The rich prick nodded and grinned. "Let's cut the shit, shall we? We both know why I'm here."

Sullivan was set to continue the game, then decided there really was no point, since he appeared to be the only one playing it. "All right," he said. "But first things first. Are you wired?"

"Don't flatter yourself."

Sullivan nodded, swallowed hard, and delved into the short speech he'd informally rehearsed. "Okay, then, let's see. I got ten for ignoring those attempted rape rumors a couple years ago, and five for turning my head when that steroid monster beat the teeth out of that Navy pilot. You guys have been such regular customers that I considered offering you a discount, but this time you managed to kill—"

"How much to let a sleeping dog lie?" said the rich prick, smiling calmly.

His oration interrupted, Sullivan felt the first touch of discomfort creep into his soul. Not only was this jerk entirely unashamed of the transgressions committed by the big white fraternity house on the corner of College and Maine, he seemed to regard Sullivan as a trivial nuisance, a garbage feeder who'd cease his irritating whine in exchange for a small bone of his own. Sullivan didn't know whether to be incredulous or indignant, but he also knew he hadn't the time to sort between the two, for though he'd taken an hour or so to rehearse an inconsequential speech, he hadn't taken five seconds to set a price.

While the rich alum shifted impatiently, Sullivan studied the mound of trash. "Uh . . . forty."

"Done."

Done. Just like that. No haggling. No hesitation. Just *done.* The shock of the transaction's swiftness stunned him at first, then he felt a pang of regret at not having asked for more.

"How about fifty?"

The rich prick smiled condescendingly and said, "Let's make it seventy-five."

Now floored, Sullivan just stared at the dark eyes beneath the blue bill of the baseball hat, wondering (oddly) how he was going to split seventy-five grand evenly with Ames, and (darkly) what sort of power and resources were available to a fraternity whose "representative" could drop seventy-five grand as if it were a two-dollar tip.

The rich prick pulled a pad of paper and a pen from his jacket pocket. "Here," he said, handing both to Sullivan. "Write down your bank, account number, and any wire transfer info we'll need. You know the drill."

Sullivan blinked in hesitation, then accepted the pen and pad, and scribbled the requested information.

The alum took back the materials and returned them to his pocket. "The money will be wired first thing Monday."

Turning abruptly in blatant dismissal, he got back in his black BMW, fired up the horses, and nearly reversed over Sullivan's foot. The vehicle paused a moment to find the first of its five speeds, and in that instant Sullivan felt the urge to pump his fist at the tinted window and shout vindication on behalf of the locals who'd shed blood in Southeast Asia, the locals who'd shed blood at Chewnocker's, and the locals who'd shed mom-and-pop tears.

But his fist hung limply at his side, and his silent shouts were squelched by the peel of tires, a shriek challenged only by the losing seagull, who emerged from the junk heap long enough to flare its grimy wings and screech at the machine that had disturbed its scavenging.

For a moment, the bird seemed to watch the mocking wink of departing taillights.

Then it gave Sullivan a look of pity and returned to its scraps at the bottom of the food chain.

9:46 A.M.

Twenty-seven hours after waking with a nightmarish gasp, Mark awoke with a contrary demon.

An inability to breathe at all.

His first thought was that he was still sleeping. Having endured dreams in which he couldn't run, lift his arms, or get an erection, he figured his not being able to get air was just a new wrinkle on an old theme.

Reality presented itself in furry form, however, as Casey pounced on his chest and smacked the wind back into him. Coughing dramatically, he swept her to the floor and rolled onto his side.

And as oxygen filled his lungs, a new sensation paralyzed him.

Pain.

Had this been an amnesia ward rather than college housing, he might've interpreted his all-over agony as the aftermath of some sort of car or boat wreck that had knocked the memory out of him. However, he recalled enough of the prior evening's footwork and fisticuffs to know that his current condition had nothing to do with an accident, and everything to do with the alcohol that now pressed its merciless remnants on his bladder. Fearing that if he lay there too long he'd do to his boxer briefs what his nose told him Casey had already done to the rug, he pushed aside his body's plea for daylong bed rest and labored from his mattress.

He dragged himself to the bathroom, did his thing, then twisted the shower knob all the way to the left and limped to the neighboring living room. He dialed Shawn's number and gently poked at his ribs while the phone rang and the shower jet spray blew steam in his direction. On the fifth ring, he remembered that Shawn had a ski tournament in Vermont. She'd be long gone by now, and it was probably just as well; he was certain his face bore evidence of activities she'd disapprove of.

He stepped into the shower, and as the hot water drummed his bruises, he pieced together the previous night's events.

As he'd feared, the boys' night out had ended in a slugfest that began when Sigma Kevin Daly, the senior who'd set a school record for touchdown receptions and who wanted to be a surgeon someday, dropped a pitcher of beer on the lap of a very hairy, very large, local resident. The townie had taken offense to the spillage, and Dominic had taken offense to the townie's taking offense. Dominic had also taken charge of the ensuing eleven-man brawl, proving first in the bar and then in the parking lot that his dominant hand-to-hand combat skills were second to none. He'd almost single-handedly whipped six of the most grisly-looking men in Southern Maine, saving Mark, Ran, Fairchild, and Daly from suffering more than just a moderate level of rumble damage.

The college boys had run at the first siren whoop, in neither the mood nor the condition to explain their actions to the local police. They'd sprinted back to Sigma, stopping on the snowy lawn to catch their breath, hug like comrades, and bask in moonlit victory.

And that's what Mark knew he'd take with him. He'd forget the sights, sounds, and sensations of the bar war, for there really was nothing material he could take from the experience, except some wounds that would fade over the course of days. But he'd *always* remember the warm wrap of brotherly arms that thwarted the chill breeze trying to tunnel through the fresh rip in his flannel. And he'd remember the three glorious revelations he'd reached during the five-man embrace.

He'd always been a Sigma.

He'd always *be* a Sigma.

And Sigma would always win.

The fight at Chewnocker's had proved it, vanquishing the insecurities that had hatched during Thursday's D-Squad hearing and FBI visit. Mark and his friends had spilled and shed a *good* brand of blood, in defense of the blood they'd once dripped on three Greek letters.

Long live the brothers of Sigma Delta Phi.

10:23 A.M.

As the brothers of Sigma Delta Phi filtered into the house kitchen for fancy omelettes and Belgian waffles, they traded embellished war stories regarding what they'd heard of the brawl at Chewnocker's.

They couldn't wait to hear a blow-by-blow description.

And they couldn't wait for the next pledge activity, for all this talk of violence had them yearning to throw a few punches of their own.

11:02 A.M.

The shower had shelved some of Mark's pain, and Advil was veiling the rest. Standard daily motion, impossible just an hour earlier, was now in progress. He dressed warmly, leashed Casey, and ventured outside.

The air was bitchy, the sun friendly, and the seven-minute walk to the Student Center neither pleasant nor unpleasant. He secured Casey to the hibernating bike rack and shuffled up the steps.

In the dining hall he ordered an egg sandwich from a hair-netted dining hall matron who could barely peel her horrified stare from Mark's scratched-up face. He offered his most charming, I'm-really-a-peaceful-guy smile as he scooped up his breakfast package, a bag of oyster crackers, and two plastic bottles of orange juice, one of which he guzzled as he made his way down the hallway that connected the dining hall and the mailroom.

He knelt stiffly, spun the combination, and opened his mailbox.

Though he hadn't checked since Thursday, there wasn't much in his box to crow about: three pieces of campus junk mail, a phone bill, and a stampless envelope addressed simply to "Mark." Gripping his brunch bag in his teeth, he pocketed all but the personal envelope, which he opened right away.

Inside was a card that hollered *"Happy Birthday!"* in bubbly letters surrounded by confetti, party hats, and balloons.

Mark frowned. His birthday was in October. He examined the envelope again, making sure it was really addressed to him, then looked around to see if he was on candid camera or something. Discovering himself to be the only person in the mail room, he shrugged and opened the card. What he found written inside baffled him even more: *"There were three of us."*

What the hell? Mark reviewed the message several times, making sure he'd read it right. It just didn't make any sense . . . and then, suddenly, it made perfect sense.

The three SWA women from the other day. They were writing to remind Mark never to wear his *De-baitable Babe* hat. They were writing to remind him that they were always watching him.

They were writing to remind him of Angela McSheffrey.

Stop it, he commanded himself. *They're trying to get a rise out of you, but you won't let them, because you're a returning All-American with tons of friends who'll back you up in bar fights . . .*

On his way back outside, he smiled at the cute junior who sometimes worked at the information desk. She smiled back.

He skipped down the steps, untied Casey, fed her the entire bag of oyster crackers, and headed for home.

4:02 P.M.

Nine of the twelve seniors met briefly in the Brother-hood Room and huddled around a freshmen face-book. They found the name they were looking for on page eight, and eighteen eyes studied the accompanying picture. They took a quick poll to decide which two of them would best be suited for that night's mission, and with secret handshakes they confirmed the assignment.

They left the room a short time later, confident that by midnight they'd be one step closer to exoneration.

Alpha would be pleased.

9:39 P.M.

For the first time in his life, freshman Jason Lyle was the most popular boy in his school.

And he hated it.

Growing up, he'd harbored no illusions about his looks

(short, slight, and pale-faced), his athletic ability (none to speak of), or his personality (more suited to Dungeons and Dragons than keg parties). He'd always been a spaz among jocks, a forgettable face in a world of beautiful people, so he'd felt perfectly at home when, upon enrolling at Simsbury, he'd fallen into his high school role of background boy, one who walked the campus in relative obscurity, blessed not in face or body but merely in mind.

Literally overnight, however, he'd become a campus celebrity. His journeys to class, once low-key and greeting-free, now featured finger-points, whispers, and stares. The door to his dorm room, once tidy and practically bare, now bore thumbtacked notes from well-wishers he didn't even know. His mailbox, once receptacle to only campus bulletins and letters from Mom, now overflowed with sympathy cards and care-package cookies wrapped in foil.

All because he was the roommate of the late Chad Ewing.

He was mortified by the newfound attention and, despite the thoughtfulness displayed by his fellow students, slightly disgusted. Where had all the well-wishers been in the weeks leading up to Chad's death? Where had they been the night Chad returned to the room with blood gushing from his nose? Where had they been the night Chad returned with blood pouring from his mouth? Where had they been the night Chad returned with blood streaming from a dozen different spots on his body? Where had they been on *all* those nights, when Chad had left for Sigma wide-eyed and terrified, returned home puffy-eyed and mentally fried, and crawled into his bed like a wounded animal?

Of course, Jason knew that only he, as roommate, had been privy to these nightly horrors. Still, someone should have noticed the stress-induced acne on Chad's chin. Someone should have heard Chad practicing his shaky-voiced Sigma songs in one of the two showers shared by the eighteen freshmen on their floor. Someone, apart from the professors who had sent pink slips, should have noticed the drop in Chad's grades. Someone should have noticed the droop in Chad's posture, the flinch in his expression, and the dart in his eyes that had begun roughly four weeks earlier, when he'd first pledged his lifelong loyalty to Sigma.

Someone should have realized that Chad was being more than just hazed.

Someone should have put a stop to it.

Someone like Jason.

And that, Jason knew, was what really disgusted him the most, the knowledge that he could have done something that might have saved his roommate's life. He could have called Chad's parents. He could have sent an anonymous letter to the dean. He could have called the police.

But he'd done nothing.

And he'd have to live with that knowledge for the rest of his life.

He had spent the day at his computer, pecking a letter to Chad's parents, but had yet to draft anything other than a jumbled array of words and sentence fragments, guilty feelings and accusations. He knew that he'd never send the letter and had never intended to. Still, he tapped away, hoping this cathartic outpouring would help him forgive himself.

He was in the middle of a long, rambling emotion when he realized that the dull pounding in his head was actually someone knocking on his door. Stopping mid-word, he looked up. *Who could that be?* Had this been a normal Saturday, he'd be expecting visitors; his room was the site of the weekly round of Dungeons and Dragons. This week's game, however, had been can-celed, for obvious reasons, so whoever was at the door was someone who didn't know Jason very well, which meant it could be all but seven or eight people on cam-pus.

He walked to the door and opened it.

One of the men was big, the other, huge. Jason imme-diately recognized both as Sigmas, and his heart began to hammer. They had killed Chad, and now they were going to quench their thirst for blood on Chad's pitiful little roommate.

Just as he was wondering how they were going to ex-terminate him, the less-gigantic of the two smiled and held out his hand. "I'm Mike Scully," he said, "and this is A. J. Dominic. We were friends of Chad's."

Jason accepted the handshake. "Hi."

"Hi," said Scully, as both he and his huge companion stepped into the room and closed the door. "Got a minute?"

Jason nodded slowly, and as he backed away from the advancing Sigmas he reached behind him and flicked off his computer screen.

10:32 P.M.

Throughout the day, the Freshman's mood had been one of nervous anticipation, laced with shards of panic. Though he didn't know what he was waiting for, he knew it was Saturday, two days after Thursday, and he now sat on the edge of his bed, obsessing on the same artless questions.

Did he get it yet?

Did he read it?

Does he get it?

Does he care?

Of course, it was only a matter of time before his mind overpowered the simplicity of these haunting quizzes, and when it did, a new question spun off:

Do I want the answers to these questions to be yes or no?

He crept to the window, pulled opened the shade, and peered out at the starless sky.

Then he bolted the window, closed the shade, and sank into the darkness of another sleepless night.

CHAPTER TWENTY-SIX

*The 200th Year
Sunday, March 1*

12:44 P.M.

The ten-minute walk across the quad ran fifty minutes longer than scheduled, as every cute coed stopped to kiss Casey's pink nose and make baby noises. It was great fun, an opportunity for both Mark and Casey to get some harmless attention. And since Mark had nowhere particular to be, he hammed it up as long as possible.

All went well until the same three-woman army of SWA members who'd condemned his *De-baitable Babe* hat approached him with the force and focus of a three-headed locomotive. They chugged to a halt several feet from Mark and his puppy and hipped their hands in unison.

Mark swallowed hard, then adopted a jolly face and met each of their glares in sequence. "Marcia. Caitlin. Hitler."

"Well, well, well," began the pudgy general, ignoring the Nazi label, "if it isn't our favorite rapist. How goes it, penis boy."

"Just fine, ladies. How are you?"

"Shitty!" barked the general, with a suddenness that suggested she and her comrades had premeditated this attack. "Because it turns my stomach to see you use a trusting puppy to sucker what you *assume* to be the maternal instincts of the women on this campus, in hopes that their attention might be diverted while you aim your oppressive male hardness at them!"

Mark shook his head, as if to clear water from his ear. "I think that was a run-on sentence, ma'am."

"Don't you dare call her ma'am," hissed Marcia. Or Caitlin.

"What should I call her?"

"Nothing!" shot the general. "Because the thought of you even *addressing* me makes me want to pull out my rape whistle and blow it till I faint!"

"Fine. I won't address you."

"Don't even look at me."

"Now, that'll be difficult, since you get in my face every few days. By the way, thanks for the belated birthday card."

There was a silence, animated only by the general's cloudy bursts of spiteful breath. Then she stepped forward cautiously, as if approaching a tethered tiger. "I'll tell you what, Mark Jessy. I'll stop getting in your face when I feel you've been suitably punished for what you did. You got off scot-free, and now you're sitting pretty on the D-Squad, getting ready to help your disgusting Sigma buddies out of some really big trouble. It makes me sick."

"Believe me, I'd trade places with you in a sec—"

"Shut up!" The general fumed. "Just shut up!" She

glared at Mark a moment, her entire body sputtering. "For the life of me, I don't know what a self-respecting woman like Shawn Jakes sees in trash like you, but I've got a right mind to slap some sense into her."

"You just try and slap her," said Mark, his own anger rising, "and she'll shove a ski pole straight through the hair across your ass."

The general stepped back, visibly stunned. Marcia and Caitlin exchanged looks of horror.

Now Mark pressed the attack. He stepped forward and pointed directly between the general's eyes. "And the next time you send me any unwanted mail, I'll charge the three of you with postal assault and attempted annoyance."

He turned his back on the women and scooped up Casey, who was cowering between his legs. "C'mon, girl," he whispered, loud enough for the women to hear. "I see some maternal instincts over by the art museum. Let's go flirt."

1:05 P.M.

The seniors gathered briefly in the Brotherhood Room, but long enough to discuss a phone call, decide on a mission, verbalize a script, and doom a career.

2:08 P.M.

Penny Ward chucked the last of the breakfast cookware into the sink, then ducked as the resulting splash backfired slugs of soap at her head. She shook her head and turned her back on the dishy swamp, since pots, pans, and all afternoon duties weren't in her job description. Rita, the dinner cook, would be in at three to bake the

Sunday-night lasagna. By then, Penny would have scratched the silver mask off ten or fifteen "Lucky Dime" scratch tickets and would be planning a much-deserved dream vacation with the ten-thousand-dollar booty she'd won.

She donned her freshly cleaned white leather and was all set to scram when Aaron Snow and Pete Thresher strutted into the kitchen and began playing catch with an escaped apple. Normally, Penny would have given them a standard hello and been on her way. However, Snow was the Sigma steward and the signer of her paycheck, of which there had been none this week.

"Hey, Aaron. Think I might get paid this week?"

Snow and Thresher exchanged looks, then Thresher turned his unreadable eyes on Penny. "Could you come into the other room for a moment, Penny?"

"Sure. As long as I get my check."

"You will."

She followed them out of the kitchen, through the dining and living rooms, and into the upstairs libes. Once inside, Snow heaved the door shut, Thresher motioned for Penny to sit, and both took seats across from her.

"What's this all about?" said Penny, thinking this was starting to look like an interrogation.

Snow reached into his pocket, pulled out an envelope, and handed it to Penny.

"What's this?"

"Your check."

Penny regarded Snow curiously, then opened the envelope. It was her check, all right, but when she read the amount her heart almost stopped.

Ten thousand dollars.

"Is this some kind of joke?"

"Actually," said Thresher, "it's severance pay."

Penny blinked. "What?"

"Severance pay. You're fired."

"I am?"

"Yup."

Penny looked at the check, then at Thresher again. "Can I ask why?"

"Sure, you can ask," said Thresher calmly, "but I think you already know the answer."

"Actually, I don't think I do. Would you mind telling me what I did wrong?"

Thresher looked to Snow, who cleared his throat and straightened in his chair. "Penny, the last four monthly kitchen-fund bank-statement reconciliations have turned up unexplained variances, ranging from one to five thousand dollars. We took the liberty of searching the kitchen lockers—"

"That's an invasion of privacy," said Penny, immediately regretting her desperate tone.

"And skimming is a violation of your employment terms." Snow pulled a rubber-banded stack of bills from the belly pocket of his hockey sweatshirt. "We found this in your locker."

Penny squinted and nodded wryly. "Oh, I get it. I stole from the kitchen fund, then conveniently hid the cash in my kitchen locker. What sort of idiot do you think you're dealing—"

"One who clearly didn't cover her tracks well enough," interrupted Thresher.

Penny opened her mouth, then clamped it shut and crossed her arms huffily. "You're full of crap."

Snow shook his head sadly. "Don't do this, Penny. You've done a good job here, a real good job. Let's not end it like this."

Penny felt her eyes fill with tears. "You can't do this to me."

"Unfortunately, we have to."

"I've never stolen a damn thing in my life."

Snow shrugged and shook the wad of money. "The evidence says otherwise, now doesn't it?"

Speechless, Penny just stared at the cash. This was not happening. This was not happening.

"You're lucky we gave you any severance pay at all," Thresher said. "By law, we're not required. You broke your agreement with your employer."

Snow pointed at the check. "That check is more than generous."

"Excuse me if I don't do cartwheels," said Penny, her voice trembling. "I have rent to pay. How long is this money supposed to last me?"

"Until you find another job. Oh, and by the way, don't look for a position with another house on campus. We can't allow that."

"Why?"

Snow and Thresher looked at each other, then at Penny. "We have our reasons," said Thresher.

"I'll just bet you do. I hope your next cook poisons your food."

The two seniors stood. "One more thing," said Thresher, his voice low. "I wouldn't go spouting your mouth off about this. *Or* about what you saw here last

Sunday morning. That would be a big mistake on your part."

As the gruesome image of last Sunday merged with the tandem towering over her, Penny suddenly understood. "Oh, do you mean how I walked into this beautiful fraternity house and nearly tripped over a dying pledge? You mean I shouldn't tell people that he was *naked*, and he had *weird things* written all over his body? I could *ruin* you guys if I wanted to."

Thresher inched forward and peered down. "Don't be a fool, you peasant bitch," he rumbled through gritted teeth. "We're smarter than you, and we outnumber you. Any action you take against us will be dismissed as sour grapes, then avenged by us."

He leaned closer, and Penny could feel the heat from his core on her face. "Don't fuck with us, Penny," he warned, "because you may live to regret it. Then again, you may not."

For a long moment, Penny stared up at the two young men, and for the first time she saw them not as two of many spoiled brats who'd had every possible opportunity handed to them because of their names and their family money and the wonderful things they could do with footballs and hockey pucks. Instead, she saw the mean glint in their eyes, the hard set to their mouths, and the hostility in their stances, and it struck her that they'd stop at nothing to protect this fraternal thing, about which she had no concept.

It struck her that they were two of many ruthless men, and that their ruthlessness might not be reserved only for pledges.

Forcing her legs to move, gripping her check tightly,

she left without another word. Her children were grown, their father was rutting with his secretary, and she was on her way home to plan a much-deserved dream vacation.

8:40 P.M.

"What happened to your face?" asked Shawn.

She'd returned from her ski race euphoric; she'd qualified for the Nationals again, and this year they were going to be held in Aspen, minutes from her house. Mark had congratulated her effusively, hoping to steer her away from questions like the one she'd just asked.

"What do you mean?"

"Your face, Mark," she said impatiently. "You look like a special effect."

"Oh that," said Mark, as if it were nothing. "Casey scratched me."

"With what? A hunting knife?"

Mark chuckled. "No, no. She got a little too excited and clawed me."

"What were you doing? Holding a steak in front of your head?"

"Nah. Just wrestling." He put up his dukes. "I was teaching her how to fight."

"Hmm," Shawn grunted, as she tossed her overnight bag on the kitchen table. "Maybe *she* should be teaching *you*."

She kicked off her boots and headed for the bedroom.

10:51 P.M.

Surrounded by black-robed brothers and shadows, the Triumvirate Leader stared down at the pledges, and then began to rhyme.

I begin this grave poem without wait or wonder,
Twelve couplings that voice this brotherhood's thun-
der.

I speak once again of an unfortunate morning,
And cite reasons for caution, reasons for warning.

There are those at the school, who want us to pay,
For a pledge's sad death, for his subsoil lay.

Therefore questions will come, suspicious and tricky,
Making an already tense situation more sticky.

So remember your oaths, and hear my voice boom.
We command you to keep secrets locked in their
tomb.

Or else you will join them.
There's a short path to doom.

CHAPTER TWENTY-SEVEN

The 200th Year
Monday, March 2

9:16 A.M.

Fresh off an outrageously sexual weekend, Templeton unlocked the door to his office and turned on the light with fingers that had recently explored every exciting inch of Linda's body. He hung his jacket, floored his briefcase, and chaired his happy ass. He buzzed his secretary, ordered coffee, and leaned back to reflect momentarily on some of the weekend's highlights.

Then he straightened abruptly, reached for the phone, and commenced moving human pieces around life's chessboard.

12:06 P.M.

As she watched Jocelyn flirtatiously nod her brown bob at a cluster of admiring freshmen, Shawn smiled and wondered how the youngest Patricola daughter would've survived the dearth of male attention had she attended Smith, the all-women's college that had refined every other woman in her bloodline. *She simply wouldn't have,* Shawn concluded.

She was about to shout a greeting, when Jocelyn beat her to the punch by smiling whitely, wiggling her carefully maintained butt, and raising a pita stuffed with greens.

"Hey," said Shawn, as the two converged in a sunny patch between Watson's and Driscoll's high brick shadows.

"What's up?" Jocelyn said, pausing to take and chew a bite of lunch, most of which she spat into the snow and cursed for containing croutons. "You would think," she said scornfully, her tongue working to purge every evil crumb, "that they'd understand by now what *fat-free* means."

Shawn nodded, though unable to fathom how Jocelyn's meal, a clearly undressed heap of lettuce and sprouts wrapped in wheat, could contain any fewer calories. "I don't know how you do it."

Jocelyn looked down, then up. "Do what?"

"*That*," replied Shawn, pointing at the pocket. "It looks so bland."

Jocelyn glanced down again and shook her head. "I squeeze lemon on it." She took another bite and grinned while crunching. "Besides, I'm on a bikini diet. Spring break's two weeks away, and I'm gonna be the hardest body on the beach."

"Which island?"

Jocelyn swallowed and beamed. "Aruba."

"With?"

The beam broadened. "Pete."

"He's not going to South Padre with the rest of the meatheads?"

"Nope. We made a deal before last year's break. If I

stayed home while he went to Cancun, he'd let me go away this year."

"He'd *let* you?"

"He gets jealous," Jocelyn confided. "Anyway, we leave a week from Friday."

Shawn nodded diplomatically, unsure whether she was more disgusted with Pete or Jocelyn. Of all Mark's Sigma friends, Pete Thresher was her least favorite, the kind of pig who insisted his girlfriend wear circus tents for sweaters while he himself salivated at every pair of tube-topped tits that crossed his leer line. She'd always tolerated him, though, clinging to the assumption that Jocelyn was simply passing time with Pete until graduation sent him back to Kentucky and her to somewhere like Manhattan, where a challenging career and a deeper relationship would make her chuckle at the time she'd spent with a moron like Pete Thresher. However, the last ninety seconds of dialogue caused Shawn to wonder if Jocelyn wasn't closer to the unflattering image Mark had painted of her.

"What about you?" asked Jocelyn, bagging the remainder of her food and pulling a water bottle from her backpack. "You going anywhere?"

"Aspen, for Nationals."

Jocelyn sucked on the bottle, then recapped it. "Congratulations," she said with a smile. "You and all your accomplishments. I don't know how *you* do it."

"Keeps me out of trouble."

Jocelyn chuckled. "And on the trail of it, right?"

Shawn smiled, then rearranged some wind-tossed strands and segued to the opportunity she'd been seeking since Monday. "Speaking of which . . ."

Jocelyn nodded vaguely and concerned herself with returning the bottle to its appropriate pouch.

". . . Do you remember Monday, when I saw you in the library?"

Jocelyn halted her project mid-zip and warily turned her attention to Shawn. "Uh . . . yeah."

"You mentioned being at Sigma when they found that kid."

Jocelyn looked down and resumed her fidgeting. "What kid . . ."

Shawn blinked. "Chad Ewing. The kid that died."

"What about him?"

"You . . . said you were there. You said you went downstairs when you heard all the commotion—"

"I don't know why I would've said *that*," Jocelyn said with an anxious giggle. "I was upstairs sleeping. I missed all the excite—"

"You *told* me you saw the body."

"I don't know what you're talking about."

"You *told* me you saw the body," repeated Shawn, growing frustrated. "You told me Chad was naked, with poetry all over him. You told me there was so much blood—"

"I never said that!"

"Yes, you did!"

"Why would I make up something like *that*?" Jocelyn said, her eyes darting every which way but toward Shawn.

Shawn threw up her arms. "Why would *I*?"

"I don't know, but you must've misunderstood me."

Arms still raised, Shawn shook her head in disbelief. Then, a new realization slowly lowered her arms.

"Jocelyn," she probed softly, "is it Pete? Did he tell you to change your story?"

Jocelyn stared at the ground. Then she suddenly grabbed Shawn's wrist and yanked her through a maze of passing denim and flannel, out of the sun's spotlight, and into the combined shade cast by Watson Hall and a wilted tree.

"Wha—"

"Shut up," urged Jocelyn, turning to face Shawn beneath a dead branch that threw dark bones across an already shadowed face. "Look," she admitted, her gloveless hand still raw on Shawn's wrist, "I remember what I told you. But the truth is, I forget what I saw."

She gripped harder. "And if you care about me at all, you'll forget what I saw, too."

12:44 P.M.

Mark jogged around the frozen basin that nozzled springtime spray at the statue of General William Q. Simsbury and, using Ran and Fairchild's unsuspecting, side-by-side shoulders, propelled himself skyward. He concluded his trick with a finishing kick, the downward push of which buckled the four friendly legs supporting him. Recovering, Ran and Fairchild fired retaliatory jabs, which Mark absorbed and returned. For a few seconds the three circled and postured, swiping at each other and talking trash. Then, remembering their age, their hunger, and the still-tender aches they'd earned at Chewnocker's, they reassembled their flannels and set a pace and a course that would put them in Sigma's dining room within minutes.

"What's on the menu today?" asked Mark.

"Chicken pucks and onion hoops!" shouted Ran, patting his belly.

"Nice," said Mark. "Go Penny."

The two Sigmas exchanged a quick look. "Actually," said Fairchild, "Penny doesn't work for us anymore."

"No way! Where'd she go?"

"She was fired."

"Fired? What'd she do, burn too many pancakes?"

"No," Fairchild replied, his voice oddly edged. "She skimmed too much cash."

"She stole!" Mark nearly shouted. "From the house?"

Nods.

"Shit," said Mark softly, trying to picture a harmless matron like Penny Ward stealing so much as a butter pat. "How much did she take?"

Neither Ran nor Fairchild had a response for this, and neither offered another word on the way to Sigma.

During the hour that Shawn, Jocelyn, Mark, Ran, and Fairchild traded body talk and body shots, Sigma alums across the country earned more than most other American families earned in a lifetime, one percent of which would be earmarked for a specific bank account in Lexington, Massachusetts.

3:01 P.M.

After listening to Chairman Davenport holler that there *was* no freedom of the press at a private school, after listening to him screech that *no* father would pay six figures for a collegiate setting that might send his beloved child home in a *box,* after listening to him point out that Simsbury's elite were *supposed* to die peacefully (not violently) at ninety (not nineteen) in south Florida, after listening to him stress the importance of both finishing ahead of the competition in the upcoming *U.S.News & World Report* survey and finishing the Chad Ewing investigation by spring break, Templeton politely excused himself to pursue these two objectives and hung up the phone. He rubbed his eyes and ears, swallowed a cup of water, then headed to see Mr. President.

"Good afternoon, Dean Templeton," said Carlisle's secretary when he'd arrived at the other end of the third-floor hallway. "That's a great tie."

"Thank you, Janet. My wife bought it for me."

"She has classy taste."

"I'll tell her you said so. Is the boss in?"

"He is, but he may be napping. Shall I wake him?"

"Only if you were about to."

"Let me check." Janet pressed a button.

Several seconds later, a groggy voice came over the intercom. "Whitney?"

"No, dear," said Janet sweetly, "but your wife *did* call. Are you awake?"

Pause. "Yes."

"Dean Templeton is here to see you. Shall I send him in?"

Another pause. "Okay."

Janet smiled at Templeton and said, "Go ahead in." Then leaning forward, she whispered, "But be patient with him."

Templeton gave her a thumbs-up, knocked once on the door behind her, then pushed it open.

Carlisle sat behind a desk so enormous it accentuated his advancing frailty, wearing a face as blank as the desktop itself. His tie hung loose and lopsided, the white hair on one side of his head pointing toward the window.

"Hello, Edison."

"Hi. Did you get my message?"

"I did. I just got off the phone with him."

"He was all upset about some picture in the paper."

Templeton nodded. He, too, had been disturbed by the published photo of the Ewings at the memorial service, but for different reasons.

"He also asked me all sorts of questions about the investigation—"

"We talked."

Carlisle licked his lips and buzzed Janet for some water. Then, to Templeton, he said, "What *is* going on?"

"Thursday's preliminary hearing went pretty much the way I expected."

"Is it over?"

"Almost. I expect a formal exoneration later this week."

"Oh," Carlisle said absently, his expression full of Alzheimer's. "That's good, right?"

"Yes, that's good."

Carlisle nodded deliberately. "Okay. Just keep me in the loop, Anson."

"Of course, Edison. I wouldn't dream of excluding you."

1:56 A.M.

The concept of insomnia had always been foreign to Fairchild, significant only in that he'd connected its eight meaningless letters to win the second-grade spelling bee and garner the first of the skillion trophies now shining from a cedar case in his bedroom back home. To him, sleep had always seemed the most humble of life's rewards, granted simply by being born. And since that day, it had come nightly, in the form of a locomotive that rolled through, minutes after his head hit the pillow.

But tonight, about a hundred and seventy-five minutes had passed since he'd drawn up the covers around him.

And the train was long overdue.

He'd initially blamed the noises native to frat life. His first hour in bed had been dominated by the downstairs calamity of a post-Triumvirate, full-contact game of hallway football. His second hour had been scored by strains more subtle: toothbrushes and soap dishes rattling bathroom baskets on the move . . . twisted towels rat-tailing thighs. However, in time, the late hour had stilled even the drowsiest shuffle, and complete quiet enveloped all three floors of the brotherhood, leaving Fairchild still very much awake and frustrated by the knowledge he'd beaten every last Sigma to bed, but none to sleep.

And that's when unease had taken hold, the feeling that each relentless, clock-radioed minute shoved him further away from a good night's rest. Not long after, panic had struck, as he concluded above the faint pounding in his ears that slumber was the most *difficult* of life's activities, and that he was never going to sleep again.

Relax, he now thought, pressing a damp hand to his equally clammy forehead. *Get a grip on yourself.* He took several deep breaths, and as the tempo seemed to subside he began analyzing the situation.

There had to be a reason for this, a certain something he hadn't yet identified. Perhaps he was too warm. He kicked his comforter to the floor and shed his tee. And maybe he should try his stomach. He flipped onto his belly and settled cheek-first into the pillow.

He closed his eyes.

But opened them almost immediately, as the thumping returned.

Disregarding the comfort factor, he returned his focus to sound, but this time to the almost imperceptible whispers that subconsciously threw off his sleep rhythm. Like that breezy brillo of pine brushing against a frosty pane. And that pipe-to-pipe run of excess water through the veins of the house. Wondering why he hadn't thought of this earlier, he swung his feet to the floor and switched on his reading lamp. He rubbed nearly three hours of darkness from his eyes, then stood and stepped to his desk, wiggled open the top drawer, and managed a smile as the earplugs from Chem 372's combustion lab rolled conveniently to the front. He positioned them on opposite sides of his tired head, then fell once more into bed. He turned off the light, closed his eyes, and welcomed a world without senses.

For one brief moment, he barely existed.

And then he heard it again.

It began as a hum, so distant he first dismissed it, but it increased exponentially, the drone of an advancing swarm giving way to the wail of approaching sirens, and as the clanging joined the revived hammering, a suppressed image threw his lids open and the plugs to the floor, and identified itself as the certain shoutless, treeless, dripless something that had denied him sleep.

Something that had chased him for nine days.

Something that had finally caught up to him.

At some point, the rickety-wheeled carriage of sleep

wobbled through the presidential suite on the third floor of Sigma.

And at some point, Fairchild labored aboard its ghostly frame.

But brought a stowaway along for the ride.

CHAPTER TWENTY-EIGHT

The 200th Year
Tuesday, March 3

NOON

For the second day in a row, Carla Ewing broke early for lunch. She loaded herself and her nearly empty brown bag into her family-sized Land Rover that still beamed the words "Simsbury College" on its back windshield, and headed for Parkview Cemetery.

And for the second day in a row, she had lunch with her son.

12:43 P.M.

Lunch hour had bombarded the mailroom with mail checkers. Fellow students elbowed each other aside, wormed their way toward issued slots, then stood smack in the way of chaos, giggling and hooting and dealing with the jostles as they paused to read eight-page discourses from friends at Dartmouth and Colgate and Williams. A freshman showed her inexperience by opening a care package right away, then shrieked with horror as an errant backpack batted the lidless cookie tin end over end, spewing chocolate chip congo bars all over the floor. She stood there helplessly, near tears, as dozens of feet made congo patties, each bearing the unmistakable grooves of the L.L. Bean–patterned boot sole.

His belly creamed with Seafood Newburg, his next class not till two, Mark was in no real hurry to retrieve the minimal contents he expected to find in his box. So he stood back from the rush, watching amusedly as cursing students grappled with the tricky combination locks.

When the area around his slot finally vacated, he moved in, turned the tumblers, and opened the tiny door that connected him to an outside world. He groped within the box and found a single envelope, which he extracted and opened absentmindedly, his focus more directed toward the hopeless cleaning efforts of the freshman whose baked goods now muddied the floor.

He pulled the contents from the envelope.

It was a Christmas card, the cover of which depicted a shiny gold tree, the words "Season's Greetings" scripted greenly beneath it. *A little late,* thought Mark, as he opened the card and read the message inside.

"*We were blindfolded.*"

4:05 P.M.

"Name?"

"Jason Bradford Lyle."

"Hometown?"

"Ridgewood, New Jersey."

"Could you state your relationship to the late Chad Francis Ewing?"

"He was my roommate," said Jason. "And a friend."

"Thank you," said Schwitters, as he turned to Shawn,

who nodded her approval. They both looked at the dean, who was observing from the corner of the conference room. No one looked at Mark, and he scored one for apathy.

Shawn cleared her throat. "Did you get along well with your roommate?"

"Pretty well."

"What did you guys talk about?"

"Lots of things."

"Did he confide in you?"

"Sometimes."

"Concerning what?"

Jason glanced nervously at the dean. "Um, he confided in me because he was hoping I wouldn't tell anyone. I don't think it would be appropriate for me to discuss it now."

"Me neither," mumbled Mark, scoring another one for sabotage and invoking harsh glares from Shawn and Schwitters in the process.

Shaking his head, Schwitters turned back to the witness. "Jason," he said, his tone overstuffed with sympathy. "We didn't mean it that way. I guess we should get to the point. We're looking for any evidence that Chad's affiliation with Sigma caused him to be unhappy, worried, or scared."

The freshman took a deep breath. "I think pledging was difficult for Chad. It . . . took up a lot of his time."

"What sort of effect did this have?"

"Well, his grades suffered."

"Did he ever mention that he was physically abused during a pledge activity?"

"No."

"Were there ever any *signs* of physical abuse? Bruises, cuts, that sort of thing?"

"No."

"Did he drink a lot?"

Jason hesitated before saying, "I don't know what you'd call 'a lot.' "

"How many nights a week?"

"Once or twice during the week, and I assume both weekend nights. I'm not really sure, because we never hung out like that."

"Did he drink on nights he had pledge activities?"

"He never told me when he had pledge activities. Those things are secret."

"Jason," said Simon, "did Chad ever mention suicide?"

Mark expected the freshman to gasp at the bluntness of this question, but instead he closed his eyes and said, "Not directly."

"What do you mean by that?" Shawn asked.

"Well," began Jason, "like I said, his grades were suffering."

"I gather," said Shawn. "But to the point where he would consider *suicide*?"

Jason shifted in his chair. "His parents put a lot of emphasis on grades."

"So do mine," argued Shawn, "but they place a far greater premium on my staying alive."

Jason half-shrugged, half-nodded, then looked down at his folded hands. "Well, you know . . ."

Shawn waited for elaboration, and when none came she leaned forward. "No, I don't think I *do* know."

"Shawn," the dean cautioned in a low voice.

She waved him off. "Jason, do you think Chad was the kind of guy who'd drink himself stupid, strip himself naked, write words on himself, then dive off a balcony just because his grades—"

"Shawn!"

Jason's head snapped back, dragging his slight frame into a cowering, bullied posture, and Mark felt a sudden, strangely paternal urge to protect him. He was just about to jump to Jason's defense when the freshman said meekly, "His girlfriend dumped him, too."

Shawn bit her lip and studied the witness. "When?"

Seeming to gather strength, Jason replied, "About a week before the accident, maybe two—"

"Accident or suicide? Make up your mind—"

"Okay, Shawn, that's enough," said the dean. He turned to Schwitters, motioning for the junior to assume command of the inquisition.

Schwitters nodded dutifully. "Jason," he said smugly, "would you say Chad was depressed?"

Jason nodded quickly, almost gratefully. "Yes."

"On what would you base that conclusion?"

"He was sleeping late, missing classes. He was getting zits, too."

"Sounds like a typical freshman to me," said Mark.

"Shut up, Mark," said Shawn.

"Go on," said Schwitters.

Jason glanced at Mark, then refocused on Schwitters. "He never smiled anymore, which was odd, because he'd always been such a happy guy."

"Could this have been a reaction to hazing?"

"Oh, I don't think so," said Jason. "I think it was more a reaction to his grades, or getting dumped."

Schwitters nodded slowly, jotted a few notes, then looked to Shawn, who made a hopeless sort of face and dropped her pen. Mark digested the exchange and gave a silent cheer, for it was clear the D-Squad's two active members were done with this witness, which meant they were one witness closer to dropping the case.

The dean thanked Jason for his time and led him out. Returning, he closed the door and sat next to Schwitters.

"Well," he said, almost cheerfully, "that's that."

Schwitters nodded, while Shawn stared sourly at the table.

"What's wrong, Miss Jakes?"

She shook her head and said nothing.

"Okay," said the dean, "as long as everyone's so happy, I have some news that will enhance the mood." He paused, peered into his mug and, finding it empty, pushed it away from him. "I've set up two depositions for tomorrow. One o'clock with the coroner, Dick Finnerty. Three o'clock with the hospital administrator, Meredith Lacroix."

Great, Mark thought, with a roll of his eyes.

"Great!" bubbled Schwitters.

"Oh, that's just great!" Shawn said, her irritation evident.

The dean made a show of looking surprised. "Why the sarcasm?"

She returned his look with one of disbelief. "Could you have given us any *less* advance notice?"

The dean shrugged. "Neither confirmed until today."

"So what? That doesn't mean we have to go see them *tomorrow.* What's the big rush?"

"Well, for one," replied the dean, "spring break's coming."

Shawn frowned. "And?"

"We've got to get this whole thing resolved by then."

"Why? Is Chad Ewing going somewhere for spring break?"

The dean's eyes narrowed. "Watch yourself, young lady."

"I can't. I'm too busy watching *you* apply a cost-efficiency equation to the death of a student."

The dean responded with a blameless shrug. "This is the Board's decision, not mine. They don't want this investigation running into April."

"Why not? Too close to Prospective Student Weekend, or is that when they start polling for the *U.S.News and World Report* survey?"

"Don't flatter yourself, Shawn." The dean smiled. "I think you're exaggerating the importance of this investigation."

"Gee, I don't know," mused Shawn. "I think death is a pretty important issue. Don't you, Simon?"

Schwitters looked at Shawn, then at the dean, then at the table.

"I fail to see the problem here," the dean said. "You have tonight to prepare. And what's to prepare, other than a few basic questions?"

"I have two midterms tomorrow," said Shawn, "and a take-home due Thursday."

The dean held up his hands. "No one said life was easy. These people are taking time out of their busy days to talk with you, and I wouldn't feel right postponing just because you've got some homework to do." He nodded knowingly at Shawn. "Sounds to me as if you've spread yourself a little thin with all your extracurricular activities."

Shawn poked the table with her finger. "My service on

the D-Squad is for the good of the college. I consider it to be more than just a résumé builder."

"And we all appreciate your dedication, but let's not forget why you're really here."

"And why's that?"

"To get an education and prepare for the real world."

Shawn took a breath as if to respond, then stopped herself.

The dean grinned smugly and pocketed his pen. "Oh, by the way, Shawn," he said, "how's that anonymous source coming along?"

Shawn shifted in her chair. "Okay."

"When can we expect to meet her."

"Soon."

"Good. Let us know when she's ready for a formal deposition." The dean gathered his papers together. "All right then. I'll leave it up to you three to conduct the depositions tomorrow. I do, however, expect that you'll represent the school well. And remember, these people are doing us a favor."

Schwitters nodded dutifully, on behalf of Shawn, who appeared ready to throttle someone, and Mark, who was guessing that he'd be the inevitable victim of her wrath.

"Let's meet Thursday," the dean said as he squirmed into his tweed. "Three o'clock."

5:02 P.M.

The Freshman knew by now that his second message had been read, for he'd mailed it three days ago. He tried to imagine how it had been received, and whether the recipient had recognized the connection with the first letter.

Then, without wanting to, he tried to imagine what it

had been like, for that one awful moment, to be falling through space, just waiting to land with all the destructive force that gravity could muster.

He closed his eyes, dug his nails into the flesh of his arm, and willed himself not to scream.

5:14 P.M.

Despite his complete baldness, Tom Davis was by far the youngest Board member, and regarded by the others as the most levelheaded, exhibiting unique skill at dealing with politically sensitive issues. It was Davis who'd overseen the near-riotous discussions between the faculty, administration, and Board when the student body had demanded that Gay and Lesbian Studies be offered as a major, and it was Davis who'd helped unruffle feathers when Theodore Lipshit complained that his name wasn't emblazoned prominently enough on the twelve-million-dollar athletic complex he'd donated. It was also Davis whom Davenport had yet to speak to regarding the current crisis, so he picked up his phone, pressed a preset speed-dial button, and waited.

"Hello, Hank," said Davis, after four rings.

"How . . . ?"

"Caller ID, friend. Get with the times."

Davenport shook his head and grunted.

"What's on your mind?"

"This year's Simsbury calendar," said Davenport. "Did you get yours in the mail yet?"

"Just got it Saturday, matter of fact."

"Any idea why there's a picture of Sigma House on the cover?"

"Probably because it went to production before Sigma

House dropped one of its own from a balcony," answered Davis. "Besides, other than our great big pines, that mansion's the prettiest thing on campus. My wife calls it the Eighth Wonder."

"But it's on the *cover*."

"Call it a last hurrah."

Davenport nodded into the phone. "So you think Sigma should be shut down."

"Whoa! You're putting words in my mouth."

"Now's your chance to put some words in mine. What's your feeling about all this?"

There was a long silence from the other end. "Well," Davis said finally, "it's our nation's classic dilemma, a microcosm of the American legal system. We've got justice on one side, money on the other. Without financial contributions from Sigma alums, we might as well be a state school. Then again, if we're going to let intimidation tactics define right and wrong, we might as well be a state school, too."

Davenport frowned, then shook his head. "What are you saying, Tom?"

Pause. "I'm saying I think I'll send my kids to University of Maine."

5:29 P.M.

Templeton poured himself a cup of decaf, for on this day, with Judith returning from a two-day foray to Boston and probably right now envisioning a night of lovemaking with her husband, he'd welcome drowsiness. If he could manage to pass out right after supper, he was pretty sure he could postpone intercourse at least one more night.

He had to admit, though, he *was* in a somewhat upbeat mood, having successfully arranged the D-Squad interrogations of Dick Finnerty and Meredith Lacroix that were scheduled for the following day. Neither witness had been particularly easy to schedule. During three separate, one-way phone conversations, each running at least twenty minutes, Finnerty had blustered about rights to privacy of decent U.S. citizens, especially dead ones. And Lacroix, after needing to be reminded who Chad Ewing was, had expressed all sorts of golly-gosh over possibly having to miss her weekly Southern Maine Teddy Bear Collectors Club dinner. In the end, however, after repeated assurances from Templeton, both had agreed to give Wednesday-afternoon depositions, and the memory of their initial hesitations now served to bring a smile to Templeton's face, for each witness had displayed the exact sort of cooperative traits he and T-Bone had identified over a week ago. Finnerty and Lacroix's testimony, or lack thereof, would help Sigma.

This time tomorrow, the investigation would be over.

Templeton washed away his smile with a gulp of coffee, picked up the phone, and began to dial.

11:04 P.M.

Mark was in that half-sleep state where reality and illusion mix behind closed eyes to make for surreal theater, when the phone's simple shrill snapped him fully awake. He blinked good-bye to the random absurdity of the night's first dream, gently removed Casey from his chest, and stretched for the receiver.

"Hello?"

"Hey. It's Shawn."

"Oh. Hey."

"Sleeping?"

"Not really. You coming over?"

"No, I don't think so," she said, then sighed. "I just want to apologize for being such a bitch today."

"Don't worry about it."

"This whole investigation just has me so frustrated."

"I know the way you are."

"You're used to it, huh?" she said, and Mark could almost picture her smile.

"Pretty much," said Mark with a yawn, while scratching his stomach. "Can I give you some advice, though?"

"Am I going to like it?"

"I don't know."

Pause. "Okay. Enlighten me."

"Stop getting so riled about this. There are a million people dying of AIDS, and there's a new war every day. The groundfish on Georges Bank are disappearing as we speak, and you've got an honors project to work on. It doesn't make sense to expend all your emotional energy on *one* discipline issue, even if you believe somebody bears partial responsibility for Chad's death, which I *don't* think is the case."

There was a long silence, followed by the soft, sweet sound of Shawn saying good night.

Mark kissed the broken connection, hung up the phone, and rolled over. Minutes later, he returned to the night's first dream.

11:39 P.M.

After an emotionally charged Triumvirate, the seniors reconvened in the Brotherhood Room. There was a minute or two of spirited chatter, and deep-voiced concurrence that Chad Ewing was dead and buried and that the pledge class was now nearing rock solidity and solidarity.

"We own those pledges," said Gamma. "We own their hearts and souls."

"Let's not get cocky," warned Beta. "We should still keep a low profile. No parties. No more fights. If for no other reason than respect for Chad's memory."

"What respect?"

Too tired to argue with Gamma, Beta let the comment slide. "Yeah. So anyway, the D-Squad met with Jason Lyle today. It sounds like he didn't say much."

"Very wise."

"What'd they ask him?"

"Pretty predictable stuff. You know, signs of hazing, drinking habits, mood swings, and so on."

"Who are they harassing next?"

"The coroner, apparently, and some woman over at St. E's."

"Are you serious?" shouted Omega.

"Sure, I'm serious. What'd you expect?"

"What do they think this is, *Murder, She Wrote*?"

"Who gives a shit!" dismissed Gamma. "These issues have been dealt with. And if they haven't yet, they will be."

"How do you know?" Theta asked.

"You think the alumni are gonna leave us hanging?" Gamma replied.

The meeting ran another ten minutes. All concerns were soothed, all doubts laid to rest. When it was over, ten of the twelve seniors retired to the barroom, where they met up with the rest of the brotherhood.

They would keep a low profile, low in the basement, that is. It was Tuesday night and there was beer on tap.

CHAPTER TWENTY-NINE

The 200th Year
Wednesday, March 4

1:01 P.M.

Canada had unleashed its fierce hound on Cumberland County, and it tore across the semirural land, sinking its teeth into all who dared venture outside. News of the minus 44° wind chill had even penetrated the isolated, self-contained ecosystem of Simsbury College—partly because it was the weather, and how could it not, but also because a portable ice-fishing hut had blown off April Pond and collided with Professor Jerace's Volvo, breaking his grading arm and providing some moderately intriguing fodder for Madame Rumor. Simon Schwitters had apparently heard the most foreboding of the Madame's accounts, for he now kept one eye on the lookout for flying houses as he drove his "custom turbo Saab" toward the Cumberland County Coroner's Office. Shawn, from the passenger seat, told him to relax, this wasn't the Land of Oz. But if they *should* find themselves at the end of a yellow brick road, piped Mark from the back, Schwitters should be sure to ask the man in charge for balls.

Of course, five minutes later Mark was the one whimpering as he led a desperate foot race across the brutally cold stretch of lot separating the parked Saab from the coroner's office. Ignoring Schwitters's trailing remarks regarding who *really* needed new cajones, Mark scampered up the steps to the office and pounded on the door for mercy.

Thankfully, they were immediately rescued by a little fuzzy woman wearing thick bifocals, too much perfume, and a white sweater covered with black dog hair. Her name was Dorothy, she said while ushering the three frozen D-Squad members into the waiting area, where she invited them to sit and warm their fingers and toes. There were only two chairs, however, so both Schwitters and Mark opted to stand, neither wanting to appear weaker than the other. Shawn settled in one chair and began to thumb through an issue of *Field and Stream*.

Even by Georgeville's humble standards, the office was tiny. The reception area was the size of Mark's freshman dorm room, and of the three doors visible, one said "Bathroom." Mark was busy hazarding guesses as to what mysteries lay behind the two unmarked doors when one suddenly opened, and out popped an old man.

"Dick Finnerty," the man said without warmth. He gave each of the three students perfunctory handshakes. "Come with me."

He led them into his office and motioned to the metal folding chairs facing his paper-strewn desk, then lowered his white-coated frame into a primitive-looking chair on the other side. He leaned back, crossed his arms, and eyed the D-Squadders until Mark felt unnerved. A quick sideways glance told him the other two felt the same.

Shawn alternated her nervous glance between Finnerty and the many framed degrees and certificates hanging on the wall behind his head. Schwitters looked this way and that, and bounced his knee.

"Did you say your name was Mark Jessy?" Finnerty suddenly asked.

Mark hesitated, then said, "Yes."

"The lacrosse player?"

"That's right."

Finnerty shot forward with a smile and slapped his desk. "Well how about that! My grandson's a big fan of yours."

"He is?"

"Sure! He plays for Brunswick High. *Loves* to watch the college games."

"Really?"

"Ayup. He's a midfielder, just like you."

"Cool."

Finnerty rummaged through the papers on his desk, found a scrap, attached it to the clip of a pen and handed it to Mark. "Could you sign this for me?"

Mark nonchalantly accepted the paper and pen as though he signed autographs all the time. "Sure."

"Make it out to Jamie."

"Jamie. Okay."

As he signed, he sensed Schwitters and Shawn shifting restlessly, their ridiculous quest for justice put on hold by Mark's status as an apparent local celebrity. He'd catch hell for this later, but would love every second of it.

He handed the signature to Finnerty, who pocketed it and thanked him.

"You're welcome. Come watch us sometime. I'll leave two tickets at the gate."

"Why, thank you," said Finnerty. He nodded appreciatively a few times, then opened a desk drawer, pulled out a manila folder, and held it up in the air. "Chad Ewing?"

Shawn and Schwitters nodded eagerly.

Finnerty extended the file, then retracted it. "Before we begin, I feel compelled to make a comment." He crossed his arms again. "When I see students from one of this country's great bastions of intellect with nothing better to do with their time but dress up as district attorneys and *snoop* into matters best handled by God and professionals, I fear for this nation's future." He looked at his desk a moment, then up again. "That you sit before a county coroner, ready to dig up a fellow student's grave, rather than humbly plant a flower and learn the lessons taught by his passing, is an unqualified abomination."

He waited for a response, but when met by silence, continued. "Very well. I've said my piece." He opened the folder and removed a single piece of paper, which he placed in Schwitters's cautious hand.

Schwitters thanked him effusively, studied the paper a moment or two, then looked up. "Uh sir," he said timidly, "is this the entire file?"

"Of course not. It's the death certificate."

"Can we see the rest of it?"

"Of course not. That would be unholy." Finnerty pointed at the certificate. "All that matters is what you've got right there in your hand, son. The Lord decided it was Chad Ewing's time, and we can only hope the angels are teaching him their songs."

Schwitters and Shawn exchanged looks. Mark sank lower in his chair and leaned away from his brethren.

"Okay," Shawn said hesitantly. "Can we ask you a few questions, then?"

Finnerty eyed the two active D-Squad members warily. "What sort of questions?"

"The snooping kind," she replied, sounding more like her confident self. "We're looking for evidence that this death wasn't accidental."

"Well," said Finnerty haughtily, "you're not going to find any."

Bolstered by Shawn's boldness, Schwitters leaned forward. "During your examination, did you uncover any unusual pathological findings."

"Findings?"

"You know, abnormal levels of alcohol in the blood, signs of drug use?"

Finnerty nodded slowly and critically. "I see," he said coolly. "I can tell you right now, he was drunk at the time of death."

"How drunk?" asked Shawn.

"Quite."

"Point three?" asked Schwitters.

Finnerty paused, eyes roving suspiciously. "In that neighborhood," he finally confirmed.

"And that was at the time of death?"

Finnerty nodded.

Schwitters turned to Shawn and said, "About twelve hours after he stopped drinking!" He turned back to Finnerty. "Sir, can you estimate what his blood content would've been at roughly midnight the night before?"

Finnerty shifted in his chair. "It would be impossible to

pinpoint. Each individual processes alcohol at a different rate."

"Could you make an educated guess?"

"It's really not my place to speculate on matters such as this."

"You're the county coroner," Shawn said, her tone laced with a touch of bite. "If not yours, then whose?"

"I'm aware of my position," Finnerty retorted, "but I'm also aware that I'm first a man, and as a man I warn you to mind your p's and q's, young lady, before you earn an escort to the door."

Shawn set her jaw and nodded.

"Mr. Finnerty," said Schwitters. "Is it safe to assume that Chad Ewing was *considerably drunker* at midnight?"

Finnerty slowly turned his attention from Shawn to Schwitters. "Yes. Of course."

"Point three-five, maybe?"

"Isn't that, like, legally *dead*?" asked Shawn.

Finnerty shook his head and said, "Generally, death will occur at point four-oh." Then, folding his hands, he said, "Folks, if you're looking for the cause of death, I can tell you right now it was massive head trauma, teamed with complications due to a broken neck."

"From the fall?"

"Yes. It's right there on the death certificate."

Schwitters eyed the certificate again, then angled it toward Shawn. "Maybe we should take a closer look at this."

Shawn shrugged.

"You're welcome to take a copy of it," said Finnerty. "But I don't know what you plan on proving with it." He shook his head, then nodded righteously. "Chad Ewing should be resting in peace."

"He will," said Shawn. "When we're done asking questions."

The hint of an incredulous smile tweaked the coroner's face. "That's a very arrogant thing to say in the presence of your Maker."

Shawn made a face. "My *Maker*?"

Finnerty nodded, then turned and motioned reverently toward the upper part of the wall, where between and above the credentials hung something that perhaps Shawn hadn't spied during her earlier inspection, or, more likely, had chosen to ignore: a deep bronze mold of Jesus, pinned to a crucifix.

Eyes narrowing, Shawn cocked her head, folded her hands, and leaned into a caustic pose that Mark understood from experience. "My *makers* live in Aspen," she said, brandishing her agnosticism. For a spell she locked eyes with Finnerty, as if to drive her beliefs home. Then, suddenly finding the cause hopeless, she pushed back her chair, which crumpled as she rose to her feet. "Let's go."

Mark and Schwitters stood obediently and followed Shawn toward the office door, but ducked away simultaneously as she turned, grabbed the death certificate from Schwitters, and waved it at Finnerty. "Can we take a copy of this, or what?"

Finnerty regarded her a moment, then shifted his eyes perceptibly and called, "Betsy?"

An instant later, a girl appeared in the doorway. "Yes?"

"This is my intern, Betsy Kimball," said Finnerty. "Betsy, these folks are here visiting from Simsbury College. They were . . . *friends* of Chad Ewing. Could you make a copy of his certificate and then show them out? I've got to get back downstairs."

Betsy smiled pleasantly. "Sure. Follow me."

Finnerty shook hands with Mark and Schwitters— Shawn had already chased Betsy out to the reception area—and wished Mark luck in the upcoming season. Mark and Schwitters joined Shawn at the copier just as Betsy was asking how many copies they'd need.

"Just one will be fine," said Shawn.

Betsy ran the death certificate through the machine, then handed the copy to Shawn. "Here you are. I'm sorry about your friend."

"Thanks," Shawn said as she folded the copy and secured it in her parka. "But actually, we're affiliated with the Simsbury Disciplinary Squad. We're investigating Chad's death."

"Really? We have one of those at Bowdoin. The Judiciary Board. Everyone calls it the J-Board."

"Interesting."

"Yeah. Well, if there's anything I can help you with, don't hesitate to call. What did you say your name was again?"

"Shawn Jakes. This is Mark Jessy and Simon Schwitters."

Betsy smiled at Mark and Schwitters, then closed the copier lid. "Let me show you out." She led them to the door. "Be careful. It's cold out there."

Mark smiled and winked at her. "Don't we know it."

4:31 P.M.

Hungry for oatmeal cookies, thirsty for milk, Meredith Lacroix opened the door to the physician's lounge, but stopped in her tracks and nearly squealed with excitement at the sight of Dr. Charles Marston and Nurse Janine Hammond, both still capped and scrubbed, standing by the vending machine.

"Well," she said, superstitiously fingering her St. Christopher's medal, "do you have good news for me?"

"I do." Marston beamed. "It's a girl."

Meredith gasped. "Oh, bless her heart! What's the name?"

Janine recycled her empty Diet Coke bottle. "Darcy Brooke."

"Darcy Brooke Chamberlain," sang Meredith. "What a lovely name!"

"She's a beautiful baby."

"I'll bet! Sarah's an utter doll."

"Go on up," Marston suggested. "Everyone's there. Lenny's passing champagne around the waiting room."

"I'll bring my cookies with me! Oh, happy day!" She hurried to the vending machine, fed it some coins, and was rewarded with a three-pack of her favorite snack. She turned to leave and was almost to the door when she remembered. "Oh, by the way, Charlie," she said. "Those Simsbury students just left."

Marston frowned. "What students?"

"Oh dear," said Meredith, "I don't remember their names. Didn't I tell you that they were coming?"

"No."

"Oh dear. Well, the dean of Simsbury called yesterday. He wanted to know if he could send some students over to discuss the death of that boy."

"Chad Ewing?"

"That's right. They're doing some sort of investigation into his death. Isn't that ambitious?"

Marston cocked his head and squinted. "What sort of investigation?"

"They wanted to know if we noticed anything suspicious about the death."

"What did you tell them?"

"I told them that there was nothing unusual that I knew of. Of course, I told them that you were really the one to speak to, and that you couldn't right now because Sarah Chamberlain—"

"Are they still here?"

"No. They left about fifteen minutes ago."

While Janine read the inside of her bottle cap and wandered toward the door, Marston put down his can and walked slowly toward Meredith. "Did they leave a number where they could be reached?"

"No," said Meredith. "Anyway, they didn't have any more questions. Not after I read them the report."

Marston frowned. "What report?"

"The one in Chad's file."

"I never wrote any report," Marston said. "The attending EMT hasn't called me back yet."

"But you signed it."

"I did *what*?" Marston put a hand to his forehead, then shook his head. "Meredith, what did this *report* say?"

"Well," said Meredith, suddenly apprehensive. "It mentioned a skull fracture and a broken neck . . . compound fracture of the clavicle . . . broken rib . . . broken hand—"

"Did it mention," said Marston slowly, "anything about the condition of the patient's skin?"

"I . . . no."

Marston stared at this response a moment, his expression shocked to the point of blankness. Then, shaking life back into his face, he said, "Well, I'm telling you, I sure as hell never wrote a report. Janine was in charge of the graph results and the general paperwork, and then she was going to forward it along . . ." He turned suddenly. "Janine, did you—"

He stopped.

Janine Hammond was gone.

CHAPTER THIRTY

The 200th Year
Wednesday, March 4

6:01 P.M.

The black BMW turned into a charcoal van at the Kennebunk rest stop off the Maine Turnpike, then resumed racing northward past pickup trucks with antlers fastened to the grills and fishing-gear endorsements bumper-stickered to tailgates. The driver, though, remained unchanged, his expressionless face half-hidden by the bent bill of a New York Yankees cap, his left arm draped over the steering wheel and his right hand loosely gripping the knife he hoped he wouldn't need.

6:58 P.M.

Mark's hip flexor had conveniently waited until the last of the optional, post-practice shooting drills to desert the leg beneath it, nullifying a solid week and a half of rehabilitative progress and putting the perfect cap on a perfectly shitty day. After swearing a blue streak and throwing his stick halfway across the Cage, he'd limped to the trainer's room. He now lay on his usual table, enduring his second twenty-minute go-round with the ice pack and blaming his recurring physical flare-up on his distracting D-Squad duties. The student trio's completely useless meeting with St. E's administrator, Meredith Lacroix, had run forty-five minutes longer than it should have—which meant he'd been unable to properly heat his hip before practice. And now look at him!

He sighed with disgust and settled deeper into the lacrosse glove supporting his head. Alone, he had only himself to chat with, and he'd exhausted that activity midway through the first ice bag. His entertainment now consisted of what he could see and hear, a ludicrous prospect given the setting.

Had this been his first-ever stint in this particular location, he might've found a minute or two of mild amusement in two of the walls. Behind him, touching the crown of his scalp, a grated circulation vent provided an auditory window on the world of the neighboring men's locker room. And positioned directly across from him, at a height visible to the listless gaze of an injured athlete, was one of the Cage's countless team photos—this one depicting the Simsbury College baseball team, circa twenty years earlier—hung between a musculoskeletal diagram and a schedule of every overlapping winter and spring athletic contest.

However, he'd been here often enough to know that the locker room vent rarely provided anything more than the misty hiss of shower spray alternating its jet between slick tiles and soapy young men insulting the hang of one anothers' dicks. And he'd long since tired of skimming the names and hokey aliases (Richard "Goose" Gosselin, Timothy "Captain" Hook) of the twenty bad-haircutted members of the first and only Simsbury baseball team to ever advance to the Division III Final Four.

So there really wasn't anything for him to do here but take a nap.

He closed his eyes, listened to the shower clamor fade over time, and wondered offhandedly what sort of observations his *own* team photo would inspire twenty years from now.

A tap on his shoulder opened his eyes. What he saw gave him a start.

"Jesus!" he exclaimed, as the close-range view of Simon Schwitters in his swimming goggles sharpened its focus.

"Didn't mean to scare you, man," Schwitters said with a nose-pinched, ducky laugh, his arms swinging through the motions of a bare-chested, back-and-forth thrash.

"For crying out loud," said Mark. "Why can't you be like everyone else and wait until you're in the pool before you put those stupid things on?"

"The meet's over. I took first in the fifty free."

"Then why don't you take them off? You look like a freak."

"Ha! I'm not the one lying here in my jockstrap."

"Good point. I'd much rather be standing here in a Speedo, making comments about another man's crotch."

Schwitters stopped his arm-flapping long enough to make an eyeless face, then continued his dance.

"What do you want, Simon?"

"I just wanted to remind you we're meeting tonight at nine, in my room. Not that we need you, of course. Shawn and I have better sex when you're not around."

Mark lifted his head and looked at him. "That was *almost* funny."

Schwitters shrugged and continued swinging. "So . . . are you coming?"

Mark shook his head, lowered it back to the lacrosse glove, and closed his eyes again. "We spent all *day* on this thing."

"I know. And now we have to figure out a strategy after today's setback."

Mark yawned. "And exactly what about today was a *setback,* other than that we wasted an entire afternoon investigating a nonexistent crime?"

"We didn't find the evidence we need."

"What's this 'we' shit? And my point exactly—there *is* no evidence, which means we should fuck tonight's meeting and just drop the case."

"You wish."

Mark opened one eye and pointed it at the swimmer. "Don't tell me Shawn's got you believing in fairy tales."

Schwitters halted his waving and began to run in place. "Like any good lawyer, I'm not concerned with what *I* believe. I'm only concerned with what I can *prove.*"

Mark propped himself up on his elbows and made a face. "When exactly did you pass the bar, Simon?"

"You know what I mean."

"No," said Mark. "I don't think I do, but it *sounds* like you're saying this whole thing's a game."

"It *is* a game," said Schwitters, intensifying his jog. "A game I intend to win."

Mark stared at him a moment. For an instant, he'd flashed on a misty image of Cherry Plain, of thwarted justice. "You know, when you say things like that, it makes me want to beat the shit out of you."

Schwitters laughed lightly as he allowed his stationary trot to dwindle. Then, stepping side to side, he leaned forward. "*Beat* the shit out of me, Mark," he said with a smile. "And you'll find out once again just how cruel a game law can be."

He patted Mark on the shoulder, turned, and slapped on bare feet across the damp tiles until they met with clay. And then he was gone.

But his words remained, and Mark blindly watched the space where he'd last seen their Speedoed source. He worked his neck beads until he could barely keep from tearing them off. Then, filled with sudden fury, he lurched from the table and whipped the ice pack across the trainer's room, where it caught the innocent lip of a tin trash bucket and smashed it against a crisscrossed pair of crutches. The barrel teetered a moment on its circular foundation, then toppled to the tiles, reverberating a two-bounce clang that echoed to silence.

Then murmured Mark's name.

He froze.

". . . Jessy."

There it was again.

For a moment, he stood motionless, the only sound and movement coming from the pound of his pulse and the cold skim that dripped from his hip to the floor. Then, as Schwitters's final words crawled completely inside the felled trash bucket, new ones slithered into the room.

From the grated circulation vent that audibly windowed the men's locker room:

"How do you know . . ."

"Easy . . . as good as over . . . on *our* team. When we need . . . he'll make sure we don't . . . trouble."

Dominic, thought Mark, recognizing the tone. His heartbeat sharpening, he edged closer to the vent.

". . . thought he was kicked out . . ."

"Yeah, but he thinks it was . . . *college's* decision. Why do you . . . still comes over?"

"I never see him . . ."

"That's because you spend all your time . . . !"

Three shades of laughter.

"Didn't he rape . . . barroom?" said a new voice. A sophomore, Mark guessed. Someone who clearly hadn't been around for the Angela McSheffrey disaster.

"Ha! He didn't . . . anything he wasn't set up to do!"

"Don't you think he's figured . . . ?"

"No way. There . . . some things Mark Jessy doesn't . . . the *balls* to question."

A pause.

"C'mon. I'm fucking starving, and I want . . . before I gotta . . . more fucking rhymes . . ."

Lockers slammed. Voices receded, then picked up a new pitch as they entered the cavernous Cage and moved toward the trainer's room. Mark tiptoed quickly across the tiles, swiped off the lights, and ducked behind a whirlpool.

The voices approached rapidly, then careened past the entrance to the trainer's room, and faded out.

Dominic, Mark confirmed.

He stayed in his hiding spot until he thought he might scream, then wandered numbly to the showers, where he let the water beat on what he'd heard.

7:21 P.M.

With a total of six hours sleep in the past two nights fueling his weary walk, Fairchild nearly bumped into a wall as he veered off the downstairs hallway and into the Sigma dining room. He avoided the milk dispenser, paralleled the salad bar, and nodded listlessly to four juniors playing football with a baked potato as they discussed whom they were going to fuck this weekend. He entered the kitchen, pulled a fresh plate from the highest shelf, and served himself the dinner he'd almost skipped.

He wasn't really hungry. However, having missed lunch due to the whispering nausea he'd dragged from his first bout with insomnia, he was now roughly twenty-eight hundred calories shy of the mass-building per diem recommended by all three of the strength and conditioning coaches he and his agent had consulted. So he piled the plate high with steak, spuds, and greens, lifting and eyeballing every few scoops to gauge its plenitude.

Deeming the meal substantial, he backtracked to the dining room, found a seat far away from the game of potato football, and prepared to eat.

But never did.

For the nausea was now more than whispering.

8:16 P.M.

The muted television set cast a bluish hue on the otherwise darkened living room, dimly lighting the long, college-issued sofa, in the middle of which sat a young man who hadn't needed a quip from Simon Schwitters to understand how cruel a game the law could be. His eyes, as if paralyzed by the shock of early morning awakening, were fixed somewhere beyond a bare beige wall. His ears rang with words overheard. His skin tingled with uncertainty.

His hand held a letter.

Mark's past, always simmering beneath an unreliable lid, had begun to boil.

He didn't *want* to believe it, of course. He didn't want to believe what he'd overheard in the trainer's room—that as Dominic had bragged, Mark Jessy hadn't done anything to Angela McSheffrey that he hadn't been set up to do. He didn't want to believe that he lacked the balls to ask questions, that the past two years had been a lie, that maybe he'd taken a cowardly fall, that the Sigmas (his *best friends*, his *brothers*, his *family*) sometimes told mocking locker room stories about him.

He didn't want to believe that he'd been had, that he was *being* had, and that his only worth to the Sigmas was as a dull-witted puppet who could, if properly manipulated, botch the Chad Ewing investigation on their behalf.

He didn't want to believe the unbelievable.

He closed his eyes slowly, allowing his mind to sprint back to the Sigma barroom, two years ago. He was drunk as a skunk, watching the brotherly world dance confusingly about him. Manly limbs proving their manly strength. Plastic cups passed from hand to hand, finally to his own, the choreographed steps of "Seniors Serve the Sophomores" Night, that new and delicious jig. Boisterous shouts of sex and violence making the drink taste, inexplicably, a little better. Alien Phi Omega intruders arriving on the scene, the dance heating up. Fists pumping and smacking and spilling blood. Winners and losers, all of them boozers.

Three strange girls, doing a strange routine. Words

meaning nothing to his intoxicated ears, then telling him
to come with her. Fingers guiding him on a waltz toward
infamy, blue eyes beneath red bangs telling him he was
stepping just fine, and to keep coming, boy. A new dance
floor, secluded by books and bolts, built for two.

The dance turning clumsy.

The dance turning ugly.

And that was all he could remember about the drunken
night on which he was supposed to have gotten way too
aggressive with a local girl named Angela McSheffrey.
All that remained were fragmented scenes and short,
catchy snippets of dialogue, as if "Seniors Serve the
Sophomores" Night had been a movie he'd seen while
half asleep, long ago. Still, although he remembered next
to nothing of that night, he could pluck three suspicious
items from his memory, items worth finally questioning,
two years and a day after the fact.

The first was the party theme itself. He'd been just too
damn content to question this at the time, but a party at
Sigma—the fraternity where seniors were worshipped
like religious idols, and sophomores were viewed as little
more than worker bees—that centered around seniors
mixing and serving drinks for sophomores (something
Mark hadn't heard of in the two years since) went against
everything hierarchical that made Sigma so great . . . unless, of course, the seniors had wanted to ensure that he
got *more* than his manageable fill of margarita mix, in
which case the party theme made perfect sense.

The second concerned the brutal beating that had been
handed the Phi Omega party crashers. Phi Omegas were
generally welcome at Sigma parties. But on the night in
question, they'd been flogged into retreat. Even for the

quick-to-punch Sigmas, the unprovoked attack had seemed out of character . . . unless, of course, the seniors had wanted to ensure that the barroom contained *only* Sigmas, perhaps because something big was about to happen, an event whose success would hinge on keeping it "all in the family."

Which brought up the third question: On a night when the seniors had made it clear that outsiders wouldn't be welcome, how come Angela and her two slutty buddies had been allowed free entrance? Of course, they were women, and dressed for sex, which made them something along the lines of walking party favors. Still, their arrival had been sudden, peculiar, and inconsistent with the all-male theme of the party . . . unless, of course, the *real* theme of the party centered around something much more sinister.

Shifting his eyes from the wall to the space above his lap, Mark once again read the letter in his hand.

Dear Mark,

Angela McSheffrey, a resident of Georgeville, has filed a formal complaint with the school, charging that on Saturday night, March 3, you sexually assaulted and attempted to rape her during a party at the Sigma Delta Phi fraternity house.

Ms. McSheffrey has indicated that she would like this matter handled by the college . . .

He stopped reading and, after two years of blindly accepting the content of this letter, began to truly dissect what he'd just read. A disadvantaged local girl had been

nearly raped by a snotty college boy, yet had opted not to
press charges with the police; instead, she had decided
that Simsbury College could better officiate the judicial
proceedings. This made no sense at all. The local newspapers were constantly filled with anti-Simsbury letters
to the editor: A group of Simsbury students had ditched
on a bar tab at Chewnocker's . . . Simsbury students, rich
as they were, shouldn't be entitled to discounted haircuts
in town, and feeless bank transactions . . . A local boy's
teeth had been knocked out by a Simsbury student (take
a bow, A. J. Dominic).

The fact was, townies nurtured a tangible animosity
toward their Simsbury neighbors; a local girl should
have *orgasmed* over the prospect of sending a college
prick to jail. But no, Angela had fled in terror from
Sigma, endured two nights of supposed rape nightmares,
then graciously agreed to have the Simsbury D-Squad
handle her case. It was almost as if she'd known she
didn't have a case that would hold up in a court of law,
but *did* have a case that would hold up in a politically
correct, bleeding-heart *college* courtroom—a courtroom
ruled not so much that day by the D-Squad, but by liberal arts sensitivity and a fat feminist named Marily
Greenledger. In a real court of law, Angela would have
had to answer some questions. In the D-Squad's court of
law, she merely had to look and act like a victim.

Oh, you stupid fool, Mark.

And what about the hearing? He'd sat so paralyzed by
what he'd done, so intent on clutching the little blue eagle
and waving the white flag in defense of his brotherly
family—the only real family he felt he'd had since the

loss of his parents—that he'd completely ignored his instincts.

He'd trust them now.

He leaned back on the sofa and thought again about Angela's testimony. There was something . . . yes, something about it that he now just couldn't accept.

"Me and my two friends, Tanya and Becky, went to the Hayloft for a few drinks, then decided to head on over here to see if maybe we could hang out at one of the frats. We'd done that before, although this was our first time at Sigma House . . .

"I took him into the downstairs library . . ."

And suddenly, there it was. Connected sentences that, at the time, had seemed like judicial window-dressing, minor details surrounding a terrible crime. Connected sentences that, linked to logic, hinted that Angela wasn't quite the innocent victim she'd claimed to be.

Angela had never been to Sigma House before. Yet, through some sort of cosmic intuition, she'd known there were *two* libraries, an upstairs one (which was always sealed off, and hidden from view) and a downstairs one. Somehow, she'd known to call the downstairs library by its proper name.

Oh, you stupid fool, Mark.

Slowly, very slowly, he returned his pounding stare to that point beyond the bare beige wall.

And began to believe the unbelievable.

CHAPTER THIRTY-ONE

The 200th Year
Wednesday, March 4

9:10 P.M.

Dr. Marston finished briefing Simsbury professor Daniel C. Jerace on what the next eighteen to twenty-four months would be like with a steel rod supporting his smashed left arm, then fetched him a bowl of raspberry sherbet to take with his painkillers. He administered the drugs and started to offer his usual you're-actually-quite-lucky-it-could've-been-worse spiel, but stopped it short. The man's Volvo had been sideswiped by an airborne ice-fishing hut; it didn't get more Fate-cursed than that. Concluding he'd done all he could for Jerace, Marston wished him a decent night's sleep, then left for one of his own.

In the three decades Marston had worked at St. Elizabeth's, he could count on two hands the number of times he'd driven to and from work. He owned a pickup, but was more inclined to plow his driveway with it than use it as a mode of transportation. He was a rugged man, a man's man, who saw nothing taxing about a half-mile walk to and from work each day. In fact, he found these jaunts beneath the crisp skies a refreshing way to gear up or wind down, or simply to reflect on the essence of life.

Now, as he made his way out the ambulatory entrance of St. E's and into the absolutely frigid night, he recapped the day's wins and losses, and gratefully inhaled nature's scent.

The world smelled clean.

St. E's was the only nonresidential structure in a two-mile radius, and as Marston moved away from the eternal lights of the parking lot, darkness enveloped him. After comporting itself all day as a harsh gale, the breeze now whispered a soft lullaby. Powdery snow hissed harmlessly as it fell in clumps from straining branches.

His wife thought he was nuts, walking to and from work in the dead of night and winter. She feared he'd be attacked by a bear or trampled by a moose, and that the paperboy would find him mangled on the side of the road one morning. He always humored her horrific scenarios, having learned during courtship that his wife needed to verbalize her biggest fears in order to gain some sort of upper hand on life's unknowns. Her husband, of course, knew better. No one had the upper hand on Nature.

Which was why he'd always found it easy to leave his work on the operating table, even after tending to violent death or dismemberment (rare occurrences in Georgeville). He'd never seen any point in dwelling on Nature's sometimes nasty work, never seen the use of dragging medical matters home with him.

On this night, however, he was within three hundred yards of his house, and there was still one work-related issue nagging at his subconscious.

Chad Ewing.

Marston knew better than anyone that Meredith Lacroix was getting on in years and prone to fits of "mix-up," as she called them, so he'd been tempted to completely disregard her recollections of a medical report on Georgeville's most recent violent death. He simply hadn't written one, so his first logical conclusion, after frowning his way from the confusion of the physician's lounge to the sanctity of his office, had been that Meredith must have pulled the wrong file for her ambitious visitors from Simsbury, one that, by some fantastically cosmic coincidence, had listed injuries similar to the ones that had killed Ewing.

But then something else had dawned on him, something he should have considered more than a week ago. If the Ewings had indeed positively ID'ed their son and hadn't yet raised holy hell over any obscene poetry on his dead flesh (and to his knowledge, they hadn't), then he could only surmise that someone, for some reason, had cleaned the corpse. And if that was the case, it was entirely possible, perhaps probable, that a bogus medical report would have been manufactured to jibe with the new-and-improved state of Ewing's skin.

Though Marston couldn't conceive of a reason for anyone on his staff to do this, all signs pointed to Janine Hammond, the nurse who'd served three unpaid suspensions for excessive tardiness and overall sloppiness since beginning work the previous July. She'd been in charge of statistical record keeping for Ewing. She'd also disappeared during his conversation with Meredith and hadn't returned for the rest of the day.

But still, what would she have to *gain* from all this?

Nearing the humble intersection of Maine and Maple, Marston made a mental note to call Dick Finnerty first thing in the morning, even before dealing with Nurse Hammond, assuming she showed up for work. There was some fishiness about Georgeville's most recent violent death.

Marston cast Ewing and Meredith and Janine from his mind as a small cluster of not-too-distant lights peeked meekly through a swarm of pine. Home. He let a smile warm his body, as he envisioned Miriam standing watch in the kitchen, running up a phone bill with one of their six kids and sixteen grandchildren, waiting for her lunatic husband to hoof his way home.

He paused at the crosswalk that carried Maine across Maple, for at that instant a dark van eased around Maple's final bend and squeaked to a slow stop. Marston momentarily hesitated. As a pedestrian, he clearly had the right of way. However, the van wore a Massachusetts plate beneath its chrome grill, and he knew all about crazy Massachusetts drivers from his occasional conferences in Boston.

This particular Massachusetts driver seemed to know the rules of the road, however, because he waved for Marston to cross. Smiling and gesturing his thanks, he started across, and as he did he noticed the interlocking "NY" glowing whitely from the face of the driver's baseball cap.

The last thing Marston thought was *A Yankees fan in the heart of Red Sox nation?*

And the last thing he heard was the roar of the engine, swallowing Nature's nighttime silence and his own unnatural scream.

9:47 P.M.

With hands that had recently written and shredded three different letters of apology to Dr. Marston (*What's the point of apologizing,* she'd finally decided; she'd violated the terms of her employment and probably broken the law, on behalf of people she didn't even know), Janine Hammond held the satchel containing twenty-five thousand in cash tight to her body as she handed the boarding pass to the suntanned flight attendant at Gate 22. The attendant glanced at the pass, ripped it at the perforation, and smiled as she handed the seating stub back to Janine.

"One way to St. Thomas," said the attendant with a trained, envious smile. "Aren't you lucky. It's beautiful down there this time of year."

"I hope so," said Janine, hugging the satchel closer, trying to squeeze guilt out the pores of skin that generally burned before it tanned. "Because I think I'm going to be there for a long time."

CHAPTER THIRTY-TWO

The 200th Year
Thursday, March 5

7:10 A.M.

The two stacks of *Portland Press Heralds*—each containing over one hundred front-page headlines screaming, in laymen's terms, that St. Elizabeth's chief of staff Dr. Charles F. K. Marston had been found mangled on the side of the road—were tossed from the delivery truck to the sidewalk in front of the Simsbury Student Center. As the truck rolled away, both stacks wobbled for a moment, then sat upright, just waiting to be divided, distributed to student mailboxes, and read.

A minute or so later, a charcoal van pulled up. The driver, an apparent Yankees fan, hopped to the pavement, rolled open the vehicle's sliding door, and tossed both newspaper stacks into the van. He then returned to his place behind the steering wheel, pulled a neat U-turn, and pointed the dented grill toward Kennebunk, where the charcoal van would turn back into a black BMW.

9:21 A.M.

Despite the new nightmare that had robbed him of sleep, Mark actually managed to clap for Casey's impressive yellowing of the snow, as seen from the warm side of his sliding glass door. He let her back in, told her what a good girl she was, and tossed a pretzel rod on her uneaten puppy kibble. He threw on jeans, a sweater, and a baseball hat turned backward, brushed his teeth, and left.

The previous day's murderous gust had blown itself out, and the sun's unfettered rays actually reached the ground, six feet above which Mark's eyes squinted as they watched the tree line separating the athletic complex and the academic buildings grow taller. His breaths shot forward, then curled around his advancing head. His jacket zipper clinked against its halfway-fastened path with each boot step that punched a size-ten hole in the snow.

The many questions swirling through his head for the past fifteen hours had, for the sake of sanity, been reduced to two. Sure, he wanted to know why Angela had chosen to go the D-Squad route instead of through the police, and how the fuck she'd known to call the scene of her assault "the downstairs library." And yes, he'd like to know why there had been only one "Seniors Serve the Sophomores" Night in the history of Sigma and whether its proximity to the only sex crime trial in the history of Simsbury had been merely coincidental. And he'd love to track down former Sigma president Scott Patterson, somewhere on Wall Street, and ask the droning son of a bitch just exactly why he'd been so adamant that Mark "wave a white flag" rather than fight in true Sigma style.

But all these details lay beneath two simple questions,

the worst-case possible answers to which made him want to vomit into the snow.

Had he been set up by his brothers?

And if so, why?

His sunrise temptation had been to just call up Fairchild and, in an apologetic, almost joshing voice, ask his best friend to ease his confused mind about something. But the topic of the ensuing conversation seemed so outlandish, so *unthinkable,* he couldn't imagine himself doing so.

So, ultimately, he'd decided to pursue a more subtle path to the truth.

He emerged from the throng of trees and immediately angled toward the Administration Building. Two minutes later, his slippery-soled boot touched down on the first of seventy-two steps that would carry him to the third floor.

He found the entire floor looking deserted. Every empty receptionist chair was swiveled away from its desk, and every executive office—those with doors ajar, anyway—appeared to be lit indirectly by the sun as opposed to brass lamps and track lighting. Mark guessed that there must be a meeting somewhere.

After a brief hesitation, he moved cautiously to the dean's corner office, where he found a tightly shut door.

He knocked tentatively.

No answer.

He knocked louder.

Still no response.

He glanced left and right, then twisted the doorknob. The door popped open.

Did he dare walk in? Did he dare risk being caught by

the dean while he snooped through the most personal information on campus?

Yes, he dared.

Stepping back, he surveyed the hallway one final time. Then he nudged the door open with his thigh, stole inside, and closed the door gently behind him.

Heart pounding, he quickly scanned the room, knowing what he was looking for, but not knowing where to find it. It could be anywhere, and he didn't have the time for a methodical search. He'd have to play the percentages and hope to get lucky.

The file cabinet against one of the two windowless walls looked most promising, so he hurried to it and pulled open the top drawer, grimacing as it squeaked. He inspected the contents. Loose papers, two blank folders, but otherwise empty. The second drawer yielded physical-plant blueprints and inventory reports for the campus's two dining commons. The third drawer, faculty files. Interesting, but not what he was looking for.

A metal divider split the fourth drawer into two sections, each of which nearly overflowed with what appeared to be student personnel files, some tattered, some crisp. Mark pulled one from the left side, opened it, and swore softly as a half dozen or so of Kevin Hathaway's accumulated pink slips flipped into the air and fluttered every which way. Mark scrambled to collect them all, arranged them in some sort of reasonable order, then closed the file and jammed Kevin Hathaway and all his academic woes back in the drawer. Concluding that the left side contained academic probation cases, he turned his attention to the right side and selected a file at random.

Simsbury College v. Montgomery Ford

Here we go, thought Mark, recalling Mississippi Monty and the notorious Dixie flag he'd aimed at the African-American Society House. He'd found the D-Squad cases. He put poor Mr. Ford back in the drawer and began systematically thumbing through the remainder of the files. A complete left-to-right search, however, turned up no folders with his name on it, which he found remarkably odd and, on this day, suspicious. He bit his lip, frowned, and had nearly finished closing the drawer when a quick flash of something made him do a double take. He reopened the drawer and peered inside.

Shoved in the back, on the other side of a seemingly unnecessary divider, was a thin, blank folder. It almost resembled trash, and on any other day Mark would have ignored it. However, he was breaking and entering and pillaging private information, so this clearly wasn't just any other day. He grabbed the folder and opened it.

The first thing he saw was a copy of the letter the dean had sent him.

He'd found it.

There was something different about his file, though. There were no notes, and no documentation of testimony given during his hearing. Just the letter, and a copy of the dean's stipulated punishments. There had to be more. He examined the back of each document, then shook the folder.

A sliver of white caught his eye, and he glanced downward in time to see a wispy strip of paper twitter to the floor. He knelt, retrieved it, and inspected it.

It was a fax transmittal receipt, smoky and flimsy and pretty well worn. Eight of the eleven digits beside the fax-destination heading had faded beyond legibility, and the first four hyphenated date-sent characters had run together to form a black smudge. However, the fax description seemed to be missing only a letter or two, and a quick run through the alphabet, teamed with an even quicker assessment of the number of pages sent, hinted that at some point two years ago both items in his D-Squad file had been faxed to a company called Great White Industries.

He was beginning to wonder why when he suddenly heard the dean's voice advancing down the hallway. He stuffed the fax receipt in his pocket and his file back where he'd found it. He closed the drawer quickly and quietly, then turned to face the music.

The dean twitched upon finding Mark in his office.

"Mark . . . what are you doing in here?"

"Good morning, Dean. I just dropped by to see what time the meeting is today."

"Three o'clock. I told you that the other day."

"I know," said Mark, smiling apologetically as he inched toward the door. "I just forgot to write it down. I'll see you this afternoon."

He turned and left the office, and as he made his way back down the hallway he heard the dean call after him.

"Get yourself a day-planner, Mr. Jessy."

12:02 P.M.

Shawn shoved her day-planner in her backpack and shouldered the strap as she hustled for the door, but the phone's ring doubled her back.

"Hello?"

"Yes," said a female voice, "may I please speak with Shawn?"

"I'm Shawn."

"Hi, this is Betsy Kimball, from the Cumberland County Coroner's Office. Remember me?"

"Sure, I remember. How are you?"

"Fine, thanks. Did I catch you at a bad time?"

"Not really. I was just on my way out to lunch."

"Then I actually caught you at a *good* time," said Betsy. "How'd you like to have lunch with *me*?"

"Huh?" Shawn grunted, before she could help herself.

"Are you free for lunch?"

"Where?" said Shawn, buying time as she scrambled for an excuse, for it was suddenly occurring to her that Betsy was a lesbian. Not that she had anything against lesbians (her roommate was one), but—

"Here at Bowdoin."

"Geez, Betsy," said Shawn, filling her voice with regret, "I'd love to. But I've got lab at one, and I'm not sure I'd be able to make it back here in time—"

"There's something I need to show you, Shawn. It concerns Chad Ewing."

"Oh?"

"That's right. Are you interested?"

"Uh . . . of course. What is it?"

"I'd rather show you myself. Come on over. I'll order from Monty's, and we can go over what I've found."

Shawn bit her lip and quickly pondered the invitation. She really did have lab at one, and having only met Betsy once, and very briefly, she was a little leery about sitting down to lunch with her. Then again, the previous day's depositions of Finnerty and Lacroix had yielded little in the way of solid leads. If Betsy really possessed quality information, then missing the first fifteen minutes or so of salamander dissection seemed like a worthwhile gamble.

"Okay," she found herself saying, "lunch sounds great."

"Super. Do you know how to get here?"

"Yeah. What dorm?"

"Coles Tower. Know where that is?"

"Of course. Tallest building north of Portland, right?"

Betsy laughed. "So they say. I'm on the eleventh floor. Suite C."

"Floor eleven. Suite C. Got it."

"Good. How do you feel about mushrooms?"

"The drug or the salad item?"

"The pizza topping," giggled Betsy.

"Love 'em. See you soon."

She hung up, repositioned her backpack, and grabbing her car keys, left for Bowdoin College.

12:06 P.M.

Templeton hung up the phone, then walked out into the hallway to retrieve his mail. He thumbed through the pieces as he turned back to his office, but a slow, hesitant movement caught his eye and caused him to look up.

Carlisle was moving slowly toward the stairs, his arms spread slightly to balance his gait. He paused at the top landing, seemed to collect himself, then began his descent, and when he'd finally drifted out of sight, Templeton smirked.

Have fun at your doctor's appointment, he thought, *you crazy old fuck.*

CHAPTER THIRTY-THREE

The 200th Year
Thursday, March 5

12:26 P.M.

Shawn parked her Jeep beside an uninhabited, ice-glazed bicycle rack in front of Coles Tower, and as she got out of her car she was almost run over by a Monty's Pizza delivery car as it screeched to a halt. The delivery man tumbled from the car, smiled his hurry at Shawn, then scrambled for the building, desperate to deliver in thirty minutes or less.

"Excuse me," Shawn called. "Is that pizza for Kimball? Eleven-C?"

He looked down at a slip of paper. "Yeah. That you?"

Shawn nodded. "What do I owe you?"

"Eight-ten."

Shawn reached into her pocket, pulled out a ten, and handed it to him. "Keep the change."

Pizza in hand, she entered the path leading to the Tower's main entrance. On the cement slant of the handicap access sat several young men in baseball hats and earth-tone jackets, happily calling out to passersby and

laughing at those who slipped on the ice. Heads turned
and eyes lit as Shawn entered their chamber of loiter.

"Hey," shouted one. "Do you deliver, pretty pizza
girl?"

His friends cracked up and slapped each other.

Freshmen, Shawn thought as she stopped and peered at
the boy through her sunglasses. "Yeah," she said suggestively, "I deliver. How much you got?"

"Oh geez," howled the freshman, smacking his forehead with an open palm. "A hundred bucks."

Shawn pretended to consider the offer, then nodded.
"Okay, deal. Go call your daddy and ask him to wire the
money." She moved closer. "Then shove it up your ass.
Your buddies and I will sit here and eat pizza while you
give yourself a hundred-dollar enema."

There was a moment of stunned silence, then whoops
of laughter. As Shawn breezed away, she heard the rest of
the guys ragging their bold friend. Once inside the Tower,
she allowed herself a smile.

She elevated to the eleventh floor and, finding Betsy
waiting in the hallway, held the pizza over her head. "Did
someone order a pizza?"

Betsy laughed. "How much was it?"

"Don't worry about it. I'm just glad you called."

"Come on in," said Betsy as she took the pie and
opened the orange door to her suite. Once inside, she set
the box down on a coffee table and pointed to two cans of
soda. "I bought some Cokes from the vending machine
downstairs."

"Great."

"Have a seat."

They ate and made small talk. They discussed majors,

job interviews, and life in general at small liberal arts colleges. Betsy proved easy to talk to, and Shawn got the sense she was extremely intelligent.

When the pizza was gone, Betsy tossed the empty box into the corner. She wiped her mouth with a napkin, then gave Shawn a serious look.

"Here's the deal," she began. "I think there's something unusual about Chad Ewing's death."

"How so?" asked Shawn, taking out the notepad she'd brought.

"Okay," Betsy said, leaning forward. "Last Wednesday, I dropped by Finnerty's office around two in the afternoon. His door was open, and he was talking to a man whom I'd never seen before. I assumed him to be the relative of one of our 'clients,' if you know what I mean."

Shawn nodded.

"Well," Betsy continued, "I listened at the door for a minute or two, and sure enough it was Chad Ewing's father. Or at least, that's who he *said* he was."

She paused to drain her Coke, and as she did, Shawn looked up from her notepad. "What do you mean, 'that's who he *said* he was'?"

Betsy stood, walked to her desk, and grabbed a newspaper, which she brought back to the coffee table. She set the paper down, opened it to the middle, and put her finger on a photograph.

"See this? This is a picture of the Ewing family at the memorial service for their son. It took place right on your quadrangle."

"I was there."

Betsy pointed to the face of Chad's father. "This isn't the same guy I saw in Finnerty's office. I'm sure of it.

The face is completely different!" She looked at Shawn, her eyes wide with excitement. "What's more, this memorial took place at the exact same time that Mr. Ewing met with Finnerty." She shook her head. "He couldn't have been both places at once!"

Shawn dropped her pen and squinted. "Are you *sure*?"

"Positive. Look." Betsy pointed at the caption. "This paper is from last Thursday. I'm assuming it contains all the news from the day before, which was Wednesday. Was the memorial service last Wednesday?"

Shawn thought for a moment, then nodded.

Betsy slapped the table. "Well, there you go!"

Shawn eyed the photo for a moment, then shook her head. "Not to doubt you, but are you sure you saw this guy talking to Finnerty on Wednesday? Are you sure it wasn't Tuesday? Or Thursday?"

"It was Wednesday."

"Hmm. Then are you sure that he was in there between one and two? Could it have been any earlier? Or later?" Though she'd come here for a lead, part of Shawn wanted to believe that what Betsy was saying, in this world of ivy and supposed integrity, wasn't true.

"No way. I don't get in until noon, and I'm gone by three on Wednesdays for lab."

Shawn slowly shook her head and said softly, "I don't believe this."

"Believe it," Betsy said, a sincere shine to her eyes. "Believe it."

1:51 P.M.

Mark had never before been to the Office of Career Services, which made sense because he had no clue what he wanted to be when he grew up, other than a father and happy. He'd always assumed he'd split the year after graduation between fishing and coaching, save a little cash, then buy a thirdhand Jeep like Shawn's and travel the country. Now that he had the perfect travel companion in Casey, this romantic fantasy had taken on sharper detail, and with each future destination added to the itinerary (Montana was Mark's latest fascination), the Office of Career Services' personal relevance had slipped further away. The OCS had become a temple in his mind, a stressful, scary shrine to suits and salary, reserved for those who craved the keys to the kingdom.

When he got there, Mark discovered he'd only overestimated the physical *size* of the OCS; the office consumed less than half the second floor of the Student Center, much of it hallway. However, he'd grossly underestimated the tension level. No fewer than eight powergarbed seniors filled the leather chairs lining the hall, their Nine West heels and Bostonian loafers nervously tapping the deep red carpeting as they studied the exaggerations on their résumés and waited their turns behind one of two visible doors.

There was no conversation, save for the occasional whispered rehearsal of phony responses to predictable questions. In fact, there was no communication whatsoever, for on this day, each was the other's competition, and even subtle communication such as eye contact had to be saved for the corporate recruiter who'd grill them one by one and belittle their summer work experience and *maybe* grant them a second interview if they kissed enough ass or satisfied a quota. Absorbing the scene, literally *feeling* the strain, Mark savored his decision not to seek gainful employment until he was ready.

And then he remembered why he was here, and the comfort vanished.

He tiptoed past all the anxiety to the end of the brief hallway, which opened up to OCS headquarters. The walls were loaded down with paper of every grade and color, and a chest-high counter separated the world of job seekers from a large computer terminal, a series of reference shelves, and a busy-looking woman wearing a name tag that said "Hello, My Name Is Serenity."

Mark was about to ask Serenity for help when the phone rang. She motioned for him to wait a minute and began griping at her caller, so he turned away and casually studied the memos, bulletins, job descriptions, sample résumés, and model cover letters smothering the wall to his right. He was midway through a list of Interviewing Do's and Don'ts when he heard Serenity hang up the phone and ask if she could help him.

"Yes," he said, turning to her. "Is Elliot Segal here today?"

She gave him an odd look. "No. He landed a job back in November."

"Oh, I know that, but doesn't he work here part-time?"

She shook her head. "He only helps out during job fairs."

"Oh," Mark said, not understanding the difference, then pausing to think. "Well, I guess you could help me out." He reached into his jacket, pulled out the fax receipt he'd pilfered from his D-Squad file, and spread it out on the counter. He pointed to it. "Great White Industries. I'm wondering if you could tell me a little bit about this company."

She gave him another queer look. "Why?"

"I'm just starting my job search, and I was thinking I might want to send them a cover letter."

"You want to send a cover letter to a company and you don't even know what they do?"

Mark shrugged and grinned. "Isn't that what being a liberal arts student's all about? You gotta start somewhere."

She shook her head. "You should start by sitting down with me and going through a proper consultation. We'll make a list of your strengths and weaknesses and videotape a mock interview. And when you're ready, we'll mail cover letters and résumés to an appropriate list of employers."

For crying out loud, thought Mark. "Sounds like a plan. But for now, could you just help me find out what business this *particular* company is in?"

Serenity frowned, then shrugged. "I guess so." She turned, pulled eyeglasses down from the top of her head, and sat at the computer terminal. "Great White Industries," she said as she typed. She smacked the enter key, waited a moment, then turned to Mark and said, "Real estate."

Mark nodded. "Hmm. What else can you tell me?"

She made an annoyed face, then turned back to the screen. "An international real-estate development firm headquartered in Boston. Gross revenues exceeding one hundred million in each of the last three years. Taken public five years ago by chairman and cofounder Terrence Bonnell."

Mark, who'd been jotting down key information on the fax receipt, suddenly stopped and looked up. "What was that name again?"

"Terrence Bonnell."

He recorded the name, and as he did a faint familiarity painted a letter-by-letter picture before his eyes. How did he know that name?

Serenity stood up from the terminal and moved back to her imperial place behind the counter. "Is there anything else I can do for you? Perhaps schedule a consultation?"

Eyes still glued to the fax receipt, Mark shook his head slowly.

"Well," Serenity huffed. "If you'll excuse me, some *real* job candidates need my attention."

Mark nodded absently, turned away from the counter, and made his way back down the hallway.

But never took his eyes off the fax receipt.

And never stopped searching his memory.

2:15 P.M.

Templeton was headed for the coffeepot when he caught sight of the open newspaper on his secretary's desk. He veered slightly, grabbed it, and skimmed the front page as he continued his walk.

Then stopped in his tracks.

Midway down the front page was the following headline: *Longtime St. Elizabeth's Chief Dead in Apparent Hit-and-Run: Georgeville mourns the loss of model citizen, family man.*

The briefest of chills passed through Templeton's body, then the busy dean resumed walking.

2:32 P.M.

For the second time in twelve days Chief Sullivan disgustedly threw the newspaper into the nonrecyclable bucket and turned his attention to an accident report. Only this time, his disgust was aimed not at the Celtics, but at the senseless death of one of Georgeville's finest men. And this time, he read the accident report not with a sense of disdain for all parties involved, but with genuine bereavement for the community's loss.

And this time, his full review of the document left him thinking not about fortune, but about misfortune.

He massaged a temple, sighed, and put the report in the in-box. Then he stood on legs that hadn't felt this old in years, and walked to the window.

For a long time he watched the western sky, somewhere beneath which loomed the big white fraternity house on the corner of College and Maine.

2:44 P.M.

Carla Ewing swayed with the bitter breeze as she stared at the cold grave, then closed her eyes, telling herself that when she opened them, she'd be back home, fixing chicken noodle soup for Chad, who'd finished his exams and was home early for spring break.

She opened her eyes, and once again found herself staring at a gray slab of marble.

She closed her eyes again.

3:07 P.M.

"Congratulations, Shawn," said the dean. "You have officially aroused the ire of the county coroner."

Shawn looked up from her notebook, glanced at Schwitters and Mark, and then said, "How so?"

"He called this morning," said the dean with a smirk, "and said that the young lady he met with yesterday behaved both 'inappropriately and disrespectfully.'" He picked up a piece of paper and began to read from it, "In fact, 'she behaved in a manner not befitting a future wife and mother.'"

"Oh, good God," said Shawn.

The dean put down his notes. "Actually, I believe it was your *lack* of faith in God that offended him. Thanks for representing the school so well."

Shawn shook her head, muttered something, and stared down at the conference table.

"Other than that," said the dean, "how'd it go yesterday?"

"We didn't learn anything new," Schwitters said.

The dean nodded slowly and tapped the table with a pencil. "Well," he said finally, "I suspected as much, but it was worth a—"

"Not so fast."

All eyes turned to Shawn. She leaned forward in her chair, a serious, almost aggressive expression on her face. "I just came from Bowdoin College, where I had a nice little chat with Betsy Kimball, the coroner's student intern."

"The girl we met yesterday?"

Shawn nodded. "She called me this morning, said she had something important to discuss with me. So we had lunch."

The dean threw a confused look at Mark and Schwitters, then shrugged. "And?"

"*And,* it seems that there is someone out there impersonating Chad Ewing's father. What do you think about that?"

The dean blinked. "What are you talking about?"

"Last Wednesday, in the middle of the memorial service, a man claiming to be Roy Ewing showed up at the county coroner's office. Betsy Kimball saw him talking with Finnerty."

"And what were *they* talking about?"

"Chad."

The dean nodded, then stood and began to slowly pace the room. "And how does Betsy know that it *wasn't* Roy Ewing?"

"The next day, in the paper, she saw that picture of the Ewings. She said that the guy in Finnerty's office looked nothing like the Roy Ewing in the picture. Plus," Shawn tapped her index finger on the table, "the guy was there at the same time as the memorial service. And without his wife! Doesn't that seem more than just a little odd?"

"Quite," replied the dean, "which is why I don't believe a word of it."

"Of course not! You never believe a word I say—"

"Not these days, anyway."

"Why would Betsy lie?"

"Why *wouldn't* she? I mean, what do you really know about her?"

"I know she's the coroner's assistant, and she goes to Bowdoin. What's not to believe?"

"Plenty."

"Like what?"

The dean put up his hands and shook his head. "I can't believe I'm even arguing about this."

"I think it's worth looking into," Mark said softly.

The dean turned to Mark in shock, then gave him a long, disgusted look. "Oh, great! Look who's finally joined us."

"Dean Templeton," Shawn said, one surprised eye still pointed Mark's way. "My gut tells me Betsy Kimball isn't a liar."

"Oh really?!" exclaimed the dean. "Well, *my* gut tells *me* that you and all your sources have gone stark raving mad!" He put up his hands again, then ran them through his hair. "Okay, okay. Look. Roy and Carla Ewing went back to the coroner's office the next day, to pick up the body. Don't you think that Finnerty would've noticed the difference?"

"No," answered Shawn. "Because only Finnerty's assistant works mornings. That's when the *real* Ewings went to claim the body."

The dean stared at Shawn. "Suppose," he said finally, "for just one, *ridiculous* moment, that what you say is accurate. What does it prove? Nothing. *Nothing!* The police might want to know that some demented Roy Ewing impostor is on the loose, but it certainly has nothing to do with Sigma's liability. There's no link."

"Not yet. But there might be."

"I'll tell you what, then," said the dean, frustration evident. "You go *find* that link. Then you get Betsy Kimball over here to testify. Until then, don't waste our time with cuckoo conspiracy theories." He stood suddenly, knocking over his chair. "I want this whole sordid episode buried by spring break. Done! Finished!" He swept his arms through the air, the way an umpire signals a runner safe at second. "You three better come up with something more solid by Friday, or I'm calling the whole thing off!"

He stormed out of the room, slamming the door behind him.

Back in his office, Templeton paced the floor, pounding one open palm with a closed fist, and whispering the same question repetitively.

Who the fuck is Betsy Kimball?

As he ran a quivering hand over the slick of sweat on his receding hairline, he realized he was on the verge of an anxiety attack.

Okay, he told himself, *calm down.* He took a deep breath through his nose and forced his darting eyes to close for the count of ten.

Feeling somewhat calmer, he sat at his desk. He breathed deeply again, then picked up the phone and dialed the digits of the private extension that would connect him to the party responsible for more than half his personal worth.

After three solid minutes of rings, the deep voice he was waiting for picked up.

"T-Bone. This is Templeton. We're having a big problem in this small, ignorant town."

CHAPTER THIRTY-FOUR

*The 200th Year
Thursday, March 5*

9:26 P.M.

Mark finally collapsed on his couch and let his mind twist with deep, dark possibilities. He was just beginning to kick the tires of it all when the phone rang for the third time in the fifteen minutes since he'd returned from practice. Once again, he ignored it, sure that it was Shawn, eager to probe her boyfriend's change of tune. He was in no frame of mind to discuss it; besides, at this point what could he really say? So he let the phone ring itself to death while he busied himself with the unspeakable questions that had pursued him for the past twenty-four hours, led by the scrap of paper that now seared a hole in his pocket.

How the hell did he know the name Terrence Bonnell?

He'd considered every possibility, linking the name and even its related corporation to all the historically significant events of life. However, neither "Terrence," nor "Bonnell," nor any derivative of either seemed to fit with any time or place he could conjure. Which, of course, burned him all the more.

He shook his head, reached for the phone, and dialed the number for Monty's Pizza.

"Hello?" said the soft voice of a woman. "Hello?"

Mark frowned, having not yet heard it ring. "Yeah, is this Monty's?"

A pause. "What? Hello? Is Mark Jessy there?"

"Uh, this is Mark. Who's this?"

"Mark?"

"Yes!"

"Oh, I'm sorry. I dialed your number, but I hadn't heard it ring. You must've picked up."

"I guess so," Mark almost shouted in frustration, "because here I am!"

"This is Carla Ewing."

"Who?"

"Carla Ewing. Chad's mother."

"Oh. Hi." *What the . . . ?*

"Hi."

"Hi."

She breathed deeply into the phone. "Listen, Mark, I hope I'm not bothering you. I got your name from Dean Templeton."

"You did?"

"Yes. I'd heard that a student committee was investigating my son's death, and I wanted a name. He gave me yours."

"He did?"

"Yes. He said you'd be a good one to talk to."

"He did?"

"You sound surprised."

"No . . . it's just that . . . how *are* you, Mrs. Ewing?"

"Under the influence of sedatives, so please forgive me if I make no sense at all."

"Of . . . of course. I understand."

"I know you do," she said, her tone even softer. "The dean told me you lost your parents when you were very young."

"I . . . yes."

"I'm so sorry."

"So am I."

She coughed lightly into the phone. "We . . . we buried Chad last Friday. That's when it hit me he's never coming back." She coughed again, then sniffed. "Did you know him?"

"No, I didn't," admitted Mark, "but my friends tell me he was a real nice—"

"It's okay, Mark. I won't be offended if you tell me you didn't know him. I get the feeling not many people did. It was the same way when he was in high school. He was always desperate to be popular, but for some reason he never got much recognition. He wasn't a good athlete, and he was a little shy. That's why, when I was up at Simsbury, I didn't ask too many questions about his death. It was like I didn't want to embarrass him, because I *so* wanted him to be *liked*."

Her pitch sharpened a bit as she continued. "But since we got back, I've been doing a lot of thinking. There are *so many* things I don't understand. For instance, I just can't accept that he willingly got himself so drunk. I mean, in high school he'd occasionally drink a beer or two to impress his friends, but to my knowledge he wasn't a heavy drinker. And the dean insinuated suicide, which I find *completely* out of the question."

Mark nodded into the phone, but said nothing.

"After the funeral reception at our house, Chad's best friend, Cory, stayed to help us clean up. He told me something I didn't know. He said Chad used to call him up at Syracuse, crying. He said Chad was *beaten, regularly,* by the Sigma brothers. Now, isn't that hazing?"

For an instant Mark glimpsed this as the perfect opportunity to sabotage the D-Squad investigation, but his own doubts disabled his trigger finger. And amazingly—or perhaps not so amazingly—he found himself saying, "Yes, it is."

"And isn't hazing illegal?"

"I . . . probably."

"Cory said Chad thought the Sigmas might've been trying to get him to drop out of the fraternity. Aside from beating on him, they made him drink vomit and urine." Her tone took on an edge that bordered spite and disgust. "Does this sound *possible?*"

Yes, it sounded quite possible, for Mark was suddenly remembering his conclusion upon first looking at Chad's personnel file photo; the freshman simply hadn't looked like Sigma material. It was entirely conceivable that the Sigmas had bid Chad, then done everything in their power to shape him up or ship him out. Still, even with newfound mistrust of Sigma contaminating blood that had once been true eagle blue, Mark couldn't see his former brothers going to potentially deadly ends to get rid of an unwanted element.

Did they get rid of me?

"I don't know," he said, distracted. "That sounds a little extreme."

"It does to me, too. But isn't that what your generation is all about?"

Mark nodded, swallowed, and said nothing.

"And knowing Chad," she continued, "he would've endured any humiliation for acceptance, because that's the kind of kid he is . . . was." Her voice began to crack. "All he wanted was to fit in. All he wanted was to belong." She sniffed. "When he first told us he'd joined the best fraternity in the country, as he called it, we were ecstatic for him. And when he started raving about what a tight-knit family the brothers of Sigma were, Roy and I actually got *jealous,* if you can believe that . . ."

She digressed to a time where her son was alive and hopeful, but Mark stayed right where she'd left him, focusing on a single word, the search for which he and Chad had apparently both embarked on at Sigma and failed to find.

Family.

"I know nothing's going to bring my son back," she was saying, her voice soft again, "and I'm certainly not going to drag this out just for the sake of being ugly. But if you could look under all the stones . . . it would be one less thing keeping me up at night."

"We'll look into it, Mrs. Ewing," he said, and though he still couldn't fathom investigating his former brothers, something told him he'd already begun.

"Thank you," she said, her tone mixed with relief and gratitude. She uttered a few more sad thoughts, gave Mark her phone number, and said a good-bye that verged on tearshed.

Mark broke the connection, and before he knew what he was doing, his finger was punching a new number and his voice was impulsively seeking information that Sigma president Scott Patterson had once warned him would lead to a restraining order and police involvement.

"Could you say that name again?" said the directory assistance operator.

"Angela McSheffrey," Mark said slowly. "In Georgeville."

"One moment please."

He bounced his foot, watched Casey's nearby napping eyelids twitch, and asked himself if he was really doing this, and why.

Though he knew the answers to both those questions.

"I'm sorry, sir," said the operator. "We have no listing for McSheffrey in Georgeville."

"Oh. What about surrounding towns?"

She paused, said, "Please hold," and tapped furiously on a keyboard. "I'm sorry, sir. I see no listing for McSheffrey anywhere within this area code. I have a McShea in Brunswick, and two listings for McShevron in Kittery."

Mark considered other possibilities for a moment, but none seemed worth holding the operator on the line. He thanked the woman, hung up, then stood and began to pace.

That there existed no listing for McSheffrey didn't strike him as wildly odd; it wasn't a very common name, and just because it wasn't listed didn't mean that Angela didn't live somewhere within the area code. Perhaps her roommate paid the phone bill, or maybe she'd married and changed her name. Or maybe she was hiding from someone and felt the need for an unpublished number.

Hiding from *whom*?

His gut told him she hadn't moved away. Himself a townie from a small, working-class town, he knew that monumental drive was necessary to abandon the security of towns where seventy-five percent of the residents were related in some way. His own high school friends had thought him nuts to want to go all the way to Simsbury, when he could've just as easily played lacrosse in the local men's league, and what the hell good would all those fancy college facts be to a fisherman who lived on instinct? Townies, he knew, were creatures of habit. They stuck to routines. Same town, same house, same job, same boyfriend or girlfriend, same summer softball team, same bar—

He froze.

Suddenly he knew, in the instinctive manner of a true fisherman, where to find Angela McSheffrey.

9:51 P.M.

Shawn dialed Mark's number for what must have been the tenth time that night, but again there was no answer. She frowned, replaced the receiver, and sat down on her bed.

And for the hundredth time that day, it occurred to her how little she knew about her boyfriend.

10:12 P.M.

According to Sigma lore, Jimmy Walsh had once gotten laid right smack on the Hayloft dance floor, courtesy of a female trucker who'd been on the road and without a man for a while. Walsh, who'd been a senior when Mark was a sophomore, had gained legendary status with this episode, mostly because he'd embellished the story so well. For his part, Mark had taken away a vision of the Hayloft as being like the countless Cape Cod dives he'd spent his high school career sneaking into.

Upon completing the two-mile walk from campus, flashing his ID at an ambivalent bouncer, and forking over the two-dollar cover charge, he shoved open the black door and found a scene that instantly jibed with all his preconceived stereotypes. Amid a cloud of smoke as dense as any maritime fog, flannel sleeves reached for ashtrays and beers set sludgy on a squarely situated bar. Acid-washed jeans electrically slid on the dance floor. Big boots sashayed and moseyed and added inches to frames already inched by hairdos and NASCAR hats worn high. A pinball machine and its neighboring juke-box swallowed quarters and kicked back neon entertainment that clashed with the efforts of a bushy-mustachioed disc jockey.

Yup, thought Mark, feeling a bit of nostalgia for home. *This is a townie bar.*

And this was where Angela McSheffrey had begun the night of March third, two years earlier.

He took a deep breath, sidled up to the bar, ordered a bottle of Bud, and continued to scope. He'd sit here, drink a beer or two, and try to blend in while he searched for the truth.

"Yer not from round here, are ya?"

It took Mark a moment to realize that the question had been directed at him, and another to locate its source. "No," he said to the man next to him, a greasy-looking guy with a skin disorder, a lower lip packed with chew, and a tee shirt that pleaded for the legalization of cock fighting. "This is my first time."

"I kin tell."

The bartender returned with Mark's beer and traded it for three singles, which he swept off the counter before turning to ring a Liberty Bell replica with his head. The bar-stooled patrons cheered.

Mark sipped his beer, then turned back to his new friend. "How can you tell?"

"I'd have seen ya before." He spat into a shot glass and pointed at Mark. "*You* I haven't seen."

Mark nodded, smiled, and played with his bottle. Then he turned back to the man. "Speaking of people you've *seen*," he said, "have you seen Angela McSheffrey here tonight?"

The man twisted his face into what Mark guessed was a frown. "Who?"

"Angela McSheffrey."

The man continued grimacing, then shook his head. "Buddy," he said, "I've spent the last twenty-two years in this town, and the last seventeen on this barstool, and I've never heard of anyone by that name." He absorbed a violent clap on the back, turned to return the favor with a solid punch to an equally nasty looking man's chest, and chuckled as he turned back to his beer.

"Never?" said Mark.

"Never. Folks in this town are French, not Irish. F'rinstance, my last name's Chabot." He licked a hoppy drip from the neck of his bottle. "Hey, you from the college?"

"What? Yeah."

He chuckled again. "No wonder I never seen ya here. You boys stick to yer frat houses, and Chewnocker's when yer looking for fights."

Mark shrugged and looked around, frustration beginning to creep into his flesh.

"Like it?"

"Like what?" said Mark. "Fights?"

"No, dummy. The college."

"Oh," said Mark. "Yeah. It's . . . okay."

The man nodded, ripped the entire label from his beer, and secured it to his forehead. "I almost went to college. Got arrested, though. Did a little time. But, shit, I learned a lot in jail, so I guess you could say I'm an educated man." He laughed and elbowed Mark. Mark smiled, nodded, and politely excused himself.

He moved away from the bar and circled the dance floor, slowly sipping, slowly searching. He watched packs of women leap and wiggle, while hungry guys patiently bobbed and snapped on the fringe, waiting for a misguided female to venture too close. He watched three different guys converge on a single dancer, each offering a different-colored, romantic drink they'd fetched her. In fact, he was so busy watching the three guys weave and posture for first crack that it was a long, visually transitional, holy-shit-am-I-really-seeing-this moment before he realized exactly who the three guys had converged on.

Angela McSheffrey.

Just like that.

Adrenaline surged through him, and it was all he could do to set his bottle on a nearby table before he dropped it or simply crushed it with fingers that had seized into a reflexive clutch. He steadied the bottle, steadied the table, then tried to steady himself. He put his hands on his face, breathed hotly into them, then ran them moistly through his hair. He turned slowly, dropped his hands to his sides, and focused on the reborn reminder of his near and distant past.

She accepted all three drinks, handed two to friends, and cocked a lazy hip of thanks to the lucky winner, whose drink she now held but didn't sip from. She humored the guy with a few lackadaisical dance steps, but kept her blank gaze on the bar's horizon, and it struck Mark that she looked utterly bored, as if going through the motions until something monumental came along. Her hair was no longer teased, her dancing clothes far baggier than they'd been the night she'd danced exclusively for him. Basically, Angela appeared out of place on the Hayloft dance floor, like a townie who'd outgrown her surroundings.

She abruptly turned and threaded her way through the clumsy thrash until she reached the jukebox, which she consulted briefly before sidestepping to the pinball machine. She fiddled with the flippers, then pushed a quarter into the slot. Her suitor arrived just as she sprung the first ball into play, and he cheered eagerly as she blatantly ignored him and casually dallied for points.

Mark took a deep breath, looked around—for what, he wasn't sure—and set a direct course for the truth.

He arrived behind her just as she dinged a profitable bell, and watched her tap her unpainted fingernails while the points rolled and her fan guffawed and rubbed her back. For a long, awkward moment, Mark surveyed the scene from a close distance, wondering how the hell he was going to approach this.

Having come all this way for a specific purpose, he finally decided on the blunt route.

"Angela," he said meekly.

No response. She continued pulling and flipping.

"Angela," he said louder.

Still no response from her, though the guy gave Mark a look that bordered on confusion and territoriality.

"Hey, Angela."

Still nothing. The guy shook his head at Mark as if to say, "you're crazy, man," and turned his full attention back to the game.

It dawned on him slowly, lagging a step behind the horror he could feel descending over his face, but by the time his jaw had fallen slack the instinct that had hauled him to this townie bar had hauled him to another realization.

Angela hadn't yet answered because her name wasn't Angela.

Though her body might indeed represent the truth, her identity was a total lie.

He opened his mouth—to say what, he wasn't sure—but just as the first jumbled utterance reached his tongue, she turned and headed for the bathroom. Speechless, Mark watched her disappear through a swinging door, then turned dumbfounded to her admirer, who was eyeing him defensively.

"She's mine, pal," the guy said through broken teeth.

"Not yet, *pal*," said Mark, and the next thing he knew, he was pushing open the door to the women's room.

She stood before the mirror, staring expressionlessly into it as she rubbed lipstick over her pucker in a half-hearted motion that implied not so much an act of self-beautification, as an act of complete boredom. She finished the task, smoothed her lips against each other, then turned toward the figure she had to sense was there.

What she saw knocked the lipstick from her hand.

"Oh my God," she blurted.

Mark just stared at her.

"What . . . what are you doing here?" she demanded, her eyes wide with what Mark recognized as horror and fury and a little bit of fear.

He shook his head at her and said slowly, "I was set up, wasn't I?"

She glared at him for several seconds, then kicked her lipstick into a stall, sturdied her purse strap, and stormed toward him. She shoved him against a hot-air dryer and pushed her way through the bathroom door. He followed close behind.

"Gino! Hey, Gino!" she yelled toward the bar. She turned and pointed at Mark. "This fucking pervert just followed me into the can."

A massive bouncer with a tattoo on his neck peered above her and locked eyes with Mark, who a scant four or five paces from the still-swinging ladies' room door couldn't have looked guiltier.

Gino lumbered over and tucked her behind him. "That true, asshole?"

Mark looked at him, then at her, then at him again. "I just . . . want to talk to her."

Gino turned to her. "You want to talk to this guy?"

She looked at Mark a long time, and as she did, he swore he saw a range of conflicting emotions cross her face. Anger gave way to curiosity, then sadness, then pity, and perhaps even shame. And briefly, ever-so-briefly, a look of longing flitted across the blue eyes that had once seduced him into trouble.

But her facial slate quickly wiped itself clean, and she shook her head.

"She doesn't want to talk to you, buddy," said Gino. "Now I suggest you leave her alone—"

"Hey, pretty boy!"

Now what, thought Mark, as he turned in the direction of the shout.

Advancing like a bearded, bloated, slow-moving tidal wave were two of the six grisly-looking Southern Maine natives that he and the Sigma boys and mainly Dominic had pummeled at Chewnocker's.

What a week I'm having, thought Mark.

"Well, well, well," said the larger of the two. "Where's your big bad friend, college pussy?"

"I don't want any trouble with you guys."

"Too late," said the other.

"Take it outside," said Gino, and he turned back to the bar. The victim formerly known as Angela McSheffrey peeled off and vanished into the crowd.

Mark turned back to the giants and swallowed hard. He rubbed his neck and fingered his beads and searched the sawdust-laden floor for some sort of escape. He nodded at each of them and tried to smile.

Then he broke for the door.

Miraculously, no one tried to stop him, and he made his way from the Hayloft with relative ease. Once outside, he backpedaled from the door and collected himself as he watched warily for pursuers. Seeing none, he turned and started briskly for campus.

Ten paces into his walk, however, he heard the inner din of the Hayloft momentarily release itself through an

opened door. He needed no backward glance to confirm
that the two behemoths were on his tail.

"Hey, pussy!" one of them shouted.

Thinking he had the speed advantage, he decided to
run for it, but after two strides a bright red Nissan
swerved up on the sidewalk and screeched to a halt. The
passenger door flung open, and the girl Mark had once, in
barroom and courtroom, known as Angela McSheffrey
leaned her head into view.

"Get in, Mark," urged the voice that had accused him
of sexual assault and attempted rape.

Mark just stood there, his instincts inexplicably failing
him, like those of a deer caught in headlights.

"Jesus Christ, get in the damn car!"

"What is your name?"

"Please—"

"What is your name?!"

She hesitated a moment, then looked down at her lap
and sighed. Then she turned misty-eyed and said, "My
name is Kelly Devereaux, and I've got a story to tell
you."

And then she screamed, because the brutes were upon
them. Forgetting he might have reason to hate this girl,
Mark dove into her car, just barely escaping their hairy
clutches. The door swung shut as the Nissan pulled a tight
three-sixty, and he lay breathless across the front seat, his
head on Kelly Devereaux's lap, as she slammed through
the gears and sped away.

10:45 P.M.

At the rear basement door through which Kelly Devereaux had once strutted and fled, the sixteen surviving

Sigma pledges lined up for the night's activity. Each held a blindfold. Each also held an assortment of cruel possibilities in their close-to-the-skin imaginations, awful questions about the night that lay before them.

Would they be made to sit there, and just listen to rhymes?

Would they be made to march and sing?

Would they be made to do push-ups?

Would they be made to drink urine?

Would they be made to drink vomit?

Would they be made to eat shit?

Would they be made to take vegetables and other edibles up their asses?

Would they be beaten?

Would they be made to speak with Brother Beam?

Or would they be made to do something they'd never before been made to do?

And if so, how horrible would it be?

When would it be over?

When would it be over?

When would it be over . . .

11:01 P.M.

The red Nissan cruised northward on I-95.

There'd been no conversation since the getaway; the air hung tense and heavy. Mark sat as far over in the passenger seat as the confines of the sporty little car would allow, his body against the door, his head tilted covertly toward the woman in the driver's seat, while he compared her to the woman carved like an ugly scar in his memory.

This *was* the woman who'd danced into his life through a basement door. This *was* the woman who'd stood high-haired above him, who'd helped him from the floor, who'd led him like a drooling vegetable to a room she shouldn't have known the name of. This *was* the woman who'd levied some serious charges, and who'd called herself Angela McSheffrey.

And who now apparently called herself Kelly Devereaux.

The Nissan slowed as it found a poorly marked exit, then pulled onto rural Route 7 and accelerated through the darkness.

"They told me you'd never figure it out," she began, her tone soft beneath the tough. "But it didn't matter, because I was going to tell you the truth anyway. I had a letter all set to be mailed the day I leave this little shithole forever. It's just that"—she paused and exhaled a deep part of her soul into the Nissan night—"it's just that I didn't expect to see you again, and I didn't think I'd *ever* be able to tell you to your face." She shrugged. "But maybe this was the way it was meant to be." She turned to him and allowed half a satirical smile. "So, do you really want to know the truth?"

There it was. The question he'd played with for the past twenty-four hours had suddenly just been asked *for* him. And just as suddenly, he felt a last-ditch craving for ignorance. Did he really want to know that the second-worst episode of his life had been a setup, orchestrated by brothers? Did he really want to know why?

Did he really want to know the truth?

Yes. He really wanted to know.

He nodded.

She turned her attention back to the shadowy road ahead. "You know," she said in a voice both wistful and indignant,

"I've suffered far more from knowing you than you have from knowing me. *You* lost your frat status and a piece of your reputation." Her eyes narrowed into angry slits as she turned back to the windshield. "*I* lost *everything*."

She allowed her angry stare to retract on its own, then resumed her watch on the passing trees and farmland. She was silent for a long spell. Occasionally, the light from a lone streetlamp rolled up her face, then streaked away. Twice she tucked stray strands of auburn behind her ear and nudged the heat lever.

But, for the most part, stillness.

Silence.

And then the silence was broken.

Kelly Devereaux began to speak.

She was born in a trailer park that used to hunker like a dirty little secret in a cleared-out patch of forest in south Georgeville. The shitty side of Georgeville—"not that there was a pretty side." Her earliest memory was of her father burning a hole in her mother's cheek with a cigar. Her worst memory, getting pregnant while still in high school and undergoing an abortion.

She had found herself briefly as an athlete, but neither the blazing pills she threw on the softball diamond, nor the forty-one points she accumulated in the basketball sectionals, were sufficient to buy her a ticket out.

The night after she graduated from high school, she began dancing at The Naked Truth, southern Maine's seamiest tits-and-ass establishment. "Exotic dancing" was what she called it. "Stripping" was what her boss and customers called it. Basically, she took off her clothes for money, because her body was her only asset and what else was she going to do. She pulled in roughly a bill a night, five nights a week, for the next two years. She moved out of the trailer and into an unfurnished apartment.

The dream of opening her own gym began with the admission that stripping was a lowlife way to make a living, and then with the realization that there wasn't a decent place to work out in the Georgeville-Brunswick-Topsham area. Why not open a gym herself? Could she do that? Did she have enough business sense? In a fit of brave determination she plopped a down payment on a fixer-upper. She began living on noodles and tap water, and putting all her sleazy income into the project that would one day become Kelly's Gym. She took out the largest possible mortgage to help finance the project.

But it wasn't enough. An additional two nights a week at The Naked Truth provided a little extra cash, but less energy for her dream. A year after the original investment, she was the proud owner of a small building, two used Lifecycles, giant segments of an unassembled mirror, and a case of mononucleosis.

It was right about then that the man in the New York Yankees baseball cap began hanging out at The Naked Truth. The first few nights he drank at the bar and chatted up her boss. The next few found him in a seat in the back row. He eventually made a go at the front row, and for the next week or so he dropped tens and twenties into a G-string that generally accommodated ones and fives. He appeared to have a thing for Kelly.

Sure enough, one night he waited around till closing and asked if she'd like to have a cup of coffee with him. Coffee (suspicion)? Coffee (reassurance). She was *this* close to saying "Not tonight, pal," but he was easy on the eyes, and she was so bored with her lack of social life that she said yes.

In a diner down the street, he moved quickly to the point. Been stripping for long? How was the money? She was quite a performer. She had a real gift.

And would she ever consider sharing it with him?

At first she thought he was talking about sex, and she almost threw her coffee right in his face. No, not sex, he said with a chuckle. More like a derivative of sex. He paused, looked her up and down, and asked her a question she'd remember until the day she died.

How would she like to make twenty-five thousand dollars for one night of work?

After spilling her coffee and apologizing for her clumsiness, she asked what type of work he had in mind. It sounded a lot like he was soliciting sex, and she didn't do that sort of thing for money. He smiled and whispered, no, he was soliciting a *performance*.

Performance? Performance! She should have said, "Thank you very much, but I don't like the sound of this," and walked away. But instead, money's sweet jingle played in her ears, and her dream regained its glimmer. She envisioned exercise benches, barbells, and a child-care center so that single moms could work out whenever they pleased. She imagined the look on her bastard father's face when he heard that the daughter he'd said would never amount to anything now owned her own business.

Actually, said the man in the Yankees cap, she'd have to put in more than one night's work. More like one night and one day. If she did her job well, twenty-five thousand dollars would be hers.

Yeah? Well she wanted more details first.

He looked at her awhile, then explained he was just a "recruiter." If she wanted more details she'd have to come with him.

He escorted her to a black BMW (why she trusted this man not to kidnap and rape her, she still didn't know; perhaps it was destiny), paused to whisper into a cell phone, and drove her to a waterfront office building in Old Port. He led her to the elevator, pushed a button for her, and sent her up to the top floor.

In the penthouse she found a single chair and a single coffee table, atop which sat a single speakerphone. She sat and waited, for what, she didn't know, but twenty-five grand kept her there.

Eventually, the speakerphone rang. She answered it— who else could it have been for?—and listened to a powerful, nameless voice detail a scenario she'd remember for the rest of her life.

The man was a Sigma Delta Phi alum—in fact, *the* alum whose mandate it was to ensure the purity of their beloved brotherhood.

And currently, there was a certain sophomore brother who *wasn't* pure.

A certain sophomore who needed to be eliminated from Sigma.

He didn't expect her to understand the reasoning. She certainly had no way of knowing how prestigious fraternities operated at prestigious colleges, because, let's face it, she was just a townie. Bottom line, there were certain college rules—the only rules that Sigma needed to abide by—

that kept him and his concerned brothers from banishing this sophomore in the normal manner. They couldn't just *fire* him. Therefore, they needed to be creative.

There was something at Simsbury called the Disciplinary Squad, which enforced its own view of the law. And this was a good thing, because with bitter minorities running the politically correct environment, the D-Squad would probably find a sophomore frat boy guilty of a crime he didn't commit, especially in the presence of a sobbing victim, and especially if the sophomore himself was convinced he was guilty.

That was the beauty of Simsbury's homemade brand of justice. The D-Squad was imperfect. The dean was a judge. Students were in charge of the questioning. Witnesses weren't always necessary. Basically, a case that would *never* hold up in court could definitely hold up in front of this D-Squad.

All that was necessary was a plaintiff.

Was she still listening?

She was beginning to seriously dislike this arrogant character, but twenty-five grand kept her listening.

Good. On the first Saturday in March, there'd be a special party at Sigma, one that would focus on getting the sophomore drunk enough so that he'd recall *almost* nothing the next day, but not so drunk that he wouldn't remember a few foggy elements. It would be a tricky task, handled by seniors, who knew a thing or two about booze, and who'd be in charge of adding a certain disorienting ingredient to each of the sophomore's drinks.

She had no idea what he was talking about. She should have walked away. Twenty-five grand kept her listening.

She'd wait, on this special Saturday, in the upstairs library of Sigma with two colleagues of choice, who'd play her "friends," and who'd each make a grand. At some point, they'd dance into the barroom. After a while, she'd move in on the sophomore. She'd "seduce" him, which wouldn't be hard, because he was a normal red-blooded guy and by now he'd be completely wasted. She'd coax him into the downstairs library and "plant the seeds" of rape in his mind. A few days later, in a controlled setting, she'd confront him.

She should have run. Twenty-five grand kept her listening.

But first she had to ask a question or two. Why? What did this sophomore do that was so bad?

The man didn't have to answer. It was really none of her business. But then he did answer, in a sly kind of way. For him, plotting seemed to be a turn-on.

On the surface, he explained, the sophomore fit the Sigma mold. On closer review, however, he clearly wasn't Sigma material, for he had a past that just couldn't be ignored.

The sophomore—Mark Jessy was his name—had a very bad family element, potentially more embarrassing—and more dangerous—than he'd previously let on.

What the alum meant by this, she didn't know, but with a bad family element herself, she should have been insulted. She should have told him to stick his condescension up his ass.

Twenty-five grand convinced her to participate in the scheme.

Everything went as planned. On the specific Saturday night, she found Mark drooling and barely standing, looking incredibly harmless. She led him to the down-

stairs libes and locked the door. She kissed him and whispered for him to feel her breast. When he didn't respond,
she took off her halter top. She'd done it before for
strangers, and for far less money. No big deal now. He
was trashed. He was useless. She ran his hands over her
body, stopping every now and then to push him away.
She played the game, and almost enjoyed it. Mark Jessy
represented Simsbury, and all the breaks in life she'd
never gotten. She dominated him, and it felt good.

She watched the look of drugged confusion come over
his face. She helped him fumble with her zipper, pulled
him in one last time, then screamed, punched him in the
chest, and shoved him. He stood there a moment, totally
gone, then toppled perfectly into her. Together, they hit
the couch. She screamed rape, flailed beneath him, and
planted some big, final seeds. She rolled him off her and
pulled down his pants. She ran out of the downstairs library, screaming partly for show, partly for the elation
that she'd just given a twenty-five-grand performance
that would keep the dream alive.

Twenty-five grand would be coming her way.

God, what a different person she was back then.

The hearing was easy—easier than expected. She
hadn't figured that Mark would beat himself up over
what he'd apparently done. And the politically correct
mood helped clear any potential hurdles.

Her only mistake, other than agreeing to set up a complete stranger in the first place, was not using her real
name. Fearing word of her "performance" would get
around town, she'd asked if she could use a different
name. "Whatever" was the answer. So she used the name
of a cousin from Caribou who'd died as an infant.

Oh, how she wished she'd used her own name.

More on that later.

Three days after the hearing, she received a twenty-five-thousand-dollar wire transfer from some bank in Massachusetts. She instantly forgot her guilt. She ignored her mortgage. It would be there for the next thirty years. She sank three-quarters of the money into decent equipment and a billboard that screamed "Kelly's Gym." She spent the rest on a small advertising campaign.

One that featured spots on the local cable channel.

The commercial aired six months after the D-Squad hearing. She and her friends watched the dinky little clip and toasted the former "exotic dancer" who was now a businesswoman—hell, who was now damn near a television celebrity. The ad aired twice a week ("I'm Kelly Devereaux, and this is my gym"). Within two weeks, business—which had been fair, at best, since the opening in August—began to really pick up. She quit her job at The Naked Truth and began living happily ever after.

She tried not to think about Mark too often.

One night, about fifteen minutes before closing time, Mr. Yankees Cap, the "recruiter," paid an unexpected visit to Kelly's Gym. Could he see her in private? Perhaps outside? Sure. What harm could come from that? She had things under control. She was a woman now. She could take care of herself.

Once outside, he got right to the point. She should *strongly* consider canceling the ad campaign. She should *strongly* consider changing the name of her gym.

Why?

Because Sigma had paid twenty-five grand to own a portion of her identity. And the portion they'd purchased was named Angela McSheffrey, not Kelly Dev-ereaux, and what the hell was going to happen, for example, when that kid turned on the TV and discovered that one part of his rape case wasn't exactly true and, in that case, what else wasn't?

That was Sigma's problem, not hers, she said. They were the ones who came up with the plan. She didn't owe them anything. She was Kelly Devereaux, and this was her goddamn gym. She wasn't going to change shit.

The recruiter nodded, a sick little gleam in his eye. Then he turned, got back in his black BMW, and drove away.

Three days later, she received a letter in the mail, along with a check. Casco Local Access TV had been purchased, and the new owner was "revamping" the advertising scheme. Unfortunately, they wouldn't be airing her commercial anymore. Enclosed was payment for services not rendered.

One week after that, she received another letter. This one was bigger. This one had no check enclosed, but rather consisted of a bank notice stating that Georgeville Central Savings and Loan was hereby calling in her note. Her mortgage on the gym was due. Right now.

She freaked and called the bank. What the hell was going on? Was this some sort of mistake? No, this was no mistake. The bank was under new ownership, and all credit agreements had been reviewed in the process. She hadn't properly complied with her covenants. If she couldn't come up with the entire principal within thirty days, property would revert to the bank. Sorry, Ms. Devereaux, but rules are rules.

After hanging up, she cried for an hour in the women's

locker room. Why was this happening? How could they
do this to her? And on and on.

By closing time, she had some answers. The *why* and
the *how* didn't matter. It was the *they* who mattered. *They*
were the new owners of Casco Local Access TV. *They*
were the new owners of Georgeville Central Savings and
Loan. *They* were soon to be the owners of Kelly's Gym.

They were the owners of Kelly herself.

They were the cold, nasty brothers of Sigma Delta Phi.

She locked up and headed for home. She muttered as
she walked. She told herself not to give up and thought of
ways she could come up with the principal in thirty days.

She didn't notice the van following her until it was too
late.

Four men—*young* men, she could tell by their builds
and the way they moved—jumped out of the van wearing
black ski masks and grabbed her before she could scream,
before she could know *what* to scream. They blindfolded
her. They threw her in the back of the van, and piled in beside her. They shouted at her. How could she be so stupid?
How could she broadcast her real identity all over town?
How could she defy the brothers of Sigma Delta Phi?

The undergrad brothers of Sigma Delta Phi drove her
to the ocean and stripped her naked.

Then they surrounded her and sang a rhyme:

You'd be foolish to fuck with brothers devout.
Try it and see what rape's really about.

When they were done, they wrapped her in toilet paper.
Then they drove her back to Georgeville and dumped her
in the street.

She crept to her apartment and cried for three days.

But she never called the police and never even considered pressing charges. She merely stayed in her apartment for the next eight weeks. By mid-November, she'd lost the gym to the bank. By mid-December, she'd gained twenty pounds.

Finally, on Christmas Eve, she slit her wrists.

Silence returned to the interior of the red Nissan.

And, gradually, Mark returned as well. During the story, he'd moved from shock to outrage to total fury at a world that made no sense at times. Once, as she was detailing their scripted encounter, he'd checked his reflection in the frosty windshield, just to make sure he was *here*, actually *hearing* this. But mostly, he'd lost himself in her story, as if his role as audience was inconsequential, as if he existed only as a fictional character in the most ridiculous yarn ever spun.

Now, fully materialized, he sat very still in his seat, groping desperately for the right thing to say. "What . . ." he croaked, then trailed off.

She blew away some stray bangs. "Whatever question you're trying to ask, I'm sure I don't have a logical answer for you." She sighed, then shrugged. "But if you're looking to make some simple sense out of it, try this. They researched our weaknesses, then played them against us, with absolutely no fear we'd get even." She turned to Mark again. "They stop at nothing, and nothing can stop them."

She eased the car toward the side of the road. "Not in this little shithole, anyway."

The red Nissan crackled briefly on ice, then came to an uneven stop.

Completely disoriented, Mark looked up, and with his sleeve wiped the winter steam from the inside of the passenger window.

They were right outside his apartment.

He turned to Kelly, "How . . . ?"

She almost managed a smile, but reeled it in with a scowl that suggested he was wasting her time with questions that had nothing to do with the cold, hard facts. "I got pretty brave one night, and decided, *Why write him a letter when I can tell it to his face.*" She paused, reflecting on it. "It's weird, but I guess I thought the two of us had something in common. You know—we both got fucked by the same dicks."

She flipped her hair, rubbed her nose, and when she spoke again all traces of sentimentality had vanished. "So, anyway, in December I stole a student directory and found out where you lived. I drove out here and parked right over there"—she pointed—"next to the lacrosse field. And I'd just gotten up the courage to do the deed when a pretty blonde pulled up in a Jeep. I watched her go in the front door, and a minute later I watched you both come out the back door. I watched you guys walk that puppy of yours on the field. I even watched you guys kiss." She reached out and ran her finger across the dash, as if wiping a slate clean. "It's funny . . . I felt relieved when I saw that, and I'm still not sure why. Maybe because your girlfriend's being there gave me an excuse not to go through with it." She turned to him. "Or maybe because I knew you were over it."

Mark looked out the window into the night. "I don't feel so *over* it now."

"You will. In time you'll forget—"

He turned to her suddenly and grabbed her wrist. "When? *When?*" He wanted to laugh and cry and scream and punch things. "Exactly how long will it take to forget that my best friends drugged me and convinced me I was a rapist? And how long will it take to accept that something I'd thought was a *secret,* my family history, was actually common knowledge? What's the recovery time for something like that?"

She stared at him, then averted her gaze. "Look," she said finally, "for over a year now I've feared the thought of you. You're basically the reason I'm moving to California in a couple weeks. I was afraid the Sigmas would find me walking down a public street or something, and *rape* me for threatening their master plan. I was even afraid you'd figure things out on your own and come find me yourself.

"And sure enough, that's just what happened. When I saw you in the bathroom tonight, like some walking nightmare, I couldn't . . . fucking . . . believe it. But then, while Gino and those two guys were harassing you, I thought of how many letter drafts I'd written you and remembered my attempt to see you in person. I wanted you to know." She turned to him. "I *wanted* you to know."

She returned her attention to the gas pedal. "Besides, I'll be in Cally soon, three thousand miles west. The only reason Sigma would have for tracking me down is revenge, and I just don't think they're into that.

"We had a score to settle, Mark. I told you the truth because I felt I owed it to you. As soon as you get out of this car, I'm gone from your life, and you're gone from mine."

Her posture straightened suddenly, and her expression brightened. "It's over, Mark. It's all over."

He stared at her for a long moment, as this last comment registered and took on a voice of its own. *It's over, Mark. It's all over. Your mother's dead and buried, and your father's . . . well, gone . . . and everybody knows how and why and so it's not a secret anymore, and that could be a good thing. You never tried to rape this girl, and that's a good thing too. You have no real friends here, but you've got Shawn, Casey, and lacrosse. You've got so much to live for. Don't look back.*

It's over, Mark.

It's all over.

He shook his head slowly. "Only for you, Kelly. I still have some scores to settle." He popped the passenger door ajar, exited the Nissan, and walked around to the driver's side.

She gazed up at him, her expression spent and weary. "I wish there were more I could . . ." Words failed her.

"No, you've done enough. Unless, of course, you can provide me with the names and addresses of every Sigma alum, so I can go bomb their houses."

She shook her head, his sarcasm lost on her. "The only name I heard was yours . . . unless you want to call T-Bone a name."

Mark shook his head and stared at the trees that sheltered his apartment. Then, struck by something that came and went before he could pin it down, he turned quickly back to her. "What? What did you just say?"

She nodded. "Yeah. On the night you didn't rape me, that *recruiter* waited with me and my friends in the upstairs library until we were sent for. He made a call on his cell phone, though, checked in with a guy he called T-Bone." She looked up at him. "That name mean anything to you?"

Mark consulted the trees again, and when he couldn't recapture the fleeting peg, shook his head. "Not yet." He looked at her again. "T-Bone?"

"T-Bone."

Mark nodded resolutely, committing the nickname or whatever to memory, then turned away from the car. However, a few steps toward the rest of his college career, and all the blind, instinctive focus he knew would power it, he took a deep breath and pivoted on the toe of one battered boot.

"Hey," he said, catching Kelly before she closed the window. "What are you gonna do in California?"

She smiled. "Gonna work with troubled kids in a trailer park."

He took it in, nodded at the rightness of it, and said, "Good-bye, Kelly Devereaux. Good luck in California."

"Good-bye, Mark Jessy. Good luck in Georgeville."

Mark watched the Nissan pull away from the side of the road, headed for California sunshine.

Then he turned and headed for darkness.

11:22 P.M.

The Brotherhood Room was nearly empty, but sprinkled with gore. While Mu wiped the fresh spots of blood off the hardwood and surrounding antiques, Gamma, Kappa, and Beta sat huddled at the table.

"You guys went overboard," Beta said, still visibly shaken by the violence he'd just witnessed. "You can't keep beating on them like that. They're going to rebel."

"Bullshit," said Gamma, his eyes icy. "The pledges get beat on every year. That's what being a Sigma pledge is all about. And *that's* why we have the strongest fraternity in the whole damn country."

Beta shook his head. "I've never seen beatings like this. Pledging *used* to be all about head games and gut checks. Rhymes and mental tests. *Occasionally* we'd get physical, but this is out of hand."

"This year's different," said Kappa. "We need to be stronger than ever. We've got to beat Sigma pride into the pledges. Don't you ever listen to a word Alpha says?"

"To be honest, I try not to."

"Well maybe you should start trying," said Gamma. "Alpha's a winner."

"He's ruthless."

"He's a god."

"They're just eighteen-year-old kids, Gamma! And one of their friends just died."

"Chad Ewing was no one's friend. I'm sorry he's dead, but he was a wimp. A total faggot, and the truth was, he just couldn't handle being a Sigma. Survival of the fittest, man. Weed out the sick and weak."

Beta stared at Gamma. "Are you serious?"

"Dead serious. Watch the Discovery Channel some time. Lions feed on the smallest, sickest zebras. That's the way the world works. And I don't know about you, man, but I'm not going to sit around and hope that Mark will pull through for us. Do you honestly believe he alone can prevent this thing from going to trial? His girlfriend's on the squad. His *girlfriend*! The chick who fucks him and gives him blow jobs, and she hates our guts. He'll do anything she tells him to do, as long as it keeps him in the good graces of her pussy."

"C'mon, Gamma, give him a little more credit. He loves this place, too. He loves this fraternity. He's one of us."

Gamma shook his head. "Look around the room. Do you see him here?"

"That's not what—"

"Then he's not one of us. And you know what? I don't give a shit, because Mark Jessy's weak."

"Then you don't know him like I know him. He's a solid guy, and he doesn't take crap from Shawn—"

"I don't care. He used to be a brother, and now he's not, and we're strong enough to control this investigation by ourselves. We don't need anyone but each other, and that's what the pledges need to be taught. And that's what we're teaching them."

"We're teaching them how to bleed."

"No. We're teaching them how to bleed *our colors*."

CHAPTER THIRTY-FIVE

The 200th Year
Thursday, March 5

11:59 P.M.

A single flickering candle lit the darkened bedroom, its simmering strobe undulating yellow and darker across the undecorated bedroom wall against which Mark sat. His left hand caressed the beads. His right hand held the time-curled photo of his parents, which he stared at with the numb gaze of a man rudely awakened.

He put the photo down, closed his eyes, and rested his head against the wall. He watched, through shut eyelids, the wavering shades of the candle's light, until a cold draft snuffed its dance.

Sensing the darkness, he opened his eyes.

He stood.

He walked slowly from his room, oblivious to the blackness. He heard a light jingling of dog tags as Casey slithered from her laundry pile.

He opened the back door and stepped outside.

He began to walk.

Snow crunched, then gave way. Pine needles brushed,

then fell aside. Reaching the clearing, he stopped and gazed around the expanse of the athletic fields. A full, frigid moon shone down, promising to light the way, inviting him to put his memory through its horseless paces.

He began to walk again.

And as he walked, the past washed over him like a series of waves cast from offshore storms. This time, however, he hid behind no breakwater and let it roar uninhibited.

It would never drown him again.

He saw three men dressed in black robes and hoods. He heard their voices, rhyming verses that initiated him and twelve fellow pledges into the bonds of Sigma Delta Phi brotherhood.

And above these voices, he heard a new, faceless voice say that Mark Jessy just wasn't Sigma material and had to go.

He quickened his forward pace, while his memory backpedaled.

He heard Elliot Segal's freshman voice ask where his parents were.

He then heard his own voice answer that both were dead.

He walked faster, on the verge of running, his breath coming in short, cloudy bursts.

He saw new, strange faces in a new, strange town, and the confining bars of a jungle gym, holding him prisoner to the taunts of nine-year-old classmates.

"Where'd you get those clothes, kid . . . ?"

"Jessy's a girls' name . . . !"

"Hey! Ain't you a real live Indian? Does your daddy scalp people? Show us your tomahawk . . ."

He felt his crazed fists pound many faces in succession, until he was the only one standing, and those class-mates on the ground knew that Mark Jessy's parents just weren't to be mentioned.

He began to jog.

He saw the empty space where his dad had been, now filled with uniformed law men on the search, and defining the line that separated heroes from outlaws.

He saw a coffin.

On the lid, closed for good reason, he saw a picture of his mom.

He ran faster, challenging his past to either slap his face or keep the pace.

He saw the sun shine down on uniforms of a far more peaceful nature. He felt the sacred meadow grass tickle his primitively clad legs. He heard the tribal songs ring out across a lilied land.

And then he saw, felt, and heard chaos—total chaos—that began with FBI thunder and ended with his mother's life gushing away.

He sprinted, no longer aware of the bellowing elements. Tears blinded him, but still he ran, almost daring something to stop his progress, almost hoping to crash blindly into a tree or a goalpost, just to see if there was something that could hurt him worse than his past.

He lengthened his stride, quickened his fist pumps, and with a final string of one-legged leaps to the center of the lacrosse field, he stopped suddenly.

He turned in a circle, panting at and scorning a world that made no sense, and never really had. He looked up at the sky, at the moon and the darkness, and wondered if anyone up there was watching or listening.

If there was, they'd see and hear him now.

He arched his back, threw back his head, and screamed, like a nine-year-old child, for everything that had ever happened.

He screamed again and again, until finally his voice failed him.

He fell to his knees and sobbed.

BOOK III

The Game

CHAPTER THIRTY-SIX

*The 200th Year
Friday, March 6*

5:59 A.M.

The day dawned clear and cold.

Fewer than three hundred students were awake. Of these, more than two hundred were actively trying to get back to sleep. The rest were fully occupied.

Thirty were jogging or lifting, for spring break was right around the corner and bathing suits had to do more than just fit. Another fifteen were studying, for merely *good* grades weren't good enough. Ten were still drinking from the night before, for it was never too late for one more. Seven were just beginning to drink, for it was never too early to start the weekend. Six were having sex, for the time was always right and they could always sleep during class.

Two were seeing first light for very dark reasons. They sat alone, at opposite ends of the campus, at opposite ends of a four-year liberal arts education.

One hadn't slept in eleven days.

The other had been asleep for two years, and perhaps thirteen.

Both were wide awake.

9:04 A.M.

The dean paraded into the room, looked around with discerning eyes, then, exasperated, rolled them back inside his head. "All right, where's Mark?"

"I don't know," Shawn replied. "He never showed up at the meeting last night."

The dean sat with a disgusted sigh. "Well, we can't wait for him to sleep off last night's behavior. We might as well get started." He pushed his chair back and crossed his legs. "What have we all decided?"

Schwitters glanced at Shawn for approval, and when she nodded, he cleared his throat. "Dean, we have no evidence that Sigma was directly responsible for Chad Ewing's death. We've decided it makes sense to drop the case."

The dean looked warily at Shawn. "Are you in accordance?"

Shawn nodded.

"We feel," continued Schwitters, "that it might be wise for Sigma to host some sort of seminar that speaks to the dangers of excessive alcohol consumption. However—"

The door to the conference room banged open, and in stalked Mark Jessy, wild-eyed, skew-haired, and jacketless.

"Mark," said the dean with a smug grin. "Just roll in from the pub?"

Schwitters chuckled dutifully.

Mark looked at Shawn. "What did you tell him?"

"About what?"

"What did you decide about this case?"

"Ha!" said Schwitters. "What do you care—"

"Shut up, Simon. Shawn, what did you guys decide?"

Shawn hesitated for a moment. "We . . . we're dropping it."

"No."

"Excuse me?"

"We're going after them."

There was a moment of stunned silence.

"Mark," Shawn said finally, "we talked about it last night. You weren't even *there*. We have no case—"

"I'm here now, and we've got a case."

"How amusing," said the dean. "Please, grant us the basis for this decision."

"I've learned some things."

"Oh, you have, have you?"

"Yes."

"And what have you learned?"

"I've received two anonymous letters in the mail this week. Both indicated some sort of unusual activity at Sigma the night before Chad fell."

"Right. Another anonymous source. *Very* rich."

"That's right, another anonymous source. And based on what I know about Sigma, which is quite a bit, I have every reason to believe that this anonymous source is telling the truth."

The dean snorted. "This is getting quite mysterious. All these secret informants running around, each with a different, grandiose spin on Humpty Dumpty's drunken fall."

"That's not funny."

The dean's eyes narrowed. "It wasn't meant to be. It

was meant to make a mockery of you and your so-called anonymous source."

Mark smiled invitingly. "You know what I think?"

"I fear what you think, Mark."

"I think you're afraid I might be on to something. Then *I'll* have discovered something *you* missed, and Humpty Dumpty's yolk will end up all over your face—"

"You remember who you're talking to!"

"And *you* remember who *you're* talking to." Mark turned to the others. "Whether anybody here likes it or not, I'm a member of this squad. It doesn't matter *how*, and it doesn't matter *why*. The point is, I *am*, and my opinion deserves just as much consideration as anyone else's." He started for the door, then stopped, turned, and pointed at the dean. "I think we've got a case, and I'm going to prove it."

He stormed out, leaving three mouths gaping in his wake.

11:01 A.M.

Mark quickly failed a pop quiz, then hurried back to his apartment. The phone was ringing as he walked in the door.

It was Dean Templeton's secretary. "He needs to see you right away," she said.

11:22 A.M.

"Mark," began the dean, his voice syrupy. "Things got out of hand earlier. I want to apologize."

Mark nodded coolly.

The dean stood and began to pace. "But I think there's something you don't understand, and I'd like to clarify it.

As dean of Simsbury, it behooves me to protect the student body. I'm sort of like a father."

"I already have one of those—"

"Shush," snipped the dean, then continued to pace. "But . . . I'm like a father with *many* kids, and sometimes I have to choose sides. It's difficult, but it must be done. Understand?"

Mark crossed his arms, leaned back in his chair, and nodded slightly.

"Good. Because maybe it'll help you to understand what I'm about to say."

He stopped pacing and, leaning forward, placed both his hands precisely on the table. "I'm forbidding any further investigation of the Chad Ewing case."

Mark shook his head. "You can't."

"I can. And I'm doing it."

"That's bullshit—"

"I need only remind you of the power I wielded in *your* case. I stepped in and overruled then, and I'm doing it again."

"Why?"

"Because I'm D-Squad advisor, and this whole thing has become absurd."

Mark was tempted to comment that it was no more absurd than *his* case, but thought better of it. He knew the dean would never believe a story like the one Kelly Devereaux had told.

"You're the only one who wants to keep pursuing the case," continued the dean. "And I think that's because you're drunk or something."

"I'm not drunk."

"Then you're just plain stupid. I'm informing the

Board that the majority of the D-Squad feels the matter should be dropped. The case is closed."

"Then *you're* stupid."

"Excuse me?"

Mark leaned forward. "Dean Templeton, for two years you've pretty much shown me no respect. You think I'm a lazy drunk. You think I'm a dumb jock. Now, I admit I sort of play up these stereotypes. But right now I'm *telling* you I want to prosecute this case more than I've ever wanted anything in my life. True, I know *nothing* about the law, and *nothing* about trial procedure. But I know Sigma as well as anyone, and I think there's a good chance they're directly responsible for this death. I think I can prove them guilty."

The dean bit his lip, then sat down in his chair and looked at Mark thoughtfully. "I'm surprised at you," he said. "I thought the Sigmas were your friends. Why would you want to do this to them?"

"Things aren't always the way they seem."

"Is Shawn putting you up to this? Did she outline that impressive little speech you just gave?"

"She has nothing to do with it. You heard her. She doesn't want to continue the investigation."

"That makes two of us," said the dean. "Three, if you count Simon, without whom, by the way, you'd have no chance of winning. He knows the law better than you know lacrosse."

"Don't underestimate me."

The dean stood again. "There's no threat of that. You're out of your depth."

"Well," Mark said, standing to leave. "I guess we'll

just have to see about *that*, won't we? If you'll excuse me, I've got lots of work—"

"Before you go, Mark, there's something I want to mention." The dean motioned to the empty chair. "You may want to sit down again to hear this."

Mark looked at the dean carefully, then sat.

The dean grabbed a folder from his desk and held it over his head like a flag. "See this?"

"What is it?"

"It's your personnel file and transcript." The dean opened the file and began to read. "It says here you were convicted of sexual assault with intent to rape. It says here you confessed to the act and accepted all detailed punishments." The dean waved the file. "Remember this?"

"You said that wouldn't go on my record."

"It won't. As long as you complete your four years within the guidelines of your sentence. One of the stipulations is that you serve on the D-Squad for your remaining semesters at Simsbury."

"What do you think I'm doing?"

The dean closed his eyes and shook his head. "If you get kicked off the squad for unethical behavior, you'll be unable to fulfill these requirements." The dean leaned forward and smiled. "That means the charge stays on your transcript. It also means you won't graduate. Understand?"

"No."

The dean smiled again. "Let me put it in terms simple enough for a meathead jock like yourself. The D-Squad drops the case against Sigma, I drop the charges from your transcript. You proceed with the case, and I boot you off the squad for unethical behavior."

"You can't do that."

"Oh, believe me, I *can*."

"That's blackmail."

"It's also your ticket out of here. Take it or leave it."

Mark fought to control his anger. "And what sort of 'unethical behavior' would I be charged with?"

The dean scratched his head, then snapped his fingers. "I know! You used to be a Sigma, right? I may discover that you're somehow interfering with the D-Squad investigation of Sigma. I think you'd agree that's unethical in anyone's book."

"But it wouldn't be true."

"It would be your word against mine. I'm the dean. You're a student with a history of criminal behavior. Whom do you think everyone would believe?"

Mark stared at the dean a moment. "I wonder," he said, as he stood and grabbed his jacket, "if the rest of the campus knows what a complete asshole you are."

The dean approached him slowly. "I run this college, Mark, and I run it well, and if running it well means squashing a few insignificant bugs like you, then so be it."

"You manipulate people."

"No, Mark. I don't manipulate people. I use them. And when I'm done, I ruin them."

"Good for you, Dean. Your mother must be so proud."

"Unfortunately, my mother passed away several years ago. However, *she* died of natural causes. She wasn't killed while—"

Instinctively, Mark grabbed the dean by the collar,

nearly lifting the smaller man off the ground. "Don't fin-ish that sentence," he hissed.

The dean wormed out of his grasp. "It's over," he sput-tered, then smoothed his clothing and readjusted his glasses. "You just drop the case like a good boy, throw your little lacrosse ball around for the rest of the semes-ter, and maybe you won't get hurt. Otherwise, I'll be forced to put a huge damper on the rest of your life. You're going to have enough trouble getting a job *with* a diploma. Without one, dear boy, you'll be collecting cans like your uncle."

"You *bastard.*"

"Get lost, Jessy. You bore me."

Mark stared at the dean for a moment, then turned and walked slowly out of the office.

12:02 P.M.

The two Sigma pledges made their way out of the Stewart Building. Class was finally over, so now they could talk about more important things, like who was banging whom, how much they'd bench-pressed the day before, and the point spread for that night's Duke–North Carolina basketball game.

They walked slowly, casting intimidating glances at pledges from other fraternities. They knew that none of their bad-intentioned gazes would be returned, for every-one knew that they represented something scary.

They were invincible.

They decided to check mail.

Fifty yards from the Student Center, however, they both stopped dead in their tracks. For standing in front of the Student Center, looming even larger and more arro-

gant than the two pledges, were brothers Kappa, Gamma,
Delta, and Epsilon.

One pledge subconsciously fingered his bruised eye
and suddenly remembered that he'd just checked mail the
day before. The other looked at his feet and recalled
doing the same, and certainly there'd be nothing new in
their boxes today.

They turned and swaggered the other way.

CHAPTER THIRTY-SEVEN

*The 200th Year
Friday, March 6*

12:42 P.M.

The typical sights and sounds defined the independent dining hall on this late winter day.

Students shuffled forward in a slow-moving line, propelled by midterm stress and missed breakfasts. They piled their plates high with nutrition, then scattered to regular tables and saved seats, where they passed judgment on the world.

Four women spoke in righteous tones about that afternoon's planned date-rape demonstration. Three others concluded that their fourth roommate was a slut. Two isolated black men rehashed the previous day's diversity rally. One southern redneck thanked God he wasn't black.

A senior with a receding hairline chastised his sophomore girlfriend because she'd remembered to buy shampoo for *herself,* but had forgotten to buy Rogaine for *him.* A junior beauty with a stellar GPA cursed her miserable loneliness and wondered if tonight would be the night she found love. A sophomore misfit with a sea urchin hairdo and a pierced nose fed bean sprouts to his pet lizard and hoped that everyone noticed how unique and different he was. A freshman nobody sat in freshman nowhere-land, and dreamed of this time next year, when he'd be a Sigma Delta Phi pledge.

Hey dudes and good moods, and Bud is the best. What's ups and paper cups, and winter's the worst. Hiking boots, peace movements, backpacks, wool socks. Politics, term papers, dancing, deep talks.

College.

And in the middle of it all sat Mark Jessy, who right now lacked eyes and ears for the trivial clamor that surrounded him. As a procession of images from the past twenty-four hours played across his mind, he let the rage well up in his gut and claw its way toward his heart. He was feeling it clench his fists, invade his thoughts, and separate that which could be helped from that which could do the helping.

It *was* a game. Different, but the same. A game where pads couldn't protect, and the ball squirted amorphous and slippery. A game where the boundaries meandered to sinister places, and teammates couldn't be trusted. A game where the enemy, to quote a local liar, stopped at nothing and couldn't be stopped.

But still, it was a game.

A game far from over.

A game worth winning.

He stood, dropped his napkin like a discarded white flag, and marched from the cafeteria.

And outside, he began to run, like a player with a host of huge scores to settle, on behalf of many.

Like the player he was.

12:57 P.M.

The Freshman finished what little lunch he could stomach, then crept to the spot on the floor where Chad had fallen. He closed his eyes briefly, but long enough for his senses to revisit a paralyzing place.

He saw the blood and the skin and the white bones. He heard the sick commands and the silence. He smelled the suffocating odor of air fresheners and floor cleaner. He tasted the awful burn of something bad and felt the spinning presence of something more.

He opened his eyes, and as ruinous rhymes echoed through his lucky skull, he stared down once more at the smooth varnish.

That could've been me, he thought, as he turned to flee the house. *Oh my God, that could've been me.*

1:25 P.M.

From her still stance on the Student Center steps, Shawn watched the legs she loved move with a beautiful rhythm over the mounds of snow that forced others to walk circuitous routes. Mark seemed to be literally flying; he looked like a low-soaring, black-vested bird.

Except birds, though they often hovered aimlessly, never seemed to fly just for the sake of flying.

And birds didn't trouble her so.

1:30 P.M.

Feeling enormously proud of his easy handling of Mark Jessy, and the cash he'd earned in the process, Templeton whimsically picked up the phone and booked a vacation for two in Jamaica. Hell, spring break was coming, and who said fun in the sun was for students only?

Having solidified a travel itinerary, he hung up the phone, closed his eyes, and smiled, because he was willing to bet Linda Regis looked almost as good in a bikini as she did naked.

And because he was clearly master of the game.

6:00 P.M.

Inside the palatial Sigma House, the undergrad brothers sat down to their traditional Friday-night feast of pizza and beer, prepared by the new chef, paid for by the alumni, served by the loyal pledges.

Meanwhile, the alumni brothers of Sigma began to descend from their nationwide corporate kingdoms to the cash-bought chariots that whisked them nightly to their private palaces.

Templeton wasn't the game's only master.

CHAPTER THIRTY-EIGHT

*The 200th Year
Friday, March 6*

8:10 P.M.

The chartered bus idled noisily, its seats filled with seventeen varsity skiers and one impatient coach. Ordinarily, the coach would have ordered the driver to step on it, for the New England Championships were the next day, and his racers needed to get to Killington. The eighteenth skier was ten minutes late; it would be *her* fault, a lesson-learning experience, if she missed the bus.

But the eighteenth skier was Shawn Jakes, team captain and three-time defending New England Champion. They could wait another couple of minutes. Besides, she was right outside the bus, her speedy, fearless body hunched within the frosted frame of a campus phone booth.

Where are you, Mark? she was thinking, as the connection rang into silence. *And what could you possibly be thinking and doing?*

After a good minute of unanswered rings, she slowly hung up the phone. She stared bit-lip and briefly at the ground, then turned and boarded the bus.

8:44 P.M.

Had an outsider basked in the psychotic leisure of Friday night at Simsbury College, he might have concluded that the institution had no need for the majority of its property. The bulk of students screamed and whistled in the Cage, as they cheered the top-seeded women's basketball team in its first-round regional tournament game. Those who saw sports as a fascist endeavor sat huddled around bongs and pot brownies in the basements of Alpha Lambda and Phi Omega. The rest burrowed deep in the recesses of lounge sofas and lovers' arms, their sudden, infrequent scampers from dorm to dorm the only kinetic display of outdoor life. The library was as lonely as it would ever be. The classroom buildings were dark and ghostly. The walkways were snow-swept and trackless. The quad was virtually empty.

Mark steered a course that kept him somewhere between the Cage and the center of campus. His pace was troubled, his direction erratic. The muffled sounds of hoop worship emanating from the Cage told him the rest of the school was caught up in passionate loyalty. The silence of the academic region of campus told him it was Friday, and time for fun. Loyalty and fun. Fun and loyalty. Neither word meant a thing to him anymore.

Justice. Now *there* was a word. Blackmail. There was *another* word. Those two words were the reason Mark was out and about tonight, searching for the way to achieve the first while avoiding the second. There *had* to be a way. Somewhere within the ivied boundaries of Simsbury College was a solution by which Mark could try his former best friends for murder without invoking the blackmailing wrath of the dean.

For no particular reason, he veered around the crusty lawn of the Student Center and headed for the entrance. Maybe he'd grab a slice of pizza. Maybe he'd check mail. Maybe he'd shoot some solitary pool and just *think*.

Predictably, the Student Center was nearly empty; the Board of Directors had yet to bottle a social alternative more fun than frat parties. Mark shuffled down the stairs toward the mailroom, thinking that perhaps he'd fetch his new *Sports Illustrated* and take it home to read beneath the warmth of Casey and covers. Perhaps it was time to put justice to bed for the night.

The mailroom was deserted, which made sense. Only geeks or sociopaths checked mail on Friday nights, and apparently both breeds were out developing physics theorems or assembling bombs. As he fumbled twice with the combination on his box, he wondered which group he belonged to, and whether bombs were really that difficult to make.

His box contained two letters and his *Sports Illustrated*. He rolled up the magazine, shoved it in his back pocket, and focused on the letters. The first one, forwarded to him by way of Kiko's nearly illegible scrawl, was from Vaughan, captain of *De-baitable Babe*. Would Mark be working for him again this summer? Mark hadn't even thought that far ahead, and right now summertime seemed to be years away. He put the letter in his other back pocket and made a mental note to call Vaughan when his life calmed down.

He opened the second letter.

It was a St. Patrick's Day card. On the cover, a goofy-looking leprechaun held a beer in one hand, a horseshoe in the other. Mark smiled, slightly touched. It wasn't like Shawn to send cutesy cards like this.

He opened the card.

"It was Brother Beam."

Son of a bitch! He jerked upright and scanned the nearby game room and connecting hallway. The only other person in the area was a headphoned janitor who was too busy sweeping the remnants of a litter-filled week into an industrial-sized dustpan to even notice Mark's presence. Other than that, the entire vicinity was desolate.

Mark read the card again, then stuffed it in his back pocket with the other letter.

He was turning to leave when he saw him.

He was hidden behind the hinged glass of a partially closed phone booth, the side of his face stuck to a hand-held phone receiver, his wide, watchful eyes locked on Mark.

It was the eyes that gave him away.

Hopeful eyes.

Terrified eyes.

The eyes of a freshman who'd sent three anonymous greeting cards to a senior he didn't even know.

For a brief instant Mark looked right into those eyes.

And then the Freshman dropped the phone and took off.

Mark stood frozen for a second, then scrambled after him, nearly falling as he rounded the turn that led to the stairway. By the time he'd recovered, he could hear the Freshman's sneakers squeaking up the second small flight of steps. Knowing he had some catching up to do,

Mark put his head down and powered his way up the stairs.

By the time he'd plowed his way out the side exit, the Freshman was nowhere in sight. Mark jogged out from the shelter of the building, where he could better survey his surroundings.

And then he saw him again. The Freshman was running across the quad, a dark snow shrew scuttling across acres of white, moving not fast enough toward the freshman dorms.

Mark tore after him.

He was seventy-five yards behind, but gaining with each step; if he was nothing else he was fast, especially when chasing someone. Within seconds he'd cut the deficit in half.

Hearing Mark's footsteps, the Freshman looked back over his shoulder and panicked. Apparently deciding he couldn't make it to his dorm, he foolishly angled back toward the center of the quad. What he thought this would achieve, Mark didn't know. What Mark *did* know was that he was captain of the lacrosse team and a returning All-American, and he was going to catch the little bastard.

He executed a pursuit curve and within seconds was on top of his prey.

He dove for the barely moving legs and wrapped his arms around the buckling knees. The two went down hard, Mark's forward momentum causing them to roll over and over in the snow.

It was Mark who made the next mistake, however. Thinking he'd subdued the Freshman, he relinquished his grasp in order to stand. He was looking into the sky, breathing hard, when the Freshman rolled onto his back and kicked him squarely in the groin.

The worst of pains ripped through Mark, and he crumpled uselessly to the ground. As he moaned and gasped, he was vaguely aware of the Freshman fleeing on thankful feet.

Mark lay very still in the snow, groaning softly.

It was a full ten minutes before he felt well enough to stand, and a good twenty-minute limp back to his apartment. But during the slow stagger, as the pain in his midsection joined with the deeper pain in his betrayed heart, he found a glimmer of fighting hope; somewhere out there, perhaps huddled sweaty and snow-covered behind a locked door, was a freshman letter writer who knew of threesomes and blindfolds and Brother Beam, and who knew exactly what had happened to Chad Ewing.

A witness.

Mark had seen him.

He had felt him.

He would find him.

CHAPTER THIRTY-NINE

The 200th Year
Saturday, March 7

The weekend began with the tranquillity of predictable college order. The sun rose bright but weak, casting shadows then gradually retracting them. New ice clung pure and polished, adding depth and sparkle to an already breathtaking setting. Existing snow lay smoothed by the wind and night. Birds awoke and sang spring to each other. For a good two hours after sunup, Simsbury College sat undisturbed and glorious, while those whose parents paid for such glory slept.

In time, tummies and term papers pulled students from their hiding places, in search of nourishment and quotable sources. Nylon sweats swished and insulated. Baseball caps beat down bed-heads. Steaming coffee mugs obscured the lower halves of faces, while logoed visors kept eyes well-protected from the glare of day. The Future of America moved without a sense of urgency.

It was Saturday. The day yawned before them.

By noon, the gym tortured a few hearty souls, and the aerobics center boomed bass and screeched the squeak of sneakers and female instruction. The game room played host to a few grudge matches on the pool table. The snow slushed, dented and well worn. The ice, though pretty, had been salted and scraped away.

And so the day progressed, a perfect synopsis of life at a small liberal arts college in New England. Everything seemed to be in place.

Except at the library reference desk, where one of the freshmen face-books was reported missing.

1:15 P.M.

The Freshman finally gave up on sleep and rose from his bed. He stumbled into the living room of his shared triple and scratched his head as he looked around. The wet clothes from his previous night's tumble in the snow with Mark Jessy were draped across the radiator. On a more upbeat note, it appeared that his two roommates had followed through on their plans to go snowboarding for the weekend, which meant he had the room to himself. Donning a bathrobe, he opened the door that led to the dormitory hallway, fearfully peered both ways (a habit that had been beaten into him after several sneak attacks at the hands of the brothers), then headed for the bathroom.

"Hey," came a voice from behind him.

The Freshman flinched as he turned, but relaxed when he saw only Danny Samarel, his across-the-hall neighbor, sitting on the floor, phone receiver resting on his shoulder, his finger poised to dial.

"Yeah?" said the Freshman.

"The mailroom called," said Samarel. "You got a package. The claim slip will be in your mail slot."

The Freshman blinked sleepily, wondering for a moment why the mailroom would *call*, especially on a Saturday. Then he nodded. "Oh. Okay. Thanks." He turned and continued to the bathroom.

1:47 P.M.

Sigma House had come to life with the same lack of hustle as had the rest of the campus. The brothers had feasted on pancakes and macho talk for the better part of the morning. Now, with bellies full and hangovers on the wane, they gathered in various sophomore rooms to drink Bloody Marys and watch the NCAA hoops conference tournaments.

Forty-one young men, two weeks into a cover-up.

Another silly Saturday.

2:17 P.M.

Inside the Student Center, the Freshman descended the stairs that led to the mailroom. He knelt before his slot and twisted the combination knob this way and that, then popped open the tiny door.

There was no package pickup slip in his mail box, just a thin wrinkled envelope that looked as if it had been forced into his box from the outside. He turned it over in his hands, then opened it.

The card screamed the words "Happy Anniversary," in bubbly, exclamation-pointed letters over a painted bride and groom, a confusing message since he wasn't married, and didn't even have a girlfriend. And then, as his tired eyes scanned the cover of the card, a feeling of sick horror pounded confusion into submission, and he suddenly found himself staring at a picture that he wanted to believe wasn't really there. He wanted it to be a mirage, a hallucination brought on by two weeks of sleeplessness and paranoia. He wanted to blink twice and see the apparent anniversary card as the something else it *really* was. Perhaps a phone bill, a piece of junk mail, or an invitation to a sorority social.

But it was none of these things.

It was, indeed, an anniversary card.

One that featured the freshmen-face-book photo of his face, cut out and slapped over the face of the groom.

And the freshmen-face-book photo of Chad Ewing's face, cut out and taped atop the face of the bride.

And the pencil-drawn outline of a third person next to the bride, a question mark filling the space of the featureless face.

And the construction-papered likenesses of thin, black blindfolds glued over the faces.

And the crudely drawn likeness of Brother Beam floating in the air above their heads.

With fingers that no longer felt like his own, the Freshman who knew all about threesomes and blindfolds and Brother Beam opened the card, and read the message inside.

"Happy two-week anniversary. I know who you are."

The early March sun died during its eleventh hour, leaving a blanket of shadow holed only by the strategically spaced safety lights that lined the campus walkways. A new skim of ice took hold, smoothing the slush left by a day of thermal energy and foot traffic. The wind, merely a breeze by day, transformed suddenly into a bitter gale. The Future of America now moved with twice the quickness of the morning's pace, for speed warmed them and hastened them toward evening's endless party.

It was Saturday. The night screamed before them.

5:47 P.M.

The knocks at the door were soft and tentative, so soft they elicited not the slightest protective yip from Casey. So soft that Mark had barely heard them himself, and probably wouldn't have, had he not been waiting for them.

He walked slowly to the door and opened it.

Before him, wide-eyed and shivering, stood the Freshman, Gregory L. Turlington from Larchmont, New York, who lived in Danforth Hall, and whose mailbox number was seven fifty-two.

They made long, silent eye contact.

"You have no choice, do you." Mark said finally.

Turlington shook his head. "Not anymore." He walked past Mark into the living room, slumped to the couch, and began to cry.

CHAPTER FORTY

The 200th Year
Saturday, March 7

6:05 P.M.

Never in his life had Mark witnessed sobs like those that racked Greg Turlington. Turlington's tears were a release beyond rival, surpassing even his own athletic-field outburst two nights prior, for those tears had been tempered by the physical exhaustion of a thrashing sprint. This was a stationary bawl, so labored with moans and gasps that Mark was sure the freshman was going to pass out. It was conclusive evidence that Turlington was indeed the anonymous greeting-card sender and had indeed experienced something traumatic.

Finally, the tears subsided and Turlington's quakes diminished to convulsive snivels. When he finally looked up, his eyes wore the glassy, bloodshot look of a junkie. His face was red and moist, his lower lip still sucking in and out uncontrollably. He took two deep breaths, then inhaled a third time, closed his eyes, and exhaled slowly.

"Are you okay?" Mark asked softly.

Turlington nodded. "I guess I just needed to get that out of my system."

"You're a freshman? A Sigma pledge?"

Turlington held up his hand. He took another long, unsettled breath, then seemed to pull himself together. He smoothed his dirty-blond hair, adjusted his slight body (*very* small for a Sigma, Mark noted), and looked right at Mark. "First, we establish the rules."

"*What* rules?"

"*My* rules," said Turlington, his fugitive eyes darting toward the partially draped slider, as if expecting to spy a watcher in the woods. "And I can't slow down. I shouldn't even be here."

"Why not?"

He smiled wryly. "What do you think I am? Stupid? I *know* who you are, and what you represent. And based on the anniversary card you so nicely sent me, you've got a pretty good idea of who *I* am, and what *I* represent. We're not friends. We both know this isn't a social call."

"What—"

"Quiet. You haven't heard my rules." Sniff. Dart. "You listening?"

Mark nodded.

"Good. Rule number one"—Turlington leaned forward on the couch, ticking the rules with his fingers—"I don't know what standard D-Squad procedure is, but you can't record this conversation. If you've got a hidden tape recorder lying around, get rid of it."

"This isn't the FBI—"

"Good. Rule number two: I'll never testify before the D-Squad, so you can forget about telling Shawn or Simon about this, or about listing me as a material witness. As you're about to find out, I'm fairly intelligent, and fairly intelligent people make fairly good liars. If you call me to the witness stand, I'll testify that Sigma didn't do anything wrong, and you'll look like a fool. Maybe I'll even say that you tried to *force* me to testify against my own fraternity. You could get kicked out if I do a good enough job."

Mark regarded the freshman thoughtfully. "What makes you think I want to put you on the stand? For that matter, what makes you think I even want this thing to go to trial? I'm a former Sigma, in case you weren't aware."

"Oh, believe me, I'm aware."

"Then what makes you think I won't run off and report you to Fairchild or Dominic?"

"Because you would've done it already." Turlington pointed shakily at Mark. "I can see it in your eyes. *You* know what they did to you. *You* want revenge. Am I right?"

Mark nodded slowly. "You might be."

"Oh, I *am*. But since you brought up the subject of disclosure, that brings me to rule number three. This is more a common-courtesy rule: You can't tell any of the Sigma boys that I've contacted you. If you do, I'll be dead, and you'll feel bad about it for the rest of your life."

"I think you're overreacting—"

"I'm not interested in what you think. I've seen firsthand what Sigmas can do when they're annoyed. I'll tell you what I know, and you can use the information however you wish. Just don't quote me on it. Agreed?"

Mark crossed his arms. "You're leaving me in a tough spot."

Turlington shrugged. "Hey. Revenge is a tricky game. That's why I don't play it."

"Then what are you doing here?"

Turlington looked at Mark for a long moment, his mouth poised for retort, then settled back against the couch cushion. "Look," he began, "I haven't slept in two weeks. Not a wink. Do you know what it's like to go sleepless for that long a period? It's a nightmare. And speaking of nightmares, I have one every time I even close my eyes, so I guess I should be *thankful* I'm not sleeping." He leaned forward. "I'm terrified to be alone, but to be with anyone makes me want to scream all I know, then write my will. I feel guilty I'm alive, yet I'm glad I'm not dead. I feel . . . I'm . . . I . . ." He shook his head. "I don't *know* why I'm here."

Mark raised an eyebrow and examined his fingernails. When he looked up, Turlington was staring at him pleadingly. "But I know *what happened*," the freshman whispered. "And I think I know *why.* Isn't that enough?"

Slowly, Mark nodded. "If you're going to tell me, then I guess that's more than enough."

Turlington met his nod, then heaved a few deep breaths as he wiped his face. "You got any beers in the fridge?" he asked quickly.

He's nuts, thought Mark. "Uh, sure." He walked to the kitchen, grabbed a bottle of Bud, and returned to the living room. He handed the beer to Turlington, who twisted the bottle cap off and took a long draw from the bubbling neck. "Thanks." He dragged a sleeve across his mouth. "You got my letters, I take it. All three."

"'*There were three of us,*' '*We were blindfolded,*' '*It was Brother Beam.*' What do they mean?"

"They mean exactly what they say."

"Who were the '*three of us*'?"

"Myself, Chad Ewing, and another pledge."

"Who was the other pledge?"

"It's irrelevant."

"You won't tell me his name?"

"Not in this lifetime. All I can tell you is he's the biggest jerk I've ever met in my life. No more questions, Mark. I know exactly what I'm willing to tell you. I'm going to give you the straight facts, and then I'm going to give you a theory, so why don't you just sit back and listen."

Mark shrugged, then nodded.

Turlington leaned forward again and placed his beer on the table. "The Saturday night before the accident," he began, his tone low and confidential, "we had a pledge activity. Derby Night. Remember that one?"

"Of course."

"Okay. The squash race proceeds with its normal brutality. The brothers kick us, punch us, splash vodka and lemonade in our eyes, whip our bare backs with leather belts, drip hot candle wax on our skin. As my bad luck would have it, or as the brothers' fists would have it, two other pledges and I finish the race last, which means we get to engage in the losers' rematch. You remember what it means to race in the losers' rematch?"

Mark nodded, remembering, and for an instant he envisioned a scene he'd witnessed a couple of times during his brief tenure of brotherhood: The brothers, teeing off with all their brotherly might. Two or three blindfolded boys crawling as proudly as possible, absorbing the kind of punishment generally administered to beasts of burden, medieval prisoners, and slaves. Although he recalled little of his own time as a pledge, Mark could distinctly remember the part he'd played on the other side, as a sophomore, and he suddenly wanted to be sick.

"So we three do it again, and this time, the beating's worse. By the time we get to the finish line, Chad Ewing, one of the other unfortunate losers, has either dropped or swallowed most of his squash. A mortal sin. The Pledgemaster tells the brothers, and they give him their own private beating. They gang up on him, punching and kicking him, and he's gasping, '*You're breaking my ribs. . . . You're breaking my ribs. . . .*'"

Turlington looked down for a moment, haunted by the memory. "When they're done kicking his ribs in, they bring the three of us down to the barroom, where they make us march and sing and do beer funnels while they shout those cruel rhymes at us and beat us a little more. Remember those rhymes? The ones the brothers write and memorize before each pledge event, to be used during the event?"

"How could I not?" Mark said. During his brief tenure as a brother, he'd actually been remarkably adept at rhyming.

"Well," continued Turlington, "in the middle of all this rhyming and beating, Chad throws up, and they make all three of us lick his puke off the floor. While we're down there, one of the brothers smashes Chad's hand with a baseball bat. He screams, and gets kicked in the face till he's quiet. They make us stand and tell us there's still a brother we haven't met yet. They put blindfolds on us, and a core group of what I can only assume to be seniors leads us from the barroom to the third floor. The rest of the brothers and pledges are going to party, one of the seniors tells us, while we get acquainted with Brother Beam."

Turlington peered up at Mark. "Do you remember Brother Beam?"

Mark nodded grimly, a reflexive chill running down his spine. "Jim Beam whiskey, right? Double shots?"

"You got it. They lead us into a room and slam the door behind us. First, they strip our clothes off. Then they make us kneel on the floor, and they spout some rhyming bullshit about how we're the three weakest pledges and we're going to have to show Brother Beam how tough we can really be. Someone puts a shot glass in my hand and tells me to drink it down, so I do. Sure enough, it's a double shot of Brother Beam. That stuff doesn't exactly go down like honey, if you know what I mean."

Mark remembered pledging, and his twenty-first birthday, and countless other functions. He knew the way Brother Beam went down.

"One of the brothers hands me a refill, and I finish it. I've drunk hard stuff before, but as you can see, I'm not very big. The shots are hitting me hard. They're hitting Ewing hard, too, because I can hear him coughing and wheezing about how Brother Beam is burning his throat. I hear someone smack his face and tell him to shut up and drink.

"I do at least five Brother Beams, maybe more. I hear Ewing, then the third pledge, topple to the ground. I'm forced to do their remaining shots, and then I get punched in the head for good measure."

Sip. "One of the brothers announces that they're leaving the room and that we should wait five minutes before we take off our blindfolds. Then another brother tells us that we better shape up our acts. He says Brother Beam becomes angrier with every transgression."

"Jesus," said Mark. "What did you guys do wrong?"

"I'll get to that later," dismissed Turlington. "The door slams, and I fuck the five minutes. I take off my blindfold. The third pledge is on his hands and knees, spitting on the floor, and Ewing's curled up in the fetal position, still blindfolded, moaning, bleeding, gasping. I help the third pledge up, and together we try to help Ewing. No use. He's a dead weight, and we're way too drunk to lift him. The third pledge and I somehow make it to the second-floor bathroom, where we both get sick several times. Then we go out into the hallway and fall to the floor."

Turlington shook his head, looked away to the wall, and stared intensely at it for a few moments. "While I'm lying there," he said finally, "I gradually get the feeling I'm more than just drunk. I mean, I'm *really* fucked up. The last thing I remember is the hallway spinning so fast that I want to scream, but my voice won't work."

He ran a hand through his hair, then looked right at Mark. "I believe I was on something."

"What was it?" asked Mark, beginning to feel uneasy as he recalled Kelly Devereaux's story and the "disorienting ingredient" Sigma had used on him.

"I'm pretty sure it was a drug called Rohypnol. I'd never heard of it, but a couple of days after Chad's death I went to a psychobiology professor and explained the symptoms of a 'friend.' He told me it sounded like someone had slipped a mickey in my friend's drink. And Rohypnol tablets—or roofies—are the current mickeys of choice. Of course, then he asked me who my friend was, in the name of intervention or investigation, but I told him my friend lived in Orlando, and thanks anyway."

"So," Mark said. "Brother Beam was spiked?"

"Brother Beam was spiked."

"For the other two as well?"

"Why not? Mine were."

As Mark nodded absently, thinking more of his own drugged-up episode, he suddenly realized why this didn't make sense. "Wait a minute!" he nearly shouted. "We talked to the coroner. He mentioned that Chad was drunk, but he didn't say anything about roofies, or any other drug, for that matter. Neither did the doctor's report."

Turlington shrugged. "I'm not a pharmacist, and I don't know how long it takes the body to process the drug. All I know is that three of us were all messed up on something other than just booze, and I think it was roofie. And the next morning, one of us was found on the living-room floor, the victim of blindfolds, beatings, booze, drugs, and gravity."

Mark stared at Turlington for a long time, then shook his head. "Crazy."

Turlington said nothing.

"Can I ask you some questions?"

"It depends."

"Shawn heard that Chad was found with poetry written all over him. You know anything about that?"

Turlington opened his mouth to reply, then closed it and shook his head adamantly; Mark got the immediate sense that the freshman knew more than he was about to let on. "There's lots I'll probably never know about that night. I have no idea what happened to Chad after the third pledge and I left the third floor, and I don't know how he got down to the second floor. Maybe he fell down the flight of stairs. Maybe the seniors went back to the room, wrote all over him, then carried him down to the second floor so he wouldn't stink up their precious domain. It doesn't matter anyway. Who cares if they wrote on him? I've given you more than enough information to build a case."

Mark nodded once and said, "Can I ask you another question?"

"Again, it depends."

"There was a house party going on while you and the third pledge lay naked outside the second-floor bathroom. How come no one outside of Sigma, some independent partier, didn't see you guys and try to help?"

Turlington shrugged. "What's so odd about being naked at a Sigma party? Happens all the time. Naked football, naked fun-runs. Sigmas are often naked. That's how they bond."

Mark nodded, agreeing, and realizing that he himself might have walked past Turlington and the third pledge without thinking anything of it. He *had* been at the party, partying like a rock star, and had probably used the second-floor bathroom.

"Besides," added Turlington, "Sigmas wouldn't let anyone who couldn't handle the sight of a couple naked dudes come to one of their house parties."

"When did you leave the house?"

"The next morning. I woke up when I heard the ambulance sirens. I got scared and woke up the third pledge. We went into one of the brothers' rooms, stole some clothes, and snuck out the back fire escape while all hell broke loose on the first floor. We watched the house for a while from the trees. Then we split."

Again, Mark nodded, but less as a gesture of understanding than as an act of curiosity, for as the answers to his two previous questions settled in their respective memory banks, a new question came to mind, one that walked on the legs of an earlier observation.

For a Sigma, Turlington didn't look just small.

He also looked *young*.

"How old are you?" asked Mark, chuckling at the simplicity of his question.

"Why?"

"You look really young."

"I'm almost seventeen," Turlington responded defensively.

Mark raised his eyebrows. "Aren't most freshmen almost *nineteen*."

"I skipped a few grades."

"Oh. You mean you're a prodigy."

"I don't like that word."

"You *are*," insisted Mark with a smile. "You read *War and Peace* as a two-year-old, taught yourself to play chess as a three-year-old, and were a master cellist by the age of four."

Turlington's face broke into gradual but genuine amusement. "No, but I did get a sixteen hundred on my SATs."

"Did you really?"

Turlington nodded sheepishly.

"Wow."

"Yeah. Listen, what does all this have to do with what I'm telling you?"

"Well, look at you!" blurted Mark, and he immediately regretted his insinuation. "I mean . . . your size . . . your age . . . you don't look like Sigma material, to be perfectly honest."

Turlington stared at him a moment, his brief expression of offense giving way to allowance. "You're right," he said finally. "I'm not Sigma material. My father was, though. He quarterbacked the last Simsbury team to win the Division Three National Championship. He holds every record in the book."

"Of *course*!" Mark smacked himself on the forehead. "Bill Turlington! His name and picture are all over the Sigma walls."

"That's my dad," Turlington said proudly. "My mother's a little woman, though. I take after her."

Mark smiled.

"So I'm a legacy," said Turlington. "Born with Sigma blood in my veins, as they say. The brothers had no choice but to bid me."

"Your father must've been proud."

Turlington smiled ironically and shook his head. "My father begged me not to join."

"Huh?"

"That's right. He begged me. Told me it would be the biggest mistake of my life. I should've listened to him. He knew what was coming."

"I don't get it."

"You will," Turlington assured. "Believe me, you will." He lifted his beer bottle and noticed it was empty. "Can I have another?"

Mark nodded and headed for the kitchen. "You sure *drink* like a Sigma," he called over his shoulder.

"Another thing not to be proud of," muttered Turlington.

When Mark returned with the beer, Turlington was standing before the now-closed slider drapes, peering past the flipped-back fringe into the night. Mark rested the beer on the freshman's shoulder, causing him to jump.

"Easy," said Mark. "There's no one out there."

"Says you." Turlington took the beer from Mark and began to stroll around the living room. Eventually he wandered back to the couch and sat. He sipped his beer. "So that's what happened. One bad night. One bad fall. Chad Ewing's gone. Simple physics. Your basic cause-and-effect equation."

Mark made a face.

"*Why* it happened," continued Turlington, "is another story altogether, the sort of story that would lead one to believe that Chad Ewing was beaten and poisoned to death for a specific reason. Very complex and sinister, if my theory is correct, and I believe it is."

"What theory?"

Turlington looked at Mark for a long moment, then said, "The Related Party theory."

Mark stared blankly, then shook his head.

"Do you know what a related party is?"

Mark shrugged. "A family reunion?"

Turlington smirked and shook his head. "It's a business expression. It has to do with accounting, SEC disclosure, all that fun stuff. My dad could give you a textbook definition, I'm sure. He's a partner at a big accounting firm in New York. He could give you a lawyer-formulated definition, and you probably still wouldn't understand it. However, I spent every high school summer interning for my dad, spiking work papers and making sure all the checklists had been filled out, and during that time I got a layman's idea of what a 'related party' is."

Sip. "Let's say you and I are best friends. You start a business, make a million bucks. You then spin off a subsidiary and make me the CEO. Your business and my business are now related parties, and the nature of our intercompany transactions must be disclosed. Otherwise we could just sit there and make sales to each other, gross up our financial statements, and mislead the SEC and potential investors. Get it?"

"No."

"Neither do I," said Turlington, shaking his head. "And I probably gave you a shitty example. Anyway, it doesn't matter, because I've got my own theory on the related party, and how it pertains to Sigma. And how, in turn, it relates to the morning Chad Ewing went over the rail."

He paused, shifted in his seat, and positioned his index fingers like prongs on either side of his face. Mark almost wished the story would end here; he was in no mood to endure an economics lesson.

"What you must first understand," Turlington began, "and I'm sure you do, is that a fraternity operates as a strict hierarchy. The older rule the younger, and the richer rule all. It's really quite simple, and it actually makes a lot of sense. Can we agree on that?"

Mark shrugged. "Whatever."

"Come on, Mark. Stay with me." Turlington stood for a moment, scratched his ass, then sat again. "Now, Sigma's no different than any other fraternity. Except the Sigma hierarchy isn't just *strict*. It's the *law*. Year in, year out, for two hundred years it's been completely unbreakable. And, for reasons touted in all those archived, mystical books in the Brotherhood Room, the levels of power that can be reached by Sigmas are that much higher. Sigma's the New York Yankees of fraternities. It's the Microsoft of fraternities. With all this power up for grabs, it's imperative that all brothers wait their turn, show undying loyalty, and obey the laws of this hierarchy. Brothers in power give the orders, and brothers below carry them out, *without exception,* for the brothers that follow orders are handed the keys to the kingdom, and those are priceless keys indeed. The brothers that *don't* follow orders must be ready to suffer the consequences."

"What the fuck are you talking about?" blurted Mark, on the verge of laughter.

"Listen to me," Turlington said, smoothing the air in front of him. "Just hear me out. I think . . . I think the best way to illustrate this to you is by taking you down the Sigma brotherhood path you were once on. Only this time, I'm going to take you all the way to the palace at the end of the path, so you can see what I'm talking about."

"This is foolish. Just tell me why Chad fell over the damn—"

"Shut up. I'm *telling* you why, but you've got to give me time." Turlington shook his head with irritation, then took a deep breath. "All right, here's the thing. There are three phases to life as a Sigma. You only experienced phase one, and a fraction of phase two. Phase one is the pledging phase. Let's say you're an impressionable freshman all over again, just looking to fit in with the studly jocks at a new school. You're seduced into pledging at Sigma by supercool guys who make you feel manly and special over a keg of beer. Then the pledge process begins, and all the horror that goes with it. Getting Sigma pride beaten into you. Learning, and earning, in sick, painful ways, unconditional trust. Vowing to kill and die for your fellow pledges and the brothers that stand before you. Listening to the rhymes, thinking they're creative, scary, and cool, and following the commands within the verses religiously. During phase one, you see the alumni lurking around the house from time to time, and you hear the undergrads sometimes mention them, but you're ignorant of the domineering role they play. As far as you're concerned, the alumni barely even *exist*. And even on those instances when they enter your terrified line of vision, it doesn't occur to you that they're still brothers. Your narrow mind, incapable of peering past four weeks, let alone four years, sees undergrads as the true brothers, perhaps the only brothers, for it's *their* direct orders you follow daily and nightly, no questions asked.

"Phase two begins after initiation. This is the undergraduate brother stage, the stage you witnessed briefly as a sophomore. Three-plus years of playing hard, drinking hard, and fighting hard, side by side with the most gifted and physically awesome men on campus. Three-plus years of thinking up your *own* rhymes and firing them at pledges. And tradition so proud and sexy that it makes you feel like singing a song every time you walk through the doors of the most spectacular-looking house you've ever *seen*, let alone lived in."

"I remember that feeling," said Mark.

Turlington nodded. "During phase two, you forget what your life was like before Sigma. And you can't imagine what your life would be like without it. That's why, in two hundred years, not one brother has dropped out. Not one. Sure, a bunch of pledges have, but no brothers. And you can see why, because phase two has filled you with a sensation of invincibility. An us-against-the-world mentality. You answer to no one except your brothers. And the alumni, of course. *Especially* the alumni. During phase two, you come to fully understand how the alumni dominate the world of Sigma. And what an awesome domination it is. Need a little cash? The alumni will throw it your way. Need a summer internship? Look no further than your friendly, neighborhood alumni, the majority of whom could make you a rich man on summer wages alone. And what do they expect in return? They expect you to follow orders. The alumni think you're better suited for a major other than the one you've chosen? You better change your major. The alumni think your girlfriend is interfering with your studies, your performance on the athletic fields, or your ability to remain loyal to the brotherhood? You better dump her. Simsbury's a liberal arts college, but as an obedient Sigma, some decisions are not yours to make."

"What the—?"

"Quiet. You graduate, and move into phase three. The real world. Except it's *not* the real world, because you're now an alumnus of Sigma Delta Phi. During phase three you're rewarded for undergraduate loyalty and handed the keys to the kingdom. No need for a job interview. No need for grad school applications. You're simply *given* a job. You're simply *enrolled* in grad school. You're simply *told* where to live. One of the hundreds of Sigma alums across the country takes you under his wing and *orders* you in the direction of a career path. You're commissioned like a soldier. You won't have a choice in the matter, and you certainly won't care. Fifty, sixty grand with benefits, right out of college, with the potential for six figures and stock options within a few short years, is an offer that can't be refused. You become a tiny piston in what might be the most awesome business machine in the United States, maybe even the world."

He eyed Mark curiously. "Do you see where I'm going with this?"

"Sort of."

Turlington shifted. "Listen. The years pass. Eventually it's *your* turn to give the orders, so to speak. *You're* the big pisser, making the important decisions at your company. Whom are you going to do business with? Whom are you going to approach as a potential client? Whom are you going to hire to give you a clean audit report? Who's going to handle your litigation? Who's going to handle your private investments?" He leaned way forward. "Who are you going to trust unconditionally?"

He settled back again. "Your loyal brothers, of course. There's a Sigma for every major business need, in every major city. We're not talking about mechanics, Mark. We're talking about lawyers and brokers and corporate raiders and insurance moguls and investment bankers, each with a specific role, each with a loyal and brotherly concept of just how he became a millionaire by the age of twenty-eight, and perhaps a billionaire by forty. Sigma is one gigantic related party."

He lifted his beer bottle and pointed the neck at Mark. "But the key to phase three is the success of phase two. And the key to phase two is the success of phase one. That's why the alumni give orders to the undergrads, and that's why the undergrads give orders to the pledges. It's a bottom-on-up success equation, based on stature, intellectual intimidation, physical bullying, and fear. But it's an equation that works.

"And it starts with the pledges. Never forget that. It's *crucial* for Sigma to recruit and initiate the very best. Not necessarily the brightest, but the most capable, the most confident, the ones with the work ethic, the ones who can be team players, the ones who'll follow orders. Nine times out of ten, it's the college jocks who are going to make it big in the business world. They're the ones who are going to be willing to go the distance, to do the dirty work for a higher purpose that'll reveal itself later on down the line. It's *crucial* to get guys like that through the Sigma doors.

"And to do that, Sigma's *got* to retain ownership of that house. That's what this all boils down to. The house is the breeding ground for this machine. There's no way a fraternity can attract eighteen-year-old heroes without a big, beautiful house, smack in the middle of campus. No quarterback or lacrosse middie is going to hang out in a fraternity that operates out of a dorm room. You can't keep a keg cold in a dorm room. Hot chicks don't hang out in dorm rooms.

"The *house* is the key. *A fraternity's got to have a house.*"

"But Sigma *has* a house," said Mark.

Turlington shook his head. "Not if the college shuts them down. That house is on college property. It could just as well be the most spectacular-looking *dormitory* you've ever seen. Get what I'm saying? That's why the prospect of D-Squad involvement is so dangerous. The

D-Squad is attached to the Board of Directors. The Board makes the decisions regarding student life, and *they* decide how college fixed assets are to be utilized."

Mark sighed heavily and shook his head. "Jesus, Greg. I thought you said that pledges are ignorant. Where did you get all this?"

Turlington smiled grimly. "I'm Bill Turlington's son. I grew up with Sigma blood in my veins, remember?"

"Yeah? Well I grew up with Mohawk blood in my veins, and I know next to nothing about my heritage. I only know how to say 'hello' and 'good-bye' and maybe—"

"No offense, Mark, but it's not the same. You can take all the language classes you want, but you won't become fluent until you live in the country where it's spoken, if you catch my analogy. I spent *every* Homecoming here, and just by hanging out with my dad and his brothers, and listening to them talk, I learned a lot. But more important, my work experience with Dad gave me access to the private Sigma Business Web page. Whenever I had free time—which was pretty frequently at an accounting firm in the summer—I studied it." He shook his head. "That page is like a recipe for wealth. Detailed stock tips. Tricky tax suggestions. Elaborate venture plans. Progress updates on the Sigma retirement portfolio. Reports on who's doing what, and with the help of which brother. Every time I logged on, I learned something new about some multimillion-dollar deal between brothers going down." He raised his eyebrows and nodded. "Simple experience and research has taught me what makes Sigma's heart beat, and what can stop it cold. The other pledges don't know, but *I* know."

"Then let me ask you something," said Mark. "If the D-Squad poses such a threat to Sigma, why would the brothers go and do something stupid, like *drug* the pledges? Why would they effectively *kill* someone?"

Turlington's expression grew dark again. "That's a good question, and one I think I can answer."

"Of course. You have an answer for everything."

"Not everything. That's why I'm here. But as for your last question, I believe I have an answer."

He bent forward and tugged on the tongues of his hiking boots, then straightened up. "The way I see it, there's one communication synapse, brought on by generational and geographical gaps, where the hierarchy of Sigma breaks down."

"Speak English, please," said Mark.

"Sorry," Turlington said, and he smiled through a long breath. "Even though the alumni rule Sigma, give precise orders and whatnot, they can't be everywhere at once. They live in mansions outside Boston and New York and Chicago and Philly, which means they can't oversee everything that goes on at their beloved fraternity house in Bumfuck, Maine. And it only makes sense. I mean, the undergrads have to make *some* decisions on their own. For example, *they* have control of house elections. *They* decide when to have parties. And *they* decide who gets to be a pledge. You see? They're sort of like soldiers in the field when it comes to these activities. They're following general orders from the alumni, but they still have to react to certain situations on their own.

"But bear in mind, these are still kids we're talking about, prone to making mistakes from time to time. Example: How stupid was it to keep hazing us like that while a house party was going on downstairs? They're lucky only the drunk and ignorant were at the party, in terms of non-Sigmas."

Mark winced, but said nothing.

"Every once in a while, during phase one, the undergrads allow a couple of these mistakes to slip through the cracks. Nonathletes. Losers. Pledges with apparent weaknesses. Pledges who'll weaken the entire brotherhood, from the bottom on up. Such pledges are like insubordinate soldiers, an insult to the brotherhood, and not worth nurturing. Such pledges must be eliminated from Sigma, per order of the alumni. Chad Ewing was one such pledge. So was the third pledge involved in our private torture session."

"But not you," Mark said slyly.

Turlington shook his head. "No, not me. Mine is a different weakness. I'm a future liability of the disloyal variety. Guilty by heredity."

"I don't get it."

"Let me back up. Remember how I said how my father was begging me not to join Sigma? I couldn't understand why at the time. I mean, Sigma had been great to him. Sigma had enhanced his heroic status on this campus. Sigma had gotten him his job at a powerful accounting firm, even though he had no accounting background. Sigma had given him client after client after client. Sigma had made him his firm's leading partner, in terms of client retention and profitability. That's why it didn't make sense that my father was so desperate to keep me out of the house that had made him so successful.

"The first week of pledging went pretty much how I had expected. It was obvious that Ewing and the other pledge were out of their league—mistakes in the bidding process, if you will—and they were taking obscene amounts of punishment. It was obvious, to me anyway, that the brothers wanted these two to drop out. During the third week, however, I suddenly found *myself* lumped in with those two. Just like that, *I* was a whipping boy, too. Had I done something wrong? Not that I was aware of. I'd followed all the orders given to me. I'd proven myself to be quite capable of absorbing their humiliation. Why were they doing this to me? I had no answer. It was during this week that my father started calling me every night, asking in that fatherly voice if everything was okay. I lied and told him everything was fine. But it got me thinking: Did he know something I didn't know? I had to find out, because my life had suddenly become very painful.

"Given what I'd learned over the years, and that I'd really done nothing to warrant such abuse, I could only guess that the answer lay in my father's business dealings. He's the lead client service partner for some *big* corporations. We're talking Fortune Five Hundred. The kind of corporations that make headlines when the CEO has a bowel movement. And most of his clients have roots in Sigma. Founded by a Sigma. Run by a Sigma. Taken public by a Sigma. It's not difficult to figure out what's going on in phase three of the Sigma world. All you have to do is read the front page of any business publication. So I decided to do a little research. I didn't have access to the Sigma Business Web page, but I *did* have access to the Simsbury library. I spent an entire Sunday at the library, reading all the recent *Wall Street Journal*s and *New York Times*. And that's where I found my answer.

"One of my dad's clients, a start-up company called Spencer Gluck Industries—cofounded and chaired by two young Sigma alums, incidentally—had been working on a project that would essentially link all of post–Cold War Europe under the same telecommunications umbrella. This was a *huge* project, Mark. Absolutely enormous. They'd laid the groundwork, contracted with over half of the European countries, even started a marketing campaign.

"But the deal crashed in January, because my dad's firm had given a qualified opinion to Spencer Gluck in their annual audit report. The banks backed off on their financing commitments, Germany bailed out, Spencer Gluck was left holding the tab, and who knows what's going to happen to them now." Turlington held his hand out to stress a point. "Mark, my dad had fucked over two of his *own*. Of course, it's his job to issue an opinion that reflects his independence from the client. But something tells me he hadn't been hired to be independent. He'd been hired to keep his mouth shut, give an unqualified opinion, and collect a six-figure audit fee. Apparently, his integrity had gotten in the way.

"I called my dad's secretary, and she told me the Spencer Gluck job had been a nightmare from day one. Now all my dad's big clients, corporations run by Sigmas, I presumed, were calling to inform him that they'd be taking their audit fees elsewhere. My dad was devastated. The other partners were worried about him and suggested that maybe he take a sabbatical.

"Now it made sense. My father had betrayed his Sigma brothers. He hadn't followed orders, so to speak, and he was no longer worthy of unconditional trust from all those related parties out there. And since *he* wasn't, neither was *I*. He'd foreseen the bad timing of the Spencer Gluck fiasco and had tried to warn me away from joining Sigma. I hadn't listened, and now I lay exposed and vulnerable in phase one, at the mercy of the young men in phase two, who follow orders from the rich men in phase three.

"I decided to drop out, and was in the middle of deciding the best way to do it when the 'accident' occurred. The D-Squad launched a preliminary investigation, and the brothers told us to remember the oaths we'd taken and to keep our mouths shut. Now I *couldn't* drop out. I was a *witness*. I was sure the brothers would read too much into my dropping out, come after me, and silence me the best way they know how. Physically.

"They killed Chad Ewing," said Turlington with added severity. "Merely for being weak. I, the pledge with disloyal blood in my body, know something about his death that could *destroy* them. What's to stop them from killing *me*?"

Mark raised his eyebrows and shook his head as if to clear it. "That's an amazing story, Greg. So amazing that I find it difficult to believe."

"You don't know what you're talking about—"

"No, I'm afraid I do. I was a Sigma *brother,* something you've never been. I never heard any talk of phase one, phase two, phase three, or any of that related-party bullshit."

Turlington thumbed his chest. "Those are *my* terms, expressions *I* made up."

"Then you've got an overactive imagination."

"Mark, this is all based on experience and research. Haven't you been listening to me?"

"Yes, I have. And your story contains one glaring inconsistency. Well, not so much an inconsistency, but something that doesn't make sense." Mark leaned forward. "*If,* in fact, the alumni deemed you untrustworthy, and *if,* in fact, the other two pledges were considered too weak, why didn't they just kick you guys out?"

Turlington leaned back and smiled again. "School rules, bro. I looked it up. It's a violation of the Simsbury College Charter, Article Fourteen, dealing with social policy, Section Six, Rule Eleven, to kick a pledge—or a brother, Mark, or a *brother*"—he pointed knowingly— "out of a fraternity, once he's been asked to join. It's legal for the dean or the D-Squad or the Board of Directors to do it, as I'm sure you're aware, but it's illegal for the fraternity itself to drop the ax."

Mark blinked, vaguely remembering something Kelly Devereaux had relayed. "It is?"

"Christ," said Turlington. "You're on the D-Squad. Aren't you supposed to know these things? *Yes,* it's a violation. Always has been. I guess it's the college's way of protecting the feelings of geeks who don't disclose themselves as geeks until after they've been asked to join a fraternity. But the existence of this rule doesn't mean that a resourceful fraternity has to bear the burden of an unwanted pledge. There are several ways to get rid of the weak and disloyal, the most effective of which is to get the pledge to drop out. And the best way to do that is to drive him past his breaking point, physically and mentally. And to do that, the brothers must get down and dirty, pull out all the stops, and use a little creativity, the sort typified by the sick poems that are thrown nightly at the pledges."

"If I recall correctly," countered Mark, "that's the way pledging has always been. It's *always* been about driving pledges past their breaking point. It doesn't mean that the brothers meant to *kill*."

"I didn't *say* they meant to *kill*. I *said* they meant to *get rid of*. Which, by the way, they certainly succeeded in doing to Chad. Order given. Order followed. Mission accomplished."

Mark felt a chill scratch his scalp. "Yeah," he muttered hesitantly, becoming by the second more of a believer in Turlington's theory. "Well, I certainly don't believe that you were included in that torture session because of something your *father* did."

"Why not?" replied Turlington, his lip curled into a faint smile. "*You* were set up because of something *your* father did."

Mark felt his stomach instinctively flip. "How . . ."

"Look," said Turlington. "Believe it or not, not every Sigma undergrad knows you were set up. In fact, I think only a few do, though there are probably more every day. The only reason I know is because Pete Thresher has a big mouth, and the Monday after the 'accident' I overheard him talking to another brother about the D-Squad, which of course led to discussions about you and your family history, and how this history had made you something of a black mark on the fraternity's proud reputation, which was why you'd been set up to take a fall. I took an obvious interest in the story he told, but for some reason just didn't buy his rationale for the setup. It seemed too . . . *corny*, I guess. I figured there had to be something more, for them to go through all that effort just to get rid of you. So later that evening I went to the library again and did a news search for the name 'Jessy.' Sure enough, I found a skillion articles from about a dozen years ago, accounts of the events and aftermath of Cherry Plain. I learned about your mom, and your dad, and that sniper."

He leaned forward and looked at Mark with a mixture of sympathy and hardness. "But most important, I learned that your dad was still on the run, and one of the FBI's Ten Most Wanted. I learned that a near-riot had started at one of your Little League games because you recognized some marshal scoping the scene for your dad, and you went after him with an aluminum bat. I found an editorial condemning the FBI's insistence on interrogating young children." He settled back again. "When I read that, I knew you weren't set up for the reasons those few undergrads think. Not because your last name was tarnishing the honorable reputation of the fraternity, or some crap like that. Rather, I believe you were set up because your presence in the fraternity was attracting unwanted attention, from unwanted parties."

Mark frowned. "I don't understand."

"With this nationwide web of related Sigma parties dominating the American business scene with such complete success," said Turlington, "and with this extended family of loyal Sigmas running up huge profits, doesn't it stand to reason that, somewhere in this rich mix, something illegal is brewing?"

Mark shook his head slowly, confused and defensive. "I don't see what that has to do—"

"With your father?" finished Turlington. "Let me shed some more light for you." He tilted back his beer bottle and finished it, then set the bottle on the floor. "My father once told me that Sigma alums are required to donate one percent of their salary to a pool of money. You know what the annual personal revenues are for all Sigmas combined? According to my dad, the average yearly haul of a Sigma is just over a million bucks, which puts the combined Sigma draw somewhere around a billion. One percent of that, by the way, is about ten million. Every year. And that's just the base. The pool is shrewdly invested and reinvested, probably gets an annual return of at least thirty percent, and at any given time my dad estimates it holds over a billion dollars, some of which is disbursed as annual dividends to all those blessed and lucky enough to be Sigmas, the rest of which is disbursed whenever necessary to fund a variety of rich-boy endeavors. Sigma conventions. Interest-free loans for start-up business ventures. Legal defense. New Year's parties.

"Well, I recently got to thinking: What else might this money be used for? It might be used to lobby congressmen. It might be used to bribe judges. It might even be used to persuade small-town cops, coroners, and doctors to ignore a suspicious death."

And it might be used to pay Kelly Devereaux twenty-five grand to charge a Sigma brother with attempted rape, thought Mark.

"Get it, Mark? Sigma brothers aren't the *only* related parties in the equation. A related party can be someone, *anyone,* who can keep his or her mouth shut and benefit financially from dealings with Sigma. Theoretically, we're talking about a lot of cash, perhaps a good portion of it funneled toward questionable activities. Possibly criminal activities. Now, I'm sure Sigma tax lawyers have set up this trust so as to avoid detailed scrutiny. But still, the threat lingers that the IRS or FBI will stumble across something illegal, and that'll start a snowball effect that could mean *big* trouble for Sigma."

"What does this have to do with me?" asked Mark. "Or my father?"

Turlington made a knowing face. "I'm guessing that Sigma has been visited by the FBI only once in two hundred years. And that was when you were a brother."

Mark felt his face go numb. "Oh my God," he whispered.

Turlington nodded. "I'm sure that the alumni do background checks on all the new pledges, just like a human resource representative might do to a job applicant. But because you were so secretive about your past, they probably didn't find out who you really are until after you'd been initiated. Which is probably lucky for you, because you might've been Chad Ewing'ed had they found out in time. Still, they had to get rid of you, so they picked their spot and planned it well."

Yes, thought Mark, *they planned it very well.*

"End result and bottom line," said Turlington as he pointed at Mark. "With you, the subject of regular FBI inquiries, gone from the fraternity, there's nothing for Sigma to fear."

"Except the sudden death of a pledge."

Turlington nodded. "Exactly. You see, it all boils down to this. With all its secretive traits, a brotherhood, at each level, is tailor-made for conspiracies. Little ones, like the one that led to your attempted rape charge, and big ones, like the ones that undoubtedly lead to Sigma's mastery of just about everything. A brotherhood *is,* in and of itself, a conspiracy." He dipped his head and wrinkled his brow suggestively. "And conspiracies are almost always illegal."

Mark bit his lip thoughtfully for a moment, then said, "Let me ask you something. Doesn't it seem odd that the sort of conspiracies we're talking about would be entrusted to kids, as you call them? The same sort of kids prone to making mistakes? The same sort of kids who'd show the poor judgment to ask losers such as Ewing and that third pledge to join?"

Turlington shook his head. "They know nothing of the extent that money rules the brotherhood. Not yet, anyway. They're more concerned with what you might call nobler objectives. Keeping the brotherhood strong and, in their eyes, virtuous. Ensuring the survival of certain traditions. The undergrads, as I'm sure you know, are led to believe that the brotherhood is the beginning of the path toward manhood. They follow orders that they believe are handed down to protect this path. It doesn't occur to the undergrads that they're following orders that are driven by *money*, by *illegal, alumni greed.* They only find that out *after* they've followed every order and graduated to phase three of the brotherhood. And by then, the smell of money is too tantalizing to refuse. Someday, Mark, when they're individually rich, each of your Sigma buddies will figure out the *real* reason you were set up. And you know what? They'll probably decide it was worth it."

The freshman's eyes danced a step, then simmered. "Do you understand what we're talking about here? We're talking about more than an extraordinary business network. We're talking about a goddamned army. Every loyal brother's a soldier who serves a purpose, sometimes without knowing what that real purpose is. Every order is followed, for reasons subject to individual interpretation and justification. It's a strict hierarchy, though, a ladder of human rungs that marches an evolutionary path to the highest levels of white-collar power this country has ever seen."

Mark shook his head and glanced at the ceiling. "This is *way* over my head."

Turlington leaned way forward again and shook his head emphatically, almost desperately. "Mark, when I decided to send those anonymous messages, there was a method to my madness. I needed to tell what I knew, and I needed to tell it to someone who probably *could* do something about it if he or she were so inclined, but probably wouldn't. I needed to feel enabled, but in a dormant sort of way. Now, if I'd sent those messages to Simon he'd have used them indiscriminately to go full bore into the case and further his own law school aspirations. I just *know* he would have. If I'd sent them to Shawn, she'd have organized a one-woman rally for justice and marched across the quad with the letters held high over her head."

He paused to spit anxiety into his second emptied bottle. "But you . . . I knew you'd probably do nothing. Sure, there was a *chance* you'd turn the letters over to Fairchild or Dominic, but from everything I'd heard, you only had passion for collegiate pleasures, like playing lacrosse, drinking beer, and getting laid, so that was a chance I was willing to take in order to feel more empowered without having to deal with the consequences. And when it became clear that you hadn't done anything about the *first* letter, I knew I'd played my hunch right."

He spat again, then squinted. "But it wasn't enough. I kept pushing the limits of what I could tell you, because eventually it wasn't enough to just feel enabled. Eventually, I wanted *action*, though I didn't realize it until this afternoon. Yeah, I ran from you last night, but that doesn't change my being there to begin with. And it doesn't change your chasing me down.

"I want action," he repeated, while straightening and thumbing his chest. Then, pointing at Mark, he said, "And *you* want to take it."

He leaned forward again. "And you know what?" he continued, his voice charged. "You're the only one who *can.* I'm guessing the local police are in Sigma's back pocket, and the FBI or IRS would laugh their collective asses off if I called and told them what I just told you. Right now, Sigma's biggest threat is the D-Squad, the one force that can take their big, beautiful house away. And the most dangerous element of that force is *you.*"

He clenched a fist and shook it. "*You*, Mark, are far more lethal than Shawn and Simon combined, because *you* know the way Sigma works. *You* know their strengths and weaknesses. *You* can convince the Board, in a trial, that Sigma's guilty, and when you do, Sigma is *history.*"

He lowered his voice. "I'm telling you, they are *ripe.* For two hundred years they've literally ruled this school. For the last hundred they've damn near ruled this country. But somewhere along the line, all that good-old-boy tradition went sour, and honor took a backseat to money. Money's the only real tradition left for the brothers of Sigma." He leaned even closer. "And now," he nearly whispered, "their backs are to the wall. They've hazed one of their pledges to death. The Board of Directors already had the Ackerly Task Force aimed at their heads, and now they've got the D-Squad aimed there, too. If you look close enough, you can see the tension in the brothers' eyes. They feel the weight of a two-century brotherhood on their shoulders. They're following orders they don't understand, orders they can't justify while lying in bed at night. They're hazing us worse than ever, in hopes that fear and pain will keep us loyal. They no longer allow outsiders in the house, not even girlfriends. It's good old boys gone bad, us-against-the-world gone mad. Sigma's like . . . like a wounded lion. More dangerous than ever. But more vulnerable too.

"You're the only one," Turlington repeated, "with the power to find and exploit that vulnerability."

"Not if you don't testify."

"I *can't* testify. My life—"

"Don't give me that, Greg. Your life's *not* in danger."

Turlington's eyes narrowed critically. "Mark," he said softly and seriously, "I slept that night in the second-floor hallway, too. That could've been *me* going over that rail. And now I'm one of two eyewitnesses to the events that led to the death of Chad Ewing. Don't tell me my life's not in danger. I'm lucky to be alive. I'm going to put my head down, keep my mouth shut, and let the brothers think I'm fine and dandy. And then, when the school year's over, and all this has died down, I'm going to transfer out of here. But I'm sure as hell not going to push my luck now."

"Then you're a coward, and there's nothing—"

"Ball's in your court, Mark. That's the bottom line."

"I don't know what you want me to do."

Turlington leaned across the coffee table and grabbed

Mark's wrists. "I want you to fight the battle you're dying to fight," he whispered, "and while you're at it, fight mine."

One last harmony hung over the campus, somewhat odd for a Saturday night, but not so peculiar given the time.

Not so peculiar, given the rhyme.

It was time for red eyes and roommates to seek catnaps and coffee, and for sitcoms to air for an hour.

A time for food to digest and friends to regroup, and for cocktails mixed sweet and sour.

A time for houses and halls to pour punch bowls and plan parties, and for wise guys to sing in the shower.

A time for Simsbury to nap 'neath a last college calm, before bowing to young men of power.

CHAPTER FORTY-ONE

The 200th Year
Saturday, March 7

8:07 P.M.

To help his mind sort out Turlington's crazy theory, Mark decided to take his puppy for a walk. He donned a turtleneck and his hunting jacket, clamped a liberal leash to Casey's collar, and stepped outside into the snow. Glancing everywhere, he sniffed away the cold and set a course for the athletic fields, his head ducked low to avoid the icy prickle of pine. Casey zigzagged in front of him, snorting up every possible ground smell.

Once in the clearing he released her, and she scampered ahead, trailing a leash five times her length behind her. He followed her passively, his eyes not so much on her as on a cascade of images called up by Turlington's remarks. It was *all* so ridiculous and, like Kelly Devereaux's story, so beyond the realm of comprehension, yet Mark found himself once again believing every word.

But still, what could he possibly *do* with the information? Who was he to expose what was going on? He knew little about trial tactics, and nothing at all about big business. And even if he had possessed the skill to build a formal case against Sigma, the dean's bony, blackmailing fingers were still wrapped tightly around his transcript and personnel file, a fact that Mark kept forgetting.

A fact he was now remembering, as a gust of wind stung his face.

He plunged his hands farther into his pockets, and his fingers closed around something small and papery at the bottom.

He read the doodled-upon fax receipt he now held in his gloveless hand.

Great White Industries. Real Estate. Terrence Bonnell. CEO.

He studied the receipt a moment, putting stray pieces together. The receipt had come from his D-Squad file. The D-Squad file he'd found in the dean's office. The same dean who'd stood watch over his own farce of a D-Squad trial, and who *had* to have known that Mark was being set up. The same dean who'd essentially *ordered* him to serve on the D-Squad and who was now essentially *ordering* him to drop the case against Sigma.

Wondering why he'd never thought of this before, Mark fetched Casey, shuttled her back to the apartment, tossed her inside, and began to walk in the direction of campus.

After a few steps, he increased his pace to a jog.

8:31 P.M.

Mark Jessy's and Elliot Segal's college careers had followed drastically different routes after the first night of freshman year, when they'd shared a six-pack of green bottles and jointly followed rumors of a fifteen-kegger to

Sigma. After enduring an hour or two of revelry, beer-drenched Elliot had returned to his dorm, armed himself with the Simsbury course catalogue, and meticulously outlined a four-year educational path that would lead him to the best possible job offer. Mark, on the other hand, had danced the night away in the Sigma barroom, and ended up passing out beneath a girl whose entire body smelled like gin.

The rest, as they say, was history.

Despite their differences, however, the two had maintained a solid friendship, one not so much attributable to cosmic karma as it was to Elliot's being the most-loved guy on campus. His stocky frame could be spotted bouncing at all hours, his voice chipping away at melancholy, his hand outstretched. If Fairchild was the Simsbury poster boy, then Elliot—or "Steamer" as he was more affectionately known—at least belonged on the cover of a marketing pamphlet.

In keeping with both his goal to graduate into a spectacular career opportunity and with his natural affinity for people, Steamer had made himself the chief liaison between the students and the alumni. He'd spent the last three years organizing job fairs and becoming King of Connections, and it had paid off. He'd been the first of the current seniors to bag a job, a fancy analyst position on Wall Street that came with stock options.

As he knocked on the tidy door on the third floor of Ruddy Hall, Mark hoped that Steamer's ties to the alumni world might help *him* as well.

"Steamer . . . are you in there?"

He heard a muffled squawk, then a loud thud.

Presently the door opened, revealing Steamer, who was clad in boxers and nothing else.

"Steamer, what are you doing in there?"

"Who is it, Elliot?" called a female voice from the direction of the closed bedroom door.

Steamer bit his lip and grinned.

"Steamer!" whispered Mark, almost managing a smile despite the seventy-two-hour horror. "Who have you got in there?"

"Cori Shapiro," Steamer whispered.

Now Mark couldn't help but cackle softly. "Isn't she the one who looks like your mother?"

"They just have the same haircut."

"You dog!"

"Elliot," the voice called again. "Who are you talking to?"

"Mark," answered Steamer over his shoulder. He pulled Mark as far away from the bedroom door as possible. "What's going on, pal? It's good to see you."

"Likewise. Listen, Steamer, I hate to interrupt your nookie, but do you still have that Excel file? You know, the one that lists alumni, what they do for a living, and stuff like that."

"Of course. Why?"

"I need to look at it."

"*Now?*"

"It won't take long. I promise."

Steamer studied him a moment, then nodded. "Follow me." He led Mark to the other side of the room, sat down at his computer, and jiggled the screen out of screen-saver mode. "Every fiscal quarter," he explained, as he moused about, "I update the information. You know, change of address, change of occupation, etcetera."

He called up a file and waited for the screen to fill up with data. "Here we go. See, this column lists the alumni alphabetically, and this next column lists their address and phone number." He toggled to the right. "This column lists their occupation, the next lists how much they gave to the school during the last endowment drive, the next the year before, and so on. If there's an asterisk next to their name, it means that they're a Bart Gib contributor."

"What's that mean?"

Steamer gave Mark an incredulous look. "Bartholomew Gibbons? You know, the guy who built the library? A Bart Gib contributor is someone who donates more than ten thousand dollars to the college in any given year."

Mark whistled as if this statistic was impressive. Of course, he knew for a fact that some alumni were willing to donate *twenty-five grand* to certain causes. The same sort of alumni who were willing to donate one percent of their annual income to a—

"What do you need to know?" asked Steamer, as he toggled the cursor arrow back to the left. "I can do any sort of search."

"I need you to look up a name for me. The guy's involved in real estate. Might be a job possibility there."

Steamer nodded his approval. "There're some real good opportunities in that field. What's this guy's name?"

"Terrence Bonnell," said Mark, as he transferred the fax receipt from his pocket to Steamer's hand. "Could you see if he's an alum?"

Steamer dutifully resumed his toggling, and when he

reached the B's he slowed down and began tracking the screen with a finger. "Terrence Bonnell," he announced suddenly, poking the screen. "Twelve-forty Sagamore Drive, Wellesley, Massachusetts." He turned in his chair again. "Wellesley's a pretty cushy town."

He twirled back to the screen and continued to read. "Founder and CEO of Great White Industries. Corporate headquarters, Boston, Mass." Then he gave a low whistle and pointed at the screen. "This guy gave two million . . . five million . . . nine . . . wait a minute." He toggled, whispered to himself, and toggled some more. "This fucking guy's given *thirty million* dollars to Simsbury over the past eight years. *Thirty million!*" He continued to manipulate the screen. "He graduated twenty years ago. He was captain of the baseball team. Hey, and look at this! He was a Sigma. He was a brother of yours, Mark! You're all set!"

Steamer turned excitedly in his seat, ready to exchange high fives.

But his friend was gone.

9:01 P.M.

Mark was so breathless by the time he reached the Cage, he could barely manage a nod of acknowledgment to Pops, the ancient security guard who was a fixture at the multimillion-dollar athletic complex.

Pops seemed surprised to see him. "Late workout tonight, Mark?"

"Uh-uh . . . Pops . . . Just stopping by . . . the trainer's room." Mark patted his hip. "A little tender."

"Well, then you shouldn't be runnin' on it! Look at you. You're all hot and sweaty, you dumb bunny."

"I know, Pops. That was stupid of me."

"And there ain't no one in there, either. Facility's been closed since five."

Mark's heart sank. "Really?"

"A-yuh. All the sports teams are away, 'cept women's hoops, and they played last night."

"Shit," said Mark, wiping the sweat from his eyes. "Listen, could you do me a favor and open it up for me? I think I left a textbook in there this morning, and I really need it for class on Monday."

"Oh," said Pops, wrestling briefly with the moral dilemma. "No problem. I've got a key." He fumbled with his giant key chain, unhooked it from his utility belt, and handed it to Mark. "It's this one right here. Just bring it back to me after you find your book."

"Will do. Thanks, Pops."

Mark hustled to the trainer's room, unlocked the door, and flicked on the lights. He focused immediately on the far wall.

He walked slowly forward, never taking his eyes off the picture of the Simsbury College Baseball Team from twenty years back, those men with bad haircuts and hokey nicknames. He had a hunch that the answer to it all could be found in this picture, which meant that the answer had been there all along.

He ran his eyes carefully over the list of names. He didn't find it in the top row, nor in the middle. But as he scanned the bottom row, it jumped out at him, and his heart momentarily stopped.

Terrence "T-Bone" Bonnell. Captain.

As Mark stared at the chiseled, arrogant face and cold black eyes, his mind swirled briefly with so many emotions that he almost fell to the ground. But he steadied himself and smiled, for the emotions quickly withered, leaving him with one triumphant thought.

Sigma brothers weren't the only related parties in the bottom-on-up, army-of-loyal-brothers equation.

Dean Templeton was a related party, too.

CHAPTER FORTY-TWO

The 200th Year
Saturday, March 7

10:41 P.M.

Carefully applying organic leaves to her thickening varicose veins, Judith was engaged in the sort of hopeless self-restoration that made Templeton want to stay even farther away from her than normal, so he left her in front of the TV and put four rooms between them. He closed the door to his study halfway, collapsed in his chair, then picked up the latest issue of *Investor's Weekly* and began to read. He was a third of the way through a piece on the future of derivatives trading when he heard the doorbell ring.

Frowning, he dropped the magazine and made his way back toward the front of the house. Passing the living room, he saw Judith trying to keep the leaves pressed to her thighs as she shuffled toward the foyer, and he waved her back. "Sit down, sweetheart. I'll get it."

He slippered down the cold, tiled front hallway and unbolted the front door.

* * *

Mark had no speech planned. In fact, he had no recollection of the angry, two-mile walk to the dean's house.
All he knew was that he was here now, head down and
resolute, armed with nothing scripted, but holding something small and explosive in his right hand. He was wing-
ing it, playing the game by instinct, too fired up to allow
rational thought to dictate his actions.

He looked up as the dean's front door swung open, and
watched the dean's weekend eyes slowly comprehend the
identity of the young man standing before him.

"Mark," said the dean, surprised. "What are you doing
here?"

Mark just stared at him. At that weasel-like face. That
tight-lipped mouth. That gleaming, white forehead.
Those small black eyes.

Just stared.

Templeton sneered. "As usual, you've got all sorts of
intelligent things to say."

Mark clenched his jaw, but said nothing.

"What are you *doing* here, Mark?"

Mark hesitated, then took a step forward. "I brought
you something to eat."

The dean smiled warily. "Oh? What is it?"

"This!" shouted Mark, lunging forward. He seized the
dean's cardigan collar with his left hand, and with his
right hand he shoved the fax receipt into the older man's
mouth. Wide-eyed, the dean tried to retreat, but Mark
held fast and dragged him out onto the front porch, then
pressed him against the front paneling of the house. He
placed his hands firmly on the dean's reddening face and
pushed and pulled on his jaw, forcing him to chew on the
paper.

"There," said Mark. "Isn't that yummy?"

The dean began to thrash his head, then made a gagging sound. Convulsing, he spat out the receipt, but not completely, and it hung crumpled and spitty from his lower lip. Mark grabbed the soggy wisp, worked it flat with his fingers, and held it before the dean's bleary eyes. He watched the dean's face register the written information, then watched the dean's eyes close slowly in defeat.

"I could tell you," Mark said, calling on all his self-control to stop him from smashing the dean's face in, "where I got this snack. I could tell you who T-Bone is, and what he and his dickhead brothers were willing to pay a local girl to lie. I could tell you the *real* role you played in my so-called attempted rape case. I could tell you that I'm going to get my revenge."

Now Mark smiled wickedly. "But I think you already know all that," he said, leaning closer. "And I don't want to ruin your appetite."

He glared at the dean a moment longer, then turned and began the long walk back to campus, never once giving a second look back to a man who wasn't worth one.

11:26 P.M.

Returning home, Mark found his apartment door ajar and all the lights on. Strangely, he wasn't afraid and felt no need to proceed with caution. The past sixty hours had filled him with a sense of bring-it-all-on toughness. The prospect of an intruder within his valueless apartment scared him not one bit; in fact, he almost relished the opportunity to beat someone senseless.

He pushed the door the rest of the way open, his fist cocked by his ear.

But when he caught sight of the intruder, he dropped his fist to his side.

Standing still and purposeless in the middle of the living room was Shawn, so beautiful and rosy in her ski sweats that Mark felt the back of his throat catch. She wore a hand-in-the-cookie-jar facial expression, her eyes wider than normal, her mouth rounded into a small "o" shape. She appeared indecisive, confused even, as if not sure whether to sit or run.

They met in a mid-living-room embrace, their first-ever hug with no ensuing kiss or grope, and it occurred to Mark that it had been *days* since he'd actually spoken to her. He hadn't yet explained to her the reasons for his Friday-morning promise, made in front of the D-Squad, to prosecute and bring down Sigma. She knew nothing of Kelly Devereaux's story, nor did she know of Greg Turlington's. She knew nothing of the dean's crookedness. Nor did she understand, for that matter, why it had *always* been his tendency to hide behind a wall of silence.

Maybe it was time to break down the wall.

He pulled back from the hug and led her by the hand to the darkened bedroom. He sat her on the edge of his mattress, then turned to his desk and lit a single candle. Then he sat down beside her, found her eyes, and told her about his boyhood home of Cazenovia, about the father who'd made him a homemade lacrosse stick, and about the mother who'd made him the black necklace beads he touched when lonely or scared.

He told her about a place called Cherry Plain, a sacred Mohawk burial ground that had been approved for sale by Congress and immediately purchased by a golf course development corporation. He resurrected the peaceful

protest that had been organized by his parents and attended by every Mohawk family in a hundred-mile radius
. . . the symbolic costumes of feathered hides and moccasins . . . and the songs that had flowed from Indian-
styled sitters.

He told Shawn about the tomahawk each Mohawk had
waved as a sign of resilience and solidarity.

He painted searing images of that day: the rumble of
approaching military vehicles, the descending thump of
chopper blades, and the positioning of FBI snipers on the
perimeter of the protest. He recalled the tension and fear
. . . the thunderous report of a rifle . . . and the bullet that
traveled fifty yards before ripping through his mother's
neck.

He told her what it was like to hold a dying head in his
lap, to kneel in a still vacuum of horror while at the same
time living through the peripheral chaos . . . his father,
blind with rage, taking vengeance on the sniper who'd
shot Karin Jessy.

He called it as he saw it now: one moment in time, two
parents gone, and a son left to live with the jagged remains.

As for the rest, he said it raw, for fresher-than-ever
were the abrasions left by the ongoing manhunt for Jay
Meadow Jessy, outlaw to those with badges, hero to all
others. He introduced a puppet named Kelly Devereaux
and a puppetmaster named T-Bone. He described the
stage Dean Templeton had built, with the help of three
dozen brothers. He told the truth about the biggest lie
Simsbury had known until now, the sex crime case whose
testimony had been scripted by billionaires, yet hadn't
found its way into a simple manila D-Squad folder.

He held back only Greg Turlington's gloss on the Chad Ewing conspiracy, keeping it instead as his own personal weapon.

But he told Shawn what she'd long been waiting to hear, and when he was finished she looked at him for a long moment that bordered on belief and disbelief. Then she told *him*, in a low, hard voice, that together they'd get those bastards—for Mark Jessy, for Chad Ewing, for Kelly Devereaux, and for everyone who'd ever been bullied and toyed with by the Sigmas.

Then she kissed his forehead, pulled him down, and wrapped her arms around him . . .

Mark waited until Shawn was asleep before he crept from the mattress. He dressed quickly and quietly, grabbed a can of paint he'd never used on his walls, and left the apartment.

An hour later he returned, soothed Casey back to sleep, undressed, and crawled back into bed.

And in the morning, all fourteen-hundred-plus Simsbury students—all those smug, future pillars—awoke to the following painted message scrawled beautifully across the old, abandoned scoreboard outside the Cage, on which random messages had been known to be painted:

TAKE OFF YOUR BLINDFOLDS. CHAD EWING WAS MURDERED.

CHAPTER FORTY-THREE

The 200th Year
Sunday, March 8

6:04 A.M.

For the first time since staring down the barrels of guns intended to scare the debt out of him—years before in Britain—Templeton was afraid for his life.

His sleep had been fitful, and as he watched the morning sun slant through his living-room window, he considered his two options, the first being to blow the whistle on Sigma before things got even more out of hand. But what sort of whistle could he possibly blow, other than a vague one? He knew only what T-Bone, his real boss, had been willing to tell him over the past five years. That, and of course that the Sigma alumni matched his salary and paid handsome bonuses for his adept handling of crisis situations. He had no smoking gun in his possession that would remove Sigma entirely from the chessboard.

Besides, calling the feds and whispering murder and bribery would be more foolish than running. If the Sigmas went down, he'd go with them. He was an extortionist. He also had a feeling he was an indirect accomplice to the murder of Doctor Charles Marston and God knows what other crimes perpetrated in the wake of the Chad Ewing crisis. He was a felon, but not the kind of man who could endure a jail sentence.

Bottom line, he didn't have enough information to cop a plea and testify in exchange for immunity.

Or in exchange for protection from Sigma.

His second option, his *best*, was to shut up and keep playing the game. After all, this was still just Mark Jessy he was dealing with—just a pawn—and it was ludicrous to envision Mark even chinking Sigma's armor. He had merely, without actually saying so, turned the blackmail threat back around on Templeton. Fine. Each now had dirt on the other, which meant they were each now free to play the game with no real restrictions except those that were inherent. Which meant Templeton would *win* the game, because he had the most powerful fraternity in the nation on his side, and he was the better man.

Wasn't he?

Please, he thought, as he reached with a shaking hand for the phone. *Please, don't let anything else go wrong.* He ran jittery fingers across the eleven numbers of a private residence, and as he waited for the call to be answered, he closed his eyes. *Be strong,* he told himself. *It wasn't your fault, it wasn't your fault, it wasn't your—*

"Hello?" said a deep voice.

"T-Bone," said Templeton, trying to keep his scared voice steady. "It's Templeton. You better get yourself some student representation. This baby's going to trial."

7:00 A.M.

Dominic was halfway to three hundred push-ups when the phone began to crow, and because only physical injury interrupted his pre-breakfast pump, he pounded his way symbolically to the two-century mark before acknowledging the outside world's existence. He used rep number two-oh-one to propel his nearly naked self to his feet, squeezed his pecs together with the force that could shatter beer bottles when dared, then turned his rage on the phone.

"What!" he barked.

"Gamma, this is Alpha with a short, sweet rhyme. Get the boys ready, because it's fuckin' time."

CHAPTER FORTY-FOUR

The 200th Year
Sunday, March 8

8:33 A.M.

Nestled between his dog and girlfriend, Mark awoke to comfort, and for the first few conscious moments he forgot all about setups and conspiracies. Blinking away sleep, he shifted onto his side and gazed at Shawn as she slept beside him, then ran his fingers gently across her back and shoulder blades.

She stirred. "Mmmm . . . gives me chills."

He continued to softly scratch and rub, but as he did happiness yielded to sudden reality.

"What have I gotten myself into," he whispered.

Shawn heaved a drowsy breath, then rolled over and propped herself on an elbow, and with dewy eyes she looked right into his. For a long moment she watched him, seeming to wrestle with something.

"I'm the one," she told him.

He stared at her a second or two, trying to read her meaning.

She cupped his chin and leaned into her words. *"I'm*

the one who voted not to expel you. *Me,*" she stressed. "The one who has a target for every cause, who's supposed to hate players like you. I voted to let you stay, and not because I thought you were innocent." She drifted her face a little closer. "But because I saw something spectacular in you. Something beautiful and real, and I didn't want this precious little world of ivy to be deprived of it."

She gently rubbed the side of his face, as sleep crept back onto her own. "That's why you frustrate me sometimes. And that's why I keep coming back for more.

"That's why I love you."

She smiled the sweetest smile he'd seen in the last thirteen years, kissed him softly, and rolled over.

1:00 P.M.

The woman Mark had decided he was going to marry had left at ten thirty for a day of ski practice, research, and saving the world, and the drive to study had left Mark soon after. By noon he'd abandoned his books, and he'd spent the last hour teaching Casey the finer points of sitting. He was making little progress and was on the verge of deserting this project as well when he heard a knock at the door.

He trotted to the back door and opened it.

"Hi," said Fairchild, his weary face betraying the cheer of his voice. "What's going on?"

Mark just stared at him, in the same manner with which he'd stared at the dean the night before. He hadn't yet considered what a face-to-face meeting with his former best friend would be like. He had, however, figured that by now the Sigmas knew of his intentions, and the look on Fairchild's face told him he was right.

Still, he had nothing to say.

He had lots to say.

"Can I come in?"

Mark shrugged and stepped aside. Fairchild entered the apartment, shed his jacket, rubbed his hands together, and said, "We need to talk."

"We do?"

"I swear to God, Mark, I had no idea—"

"Bullshit."

"Really," pleaded Fairchild. "I swear. Only the seniors were in on it. Honestly, do you think I would've let that happen?" He moved forward and put a hand on Mark's shoulder. "Come on, Mark. I'm your *friend*."

Mark shook him off and smiled coolly. "Dave, if you're my friend, then I dread to think who my enemies are."

"I'm your brother."

"You're no such thing."

Looking as if he'd been slapped, Fairchild shifted his jaw to one side. Then he averted his eyes. "I hear you might prosecute."

"Oh, and who'd you hear that from?" said Mark. "Templeton, the bribe-able Brit? Or was it T-Bone?" Mark searched for Fairchild's honorable blue eyes and found them still glued to the rug. "That's right, Dave. I know about T-Bone. Terrence 'T-Bone' Bonnell, warlord to the undergrads. Did he send you over here? Does he want to know the price of my cooperation?"

"I . . . don't know what you're talking about."

"Oh, come on. Let me tell you something, Dave.

Whoever told you I *might* prosecute was wrong. I'm *definitely* going to prosecute. In fact, I can't think of anything I'd rather do than crush to little pieces the conspiracy of silence you guys have going. So you just run along back to the house and tell your sick brothers and all those sick alumni to get ready for the fight of their lives."

Now Fairchild looked up from the carpet. "Oh, would you just listen to your bad self. You're so tough."

"I'm tough enough."

"I'm real terrified. Feel free to jump at any time—"

Mark lunged suddenly, grabbed Fairchild by the jacket collar, and slammed him against the wall. The two senior All-Americans rolled the length of the wall, alternating the upper hand, until Mark succeeded in wedging the hockey player into a corner. He cocked a fist, and readied to add another chip to his former best friend's nearly perfect face.

Fairchild glared at him. "Go ahead and hit me. Hit me *hard*, and end a three-year friendship—"

"It was a *one-year* friendship, you asshole."

Fairchild opened his mouth to respond, then clamped it shut, bracing for the punch. Mark kept his fist poised, recoiling it even higher, and for a moment considered throwing it.

But something held his fist at bay.

Relinquishing his hold, he backed away.

Fairchild pried himself from the corner and smoothed his jacket as he edged toward the door. For a long minute he eyed Mark like a rival gang member. Then his glare softened with the same sort of underlying respect that had kept Mark from hitting him, and with a shaky sigh he said, "Look, you have every right to be angry. On behalf of Sigma, I apologize for what happened."

Mark shook his head. "Save your apologies for the Board of Directors. I'm gonna bury you guys."

Fairchild sighed with frustration. "*Think* about what you're saying. You've got your eye on every lacrosse record in the book, a beautiful girlfriend . . . and good friends." He looked up at Mark. "Believe it or not, we still consider you a brother over at Sigma." He tapped his own temple. "*Think* about what you're doing, and ask yourself if it's really worth it."

Mark set to reply, then stopped himself. *Was* it worth it? Was it worth forever alienating a friend like Fairchild—a guy with whom he'd shared all his hopes and dreams?

Was it worth maybe risking his *life*?

For a moment, the answer hid weakly behind the question. Then came at him in a rush.

"Get out, Dave. Get the fuck out."

Fairchild nodded slowly, resignedly. "Very well, Mark, you can have it your way. Go ahead and turn this campus upside down. Go ahead and use Chad Ewing's unfortunate soul to try and get a little revenge for yourself." He shook his head sadly. "But remember this. You're going to lose."

4:12 P.M.

Following strict rhymes, the three pledges trudged across the quad, down the snowy path, and through the Cage parking lot. The first carried a ladder, the second a bottle, and the third a bucket with sponges, brushes, and paint cans.

When they reached the scoreboard they stopped, looked up, and read the message to themselves.

Then they went to work.

As the sky turned the color of a bruise, the pledges took turns climbing, scrubbing, and painting, until finally one simple word was written across the scoreboard.

Brotherhood.

They exchanged secret handshakes of solidarity, took apart the ladder, and walked back to Sigma in silence.

Madame Rumor usually saved her best stuff for Mondays, but this was too good to pass up. For the second time on this sleepy Sunday, the old scoreboard outside the Cage had a message.

The first message had inspired wonder. *Chad Ewing was murdered? Really? By whom? And what's this about blindfolds?*

The second message had caused confusion. *Brotherhood? What the hell is that supposed to mean?*

Something is happening, whispered the Madame. *Stay tuned.*

5:20 P.M.

The Brotherhood Room was barely lit and cold, the air wired with pregame intensity. Each of the twelve faces wore a hard look—save for Mu's, which was incapable of anything fiercer than impishness.

"I just want to know one thing," Beta said, his voice soft but strained. "How many here knew Mark was being set up?"

The brothers exchanged looks.

"If you knew before last week, please stand up."

Again, they silently searched each other. Then, shrugging, Gamma stood, and Kappa immediately followed.

Beta nodded. "Why am I not surprised."

"I just found out last fall," said Kappa defensively.

"Then why didn't you tell us *then*?"

Kappa nervously eyed the faces angled toward him. "Because—"

"Because I told him not to," said Gamma. He turned to Kappa and motioned for him to sit, then sat himself. He readjusted his mass in the chair and crossed his arms defiantly.

"I see," Beta said, his lips whitening. "So what you're saying, Gamma, is that we're only a brotherhood when it suits your secret side."

"I'm saying that the matter was over and done with. It was best for the brotherhood that no one else know."

"Why's that? So the rest of us could come off looking like a bunch of two-faced pricks?"

"That was only gonna happen if Mark found out."

"Which he did."

Gamma raised his eyebrows and studied his fingernails. "As someone in the know, I felt his chances of finding out were about one in a million. He got lucky."

"Well, why the hell were *you* in the know?"

"It was a senior thing," Gamma said, shrugging. "My only role was to get heavy in the event of intruders. The Phi Omegas arrived uninvited, and I helped thump 'em because Beta Patterson ordered me to. Afterward, I asked him why we'd done that, and he pulled me aside and explained what was going on, and why."

"And what *was* going on?"

"We were ridding the brotherhood of weakness."

"And why?"

Gamma looked around the room. "Because Sigma's hallowed doors are not open to the lying son of a murderer."

Beta looked incredulous. "In what way did Mark *lie?*"

"He told everyone both his parents were dead, and we all felt bad for him."

"And why shouldn't we feel bad for him?"

Gamma glowered. "Because his fucking father killed an FBI agent who put his life on the line to protect decent Americans." He leaned forward and pointed at Beta. "Bottom line, Mark was a black mark on our proud tradition. He had no business being here."

"Did he write that message on the scoreboard?" asked Delta.

His attention still riveted on Gamma, Beta shook his head absently. "I didn't ask." Then the question seemed to register, and he turned to the rest of the seniors. "Does it matter? And could you blame him?" He threw up his arms. "Does anybody else here think what we did to him was *wrong?*"

Two or three nodded, but the rest shook their heads.

"Look, Beta," said Epsilon. "Mark's an okay guy, and I feel bad for his situation, but he really didn't belong here."

"Why? Because he never belonged to a country club?"

Epsilon shook his head. "I never belonged to one either. It's just that . . . he *seems* to have a way of finding trouble."

"And we don't?"

"He's a loser," said Delta.

"Oh really, Delta," said Beta. "And as one of his team-mates, what do you think of his ability on the lacrosse field?"

"He's good."

"Just *good*?"

Delta hesitated. "He's the best player I've ever seen," he admitted.

Gamma rolled his eyes. "Can we drop the scouting report and move on to more important matters?"

"Such as?" asked Epilson.

"Such as the phone call I got today from Alpha *himself*," Gamma said, chest noticeably swelling.

"Does Alpha know about Mark?"

"He does."

"What's he want us to do?" asked Upsilon.

"He's ordering us to proceed with Operation Blue Eagle."

"Oh please," scoffed Beta. "Operation Blue Eagle. Hey, man, this isn't the Middle East. Why don't you join the rest of us here in the real world."

Gamma glared at Beta. "Where were you while I was putting my life on the line? The mall? Your senior prom?"

"I was watching the whole farce on TV. You guys were really tough, the way you kept a lid on all those mean, scary—"

"Shut up."

"Good thing you got to kill someone, Gamma. He might've been the one to discover the mother of all chemical weapons. He might've been the one who was really gonna bring down the good old US of A."

Gamma pointed at Beta. "I said shut up! Later on, we can talk all you want about how chicken-shit you are, but right now we talk about Operation Blue Eagle."

Beta smiled, completely undaunted. "You like saying that, don't you. You like saying Operation Blue Eagle."

"Shut up—"

"You like the way it sounds. Makes you feel like the colonel you'll never be."

"*Shut up!* Shut the fuck—"

"Colonel Gamma, the Soldier of Alpha's Fortune."

"Goddammit, Beta, shut your cocksucking mouth!"

Beta's head snapped back, his eyes widened, then narrowed. There was a short silence as the other ten seniors shifted their gazes between two close friends on the verge of tearing each other apart.

"Jesus," Mu said, his voice trembling. "*Please* stop."

"Never!" hissed Gamma, his eyes filled with rage. "Mark Jessy's the enemy. He and his cute little lawyer team are showing us no respect. I have no respect for people who have no respect for us, which is why both Alpha and I agree the time's come to get physical."

"Damn straight," said Epsilon.

"Right now!" shouted Delta, and he and Omega slapped hands.

Beta looked up and sneered. "Would you listen to yourselves? This isn't the mob. We can't go around breaking arms and legs every time someone disagrees with us."

"I'd call this a little more than a disagreement."

"Definitely," said Zeta. "I say we kick the shit out of him tonight."

"You couldn't beat up Mark's girlfriend," countered Rho.

"I could fuck her, though." Zeta smiled and nudged Kappa, who laughed and spat on the floor.

"No," Rho said pensively, "you probably couldn't do that either."

"Oh yeah? And why not?"

"Because you've got big ears and a small penis."

Laughter.

Gamma exploded to his feet and threw an empty beer bottle against the wall. Glass splintered in every direction. "*Fuck!*" he screamed.

Sudden silence.

He glared at each brother who dared to make eye contact. "Is this a joke to you guys? Did you see what was written on that scoreboard? There are some people out there who want to see this fraternity shut down. Forever! Are we gonna just sit here and make jokes while it all slips away? We've got orders to follow! Now let's go kick some soft pink ass!"

Malicious hollers of agreement met this mini-sermon.

Beta hung his head and shook it amid the clamor.

When the din had subsided, Gamma said, "Chin up, Beta. And for crying out loud, relax. In Operation Blue Eagle, Mark's not the primary target."

"Oh really? Then who's the primary target?"

"*Targets,*" Gamma corrected as he reached behind him and grabbed a thin stack of word-processed documents, then stood and began to pass them out. "They're listed here, in chronological order relating to estimated time of attack." When each of the other eleven brothers had a printout, he returned to his seat. "I think target number one speaks for herself. I've done a little research into her habits, and I think we can have her tonight. Target number two is probably the most important. We need this guy on our side. As for target number three, this is merely a warning to Mark, to get him thinking about what he's getting himself into."

Beta finished digesting the list, then looked up in disbelief. "How the hell does Alpha know about target number three?"

Gamma smiled proudly. "He doesn't. That was my addition to the list."

Beta crumpled his sheet and tossed it on the floor. "You're a sick son of a bitch, Gamma."

"Enough, Beta," said Gamma impatiently. "Now, here's what we're gonna do. After dinner—"

"Aren't we going to vote?" asked Beta.

"What the fuck for? It's a goddamned order from the alumni!"

"Let's vote anyway. When it's all said and done, I want us all to be able to look back on this night and remember just who wanted to do what."

"We have no choice, Beta," Gamma said wearily, "but if it means that much to you, then call for a quorum."

"We've already got one," said Beta as he stood. "Ballot or hands?"

They all agreed it should be a show of hands and then proceeded with the unnecessary vote. The measure passed, ten to two, and Operation Blue Eagle was launched.

5:58 P.M.

On a single bed that had never seen the bare ass of a man, target number one read a work of nonfiction and dreamed of the day she was the foremost authority in her field.

On a double bed barely big enough for his ego, target number two watched C-Span and dreamed of the day his motions would be big news.

On a makeshift bed of familiar smells, target number three slept soft and sweet, and dreamed of nothing at all.

6:15 P.M.

Once nourished, they assembled in the Brotherhood Room. Dark clothes were distributed, final instructions were given, and with a final, good-luck tap from the Sword of Tradition, its blade still heavy and hard after all these years, the brothers marched out the door single file, like the army that they were.

The last soldier out brought the Sword of Tradition with him.

CHAPTER FORTY-FIVE

The 200th Year
Sunday, March 8

7:15 P.M.

Betsy Kimball had never thought twice about taking the shortcut through the woods that connected Coles Tower to Brunswick Apartments, where her boyfriend, Tom, lived. Yes, the path was dark, and it snaked intricately, but the lights of both the Tower and Tom's apartment could be seen at any point on the path, depending on the direction she was heading. And since it was just beyond the Bowdoin College dinner hour, she was heading in Tom's direction. As always, they'd study together until midnight—he lived in a quiet single, where the studying was good—and then he'd walk her back through the woods. She'd allow him to kiss her good night at the door to her suite, then send him on his way.

Because this nightly journey through the woods was practically tradition, she had grown accustomed to the darkness, the silence, the shadowy lurk of the trees and the bushes.

Which was why she almost didn't notice when the

shadows that had once been bushes and trees began to move, and then came straight for her.

The masked figures homed in from every direction. She had no time to cry out, which was just as well, because she wouldn't have known what to cry. Strong hands—ten, maybe twelve of them—covered her mouth and subdued her hands and ankles. A blindfold was forced onto her face. A crumpled rag was shoved into her mouth. She felt herself being carried silently away from the Tower.

She struggled to free herself, but abandoned all such efforts after a few ineffectual wiggles. Whoever, whatever, had control of her possessed extraordinary strength. Her best bet was to relax. Whatever it was her attackers desired, they were going to achieve. Defiant efforts on her part would only exacerbate the situation.

Though blind, she was keenly aware of her environment. A van door sliding open. Whispers. Feet scraping on pavement. Her body being shoveled forward, her palm scraping across damp carpeting. Arms and legs crawling over hers. The door slamming shut, the gag being yanked from her mouth, and the engine roaring to life.

Her world lurching into motion.

They were taking her somewhere.

They were going to rape her.

She wouldn't be a virgin much longer.

A piercing scream shattered the monotonous engine hum, and loud music began pulsing through a speaker close to her left ear. Reflexively, she rolled away from the sound, but a strong hand grabbed her face and pressed her head to the floor.

"Lie still, bitch!"

Through the blaring heavy metal, she heard the accompanying shrieks of her attackers. Men. Young. Bowdoin kids? Doubtful. Probably townies. She made a mental note of everything she heard, felt, and sensed. Did the engine sound old? Yes. What was that smell? Oil? No, bleach. She'd remember all this when she filed a police report. These bastards would be caught. She'd see to it personally.

Someone screamed in her ear, and she flinched and leaned away.

A voice close to her sang tauntingly with the music. "*Do you know where you are? You're in the jungle baby . . .!*"

The terrain became bumpy, and the van slowed. The music faded, the screaming abruptly subsided, and all fell silent again, save for a persistent rattle. She'd remember that too.

The van rumbled to a halt and its engine died.

She waited tensely.

Doors squeaked open, then slammed shut. The sliding door gave way to a distant, outside roar. Iron hands grabbed her again and dragged her from the van. A whisper ordered her to stand.

As she stood, an icy gust of wind slashed at her exposed cheeks. And then, above the moan of the wind, she heard a deeper, more distant bellow.

Ocean waves.

The hands led her from the van. The wind intensified. The surf thundered louder.

They were taking her to the water.

They were going to rape her, and then they were going to drown her.

Despite the numbness in her face, she felt her lower lip begin to quiver. The blindfold absorbed the tears, but nothing, not even the clamor of the wind and waves, could mask her whimpering.

"Please, no. Please, I'll give you anything you want. Just let me—"

"Shut up, cunt!"

She was hurled to the ground, and the frozen rocks of Maine's winter seashore broke her fall. She cried out.

There was silence for a moment. Then, a calm, mighty voice rose above the elements.

"Miss Kimball. . . . Please remove your blindfold."

They knew her name! She fumbled with the cloth that covered her eyes. Managing to peel it off her head, she let it fall to the ground, then squinted into the glare of the fire that blazed before her. Red ash peppered her face, and she turned away.

They were going to rape her, and then they were going to burn her.

A surging wave, bigger than its brethren, crashed against the beach, spraying her with a chilly mist that contradicted the flames. She was ten feet from the ocean, ten feet from the fire, ten feet from . . .

"Miss Kimball, look at us!"

Shielding her eyes, she obeyed, and what she saw made her gasp.

Fire and water were the least of her worries.

Surrounding the blaze, facing her, roughly thirty men dressed in black and wearing ski masks stood as tall as any tree. On a large rock stood three more, each cloaked by a black robe and a Klan-like hood. One held an ax, another a noose, the third a sword.

The sword bearer jumped from the rock and floated toward her, his feetless robe circumventing the flames. The light from the fire cast his long, elusive shadow as he approached.

"Stand up, Miss Kimball."

She scrambled to her feet. As she watched the sword bearer come closer, she thought about running, but realized they'd catch her easily.

The sword bearer stopped in front of her.

Raised the sword high over his head.

And then began to rhyme.

Miss Kimball, Miss Kimball alone in the light.
You are a Bowdoin student, creative and bright.

Your parents pay pretty for your education,
So commencement might bring you guaranteed
occupation.

He poked at the fire with his sword, and the kindle spat its ashy protest.

But the school skills you're learning aren't fit for
your calling,
In fact, we find the pairing appalling.

Craft is to medicine as tongue is to a foreigner.
Whoever heard of a creative coroner?

We are troubled by yarns that have spun from your
head.
Startled by your gossip regarding the dead.

He moved closer.

Simsbury College has been dealt a great trauma.
It's against your best interest to heighten the drama.

And suddenly, all these bizarre rhymes made sense to Betsy. Chad Ewing. These were his friends.

Or his enemies.

We suggest that from now on, you keep your mouth shut.
Or into your life deep danger will strut.

Tread ever-so-softly and rejoin the wallflowers.
For though death be your business, the kill is all ours.

The sword bearer raised his sword high over his head, and instantly three of his comrades rushed forward and seized Betsy. Two grabbed her arms, while the third knelt and secured her feet.

They needn't have bothered.

She was paralyzed with terror.

The sword bearer edged closer, now inches from her. He made eye contact with her (for a moment she saw icy eyes peering through the mask), grabbed the waistband of her sweatpants, and began to slash them from her body.

She screamed once, but the man to her left slapped her face hard, reducing her to quiet, helpless whimpers.

The ribbons of fabric fell from her waist and legs. The sword bearer then grabbed her underpants and ripped them off with a violent yank that propelled her forward and to the ground. She landed in a heap, half-naked and sobbing, waiting for further violation.

But it never came. All that came was a low, hard warning, from a voice savagely poetic and very close to her ear.

Don't once for a second think our threats to be corny.
Heed them well, sweatbeast, or next time we'll be horny.

And that was it. The blindfold was jammed back on her face, and she was lifted like a rag doll. She was carried back to the van, and the pound of the ocean receded.

The loading process was repeated, and the van bounced from rugged terrain back to smooth. The hum of the engine returned. Betsy sat motionless in the back, aware that she sat inches away from some serious assholes.

After a blank period of time, the van screeched to a stop.

Doors opened, then closed. The sliding door rolled open. More whispers, more hands. Cold air hitting her bare ass and legs, and then a hard, impersonal shove.

She landed awkwardly, rolling over once. The snowy ground shocked her naked bottom, but she dared not stand or even remove her blindfold. She had no desire to see the license plate. She had no desire to remember *anything* of this night. The assholes had found her once, and they could easily find her again.

She heard tires squeal, and when she was sure the van

was gone, she removed her blindfold and cautiously looked around. Amazingly, she was back at the entrance to the path that separated Brunswick Apartments and Coles Tower. It was almost as if nothing had happened, yet she knew she'd have nightmares about this night for the rest of her life.

Although she'd never take this dark, wooded path again, right now she had no choice. She was naked from the waist down. There was no way she was going to let Tom see her like this, and the main road was out of the question.

She scurried barefoot and seminude through the woods, increasing her speed until panic took hold with the fingers of a wildly imaginative child. They were following her, and would attack her from behind. There were poetic monsters in the closet of trees, and under the bed of snow, and the damn Tower seemed to be running away from her!

Her feet finally touched the slush of the parking lot. The trees and the bushes and the shadows turned back, and the bright lights of academia pulled her to safety.

By some miracle, she made it across the parking lot and up the walkway without being seen. She opened the door to the Tower, poked her head into the lobby, and after gauging its emptiness snatched a black-and-white "Go U Bears!" banner from the wall, which she wrapped around her like a towel. She scampered to the elevator, frantically called for it with a trembling finger, and did her best to conceal her identity when it arrived with three passengers, each of whom, she sensed, gave her a look of utter horror as they disembarked. She ducked into the elevator car, pressed a button, and only when the door slid shut and the elevator car began cranking upward, did she allow herself to weep.

She disembarked at the eleventh floor and crept down the hall to her four-person suite. She opened the door quietly, slipped inside, and locked it behind her. She hoped her roommates had each brought their keys with them, because she had no intention of unlocking the door for anyone on this night.

She turned on all the lights in the common area, stumbled to the bathroom, knelt in front of the toilet, and began to vomit.

A half hour later, she stood and staggered to her bed.

8:45 P.M.

It was an unwritten rule that Simsbury College, blessed as it was, owed a debt to society, Georgeville in particular. The college seized every opportunity to give back to the town, since it was good both for community relations and student character development.

Camp Cardinal, the brainchild of the current athletic director, had been an instant success. The camp was a yearlong program of instructional clinics hosted by Simsbury College varsity athletes for the benefit of local kids. In general, the Simsbury athletes were happy to help out.

Except Simon Schwitters. He hated both teaching *and* kids, which rendered his Sunday-night swimming lessons a loathsome task. His students were all between the ages of ten and twelve—young enough to be hyperactive, old enough to walk all over him. He endured the lessons, though, for one reason, and one reason only. The coach of the swim team, Davis Ballmiller, was a staunch supporter of Camp Cardinal and looked favorably upon those who volunteered. Further, Coach Ballmiller's sister was a high-ranking big shot at Harvard Law, Simon's grad school of choice. It was never too soon to start networking.

On this night, however, not even Ivy League dreams could keep Schwitters interested in the pint-sized townies making trouble in the pool. He had an International Law exam the next day, and every minute he spent teaching the butterfly to brats was one minute less he could spend studying his index cards.

"Free swim!" he shouted. "Tony, no more dunking, or you'll spend the next ten minutes swimming laps."

Tony Russo, a twelve-year-old nightmare, gave Schwitters the finger, then disappeared beneath the water.

After passively supervising ten minutes of cannonballs and waterfights, Schwitters blew his whistle, signaling the session's end. The pool spat kids into the toweled arms of mothers and fathers, while Schwitters began stowing all the volleyballs, bubbles, and water rings. By the time he'd secured the toy box, the swimming deck was deserted. He shut off the lights and left through the Cage's rear exit.

He moved away from Simsbury's twelve-million-dollar marvel into the darkness of the long, pine-covered path that wound its way toward the center of campus. The air felt and smelled like snow, true to the weatherman's call for six to ten inches. Schwitters eyed the imposing snowdrifts that already lined the path, and wondered where the hell they were going to put it all.

He heard a noise from the woods to his right and instinctively quickened his pace.

A gust of wind bombarded his face with dusty snow, temporarily blinding him. He turned and walked backward as he wiped the frost from his eyes.

It was then that he noticed the dark figure speeding toward him through the white mist.

The attacker drove his shoulder into Schwitters's stomach, slamming him to the icy pavement with a breath-expelling thud. As Schwitters gasped for air he was flipped roughly onto his stomach, where he noticed two additional boots standing before him. The first attacker pinned him to the ground with a knee to the spine, while the second knotted a piece of cloth around his head.

"Please . . ." he gasped, his world suddenly blackened by the blindfold. "Don't hurt me. My . . . my father has . . . money."

His pitiful whimper had no apparent effect on the assailants. They flipped him over once again, hoisted him into the air, and carried him swiftly away, one set of hands under his armpits, another grasping his ankles.

A car screeched to a halt, and his spirits momentarily lifted. Then he heard a young, aggressive yell, and it occurred to him that a friendly, passing motorist had not stopped to help.

Rather, the attacking troops had been fortified.

"Watch your head, pussy!"

Schwitters felt himself being tossed forward like a sack of garbage. Cold vinyl against his skin and the smell of motor oil told him he was now in the car. He heard doors slamming hard, then felt the car lurch into motion.

His one glimmering hope was that he was being kidnapped by his pledges. They'd been known to playfully abduct upperclassmen and bring them off-campus for a night of beer and pornos. He tested out the theory: "Mothball?" he asked hopefully. "Snaggletooth? Is that you guys?"

There was a long silence, broken by the scream of the car's sudden acceleration. And then, from the front seat came a frat-boy voice, but deeper and meaner than the kind he was accustomed to hearing.

This ain't no Zeta Rho tea party, you small, dickless cretin.

Now keep your mouth shut, or we'll give you a beatin'.

The car raced down the road, away from the safety of Simsbury College.

Toward the ocean.

10:21 P.M.

Mark lay contorted on his living-room couch, his textbooks and notepads dog-eared on the floor or draped upside down across his midsection and legs. What little energy his senior mind had once held for schoolwork was now wholly focused on exposing the truth behind Chad Ewing's death.

Despite his confident bluster during the altercations with Templeton and Fairchild, he realized he didn't know the first thing about trial procedure—other than, of course, what he'd learned from movies. He had no clue how he was going to try this case, and for the first time ever he was grateful that Schwitters was on his side, since the guy seemed to know a lot about the law. For the next week or so, Mark would have to pretend to like him.

He picked up the phone and dialed Shawn's number. Busy. He hung up, leaned his head over the couch backrest, and closed his eyes.

He opened them again.

Something was wrong.

The apartment was way too quiet.

Where was Casey?

With the guilt of a neglectful parent, he realized that he'd let her out almost an hour ago. Disgusted with himself, he stood and walked to the glass slider. Throwing it open, he called for Casey to come here, girl.

No response.

He cupped his hands around his eyes and peered through the snow-white blackness.

No sign of her.

He stepped out and worked his way through the trees, straining to hear the telltale jingle of dog tags. However, the piercing shrill of a snowstorm's gale dominated. All he could hear was the howl of winter.

He whistled sharply.

Disturbed, winter screamed its nasty retort, and Mark felt the first stirrings of paternal unease creep into his soul.

He paralleled the row of apartments, checking the small, dark alleys between each for a pair of glowing eyes. He looked through every matching slider, wondering if one of his neighbors had found the puppy and taken her in. Most of the apartments were dark, though, and those that were lit were filled with disciplined studiers, none of whom would have the time or inclination to care for a lost pet.

Where *was* she? He was scared now. The snow seemed to fall heavier by the second, the wind ever-freshened. If Casey were to get lost in the woods on a night like this, she'd never be found. His only hope was that she'd instinctively veered toward the athletic fields. That would make sense, since that was where he took her to play. He turned toward the snow-drifted lacrosse field and began to plow his way through bowing branches.

A faint noise stopped him.

The wind died a sudden moment, and he heard the noise again.

A high-pitched whine.

A squeal.

He pinpointed the source and whirled around.

And there, pinned helplessly against the thick trunk of a tree, no more than twenty feet away, was Casey, her large, brown eyes pleading for help.

He ran toward her.

She was bound tightly to the tree with a thin length of rope, the worn fibers of which wound, intentionally, it seemed, over her ears and around her neck. Frozen blood matted her fur. She squirmed frantically at the sight and smell of her master, causing the rope to dig deeper into her skin. Her pained squeals and frightened trembles were enough to break his heart.

How could someone have done this to a puppy?

He set to work on the rope, but the knots, covered with ice and snow, had been pulled so tight by panic that his fingers had little effect on them. He dug his bare hands under the snow, searching for a sharp rock or a piece of ice. Finding nothing but powder, he dug deeper.

His numbing fingers touched something smooth amidst the jag. He worked his hand around the object and pulled.

It was an empty beer bottle. He swung it in a swift motion, and the neck splintered against the tree.

Now armed with razor, he had Casey free in less than a minute, and she scrambled into the safety of his arms. He pulled one side of his flannel across her head and staggered through the snow back to his apartment.

Once inside, he set the shivering, bleeding puppy down on the kitchen table and examined her wounds. In the light they didn't look too bad, but the slice on her ear was oozing a fair amount of blood. And she still trembled violently.

She was in shock.

And he knew of only one person who could help her right now.

He threw on his heaviest jacket and zipped his puppy warmly inside. He stepped outside again, and headed toward the center of campus.

10:40 P.M.

All three targets successfully hit, the brothers returned to their sacred, white-paneled lair. In contrast to the unity with which they'd left, though, they returned in trooplike groups of six to ten. And unlike the blank, soldierlike expressions they'd worn during deployment, they returned with smiles of victory stretched across their young faces.

Smiles concealed by black masks.

10:50 P.M.

Mark pounded at least a dozen times on the door at the far end of Dudley Hall's second floor, then rocked on his heels and peered down at the pair of soft, trusting eyes that gazed up at him from the pouch formed by his partially zipped jacket.

The door opened.

Jessica LaChance, the woman who liked vanilla frozen yogurt and wanted to be a veterinarian when she grew up, smiled at the sight of the man she'd slept with often during her freshman year. "Mark," she said. Then the look in the eyes beneath his snow-covered hair seemed to register with her, and her smile vanished. "What's wrong?"

He unzipped his jacket, revealing the blood-crusted puppy nestled against a blood-smeared tee shirt.

She put her hand to her mouth and gasped. "Oh my God! Was she hit by a car?"

He shook his head, on the verge of tears. "No . . . she . . . she was tied up. Someone tied her to a tree . . . with some rope. I . . . Can you fix her?"

She pulled him inside, shut the door, and gently took the dog in her arms. "Okay," she crooned softly, "let's take a look at you. Ssshhhh . . ." She probed her fingers through Casey's fur, looked in her ears, peered in her mouth, and ran a hand down her chest and under her belly. "All right," she said finally. "She's got a nasty little boo-boo on her ear, but other than that, she's going to be fine. Puppies are bionic." She rubbed Casey's good ear and turned to Mark. "I'll take her to the clinic with me tomorrow. For now, I can put some Bacitracin on that ear. If it's good enough for us, it's good enough for dogs. Right?"

Mark stared at her blankly, and as the agony of concern ebbed, a new emotion streamed in. And by the time he'd mindlessly shuffled to the window on the other side of Dudley 22's common area and focused on the big white house that towered against a black, stormy sky, the sensation had filled every void to the point where its identity was unmistakable.

Rage.

Sheer and utter rage.

12:24 A.M.

The phone next to the dormant New York Yankees baseball cap rang eleven times before it succeeded in waking the soundly sleeping man. He balled his fists, pressed his eyeballs deep into their sockets, then throttled the phone and said, "What the fuck?"

"Hey," said a deep voice.

"T-Bone," said the man, suddenly more alert and respectful. "What's up?"

"I've got another job for you. The kind you like."

"You mean . . . right now?"

"No. Tomorrow night."

"Sure. What needs doing?"

A long, chill silence met this question; by the end of it the man knew what needed doing, and he gripped the phone tighter.

"Man or woman?"

"The former. A college kid."

The man paused. "That makes it harder—the college kids you know are good fighters."

"So you break a sweat. I'll make it worth your while."

The man smiled.

"So what's this kid's name?"

"Mark Jessy," said T-Bone. "The kid we set up for rape."

"What's *my* name?"

"I'm working on that."

The man paused as he absorbed the exchange. "Boy, you guys really don't like this kid, do you?"

"He keeps getting in the way."

The man switched the receiver to his right hand and began cracking the knuckles of his left. "What about disposal?"

"My boat'll be waiting for you in Cape Elizabeth. Get far enough offshore that we won't have to worry about anything being found. But before you do that, do me one special favor."

"What's that?"

"Make him suffer."

CHAPTER FORTY-SIX

*The 200th Year
Monday, March 9*

11:42 A.M.

The dean was already planted at the conference table when Mark and Shawn arrived, and he offered his usual smug nod as they took their seats. Shawn offered a strained "Good morning," speaking more to her water bottle. Mark offered no greeting at all. He took a seat at the very end of the table, fearing that if he sat too close to the dean he'd be unable to resist the temptation to take a swing at him.

The corners of Shawn's mouth turned downward as she wriggled free of her jacket. "Simon's not here yet?"

The dean hesitated and sort of chuckled to himself. "There's something we three need to discuss." He paused to polish his glasses, and after meticulously wiping away every little smudge, delivered his bombshell. "Simon has resigned from the D-Squad."

"*What?*" said Shawn.

"He informed me of his decision this morning. He doesn't feel we have anything solid on Sigma, and he's uncomfortable pursuing the case any further, despite his deep respect for the D-Squad, the college, and the institution of law in general." The dean hesitated briefly then continued. "One can only imagine the degree of angst Simon endured in reaching this verdict. I, for one, support his decision."

"Well, I don't!" screeched Shawn.

The dean closed his eyes and shrugged.

"Do you think he'd reconsider?" Shawn asked. "Maybe I should talk to him."

"I don't think so. He seemed pretty set."

"That's it, then? The case is over?"

"Technically," answered the dean, "you and Mark may pursue with the prosecution. Let me remind you, though, that the Board of Directors, who'll be acting as the jury, will weigh heavily Simon's switching from the prosecution to the defense. I'm afraid they might be skeptical—"

"Wait a minute," said Mark. "*What* did you just say?"

The dean smiled innocently. "Didn't I tell you? Simon has decided to represent Sigma during all future proceedings."

"*What?*"

"That's right, Shawn," confirmed the dean. "So, I guess he hasn't dropped the case completely. He's merely . . . switched sides."

"Oh my God."

"Can he do that?"

"Sure he can. In the event of a D-Squad trial, the defense can secure representation by any Simsbury student."

"It would've been nice for him to tell us in person," Shawn said.

"He sends his apologies. Unfortunately, he couldn't make it. He's having lunch at Sigma. After all, they've got a lot of work to do, and not a lot of time to do it." He raised a finger. "Which reminds me . . . as judge, I must request that you furnish a list of witnesses to both myself and Simon." The dean turned to Mark. "Have you such a list with you?"

"No."

Shawn threw up her hands. "No, we don't have a *list*! Simon was supposed to put it together. We're going to need more time."

The dean shrugged. "I'm sorry, but the trial's slated to begin tomorrow afternoon. I've already informed the Board of Directors, and they've graciously agreed to come. We can't push it back any further."

"This sucks."

"I remind you," countered the dean, "that you had all weekend to do this. As an impartial party, it wouldn't be right of me to grant you any more time."

Impartial. Mark wanted to gag.

"I'd like the list by one o'clock."

Shawn looked at her watch. "So that means we have barely an hour to come up with a list of witnesses."

"I guess so."

"How fair of you."

"I don't play favorites, Shawn. In fact—"

"You'll have that list," promised Mark.

Shawn and the dean looked at Mark with surprise.

"Oh really?" said Shawn. "We'll just churn out a list of witnesses, just like that?"

"If we have to."

"You have to," said the dean. "I want two copies, on my secretary's desk, at one o'clock today."

"You got it."

12:15 P.M.

Shawn had not stopped venting since they left the Administration Building, and she showed no signs of slowing down as she and Mark waited like herded cattle in the dining hall lunch line.

"Are you crazy?" she ranted yet again. "A *list* of witnesses? We don't even have *one* witness, let alone a whole list."

Mark grabbed a pear and an apple from a large bowl, and placed them on his tray next to his plate of lasagna. "What about Betsy what's-her-face?" he suggested. "You been able to reach her?"

"No. She won't return my calls."

"Keep trying."

Shawn put a hand on Mark's shoulder. "Hey, are you hearing me? We have *no* witnesses! *None.*"

"We have plenty."

"Oh yeah? Name one."

Mark leaned over and kissed Shawn lightly on the tip of her nose and winked at the server who was smiling at them.

"Be patient, my love. We'll discuss it over lunch. Now, I think you need some more complex carbs . . ."

1:05 P.M.

After a minute or two of delicate fingering, Simsbury's aged and frustrated commander-in-chief finally tore the sugar packet in half, sending very little sweetness into his cup and a granular blizzard over the rest of his desk. A defeated look on his face, Carlisle sighed and pushed the steaming cup to the corner of his desk, then turned to the dean.

"Okay, Anson," he began, "what's going on?"

"We're going to trial. Tomorrow, four o'clock."

"Really?"

Templeton nodded.

"What needs to be done?"

"Nothing. I've told Hank to call the other Board members. He'll fill them in on the details."

"Like what?"

"Like time, place, etcetera."

Carlisle was silent for a moment as he scratched his head. "Who's going to win, Anson?" he asked finally.

"Sigma. Without question."

"Is that good or bad?"

"Since Sigma had absolutely nothing to do with Chad Ewing's death, I'd say it's a *good* thing, wouldn't you?"

"Sure. Justice is a good thing."

Templeton nodded in agreement, but said nothing.

1:54 P.M.

Had Mark known he would literally bump into Schwitters as he hustled around the corner of the Economics Building, he would have led with his forearms and done the job right. Unfortunately, he was more focused on getting to his two o'clock class on time than he was on leveling a traitor. In fact, his defenses were so down that Schwitters got the best of the collision, his attaché-case-carrying elbow boning deep into Mark's side. Mark swore, twisted to one side, then dropped his backpack and began to rub the point of contact. Schwitters gave him a momentary look of fear and shame before resuming his trademark smugness.

"So sorry," he said with a nasty smirk.

Mark buried all facial winces and reached down for his backpack. "Not as sorry as you're gonna be, *counselor.*"

"Oooh, big word," said Schwitters. "Trying out all the technical legal terms you've been ignoring the last two years?"

"Only the ones I've learned from you, Mister I'm-not-concerned-with-what-I-believe-I'm-only-concerned-with-what-I-can-prove." Mark hitched his backpack higher. "Am I to assume, dickhead, that you've decided it's easier to prove Sigma innocent than it is to prove them guilty?"

Schwitters made a face. "You're to assume *nothing* about me, asshole."

Mark nodded and crossed his arms. "Well here's something I know for a fact: The guys at Sigma hate your guts, Simon. They hate your fucking guts."

Schwitters smiled and shook his head. "Not as much as they hate yours. See you in court, *counselor.*"

He turned and made his way toward Sigma.

2:02 P.M.

The intercom buzz snapped Templeton from his catnap. He leaned forward and poked his phone unit twice.

"What is it?" he mumbled.

"Shawn Jakes is here to see you."

"Send her in."

A moment later the door to his office opened and

Shawn strode in as if she owned the place. She walked right over to his desk, slapped down a piece of paper, then put her hands on her hips and announced, "Here's your list of witnesses."

Templeton picked up the paper, skimmed it briefly, then set it to the side. "This list was due an hour ago."

"Kiss it, Dean Templeton. I think it was incredibly unfair of you to not give us more time, given the circumstances."

"I'm *so* sorry you feel that way."

"I'll just bet you are. I know all about your little financial relationship with Sigma."

"Oh really?"

"Really. If I could prove it, I would. I think you're repulsive."

"And I think you've been listening to one too many of the fairy tales floating around in your boyfriend's disturbed little melon." Templeton pretended to search his desktop for something more important. "They *are* entertaining, though, and any other day I'd love to microwave a bag of popcorn and listen to the whole amusing lot of them." He swiveled in his chair and put his back on her. "Unfortunately, I've got some real work to do, so if you could just run along . . . ."

He stood and turned, but by the time he'd fully done so, Shawn was storming back down the hallway.

4:33 P.M.

The phone in Sigma's presidential suite rang a half dozen times before finally coaxing Dave Fairchild from his reverie.

He picked up the receiver. "Hello?"

"Dave!" blurted an unmistakable voice.

"Hey, Jeremy. How are you?"

"Good, Dave, good. How are *you*?"

Fairchild hesitated, tempted to blurt the truth. "I'm okay."

"Are you sure?" said Jeremy Townsend, agent to fourteen NHLers and six NFLers. "Because Coach Cote called. He's worried about you."

"He is?"

"Yeah. He said he saw you on the quad yesterday and called your name, but you didn't respond. He said you looked . . . tired and out of it." Townsend cleared his throat into the phone. "He said you looked *skinny,* Dave."

"I've been . . . I've had a stomach virus."

"I figured it was something like that," Townsend said, sounding reassured. "Cote was concerned that maybe you had a little too much going on in your life right now. I told him the Dave Fairchild I know can handle anything and everything at once, so bring it on, baby!" He laughed himself into a coughing fit. "Geez," he said finally, "you're not the only one with a bug. Seriously, though, is everything all right?"

"I . . . yeah, Jeremy, everything's fine."

"That's what I like to hear," said Townsend. "But try to get that weight back up. Remember, all the S and C coaches we talked to said one-ninety of pure muscle by training camp. Speaking of which, I've been pushing the Bruins GM to take you. If he does, we might be looking at a signing bonus of seven-fifty . . ."

As Townsend's sales pitch rambled into oblivion, Fairchild's gaze shifted to a photo on his desk—one picturing happier times. As it did, he swore he'd trade every dwindling pound to prevent what he'd already let happen, and give every bonus buck to take back what he'd done.

What he would trade . . .

What he would give . . .

8:44 P.M.

Mark and Shawn were forty-four minutes into their third regimented hour of pizza and strategy, and nearly done. The meeting had marked the first time in their eight-month relationship—that *he* could recall, anyway—that the two communicated as fellow students instead of as boyfriend and girlfriend. No flirting. No underlying sexual connection. Just a man and a woman, seniors both, working together as if on a term project.

Except the topic was a dead pledge.

And the theme was justice.

Seated cross-legged on the floor, Shawn dropped her pencil and yawned. "I should go," she groaned. "I've got a paper due Friday." Then her eyes lit as Casey wobbled into the room. "Come here, my little angel. How's my baby's ear?"

The puppy climbed onto Shawn's lap and settled in, her gauzed ear nuzzling the crook of Shawn's arm.

"Am I sleeping over tonight?" asked Mark, ready to be a boyfriend again.

"Only if you bring this little angel."

The phone rang, and Mark nabbed it. "Hello?"

"Yes, hello," said a deep Maine voice. "May I speak to Mark Jessy?"

"You already are."

"Hi, Mark, this is Tino De Lasa. I'm a Cumberland County EMT."

"Yeah?"

"Yeah. On the morning of Sunday, February twenty-second, I responded to the emergency at the frat house."

Mark swallowed hard. "You mean," he said, motioning for Shawn to stay, "when Chad Ewing fell?"

"Yes."

"You were there?"

"Yes. In fact, I just found out this morning that he died."

"Yeah . . . he did."

"Man," De Lasa said, then sighed heavily. "I, uh, spoke to Chief Sullivan today and he told me the fraternity had settled on a pretty hefty fine with the state, for violation of liquor laws. He also told me that the college was handling their own private investigation."

"Yes," said Mark. "I'm in charge of it."

"I know. That's why I called. I got your name from President Carlisle. He said I should talk to you."

"Really?"

"A-yuh. Yours was the only name he could recall," he said with a light chuckle. "He said you're a real big lacrosse star."

"I . . . play."

"Sounds like you more than just *play*," said De Lasa. "Anyway, I know this Ewing thing is no longer my business, but I feel as though I have to say something."

There was a pause.

"Go on," urged Mark.

"That boy was brutalized," De Lasa said quickly, as though he'd been just waiting for the proper permission. "He was naked and everything, and had rude poetry writ-

ten all over him. There were some other things, too—
things that had me thinking, *This is no accident.*"

Mark's heart stopped, then exploded into a sprint. He
turned and gave Shawn a thumbs-up. "Mr. De Lasa, is
there any possibility we could meet—tonight?"

Silence.

"It's *really* important."

The pause grew louder, then ended with a sigh. "Sure.
As a matter of fact, it gives me an excuse to get out of the
house. My wife's hostin' a baby shower tonight. You
know how those things are."

"Not yet, thankfully."

De Lasa laughed. "Do you know where Jack's Coffee
House is?"

Mark thought for a moment. "No, I don't think so."

"It's down Freeport Road, just past April Pond. It'll be
on your left."

Mark grabbed a pen and paper. "Okay, that sounds
easy enough. I should be able to find it."

"Great. I'll meet you inside."

"Cool," said Mark as he scribbled. "Wait a
minute. . . . How will I recognize you?"

"Shouldn't be too hard," said De Lasa. "We'll be the
only two customers under the age of fifty."

"Okay."

"Can you be there in fifteen minutes?"

"Sure!"

"See you then."

Mark dropped the cordless and shot a fist into the air.
"Yes!"

His shout sent Casey scrambling from the room.

Shawn stood quickly, her eyes blue on an expanse of white. "What is it?"

"That," said Mark, "was the EMT who worked on Chad Ewing after the fall. He said that Chad was *naked*, and he had *writing all over him*!"

Shawn shook her head in amazement. "I don't believe it."

"Believe it."

"And he wants to talk with you now?"

"Yeah. We're meeting at Jack's Coffee House."

"Where's that?"

"Just past April Pond."

"Geez. That's way out there. Watch out for flying ice-fishing huts."

"No shit. Can I borrow your Jeep?"

"Sure," said Shawn, tossing him the keys. "I'll walk from here. Should I still expect you later?"

"Of course," said Mark. "After I meet with De Lasa I'll come back here and get Casey. I'll be over after that." He reached for his jacket and dove into it. "Wish me luck."

Shawn kissed his cheek. "Good luck."

CHAPTER FORTY-SEVEN

The 200th Year
Monday, March 9

9:09 P.M.

Templeton hung up the phone, smiled, and danced to the bathroom. He splashed a little cologne on his neck, then went to find his wife. He found her lumped under a blanket on the couch, watching *Masterpiece Theatre* and, of course, eating.

He had some business to take care of in his office. He hadn't eaten, but he would pick up something at Monty's. Judith nodded absently, then tittered at something amusing on the TV screen.

Templeton shook his head, and as he turned away from his wife and toward a rendezvous with Linda, he had a brief, glorious vision of himself divorced and independently wealthy, no longer in need of a rich, aging mother-in-law.

Soon, he told himself as he headed out the front door. *Very soon.*

9:30 P.M.

All across campus, the students of Simsbury College made things.

In libraries, they made study guides.

In kitchens, they made frozen pizza.

In lounges and common areas, they made small talk.

In beds, they made love.

And in a quiet, lonely room, Jason Lyle made a decision.

Then he made a phone call.

9:32 P.M.

This end of Freeport Road was dark, desolate, and overgrown, like the forested path of a Grimm's fairy tale. Night painted the trees into hulking forms of ebony pine that hid any hint of civilization as Mark bounced his girlfriend's Jeep along the frozen, mud-bunkered road and searched through his frosted window for Jack's Coffee House. He was filled with optimism, knowing that within minutes he'd be talking with a witness to the carnage and aftermath of Chad Ewing's fall. Still, a twinge of unease scurried through his gut, whispering to him that something about this rendezvous point was . . . odd.

The unease intensified when a building suddenly leapt from the rural gloom. Skidding the Jeep to a lopsided halt, Mark studied the structure from inside the vehicle. The building was set back from the road, at the rear of a barren, unplowed parking lot at the forefront of a wooded area that seemed to extend thickly into forever. The establishment certainly didn't look like a warm, cozy coffee shop. It looked more like a broken-down, beat-up shack, livened only by a single, smoky spotlight that looked as if it might burn out any minute. Rotten boards covered the windows. Missing shingles revealed black holes in the exterior. Over the door, however, was a small, painted sign, that read ACK'S COFFEE HO SE.

This had to be the place.

He maneuvered the Jeep onto the soft shoulder and turned off the ignition. He eyed the building suspiciously one last time, wondering whether he should even get out of the car. It appeared as though the shop had gone out of business. He wondered if De Lasa would even be there.

And then he noticed the black BMW parked near a Dumpster in the rear corner of the parking lot.

It had to be him.

Nudging his doubts aside, Mark exited the Jeep and walked toward the car. A gust of wind whipped through the parking lot, and he zipped his jacket as far as it would go.

When he was fifteen feet from the car, the driver's door opened. A tall, lean man emerged.

Mark squinted through the pelt of powder. "Mr. De Lasa? Is that you?"

"A-yup," said De Lasa, his baseball-capped head bowed defensively to the swirl of wind as he came forward. "Sorry about this. I wasn't aware that the place had closed down."

"That's okay. I'm just grateful you called."

"My pleasure," said De Lasa as he stopped and lifted his head.

And revealed the New York Yankees logo etched in white on the face of his cap.

Mark froze, as if Kelly Devereaux herself had reached out and stopped him for his own good. He stood there a moment, feeling his adrenaline surge as he called up isolated details from her story . . . *a man wearing a Yankees cap . . . driving a BMW.*

This man wasn't Tino De Lasa.

This was the *recruiter.*

Sigma's errand man. And maybe something much worse.

For an instant the two men locked eyes. Then Mark turned and began to walk back to the Jeep.

"Where are you going?"

"Back to the car," said Mark quickly. "I forgot my tape recorder." He forced himself to walk calmly. If he could somehow keep an I'll-be-right-back gait, maybe he could be in the Jeep and flooring it before "De Lasa" figured out his alias had been decoded.

But then he saw the man's shadow, black against the ashen snow, following close behind.

Casual would no longer cut it.

He quickened his pace and glued his eyes to the shadow, checking its wheels for changes in speed. So focused on the silhouette's legs, he was within ten steps of the Jeep before he noticed the certain something that extended sharply from one hand.

Mark broke into a sprint that matched the hammer of his heart. The next six or so running steps were surreal, as if they existed not in the normal realm of time or space, but in a world where relativity was warped. The Jeep seemed to exist only as a mirage, a safe but unreachable base on the boundaries of a game that had suddenly turned deadly.

He finally reached the Jeep. Trusting that the man was on his tail, guessing he hadn't the time to fiddle with the cranky door handle, Mark used the driver's window as a springboard and, turning quickly, unleashed a punch that dismantled his assailant's nose. The man cried out once and collapsed to the ground, blood pinwheeling through gloved fingers, tarnishing the glint of his knife and burning burgundy holes in the snow.

Mark watched for a moment, then dove into the Jeep and started the engine.

He swung in a circle that slung frozen mud in the direction of the bleeding man, aimed the Jeep toward Georgeville, and floored the accelerator. The transmission moaned, then adjusted to the pressure. The skidding tires searched for answers, then found them, as all at once the Jeep understood the situation and exploded forward. As it hurtled down Freeport Road, back toward the relative safety of the nation's sixth most prestigious liberal arts college, Mark kept one eye fixed on the rearview mirror, checking for a black BMW crawling up his tailpipe.

He sped through the center of Georgeville and shot through the snotty, cast-iron gates that separated Simsbury College from the real world. He pulled the Jeep into the tree-infested parking lot that nearly hid his pad from view, parked it, and hurried inside. He locked the three doors to his apartment for the first time ever, turned out all the lights, scooped Casey into his arms, and hunkered low into the darkest corner of his living room.

Where he waited, listening to his breath come in ragged rasps, and fingering his beads.

10:25 P.M.

Shawn poured a glass of white wine, carried it to the bathroom, and set it down on the sink. She turned on the shower, slipped out of her bathrobe, and sipped her wine as she absently examined her naked reflection in the mirror. When the leading edge of steam began to cloud her vision, she returned her glass to the sink, stepped into the shower, and allowed the hot spray to leach out the day's stress.

She lathered and rinsed absently, then remembered Mark was coming over, so she resoaped her legs and shaved them. Finished, she turned off the water, toweled herself dry, and slipped back into her bathrobe. She retrieved her glass of wine, opened the bathroom door, and shut off the ceiling fan.

She stepped out into the hallway. The apartment was quiet and Daphne-less, the only sounds the distant ticking of the living-room clock. She padded down the hallway to her room.

As she reached for the light-switch, a hand shot out from the darkness and grabbed her wrist. She screamed and dropped her glass, and crystal shards and wine sprayed against her bare ankles. Another hand grabbed her by the hair and pulled her into her bedroom. She clawed at the air with both hands and felt a fingernail evoke a deep, low curse, and in the next instant she was thrown across the room.

Landing hard on her bed, she screamed again and tried to bounce back to her feet, but a palm closed over her face and pushed her back onto the bed. She kicked furiously at the darkness, and as she did, her bathrobe rode up over her hips and untied itself. A hand encircled her throat, and another ripped the robe from her body.

Above her, dark and massive against the hallway's thin

light, a figure dressed in black stared down at her with eyes blinkless behind a ski mask.

She lashed out with her fists, connecting twice but with little effect. One of the enormous hands slapped her hard, hurling stars at her fluttering eyes. She moaned and covered her face with her hands. Two trunky thighs straddled her, gripping her ribs. She swung her fists again, beating them harmlessly against a thick, beefy chest. The hands squeezed her wrists again and pinned her arms to the bed.

She struggled briefly, then gave up and whispered a desperate plea. "*Please* . . . don't. You . . . better get out of here. My boyfriend's on his way over . . ."

The masked face leaned close to hers. Hot, rancid breath attacked her face, and whispered, "I don't think so."

Now just one hand held both her wrists, and Shawn watched with horror as her attacker pulled the glove off his free hand with his teeth. She knew what was coming, so she closed her eyes and swallowed hard.

A burning hand closed over her breast, then found her nipple and pinched it hard. She bit her own tongue to keep from screaming and slowly opened her eyes.

White teeth grinned a warning at her through the slit in the mask.

Then the tongue behind the teeth began to rhyme.

Take my advice, pursue not one more day.
Test us and find this tit-pinch to be foreplay.

Unless you've a wish to die before motherhood,
I'm warning you, bitch, not to fuck with the brotherhood.

The attacker rose from the bed, placed both his hands under her, and flipped her into the air. She spun like an unwilling gymnast, landed like a sack of limbs, then rolled across the bed and off the other side, where she fell between the bed and the wall. Crumpled, folded, and naked, she listened while heavy steps pounded through her apartment and out the front door.

She struggled from the crevice and to her feet, then sat on the edge of the bed, placed her head in her trembling hands, and began to weep.

And as she cried, all the anger and hatred she'd once felt toward Sigma vanished like a skittish campus squirrel into a tangle of brush. The fraternity now triggered a new emotion in her.

Fear.

10:52 P.M.

Officer Ames positioned the badge carefully over his heart, then slammed his locker shut and hummed the Andy Griffith theme as he exited the Georgeville P.D.'s changing quarters into the hallway. He was headed for the dispatcher's cubicle, where he'd get a brief rundown before beginning his graveyard shift. Pulling even with the chief's office, however, he ceased his hum and slowed his pace. The light was on. The door was ajar.

It was nearly eleven on a Monday night, and Chief Sullivan was in.

Ames gently knuckled the door open. "Sully," he said with pleasant surprise. "What are you doing here?"

"Waiting for you," Sullivan answered, as he leaned back in his chair. "Shut the door."

Ames closed it, then took the seat opposite Sullivan's desk. "What's on your mind?"

Sullivan sighed and rubbed his eyes. "A whole shitload of things, none of them good."

"Problems at home?"

Sullivan shook his head, then leaned forward in his chair and looked darkly into Ames's eyes. "Did you spend that money yet?"

"I . . . no—"

"Good. Don't."

Ames frowned. "How come?"

"Because it's blood money."

"I . . . really? What do you mean?"

"C'mon, man. This might be Georgeville, but you're still a cop. You know what that expression means."

Ames stared at Sullivan, then down at his lap as he nodded. "Whose blood?"

"Doc Marston's."

Ames closed his eyes and swore beneath his breath. "Who spilled it?"

"The big white fraternity house on the corner of College and Maine."

"You know this for sure?"

"Pretty much. You know how I met with that prick in the parking lot behind Paul and Dory's? Well, he was so fucking cavalier about paying us off, so cold-blooded, that it occurred to me that these assholes would literally *kill* to keep their frat alive. Sure enough, four days later the doctor who tried to save that pledge's life gets run over in a town where only accidents and natural causes kill. Very convenient. So I checked the Massachusetts plates of the prick's BMW against police records from all six New England states, New York, and New Jersey."

"What'd you find out?"

"Nothing, except that the plates were reported stolen to the Boston DMV last year."

"Hmm."

"Yeah. So then I checked the videotape from the first set of tolls on the Maine Turnpike for the day of and the day after Marston's death." Sullivan leaned forward again. "At five-twenty P.M., roughly four hours before Marston was hit, a black BMW of the same make and year as the one I was looking for crossed the Maine border. At eight-eighteen the following morning, the same BMW crossed back over to New Hampshire."

Ames felt his eyes widen. "Did the plates match?"

"Each other, but not the one I was looking for." Sullivan leaned back. "Anyway, that doesn't mean shit. I'm sure it was the guy, and I'm sure he killed one of the best men this town ever knew."

Ames shook his head again and clenched his teeth. "You know," he said finally, "I didn't even want that money."

"I know you didn't, and I was wrong to assume you did. Shit, I was wrong to want it myself." Sullivan shook his head and sneered at the Vietnam combat medal that hung from his desk lamp. "It's just . . . that I was so caught up in making those rich Simsbury fuckers *pay*, that it never occurred to me the best way to make them *pay* was to take away all that fancy queer brotherhood shit that makes me want to puke." He pointed to the wastebasket. "If I'd acted on your original report of that so-called accident, that big white frat house would be a big white graveyard by now."

Ames raised his eyebrows and said, "What do we do now?"

"Nothing."

"Sully, we can't let them get away with it."

"We already did. I put out an interstate APB on a black BMW with a dented grill, but I know it won't lead to shit, especially since the paint they scraped off Marston's corpse doesn't match the paint they use at BMW. I checked it out."

Ames threw up his arms. "Okay, fine, but we could press charges for the death of that kid."

"And say what? That we've been so busy that we're just now getting around to it? Believe me, Amesy, you and I are the ones who'd end up on trial, and I'm not ready to sacrifice my job on the off chance that we *might* succeed in bringing down that frat."

"So we're gonna do *nothing*?"

"For now," Sullivan said as his expression turned dark. "Those pricks have fucked up before, and they'll fuck up again. And when they do, I'm gonna fuck *them* so hard up the ass that they'll fart pieces of me for the rest of their lives." He stared at Ames for a long, hard moment, then softened his visage and posture, stood, and wandered to his window, where he seemed to stare down the black western sky.

"Meantime," he said finally, "I know what we can do with that blood money."

11:40 P.M.

"We've shed all the blood we can," said Gamma, the undergrad leader of Operation Blue Eagle, and thus the new unofficial leader of the Sigma seniors, especially since Beta appeared to still be in the throes of an extraordinary funk.

"Wait a minute," said Epsilon. "Are we *sure* we can trust Schwitters?"

Gamma considered the topic, then nodded. "He won't dick us over. He values his frail little body too much. Besides, this is a golden opportunity for him to hang with the cool kids. Remember, he tried to get a bid here as a freshman."

"What a joke."

"And he can't stand Mark," offered Upsilon. "I think he's got a thing for Shawn. When we brought him back to his room to talk strategy, the first thing he did was cover all the pictures of him and Shawn being *lawyers* together. This is his chance to beat the man who's bangin' the object of his affection."

"Even if he *does* turn on us," said Gamma, "we'll simply argue that we weren't given fair representation because he was still in cahoots with the D-Squad. The Board will buy that, the case will be thrown out, and I'll personally hand Schwitters the beating of his life."

"So essentially," summarized Kappa, "we can't lose."

"Exactly."

"Unless, of course," said Beta, who'd sat quietly in the corner until now, "it leaks out that we've bullied everyone in a ten-mile radius."

Gamma looked at Beta. "What do you mean, 'leaks out'?"

"What do you think I mean? Betsy Kimball? Jason Lyle? Shawn Jakes?"

"They won't say a word. They're not that stupid."

"What if they're not that cowardly, either?"

Gamma glared at him. "Listen, Beta, I know you don't approve of the way we've gone about this, but believe it or not, what we've done is probably going to win this case for us."

"Like Alpha says," added Kappa, "nothing else matters but our house and our brotherhood."

"You're out of your mind."

"I'm dedicated," said Kappa to Beta. "Just like you used to be. What's happened to you, man?"

Beta looked at Kappa for a long time, then turned to look out the cracked window against which his left shoulder rested. The meeting continued without him, and though he heard his name mentioned a few times, he never looked up.

MIDNIGHT

As the clock struck tomorrow in the distance, Mark concluded—with neither relief nor disappointment—that a second attempt on his life wouldn't be coming, at least not tonight. Feeling as if he'd been granted some bizarre stay of execution, he reached for the phone, dialed Shawn's number, and listened as it rang into nothingness. Apparently, she'd given up on him and gone to bed. Adjusting his clutch on Casey, he settled deeper into the blackness of his living room and reflected on the status of this mortal contest into which he'd been thrust.

So, Turlington had been right. There *were* lives at stake. And since the game had evolved to a lethal level, he now had to wonder whether it really *was* worth it to play. For despite all the scores that needed settling, one terrifying realization hit home.

That man wanted to kill me.

Death. The word and all its forms and sides certainly meant more to Mark than to anyone on campus. He'd cradled his mother's ripped-open neck. He'd watched through screaming tears as the Cherry Plain trees convulsed with his father's rage. For thirteen years he'd lived with death in the way some folks lived with asthma or wealth.

Before, death had merely haunted him.

Now it was *hunting* him.

He closed his eyes, rested his head against the wall, and tried to think through the pounding in his head. He knew his safest option was to wave another white flag before he lost far more than just a brotherhood. But the thought of conceding to Sigma now, after everything he'd learned . . . well, he just couldn't. His next safest alternative, he guessed, was to call the police and try to convince them to get involved. Of course, these same police, according to Turlington, were in Sigma's back pocket, so they'd probably do more harm than good. Besides, cops wore badges and represented the law and were brethren to the FBI; Mark hadn't spent a lifetime waving aluminum bats at U.S. marshals to let bygones be bygones now.

So basically, he had no one to turn to.

Except maybe his father, who'd once claimed there was no more endangered animal than a hunter who'd suddenly become the hunted.

Mark opened his eyes, stood up from his nook, turned on all the lights in the apartment, and moved to his bedroom. He reached on top of his dresser, pulled his father's legacy—the lacrosse stick Jay Jessy had made for his son—from its memorial bed, and ran his fingers over its smoothness.

Then he snapped it over his knee and took the sharper half to the living room, where he sank once again into his safe corner of the world, worked the beads relentlessly, and summoned the resolve of a hunter.

CHAPTER FORTY-EIGHT

The 200th Year
Tuesday, March 10

6:00 A.M.

He didn't need the wake-up call. The broken nose and swelling eyes had kept him from sleep all night. He hadn't even removed his Yankees cap. He'd simply sat in the hotel room's one easy-chair, picking at room service, wincing with every deliberate chew. At dawn, he decided to report in.

"Hello?" said a voice after two rings.

"T-Bone. It's me."

"Mission accomplished?"

"No."

"*What?*"

"He . . . I don't know. He somehow knew what was going on."

"Jesus."

"Who *is* this kid, T-Bone?"

A pause. "What do you mean?"

"I mean who *is* he? This kid's got instinct."

"Don't give him too much credit. You got cocky, and he got away."

"T-Bone . . . what am I dealing with here?"

"Nothing you haven't dealt with before."

"I don't think so. Give me some background on the bastard—and I *don't* mean his grades."

T-Bone sighed a burst of frustrated static into the phone. "Cherry Plain."

The man with the broken nose began to reflexively question the meaning of this response, but stopped short. For as the words "Cherry" and "Plain" fluttered through his head and joined with what little he knew about his current target, the years suddenly melted away to a time when everyone else in America had been raging against an FBI machine that had shot a young mother dead. He, as a Marine headed for a stint in Special Forces, had been less intrigued by the death of a civilian as he'd been by the barehanded way in which the civilian's husband had exacted revenge.

By driving the sniper's nose right up into his brain.

"He's *that* Jessy?" he said, while lightly fingering the break in his own nose.

"Son of. His daddy's still on the run. My bodyguard has contact at the FBI. The talk is that Jay Meadow Jessy's the smartest fugitive they've ever hunted." T-Bone paused, then continued. "But I don't buy it. I think they're just trying to cover their asses. They got cocky, just like you did, and now they have to pretend he's more clever than he really is. But they'll get him. Soon, I hear."

The man with the broken nose nodded slowly into the phone.

"So," said T-Bone. "I suggest you drop the cute stuff

and pay a visit to our boy's apartment. Get the job done.
Now."

"I don't like giving a target the benefit of his home
turf."

"You don't understand. He's already *on* his home turf.
After last night, he'll probably never leave campus
again." T-Bone paused. "It's only going to get *harder.*"

"Not necessarily," said the man with the broken nose.
"I have an idea."

9:00 A.M.

At precisely 9:00 A.M., the doors to Southern Maine
Savings were manually unlocked by the vice president
who'd begun work at SMS as an eighteen-year-old teller.
And at precisely 9:04, two sums totalling $75,000 were
wired from an account designated "Georgeville Police
Department Retirement Fund," to the private accounts of
Paul and Dory Bunker—a mom and pop from Georgeville
who'd been forced to liquidate and retire to the hills of
Tennessee, rather than the beaches of Florida, when the
corporate franchisers came to town.

9:07 A.M.

After dropping Casey at Jessica's apartment for the
foreseeable future, Mark picked out the safest route to the
Administration Building, setting a slower pace than usual
as he scanned for evidence that he was being followed.
He arrived at the conference room just a few minutes late
and was surprised to see only the dean waiting for him.

"Where's Shawn?" was Mark's first question.

"She's gone."

Mark paused. "What do you mean, 'gone'?"

"Gone. Like your mommy and daddy."

Mark closed his eyes and took a deep breath. "Dean Templeton," he said softly. "Please tell me she's okay."

"Oh, she's fine! Fit as a fiddle and sane as Galileo." The dean leaned forward and rested on his knuckles. "She's resigned from the D-Squad, though."

Stunned, Mark could only grunt.

"That's right, Mark. She e-mailed me her resignation this morning. I'm sure she wishes you luck in the trial today."

Mark's head began to swim.

The dean chuckled and picked a piece of lint from his sleeve. "I don't know why I was worried about you," he crowed. "You're a lightweight. You can't even get your own girlfriend to believe your fantasies." He stood up from the table and glared. "It's *over*. There is no case, and there'll be no revenge for you. I win."

Mark felt the anger channel into his arms and hands, saw himself punching the dean's face again and again until the man's pompous blood stained the Asian rug a dark and wonderful red.

But then he saw himself in handcuffs, being led out of the Administration Building and past all the self-righteous Simsbury students. He saw the Sigmas smiling and waving bye-bye as he was carted off. He saw himself banished from school and serving a life sentence as Kiko's first mate, on an endless quest for fish that just weren't around anymore.

He turned and ran from the conference room.

9:12 A.M.

Having actually slept three hours, and possessing what felt like an appetite, Fairchild left a good part of his guilt at the door of the Sigma dining room and headed toward the kitchen on feet that, for some reason, felt good about everything today. He said good morning to the new cook, helped himself to a Mexican omelette and a side of black beans, and took a seat as close to sunshine as he could find. He scooched in his chair, spat his gum into a napkin, and prepared to replace some of the precious weight he'd lost.

This time the vision blindsided him with no warning hum. *Take a good look,* it seemed to command. *Take a good look into the eyes that looked up with trust, and asked when it would be over.*

Take a good look at your answer.

Take a good look at human wreckage.

Fairchild leapt to his feet and sprinted from the dining room. He careened down the hallway, past the spot where Chad Ewing had crashed to his death, to the bathroom, where he knelt before the toilet.

But there was really nothing to expel. No food, no water, and certainly not the hum that followed him in and out of sleep and to meals and asked him every so often what he would trade and what he would give. So he dipped his head low and gagged a few times, the final heave of which clunked his gaping jaw against porcelain with a force that threatened to chip another tooth.

He rested there a moment, then stood and stumbled to his room, where he'd wait until it was time to defend a brotherhood.

9:19 A.M.

Throwing his pissed-off shoulder into the Administration Building's lobby door and tumbling into caustic wintry sunlight, Mark's one and only urge was to grab Shawn by the shoulders, shake her hard, and scream, *What the hell are you thinking? Who the hell got to you?*

Without a moment's thought to the possible ramifications of confrontation, he broke into a jog and angled for the Environmental Studies Building on the north fringe of campus; within two minutes he stood fifty feet from its doorway. Sure enough, his heat-seeking eyes spied, amid braids and baseball caps, the telling blond ponytail hooking the collar of a varsity-ski-team windbreaker. As he watched Shawn smoothly negotiate the unsalted walkway, her eyes tossing looks of aloof impatience at those moving too slowly for her liking, her nose pointing slightly skyward, he understood how easy it would be to dislike her. In fact, as he continued toward her, his fists clenching involuntarily for the second time in twenty minutes, he understood how easy it would be to *hate* her.

Because he was suddenly doing that very thing, and was prepared to act on it.

But then she looked up and their eyes met.

And in that instant the cold block of hate melted and ran off, leaving behind an odd admiration that had no real place in this particular moment when he was twenty-two, scared, and on the run.

For this was still Shawn staring back at him . . . the woman who'd spend the next ninety minutes sitting rapt while an environmental policy professor further instilled a drive to make the world a cleaner, better place . . . who'd probably recycle her skiing trophies if she thought it would help. This was the woman who'd patiently endured seven guarded months of secrets regarding her boyfriend's family past . . . who'd seen something spectacular, beautiful, and real in him, when no one else had.

This was still the woman who pursued causes to mental and bodily limits.

Unless she had reason to fear for her life.

He'd leave it to others to hate her looks, her intelligence, her quick, sometimes brutal retorts to their sexual advances. And he'd save his own hate for the FBI and Sigma Delta Phi.

I trusted your secrecy, her look seemed to remind him. *Now you trust mine.*

Thinking he'd never forgive himself if something happened to her, thinking he'd literally *kill* if someone hurt her, he faintly nodded his trust as she disappeared into the Environmental Studies Building.

Then, never more alone in his life, he turned and walked toward the library, where he'd hide amid the studiers until it was time to battle a brotherhood.

CHAPTER FORTY-NINE

The 200th Year
Tuesday, March 10

9:30 A.M.

Amid the multitude of logos bobbing on hats all over campus, a New York Yankees logo blended anonymously halfway between Sigma House and the Hendrigan Art Museum as T-Bone's designated hitter acquainted himself with the Sixth Most Prestigious College in America.

Campus tour guide Sharon Kolojay, who'd spent the last half hour with the man, found him bewildering. He'd taken the tour alone, without a high-schooler by his side. And he hadn't asked her a single question about the curriculum. Strangest of all, he *had* asked several questions concerning the level of nighttime safety provided by security guards, and a couple more regarding which buildings had "antiquated electrical systems," as opposed to those with "more modern utilities."

And what was with the swollen nose and two black eyes?

Next semester, she'd get herself a different kind of work-study job. This one forced her to deal with too many parents, and they were getting weirder and weirder.

10:00 A.M.

In keeping with the Tuesday, March 10, 10:00 A.M.
deadline, the chairman of the Tenure Committee put his
signature on this year's ratification and stamped it with
the college seal. Then he quickly reviewed the list of
those faculty, administrators, and alumni who'd been
granted a sneak preview of the vote, and began faxing, e-
mailing, and phoning.

By 10:20, he was done communicating the results.

By 10:27, the sixteenth name on the list, an alumnus
named Terrence Bonnell, had reviewed the faxed copy of
the vote and smiled as he recognized the possibilities it
offered.

By 10:33, he'd done a little communicating of his own.

12:38 P.M.

Templeton scribbled his approval on the list of all
sophomores wishing to spend half or all of their junior
year abroad, then tossed the document into his out-box,
took a bite of quiche, and turned his attention to one of the
two retirement fund statements that came to him monthly
from Grand Cayman Fidelity.

He noted the recent deposits appreciatively, then
smiled, leaned back in his chair, and dreamed of the future.

2:58 P.M.

It had taken all of Mark's courage to leave the safety of
the library, where he'd spent the last five hours missing
Shawn, wondering if he'd be dead by day's end, and realizing how completely unprepared he was for the D-Squad
trial set to commence at four. However, fear and anger

and dread had taken a backseat to curiosity when his neighbor Matt Moriarty hurried past his cubby, then doubled back and said, "Hey, Mark, did you know there's an envelope taped to your door?" Weighing danger against possibility, Mark had finally chosen to be proactive and had returned, alone, to his apartment.

Though he didn't think anyone would dare take a shot at him in broad daylight, he crept through the pines that separated his and the eleven other senior apartments from the lacrosse field. Thankful for every cloaking limb, he emerged into the cold, shadowed clearing just as a blast of winter ripped north to south along the row of apartments, systematically upsetting the shriveled, leftover Christmas wreaths and other decorations.

And rippling the envelope taped to his door.

He marched forward, freed it from its perch, and opened it.

Mark,

I waited outside your eleven o'clock class, but apparently you skipped it. I tried calling, but I got no answer. Believe me, your not sticking to routines today is a good thing. There are three pieces of information you need to know.

We've found your father.

Someone is trying to kill you.

The two events are directly related.

U.S. Marshal Sehorn is watching you right now, for your protection, but I can't guarantee you'll see another sunrise if you stay here. Pack a duffel if you must, then scram. Spend the rest of the day with friends on campus, then meet me at midnight in the

Trussell Biology Building, Room 104. I'll take you to a safe place and explain what's going on.

At some point, Mark, you're going to have to trust me. I suggest you start now.

Sincerely,
Deputy Trevor Mawn
United States Marshal Service
Federal Bureau of Investigation

A new, more frigid gust swept past Mark as he read the letter twice, allowing every conceivable emotion to whip through his soul. In the end, one word lingered longer than the others.

Trust.

Turning, he scanned what passed for a horizon within this world of fir and danger. At first, he saw nothing but the expected dazzle of snow and wintergreen. But then, as the sun dappled through the hypnotic dance of branches, his eyes caught the briefest glint of glassy orbs.

Binoculars.

Watching him.

Needing no further convincing, he stuffed the letter into his pocket, entered his apartment, and quickly packed a duffel.

But not before reaching beneath the pile of linty sweaters in the corner of his bedroom.

CHAPTER FIFTY

The 200th Year
Tuesday, March 10

4:00 P.M.

In the third-floor conference room of Simsbury College's Administration Building, a simulated court trial of mammoth proportions was about to begin.

The jury consisted of twelve aristocrats, all of whom believed they had Simsbury College to credit for their success, which was why they served thanklessly but proudly on the Board of Directors. They sat in two rows, on benches of hand-carved maple, waiting to hear the case before them.

Against the wall closest to the conference room door sat the defendants, a striking trio of young men resplendent in matching navy suits. Dave Fairchild—he of the countless awards, many fans, and Christian face—struck the most impressive pose, despite looking overtired and a bit thin. His hair was parted like a Ken Doll's, and his royal blue eyes matched the color of the Sigma eagle pin attached to his lapel. Next to him sat A. J. Dominic, a mountainous man whose bulk pulled the collar of his shirt and suit tight around his neck, forcing a few boa-like veins to his skin's surface. He sat stiffly like a new recruit waiting for directions from a drill sergeant. And to his left was Pete Thresher, far less imposing than A. J., but nevertheless present, with darting eyes that read and measured the jurors, one by one.

To Fairchild's right, at the head of the defense table, sat Simon Schwitters, a young man with a young face who appeared out of place beside his three clients. He wasn't there to look good, though. He was there because he was an acknowledged legal genius, a student ahead of his time, and the briefcase from which he now plucked notepads and manila files was a testament to his precocity.

Next to the defense table, seated on a raised platform, high above it all, presided the judge, Dean Anson Templeton. He wore a robe and a look of total imperialism. Before him, on a slanted podium, lay the Simsbury College Charter and a gavel.

And seated behind an antique table was the prosecution: Mark Jessy, lonely and a bit scruffy in his borrowed blue suit. In front of him lay an open notebook, on which he'd scribbled vague annotations. Had he not been so preoccupied with mortality, he would have felt even more out of his depth than he already did.

The dean rose and pounded the gavel twice. Court was in session.

"Ladies and Gentlemen," he began, "this begins the case of *Simsbury College v. Sigma Delta Phi*. My name is Anson Templeton, and as dean of the college, it's my duty, as written into the bylaws of the Simsbury College Charter"—he hoisted the charter into the air—"to serve as impartial judge in these proceedings. When inside these walls, I shall be referred to as 'Your Honor.' Only when a verdict is reached will I again become dean, and at that point I will enforce the sanctions, if any, imposed by the jury."

With a grandiose sweep of his arm he indicated the jury. "To my right are the members of the Simsbury College Board of Directors. As peers, they fit the constitutional definition of a fair jury. It will be their duty to determine the guilt or innocence of the defendant.

"The defendant," he continued, "Sigma Delta Phi, is represented by undergraduate brothers David Troy Fairchild, Anthony James Dominic, and Peter Reginald Thresher. Sigma's legal interests have been entrusted to Simon Duncan Schwitters, the third. Mr. Schwitters has been duly advised that it is his moral obligation to represent his client fairly, and that any attempts to undermine his client's well-being will be met with disciplinary action.

"The College is represented by Mark Morningstar Jessy, who shall act as sole prosecutor in this case. Mr. Jessy is a member of the College's Disciplinary Squad. It should be noted that although this organization usually consists of three students, two of them have resigned. One of these former members is defense attorney Schwitters.

"On behalf of the school, Mr. Jessy has filed what the Simsbury College Charter refers to as 'Responsibility Charges,' alleging that Sigma was responsible for the recent death of Chad Francis Ewing."

Pausing, the dean consulted the podium. "Each side shall give an opening statement. The prosecution shall then call its witnesses, and the defense will get a chance to cross-examine each of them. Based on examination of the witness list, the defense has decided not to call any witnesses of its own, and will rely exclusively on cross-examination testimony. All witnesses have been instructed to remain in their rooms, on call, during court hours."

He looked up. "While I encourage both sides to play to win, it would behoove you to bear in mind that you are fellow students, and these proceedings are intended to resolve this conflict in a civilized manner. Inappropriate behavior will be met with the appropriate recourse."

The dean sat, put on his glasses, and adjusted his chair. "Now, if there are no more questions, the prosecution may make its opening argument."

Swallowing hard, Mark stood, faced the jury, and began reading from a notepad.

"Ladies and Gentlemen of the jury, on the morning of Sunday, February twenty-third of this year, Sigma pledge Chad Francis Ewing was found in critical condition on the living-room floor of the fraternity house. Despite efforts to revive him, the freshman was pronounced dead a short time later at St. Elizabeth's Hospital. These facts are indisputable."

He began to slowly pace in front of the jury, as he'd seen in all those courtroom movies.

"At question here are the events which led to the discovery of Chad's crumpled body. It can be assumed by the position of the body, and the nature of the injuries, that he fell from the second-floor balcony, which is approximately fifteen feet above the living-room floor. However, the cause of the fall is the subject of much debate. Mr. Schwitters will probably tell you that Chad behaved irresponsibly, drank too much the night before, and passed out in the second-floor hallway. The next morning, Mr. Schwitters will then say, Chad woke up disoriented and drunk, and in his confusion toppled over the thigh-high railing that lines the balcony. Thus, it will be Mr. Schwitters's assertion that Chad, and *only* Chad, was to blame for this unfortunate accident."

Mark looked up from his notebook and made eye contact with the jury. "The College, however, will prove a different sequence of events: On the night of Saturday, February twenty-second, the Sigma brothers conducted a pledge activity. After subjecting the pledges to extreme physical and mental abuse, the brothers then singled out Chad and, in an effort to get him to drop out of the fraternity, stripped him naked, forced him to do shots of alcohol, then wrote degrading poetry all over his flesh with Magic Marker. They left him lying unconscious in the middle of the second-floor hallway. In the morning, when Chad awoke, he was still horribly drunk. Dizzy, he fell from the second-floor balcony."

Mark flipped a page. "These are the facts, and I will prove them. And when I'm done, I'm confident you will conclude that Sigma is guilty of the Responsibility Charges filed, and that they should be punished accordingly. Thank you."

He sat down.

Schwitters stood, looking very cool and confident. He held no notebook, and his three-piece suit put Mark's to shame. He smiled at the jury and slid his hands into his pockets.

"Ladies and Gentlemen of the jury, I stand before you with no notebook, for I have no prepared script. And that's exactly what Mr. Jessy was reading from. A script.

A lie. It's my experience that only the *truth* comes naturally, which is why I'm confident that I can stand before you armed with nothing but my integrity.

"I would, however, like to thank Mr. Jessy for the wildly entertaining scenario he has fabricated. Even *I* found myself getting excited by his tale." Schwitters nodded eagerly, smiling at both the jury and Mark.

"But then I remembered that this is Simsbury College, not the set of a Hollywood movie, and I immediately calmed down.

"Simsbury College. Where the students value each other's lives in the same way we value each other's opinions. To even suggest that the Sigmas were responsible, directly or indirectly, for Chad's death, is an insult to me, my client, and every student who has ever come to this school to be surrounded by greatness."

Schwitters leaned against the defense table and rubbed his chin. "It helps us all, I think, to understand where Mr. Jessy is coming from. Did he mention he's a former Sigma?" He searched the jurors' faces. "He *didn't*? Well, let me tell you, he was once a proud Sigma brother, eager to uphold the traditions of honor and excellence established by its founders, and achieved by current members and alumni. However, he failed in his endeavors. He was found guilty—two years ago, yesterday, to be exact—of sexually assaulting and attempting to rape a local woman. Subsequently, Simsbury demanded he disaffiliate himself from the fraternity. In other words, Ladies and Gentlemen, Mr. Jessy's been in this room before."

Schwitters began to pace again, and raised his voice. "And unfortunately, that's why we're here today. Poor Mr. Jessy can't bear the thought that other young men are enjoying the entitlements he squandered. He's operating under the delusion that Sigma somehow did him wrong. Now, he's out for revenge against the very fraternity that embraced him as a brother. This became clear to both myself and Shawn Jakes, the third member of the D-Squad, who, in fact, removed herself from the case just this morning. She and I were no longer comfortable helping Mr. Jessy pull off this act of petty vengeance.

"Poor Mr. Jessy," said Schwitters, shaking his head sympathetically, his eyes fixed sadly on Mark. "All alone, because he just doesn't get it."

Mark looked away from Schwitters and found himself staring at the contemptuous grin of Pete Thresher. With nowhere to turn, he finally just looked at the floor.

"Frankly," continued Schwitters, "I don't feel that Mr. Jessy will mount much of a case here. But should he do so"—he began chopping the air with his hands—"the defense will prove that Chad was *not* hazed, was *not* forced to do shots, was *not* stripped naked, was *not* written upon. The defense will prove that Chad behaved not just irresponsibly but *recklessly,* and was the only one responsible for his unfortunate accident. In fact, new information has arisen that might lead one to question whether Chad's death was a suicide."

Schwitters stopped pacing and looked up at the jury. "But is all this really important?"

He began to move again. "What's important is that Chad has passed away. Whether this passing was by his own hand or that of God's doesn't really matter now. Can't we let him rest in peace? I'm confident that the jury will allow him to do just that, by issuing a verdict of not guilty."

Schwitters returned to his seat. Fairchild leaned close

to Schwitters and whispered in his ear, and the junior student counsel nodded and stood up again. "If it pleases Your Honor, let the record show that Mr. Jessy was incorrect in establishing a time frame. Chad died on February twenty-second, not the twenty-third, as Mr. Jessy previously stated. This careless error was brought to my attention by my client, whose members no doubt will remember that tragic morning for the rest of their lives." He sat down again.

"Noted," said the dean, and he turned to Mark. "Mr. Jessy, the College may call its first witness."

Mark nodded politely, then looked down at the pitiful list of questions he'd thrown together while hiding in the library. For a moment, he considered calling a witness and perhaps posturing as an attorney for a while. But really, what would be the point. He was grossly unprepared and would only waste both time and a witness.

Besides, how could he focus on restoring meaning to the abbreviated life Chad Ewing had led, when his own was in such danger?

He stood. "Your Honor, the prosecution rests."

The dean blinked. "Excuse me?"

"You know, I rest. I'm done."

The dean smirked. "Mr. Jessy, if the prosecution rests, then the case is over."

"No," said Mark, flustered. "What I mean is, I'm not ready to call witnesses *today*."

The dean looked offended. "Mr. Jessy, your blind ambition is the sole reason we're here today." He glanced at the jurors. "These jurors came from all over New England because *you* said you had a case. Are you now asking them to go back to their hotels and wait until you've got your act together?"

"I'm asking for a little patience, Your Honor. When this day started, I had a partner. Now I have none." Mark turned to the jurors. "Please . . . I promise I'll be more prepared tomorrow."

The Board members exchanged annoyed glances. Finally, the baldest one turned to the dean and nodded.

The dean absorbed the gesture and swallowed. "Very well. To accommodate Simsbury's eight-to-three class schedule, court stands adjourned until four o'clock tomorrow."

Mark busied his hands with his one belonging, and his mind with the night that lay ahead, as the jurors and the defense team filed out of the room.

When he looked up, only the dean remained, his grin mocking. "Nice show, Mr. Jessy. You're a real scary player."

Mark stared evenly at the dean. Then he turned and left.

4:42 P.M.

Fairchild, Dominic, and Thresher cut a tough swath across the quad on their way back to Sigma House, their collective gait forging, in two-thirds of their minds, an invisible but clear triangle of fear that extended several first-down lengths in front of them. Dominic and Thresher traded laughs over the ease with which Schwitters had handled Mark's fumblings, and they both concluded that this time tomorrow, the trial would be over.

Fairchild walked silently, his eyes focused on the ground.

Thresher nudged him. "What's the matter with you? We just kicked some serious glute."

Fairchild pressed his lips together, but said nothing.

"Come on, Dave," Dominic said. "I know he's your friend, but he deserves all the humiliation he's getting. He dragged us in there, and now he's paying for it."

Fairchild stopped walking and looked up. "You think so?"

"I *know* so."

Fairchild nodded and looked at the sky. "He knew some things, though, didn't he?"

Dominic blinked. "Like what?"

"He knew about the shots. He knew we had a pledge activity before the house party."

Dominic frowned. "For Christ's sake, he *guessed*. He used to be a brother. He knows we have pledge activities, and he knows we sometimes make the pledges drink shots."

Fairchild bent over, picked up a small stone, and flung it at a tree. It smacked against the trunk, then bounced across the path.

"Somehow, he *knew*."

"Bullshit. If he knew so much, how come he didn't mention the roofies?"

Fairchild shook his head once, then turned and began to walk in the other direction. Dominic and Thresher exchanged looks, shrugged, and continued on to Sigma.

7:56 P.M.

With thirty-six years of coaching experience under his belt, Gene Capofina had seen it all on the lacrosse field. He'd watched the Gait twins revolutionize the game, turning the act of scoring a goal into an art form. He'd watched Princeton write the book on offensive efficiency, their cold, executionerlike attack evoking comparisons to a six-man firing squad. He'd watched some of his *own* players enjoy single-game outbursts, the kind that warranted presentation of the game ball. Essentially, he'd seen enough to know that a wise man steered clear of heaping "all-time" superlatives on one player, one team, or one game.

But never in his life had he seen the sort of performance that had just been displayed by Mark Jessy.

Sure it had been a scrimmage, played indoors, and against one of New England's more run-of-the-mill teams. Nevertheless, Mark had dominated so completely that, for the first time in his life, Coach Capofina had been rendered speechless.

Mark had played as if it were his last day on Earth.

He'd played as if his life depended on it.

Now fifteen minutes after the culmination of a romp that had seen Number Ten score seven goals, assist on six others, block two shots with his chest and one with his helmet, and separate the shoulder of the other team's dirtiest player with the cleanest, hardest hit he'd ever seen, Capofina had finally found his tongue. Intent on using it to congratulate his sensational tri-captain, he opened the door to the men's locker room and leaned his head in the direction of the showers.

"Hey, Jessy!"

No response, save for macho banter.

"Hey, is Jessy in here?"

"No, Coach. He split."

Capofina shrugged and retreated from the locker room. He'd talk to Mark tomorrow.

8:09 P.M.

Turlington sat alone in his dorm room, letting the sounds of a Springsteen CD soothe his soul. He had to admit, he'd felt better since spilling his guts to Mark Jessy, and his relief showed in his hands, which were tremble-free for the first time in weeks. He felt as if the weight of his secret had slipped almost completely from his shoulders.

Although still a Sigma pledge, and aware of the dangers that traveled with such status, he had the comforting sense that his battle was someone else's now.

It was over.

Perhaps tonight he'd finally sleep.

8:17 P.M.

A thousand miles to the west, Carla Ewing thumbed mindlessly through the family photo album for the tenth and final time since Jason Lyle's phone call the night before. Then she put the album away, wiped a remaining tear from her cheek, and reached for the Simsbury phone directory she'd been issued during Simsbury Parents' Weekend, back when she'd been a Simsbury parent.

But this item she thumbed through only once.

And only until she got to the J's.

8:28 P.M.

Because each of the two hundred and thirteen campus phones required only a 9 to dial out, there was little need for the pay phone located across the street from Sigma, on the piney fringe of the deep woods that separated this part of Georgeville from the next town over. In fact, the booth had yet to receive coinage from a single patron during the month of March.

Until now.

The dark figure leaked from the first thick row of trees, a shadow's shadow that, to a witness, would have seemed tailor-made for the blackness that covered his mission, whatever that mission might be.

Of course, no witness existed.

So no one saw the shadowy man duck briefly into the icy light of the phone booth, roll a silver series into the coin slot, and punch eleven numbers. No one heard him speak without using his name, and no one heard him hang up without saying good-bye.

No one saw him slip back into the shadows.

But on the other end of the recently broken phone connection, no less than five powerful men watched the call's even more powerful recipient sit completely motionless while digesting the enormity of what he'd just been told, then drop everything, and reach for a weapon.

Immediately, all five followed his lead.

9:16 P.M.

For the second time in as many nights, Shawn stood before her bathroom mirror.

This time, however, she was clothed.

With Mark's morning look of trust adding spine to her posture, and Carla Ewing's recent telephone words still ringing in her ears, she nodded at her intense image.

Then she smacked the nearest wall with an open fist, stormed from the bathroom, thundered down the hallway that led to her living room, ripped her jacket from the peg beside her Phi Beta Kappa certificate, and exploded out the front door.

She also had a score to settle.

And now she knew exactly where to begin.

11:01 P.M.

Robes, hoods, shadows, and candlelight.

The Triumvirate.

Again.

The Leader stared blackly at the pledges, then slammed the table with a sword and began to rhyme:

I begin these grave rhymes with the usual demand.
Pledges shed blindfolds, the standard command.

I rhyme to you now of birthrights and royalty.
I remind all you pledges of death vows and loyalty.

This war will be escalating 'neath the cover of query.
But it's of D-Squad questions you should truly be leery.

And so keep the secrets, when you're asked who's to blame.
Keep them locked in your heart, and we'll win the game.

The end of the rhyme gave way to dramatic stillness, as the long shadows had silent sex with the wall and the ceiling and the flags and the secrets. Finally, the Leader ordered the pledges to replace their blindfolds, and they did so quickly.

They crawled from the room, enduring scattered kicks and punches. When they reached the second-floor Dennehy Room, they were allowed to stand and remove their blindfolds. From there they were permitted to leave, one at a time, of course, so as not to arouse suspicion.

One by one, they dragged their battered asses back to their dorm rooms, where they would crawl wearily into their beds.

And where the inevitable nightmares were waiting.

11:22 P.M.

An hour or so before the Triumvirate, Rho had finished whipping up a batch of his famous pot brownies, and to celebrate Mark Jessy's pathetic showing in court, seven of the twelve seniors had indulged. Now, all seven were high (in fact, two hadn't even been able to attend the Triumvirate, for fear they'd begin giggling), and all seven were feeling paranoid. The trouble began when Rho, who was *extremely* high, said he thought the pledges were showing signs of buckling under the pressure and what should they do about that? Mumbling, he then exited the room in search of snacks, but left behind some doubt.

Gamma, who wasn't high but perpetually belligerent, suggested that they call the pledges back to the house for some additional hazing. Kappa, of course, concurred. Delta, who never handled pot well, said that maybe Kappa should worry a little about his fucking girlfriend, who'd opened her dick-sucking mouth before, and how could they be sure that she wouldn't do it again? Kappa replied that Jocelyn would keep quiet, and Epsilon said of course she would, because why would she want to risk another beating? Kappa took a swing at Epsilon, Epsilon retaliated, and Gamma jumped in and slapped each of them silly for a few moments. Rho returned in the middle of all this, unaware that he'd started the paranoid chain reaction. He sat on the floor in the corner, eating ruffled chips, and reminding his battling brothers that pot wasn't supposed to make people violent.

When the dust had settled, Gamma sat down, twisted the cap off a beer bottle, and threw it at Rho. "You fucking hippie! You're scaring everyone!"

Rho munched his chips. "Hey, I don't trust a few of them."

"Like who?" asked Zeta.

"Drew Silas and Greg Turlington, to name a couple."

"Why not?"

"Why do you *think*?"

"Do you really think they'd turn on us?" Delta asked Gamma.

The larger man shrugged and slugged his beer. "Turlington might."

"What about Silas?"

"No way," Sigma said. "He worships this place."

"I agree," said Kappa, still a little shaken from his altercation with Epsilon. "As much as I hate him, he's in it for the long haul."

"Then thank God I'm graduating," said Delta, "because I can't stand that kid."

"Me neither," said Epsilon. "I can't believe he hasn't dropped out yet. Who the hell gave him a bid?"

"Walker," Rho answered scornfully. "They're from the

same hometown. Very controversial, though. If I recall, the vote was close."

"It definitely wasn't unanimous," Upsilon remembered.

"Can we get back to the subject?" asked Gamma. "We can recap every little political moment in our history some other time. Jessy's going to start calling pledges as witnesses tomorrow, so I propose we do something about Turlington *tonight*."

"Wait a minute," Beta said. "When did we decide to do something about Turlington? What did *he* do?"

"Nothing yet. It's what he *might* do that worries me."

"Oh, so now you're a psychic."

"Go fuck yourself, Beta. I'm not in the mood for your holier-than-thou act tonight."

Beta poised to respond, then crossed his arms and huffed a few times. "Okay," he said finally. "What do you propose we do?"

"Beat a little Sigma pride into him."

"And where will that leave us? Suppose Mark calls him to the stand. Turlington's going to look awfully suspicious with cuts and bruises all over his face."

"Not if we get him in places that don't show," Gamma said calmly. "A couple of punches to the ribs, maybe a brand on the ass. Something to remind him to keep his mouth shut."

"Why stop there?" Beta said sarcastically. "Why not just kill him?"

"Beta," reasoned Epsilon, "we don't exactly enjoy inflicting pain, but sometimes it has—"

"Oh, that's comedy. This from a guy who wears steel-toed boots on the nights we get physical."

"Hey, Beta," Gamma said, a gleam of knowing malice in his eyes, "your hands are as bloody as ours. So are your boots, for that matter."

Beta's entire body recoiled, and for a moment he looked as if he himself had been hazed to the brink of death. The bags that had recently hung themselves beneath his eyes blackened, and his cut cheeks grew suddenly gaunter. "I . . . I can't believe you just said that," he said.

"Believe it, man, since you clearly believe in nothing else these days."

Beta stared at Gamma for a moment, then hung his head, and said, "Leave Greg alone, Gamma. Just leave him alone."

"No way," said Rho. "I don't like the look in his eyes lately. He's up to something, and I don't trust him."

"Me neither," said Delta. "And the alumni obviously feel the same way. Otherwise, they wouldn't have told us to get rid of him. Turlington's a liability, and I'd sleep better tonight knowing we'd done something about it."

Silence, long and threatening.

Gamma stood suddenly and pointed at Kappa. "That's it. Call Turlington. Tell him to be at the Rock at midnight."

Kappa smiled cruelly. "What are we gonna do to him?"

"We're going to remind him he's a Sigma forever."

11:34 P.M.

The chronically high-strung freshman was almost to the end of the path that connected the Cage to the westernmost edge of campus when a faint noise caused her to stop and whirl.

What was that?

She scanned the darkness behind her, wide eyes searching for trouble in every pine thicket. Satisfied that only breezy shadows trailed her, she shook off her fright, turned, and continued to her dorm.

In that instant, the trailing shadows took on breezeless and darkly dressed lives of their own, as six who'd dropped everything for weapons emerged like black puffs of gun smoke from the pine thickets that, by day, beautified the grounds.

Then simply dropped low, and penetrated Simsbury College.

CHAPTER FIFTY-ONE

The 200th Year
Tuesday, March 10

11:45 P.M.

Security guard Ralph Deeble yawned with boredom, then swept his eyes across what had to be the safest pocket of an extraordinarily safe part of the world: the quarter mile that called itself the Simsbury campus.

There was no need for him to be here, he concluded, as he leaned back against a tree and closed his eyes.

At that moment, two dark figures emerged from separate but equally thin shadows, then cast their own on the snow surrounding the Trussell Biology Building. Though each man held out hopes of seeing the other—with different purposes in mind—neither had detected the other's presence.

Nor could either be heard by Ralph Deeble.

For one walked like an Indian.

The other, like an assassin.

The door to Trussell creaked open, then swung shut.

And the Sixth Most Prestigious College in America fell once more into a deadly hush.

MIDNIGHT

The man with the broken nose, two black eyes, and a gun in his hand smiled as the darkness enveloped him. For a moment, he peered through gloom punctured only by secondhand light from other campus structures. Then he donned his night-vision goggles, stepped to his right, and in one swift motion disabled the antiquated fuse box he'd singled out during his earlier campus tour. Satisfied that the blackness was now permanent, he hunched his shoulders, focused hard on the closed classroom door at the opposite end of the brief hallway, and moved silently toward a substantial payday.

In no time he'd traversed the corridor and stood within a yard of Room 104. Pausing, he tightened his hold on his gun. Then he set his jaw, wiggled the fingers of his free hand, and reached for the doorknob.

He froze.

Posted to the door to Room 104, glowing white amid the goggled brightness of countless other posted bulletins, was a folded piece of paper addressed simply to "Mawn."

Frowning, he stepped back from the door and gave a quick recon of the hallway. Seeing nothing but blackness, sensing nothing but emptiness, he relaxed his grip on his weapon, then holstered it entirely. He snatched the paper from its tack, unfolded it, and began to read.

Deputy Mawn,

U.S. Marshal Sehorn disappeared about four hours ago. Though such ineptitude on your agency's part doesn't surprise me, it certainly leaves me feeling exposed. Obviously, I need to be more proactive in my attempts to remain safe. I will meet you, but not here.

On the north end of campus is a building called Unter-Vessey Hall. On the second floor are a series of small psychology-department-survey studios that can be secured from the inside. By the time you read this, I'll be locked inside the easternmost room (I'm assuming even you know which direction east is). Knock three times, then two times, then say the word "Tomahawk."

Frowning, he read the letter twice, then crumpled it slowly as he stared at the floor and considered aborting this mission before it even began. He knew enough about killing to know that it should be carried out quickly and cleanly or not carried out at all, and that jackassing all over campus in search of his target was just plain foolish.

Then again, "quickly" and "cleanly" were adverbs he'd already forfeited in connection with this particular assignment.

He shook his head, straightened his spine, and pocketed the balled-up letter. Then he turned from Room 104, backtracked down the corridor, and exited into the night.

12:14 A.M.

Simsbury security guard C. C. Marino paced her usual beat, grinding a dotted line of snow prints between the northernmost and southernmost coordinates on campus. Her left hand twirled a ring of keys. Her right dangled a half-sucked lollipop. She was bringing the pop to her mouth for a lick and watching a dormitory window shade batten down for the overnight, when a silent disturbance in the pulse of the night caught her attention. Halting abruptly on the midpoint of the quad, she tongued her lolly and turned to the west.

And watched as six black shadows moved like thunderheads across a calm lake of snow, then vanished into the trees.

12:18 P.M.

The man with the broken nose, two black eyes, and a commitment to killing crouched low against the wall as he arrived on the second floor of Unter-Vessey and fixed his dead ahead stare on the easternmost of five identical doorways. He paused a moment, listening. Then he took a deep breath, centered his goggles, and squeezed his gun as he skulked across the carpeting to where a single closed door separated him from his bounty.

Drawing even with the studio door, he palmed it lightly, feeling for life, then clenched his hand into a knocker. He rapped three times, then twice more, then put his lips to the thin crevice segregating the bolted door from its frame.

"Tomahawk," he said, as he raised the gun to firing level and snaked a finger across the trigger.

No answer.

He leaned away, waited through a moment or two of silence, then leaned back in again.

Knock-knock-knock.

Knock-knock.

"Tomahawk."

Nothing.

Absolutely nothing.

For the second time in twenty minutes, he stepped

back from a doorway that was supposed to open on a twenty-two-year-old target. And for the second time in twenty minutes, he concluded he was the only live body within a building that should have housed two.

For an instant longer he held his stance, mouth slightly ajar, gun still pointing in what should have been a deadly direction.

Then he clamped his lips shut, dropped the weapon to his waist, and kicked in the door.

And, so doing, confirmed the nothingness he'd sensed.

Unter-Vessey's easternmost survey studio was indeed empty.

He swore softly at the lifelessness before him and was set to turn back toward the hallway when a small, solitary something, midway up the rear wall of the vacant studio, caught his attention.

A single piece of paper.

Folded in half and addressed to "Mawn."

He stepped to the wall, ripped the paper from its post, and once again began to read.

Deputy Mawn,

I can't stay here, and I don't have the time to tell you why. Meet me inside the north entrance (back-stage—hidden from view—no one will see you go in, I hope) to the Janis Performing Arts Center, on the far west side of campus.

Please hurry.

Again, he read the letter twice, then crushed it in his hand.

And again, uneasiness pinched his nerves.

But as before, he turned his back on the sensation, for to acknowledge it was to give in to it. If anything, he was annoyed. Annoyed because he was halfway through the hour he'd given himself to get the job done and get out of here, and still hadn't even spotted his target. Annoyed because with each passing minute this was beginning to feel more and more like something it had no business being.

A game.

That someone else was controlling.

Fuck that, he thought. College kids simply didn't play games with their lives, and while a cocky one with a scarred past might toy with a badge-carrrying, law-enforcing U.S. marshal, no one toyed with *him.* No, his target hadn't been at Trussell—nor at Unter-Vessey either. Still, Simsbury College was a tiny little haven for rich, precious cherubs, and his target had to be somewhere— as scared as his notes suggested him to be.

T-Bone's man retraced his steps until his feet found snow again. Then he concealed the items that defined him as dangerous and, with the east wind showing him the way, continued to hunt.

12:31 A.M.

His name was Johnson, but on this night that was hardly of consequence. On this night, he was simply one of six who had dropped everything for weapons, one of many who would have done the same. With the rest of his team, he was crouched in shadow behind a wall of bushes, forty yards to the west of a building that loomed electrically lifeless behind a wall of evergreen.

"I've never seen so many trees in my life," Johnson whispered, his eyes trained dutifully in the direction of the Janis Performing Arts Center. "How long are we going to give this?"

"As long as it takes," replied the man to his right.

"What if nothing happens?"

"Something's gonna happen. I can *taste* it."

Johnson turned to the man a moment, watched him fiddle with the settings of his gun, and shook his head in admiration. Then, angling his face toward the ground, he let a gob of adrenalized spit fall from his lips before returning his attention to the academic scene forty yards off.

But because this hunt had accustomed his eyes to objects of grand scale—giant pines that jostled for space and scraped the black sky, and the massive three-story building just beyond—it was a long moment of adjustment before his squint zeroed in on a single human figure that hadn't been there just moments before.

"Is that who I think it is?" he whispered, shaking the thigh squatted next to him.

The man to his right looked up. "Jesus," he exclaimed softly. "It's Mark. I told you it was gonna happen."

He turned and began signaling to the other four. Meanwhile, as one who had heard a lot about Mark Jessy but never actually seen him, Johnson reached into his pocket, pulled out a pair of infrared binoculars, and put them to his face. He worked the focus knob until features took on their appropriate definitions, then slowly ran the scope head to toe. The magnified image jibed with his expectations. Mark's white-brimmed eyes darted anxiously, and his frequent frosty breaths suggested his heart was working overtime. His arms angled downward, as if attempting to keep the rest of him in balance, and his legs fidgeted for a footing he couldn't seem to find. The kid looked vulnerable, exposed, and scared, like hunted quarry, which was exactly how he *should* look, given the—

Wait a minute. What was that?

He lifted the binoculars a fraction and focused on the hips. Then he scanned slowly to the left, until his sight fell smack on the right hand.

And the brutal item it clutched.

"Hey," he whispered, passing the binoculars to his right. "Is he holding what I think he's holding?"

He felt the binoculars leave his hand, and an instant later heard the man to his right mumble, "Holy shit. It all ends tonight."

"Should I—"

"Not yet. We wait for our man."

Johnson peeled his eyes off Mark and gave the area's darkest alcoves a hard, probing search. "I don't see him anywhere."

"Which means he doesn't see us. Give it time. We've waited this long, we can wait a little longer."

The six who'd dropped everything waited in signaled silence until Mark Jessy had been struck by whatever urge he'd been waiting for and disappeared into the trees surrounding the Janis Performing Arts Center.

Then they dropped the hammer on waiting, crept from their hiding spots, and closed in for the kill.

12:40 A.M.

T-Bone's man studied the Janis Performing Arts Center, then, as a cloak of wind hissed through the high limbs, began to move. He darted from shadow to shadow, his steps touching down just long enough to leave tracks.

He moved at his own professional pace and only altered his course for trees.

He'd just bounded up the steps of the building's north entrance, when he saw it—something that froze him in his tracks. Disbelievingly, he stared at the object that jutted from the door, at the iron that glinted dully in a hairy flux of moonlight.

It was a bloodstained tomahawk.

And beneath it, impaled to the door, was an unaddressed note.

The man swallowed hard, pried the weapon from its gash with one hand and, with the other, caught the note as it fluttered toward the ground.

He opened it, and in a cube of misty light cast by something distant, began to read.

Dear Whoever You Are,

Your research failed to uncover that I would never trust U.S. Marshal Mawn. I trust one thing only: my instincts.

But come inside, anyway.

I'm waiting.

This time, he read the letter only once.

Then he let his gaze drift slowly from the page to the snow-covered ground, where fresh, one-way boot prints, a shade smaller than his, left undeniable proof that a man had recently entered Janis from the north.

And was still inside.

Waiting.

As the man with a broken nose and two black eyes stood there, fixated on the thinly slit moon that scarred the night, he consulted his own instincts, none of which befitted a former Marine. He had a sudden urge to walk away, to run, to get in his car and drive back to Boston, where the targets were more one-dimensional.

But eclipsing that urge was a far more powerful one.

The urge to kill.

Right now.

He tossed the tomahawk aside, drew his gun, and slammed the ammo cartridge with his palm. Then he turned abruptly, donned the night-vision goggles once more, and as his world of previous blackness exploded into militia-green luminescence, he opened the door and penetrated the cluttered, backstage world of Janis.

He moved to the stage curtain's slit and stole a quick look through it.

Then he raised the gun to his shoulder, slid through the opening, and attacked.

And for a moment, the audience of empty seats watched him kill nothing but a unit of time.

Then the shadows pounced.

The first figure rose like a fifth-row phantom, arms, head, and torso unfurling from what had been one of a thousand empty seat backs. The second shot to life ten rows farther back, and the third exploded into the form of a man from behind the balcony eave. The fourth and fifth converged from opposite stage wings, and as they crouched, a sixth sprung from the depths of the orchestra pit.

And as the ambushers aimed their arsenal and left him nowhere to go but a morgue, the man with the broken nose, two black eyes, and loaded assault weapon could do only one thing.

Watch.

And so he did, until his one-target world had fully evolved into a world that featured six still-life reflections of himself.

Six black-clad men.

Six sets of night-vision goggles.

Six raised guns, pointing at his head.

And then a single voice made clear the distinction.

"Jay Meadow Jessy!" shouted the man in the fifth row, as he unzipped his jacket to reveal the star-shaped badge that hung from his neck. "Deputy Trevor Mawn, United States Marshal Service, Federal Bureau of Investigation. Put down your weapon, put your hands behind your head, and take two steps back!"

The man with the broken nose and two black eyes just stared at him.

"Drop the gun, Jessy!" warned another voice.

"Drop it, scumbag!" hollered a third.

"Put it down, asshole!"

"Drop it!"

"*Drop the fucking gun!*"

And then, from the orchestra pit, a low, urgent murmur snuffed the screams of escalating tension.

"That's not Jay Jessy . . ."

And as the four simple words confounded the six-man chorus into a confused silence, the man with the broken nose and two black eyes slowly realized what was happening, what he and his six gun-toting, ready-to-fire reflections had been manipulated into doing. Had his mind been less consumed with a way out of this fiasco, he might have smiled to himself and shook his head in grudging appreciation, for he had to concede the obvious. This Jessy kid was clever.

But not clever enough.

Making a split-second decision, T-Bone's designated hitter lowered one hand, calmly called, "Don't shoot," and, with peaceful intent, reached slowly beneath the zipper of his jacket.

And pulled out a star-shaped badge of his own.

He held the star high. "United States Marshal Kenneth Sehorn, Portland Precinct. I'm one of you."

He watched six reflections reluctantly ease, followed by six guns lowering.

CHAPTER FIFTY-TWO

The 200th Year
Wednesday, March 11

1:22 A.M.

The sorting of events took place over doughnuts and coffee laid out on the trunk of an unmarked government car, and ran only thirty-two minutes. However, in terms of time and money wasted on behalf of their respective taxpaying, bounty-paying constituents, the cost to both sides—the six U.S. marshals from the FBI's Boston office, and the broken-nosed "marshal from Portland"—was dear. Not that either side would acknowledge it, of course.

As far as the six Boston marshals were concerned, only one party had been on the hunt tonight, the United States federal government, and though the six had certainly been surprised by the unexpected appearance of Marshal Sehorn, it was encouraging to see that the search for a killer like Jay Meadow Jessy was indeed of national concern.

For the record, at roughly 8:30 P.M. Trevor Mawn had received an anonymous phone call, traceable to a pay phone on Maine Street in Georgeville, from a nervous, almost reluctant-sounding someone who would only say that he was a patriotic Simsbury student and knew for a fact that Mark Jessy was planning to meet his fugitive father for the purpose of giving him something, sometime around midnight, in the Janis Performing Arts Center. The caller had provided details that only someone close to Mark would know, and for that reason had been deemed credible. Mawn and his five colleagues had arrived on campus at 11:30, and after spotting Mark in the vicinity of Janis, holding the tomahawk stained with his mother's blood, they'd penetrated the building and lain in wait.

It must have been right around then, Marshal Sehorn intoned, that the call for backup was routed from the Boston office to Portland, requesting at least two men with working knowledge of the Greater Portland wooded areas, should the manhunt evolve into an outdoor foot chase. The only man available for duty, Sehorn had arrived on campus around half-past midnight. Almost immediately he'd thought he spotted an individual fitting Mark Jessy's physical description enter Janis from the north. Unaware of the Boston team's location, and thinking the son would lead him to the father, he'd followed.

Clearly, Sehorn now concluded, it had been a false alarm.

Shaking his head, he trailed off, and while the six from Boston communicated their own silent frustration, he pocketed his badge and credentials, and lightly rubbed his deeply bruised eyes.

And that was that.

Final apologies were issued, handshakes exchanged,

and with a mutually rendered vow to one day get their man, the six marshals from Boston piled into two tan sedans and split.

The single marshal from Portland watched until their taillights had dissolved into the horizon. Then he walked to his black BMW, slid into the driver's seat, and disappeared into the night.

2:11 A.M.

The ungodly hour had presented Marshal Johnson with only two choices of television programming, the ESPN World Canine Championships or pay-per-view smut, and since Deputy Mawn, his roommate for the evening, was vehemently opposed to pornography of any kind, dog show it was. Johnson sat at the foot of the hotel bed, sipping a beer, watching an Irish Setter misunderstand its master's commands, and momentarily wishing he'd pursued a career as a gym teacher.

"I wish we'd brought the chopper," he groaned, thinking how nice his own bed would feel right now.

"Oh sure," replied Mawn as he undressed. "We respond to a hush-hush tip with helicopter blades a-thumpin' over the woods of Southern Maine." He threw Johnson a critical glance. "That's one way to scare off a fugitive."

"What fugitive?" muttered Johnson, and immediately wished he hadn't.

Mawn gave him a long, calculated look, then threw his jacket on his bed. "Do you have a problem with the way we operated this evening?"

Johnson started to give his usual subordinate response,

then stopped. "Yes," he admitted finally, recklessly. "I have *big* problems with the way we operated."

Mawn sat and crossed his arms. "Enlighten me."

Johnson hesitated a moment, then delved in. "Okay. First we respond to the sort of hush-hush tip that we usually ignore. Then, after hauling our asses to East Jesus, we sit and watch a building for a while, and even though our fugitive's son is running around with the most telling object he owns, we're going to wait until we see our man before we make our move. Then, *without* seeing our man, without even knowing whether he's in the fucking state, we storm a great big puppet theater, and in the process almost blow a colleague's head off." He shrugged, then motioned toward the TV. "And now I'm in a hotel that doesn't have room service, watching wiener dogs piss on each other."

Mawn glanced at the TV, then shook his head and turned back to Johnson. "First of all, every man who wears our badge takes an oath to do whatever is necessary to bring pieces of shit like Jay Jessy to justice. I'm fully prepared to kill for this cause, just as I'm fully prepared to die for it. I assume that Marshal Sehorn feels the same way. I also assume that he has rocks in his head, because what he did tonight was just about the most idiotic thing I've ever witnessed, and tomorrow I'm going to call his supervisor."

"It *is* tomorrow, Trevor."

Mawn waved him off. "As for the rest of your comments, I can only say that I played some split-second hunches and lost. But even if I'd played 'em right I *still* would've lost, because Jay fuckin' Jessy wasn't within fifty miles of here." He paused, then added, "As far as I know."

"Which leads me to my next comment," Johnson said, leaning forward. "Let's go back to Simsbury and arrest Mark Jessy."

"On what charge?"

"C'mon, Trevor. He obviously made the phone call—"

"On what charge, Steve? All we have is an anonymous call from a phone booth near Simsbury."

"He baited us with that tomahawk."

"Oh please, he had no way of knowing for sure whether we were even there. And again, what could we charge him with? Unlawful possession of a family heirloom? He could say he was taking it to show his girlfriend. He could invoke his constitutional right to bear arms." Mawn stood from the bed and took off his undershirt. "Bottom line, we have nothing to pin on him, and I'm sure as hell not going to give him the satisfaction of knowing he got under our skin."

He strolled to the mirror and stared at it, his fingers absently balling a pair of wool socks. "Mark Jessy," he said, "can have his moment. He can go to bed thinking he played a cute little trick on his father's pursuers. But deep down, he'll know that all the childish games in the world can't change two simple facts."

He dropped the socks, leaned on the dresser, and moved his face within inches of the reflective glass. "His father's a killer," he said softly. "And I'm gonna catch him."

3:38 A.M.

As the echoes of yet another freshman's screams ripped through his mind, Fairchild gazed numbly upward in the darkness.

He rose from his bed and maneuvered through his

suite's gloom to the third-floor hallway, which was lit by a single indicator light. He wandered down the corridor, with no concern for any of the clamped doors, save the one he was focused on. He arrived at it quicker than he'd expected to, twisted the doorknob, and entered.

Again he bumped through a suite, this one less dark but also less familiar. He was vaguely aware of strewn laundry underfoot. He had a detached sense of jocks and bikini babes watching him from posters.

Judging him.

He paused at the bedroom door, then pushed his way in.

And as his adjusting eyes guided him through the deeper darkness, the slumbering form of Ran Robinson materialized.

Fairchild knelt to the floor next to the bed, and for a long time watched his friend sleep. And as he did, he wondered, with undisguised wistfulness, what it would be like to live life without the burden of heroic expectations.

He watched until he thought his throat would burst.

Then he leaned imperceptibly forward and, in a soft whisper, began to confess.

"Ran, there's something I need . . . I want to tell you." He paused, and swayed back to a full upright position. "A couple nights before Chad died, he came to me . . . and he asked . . . he *told* me he wasn't sure he could take the abuse much longer, that he was thinking about dropping out. And . . . and you know what I told him?" He shook his head at the ceiling. "I told him to stick it out, buddy, because it would be over soon." He shook his head again, then turned his imploring look back to Ran's unconscious eyes. "And *then* . . ."

He stopped himself.

He reached out tentatively and poked Ran's shoulder. Satisfied his friend was still sleeping, Fairchild stood and escaped to the hallway.

But the sacred passageway provided him little refuge; he doubled over, and in the murky glow stared at the hands that had poured shots for Chad Ewing, at the feet that had kicked in Chad Ewing's ribs.

It was all just a matter of time now.

Time. The one thing he'd never had mastery over. The one thing he wished he could turn back.

CHAPTER FIFTY-THREE

The 200th Year
Wednesday, March 11

6:16 A.M.

The man with the broken nose flung his Yankees cap into the hotel easy-chair, grabbed the telephone, and fuming, punched in an eleven-digit long distance number.

"Hello?"

"T-Bone. It's me. The little fucker's still alive, but he won't be for long—"

"Forget it," interrupted T-Bone. "We're destroying him in court. Let him—"

"No. You don't understand. I *will* kill this kid. Pay me or don't pay me, I don't give a shit, because this no longer has anything to do with you. It no longer has anything to do with money."

The hit man squeezed his leg. "I swear, on every grave I'm responsible for, that this cocky little fucker will be in a watery one by sunrise tomorrow."

9:47 A.M.

The three-car caravan of unmarked government cars

obeyed the speed limit as it traveled south on the Maine Turnpike, its three drivers sipping coffee as they watched the road, and two of its three passengers sleeping off a night of insufficient sleep. The sixth man, however, hated both coffee *and* sleep, and since he'd managed to shirk driving duties for the second time in twelve hours, he was free to focus his alertness on something else.

Something that bothered him.

He scooped up the car phone and punched some numbers.

"U.S. Marshal's Office," said the answering voice. "Hannah Kelly speaking."

"Hey, Hannah. It's Trevor."

"Deputy Mawn," sang Hannah. "I've been waiting for your call."

"The wait's over. What do you got for me?"

"Well, funny you should ask that. It seems Personnel doesn't have any skinny on a Marshal Sehorn from Portland."

"How come? They should be able to just call it up—"

"Because he doesn't exist."

Mawn felt his jaw go slack. "What?"

"There's no such man."

"From Portland?"

"From *anywhere*."

Mawn shook his head at the dashboard. "I don't understand. He had the credentials."

"That may be, but he has no *file*."

Mawn put a hand to his forehead, turned to the driver's seat, and in a moment of near lunacy watched Marshal Tasha bite off a piece of his Styrofoam cup and chew it. Then, refocusing on the dash, he said, "Try . . . try a different spelling, Hannah. Maybe add an 'e' to the end . . . or something."

"We did that already. Found a 'Richard' by that spelling, but he died in the line of duty twelve years ago in Detroit."

Mawn shook his head again and shifted in his seat. Then, as the full significance of what he was hearing finally caught up with him, he switched the phone from his left ear to his right and leaned forward in his seat. "Wait a minute," he said slowly. "Are you telling me that there has never been, *in the history of the United States,* a marshal named Kenneth Sehorn?"

"That's what I'm telling you."

10:14 A.M.

As Professor Rosenfield touted animal kingdom survival tactics, Simsbury's most secret survivor sat in the back of class and tried to stay focused on the trivial lecture. The previous night's matching of wits, however, had left Mark with an adrenaline hangover and a listless confusion. Part of this, he knew, was due to last night's culmination——or rather, the lack of it. The U.S. Marshals had clearly failed to arrest the killer Mark had hand-fed them. Nevertheless, his thoughts this morning were scattered, ranging from what he'd pulled off to what he *hadn't* pulled off, from what his parents would have thought of it all to what Shawn was thinking right now. And beneath his rhetorical ramblings, of course, lay the one question that required an answer.

How was he going to find a witness to testify against Sigma?

He wondered if he shouldn't just stand up at today's

trial session, break his promise to Turlington, quote the freshman word for word, and accuse the dean of being corrupt. Not a good strategy, he concluded. Without a supporting witness, such testimony would sound absurd. He'd lose all credibility with the jury, the case would be thrown out of court, and Turlington would be secretly beaten within an inch of his life.

He mulled other approaches, each of them hopelessly fruitless, then shook his head and drifted back to the class discussion. Professor Rosenfield was standing on the tips of his Birkenstocks and pulling down the movie screen at the front of the room. Mark felt a reflexive pleasure at the sight, borne of the many hungover mornings he'd stumbled to class and prayed for darkness. Rosenfield's movies were generally long, lacking in exam material, and ideal for naps.

Rosenfield motioned for the AV man to start the projector, and as the professor himself turned out the lights, the screen whirred to life, introducing the film's first star, a camouflaged stingray that burrowed in the sand and effectively vanished from sight. Mark watched the succession of defensive animals for as long as he could stand it; then, as a squid shot a massive, black cloud of ink that cloaked the lens of the camera pursuing it, he slowly closed his weary eyes.

But opened them immediately.

For the film's last, black image had followed him behind closed lids and shown him something he hadn't seen before. Now, having seen it, he sat momentarily blinkless and breathless, remembering and imagining, plugging pieces into parts, and exclaiming with a sudden, inner shout that the answer to it all really couldn't be that simple, could it?

He leapt to his feet, grabbed his notebook and jacket, and tore down the steps of the auditorium. He shot an apologetic look at Rosenfield, who was too amazed by the expansion of a blowfish to care.

He tore across campus, racing an invisible clock, hoping the truth would wait for him.

10:48 A.M.

"Grand Cayman Fidelity, how can I help you?"

"Yes," said Templeton into the phone, "I'm checking the amount of a direct deposit that should've been wired to my account this morning."

"Just a moment . . . Okay, account number?"

"Four-two, nine-five-nine, one-six-six-three."

Tap-tap-tap. "Thank you. One moment please . . ." *Tap-tap-tap. Tappity-tap-tap-tap.* "Here it is. We have a twenty-five-thousand-dollar transfer from Blue Eagle Corporate Trust. Does that amount sound right?"

"Yes," Templeton said. "It sounds perfect."

10:52 A.M.

In his excitement, Mark almost entered his apartment by way of a door, but remembering what would happen to the next unfortunate soul who used *any* of his three civilized entrances, he checked himself in time and heaved himself through his bedroom window. He tumbled to his rug, stood, and whipped open his desk drawer.

Beneath the photo of his parents he found the bogus letter the dean had sent him, two years and six days earlier. He smiled at it and put it in his pocket. Then he threw himself back out the window and began to run.

And as he ran, the rhymes began.

12:01 P.M.

The Sigma dining room filled with brothers and macho chatter. Sandwiches were prepared, chowder bowls were filled, and seats were loaded with large, cocky frames that got larger and cockier with each visit to the gym. The pledges followed orders and scurried about, trying to look dignified while they served juice and milk and got their heads slapped.

Morning classes were over, which meant the brothers were now one morning closer to finals, to summer, to graduation, and to the riches that awaited them in banks and boardrooms. Chad Ewing was dead and buried, the related D-Squad trial was developing into a rout in their favor, and spring break was just a couple days away.

It was a wonderful day to be a brother of Sigma Delta Phi.

12:06 P.M.

Mark pounded on the door, then shifted on restless legs as he waited for a response. *C'mon, be there,* he thought. *Be there be there be there be there be—*

The door opened slowly, and Turlington eyed Mark warily, as a housewife might eye a door-to-door salesman.

"Listen to me," said Mark, completely out of breath, and with nothing to sell but a course of action almost as risky as the one he'd pursued the night before. "Remember, the other day, when you told me how it doesn't occur to the pledges that alumni are still brothers? Remember? Remember when you said that?"

Turlington hesitated, then nodded once with little commitment.

"Okay," said Mark, with enthusiasm for two. "Okay. Now, if I told you that you could bring down Sigma, *without even testifying,* what would you say?"

Turlington looked at Mark for a long moment. Then he slowly peeled off his tee shirt and let it drop to the floor.

Mark gasped.

On the freshman's left deltoid, branded in bubbly blisters, were the words, *Sigma Forever.*

"I'd tell you I'm a Sigma forever, Mark," said Turlington as his eyes flooded. "I'd tell you I'm a Sigma forever."

12:46 P.M.

"I'm telling you," said the cranky temp filling in for President Carlisle's regular secretary, who reputedly had tonsillitis. "He's not in his office, and I don't know when he'll be back." She waved a hand in the air like a flitting, one-winged butterfly. "He just . . . wandered off."

"You have no idea where he is?" said Shawn.

The temp made a nasty face. "Do I stutter?"

Shawn opened her mouth to retaliate, then stopped herself. "No . . . you don't," she said finally, and though she could have quipped that she knew someone *else* who stuttered, she didn't. For this very thought suddenly posed as an idea, and something she should have checked into after hearing Jocelyn Patricola's initial account of the carnage at Sigma.

She turned on her heels and set off for the Campus Security Office.

CHAPTER FIFTY-FOUR

The 200th Year
Wednesday, March 11

4:10 P.M.

The dean thumped his gavel on the lectern. "Is the prosecution ready to call its first witness?"

Mark stood. "Yes, Your Honor. The College calls Sigma pledge John Andover to the stand."

The dean pressed his intercom button. "Peggy, please subpoena freshman John Andover."

As the court members waited for the first witness to arrive, Mark tried to busy himself with the roughly doodled questions on the exposed page of his notebook, rather than make eye contact with anyone. However, his curiosity finally got the best of him, and he shifted his attention to the defense table. Sure enough, Dominic was glaring at him with a famished sort of malevolence. Thresher wore the bad-tempered-yet-cowardly sneer of a wife beater. Schwitters looked imperial. Fairchild simply looked tired.

And really thin.

Strikingly so, in comparison to John Andover, who appeared to be a Dominic-in-the-making as he strutted his bulk through the door of the courtroom. Yet another in the long line of Sigma football players, he wore the cold stare of a linebacker as he stalked toward the witness chair. Mark felt like an enemy quarterback.

The dean motioned for Andover to sit. The witness obeyed, adjusted his Sigma blazer, and directed a loyal nod toward the defense table.

"Mr. Andover," said the dean, looking down at the witness, "you are reminded that any false statements made during these proceedings will be considered a direct violation of the Honor Code contract you signed on enrollment."

Andover nodded nervously. "Okay."

Guessing this was his cue, Mark stood and walked over to the witness, who dignified the advance with a cool sneer.

Mark cleared his throat. "May I call you John?"

"Of course. That's my name."

"John, are you a Sigma pledge?"

"Yes."

"Are you aware of the College's policy on pledging? In particular, the policy on hazing?"

"I guess so."

"Are you aware of what hazing is?"

"Sure."

"Could you define it for the court?"

Schwitters leaped to his feet. "Objection! Does the prosecution really expect this student to give a textbook definition of hazing?"

Mark turned to the dean. "I merely want to let the record show just where the College stands on the issue."

Still standing, Schwitters shook his head. "And *I* would like to let the record show that if Mr. Andover knows *neither* the definition, *nor* the policy, this lack of knowledge will have no bearing on the guilt or innocence of my client. Just because he can't define hazing, doesn't mean he's been hazed. The witness probably can't define triskaidekaphobia either, but that doesn't mean he's afraid of the number thirteen."

Mark rolled his eyes.

The dean scratched his head. "Sustained. Mr. Jessy, all freshmen are given an introductory safety seminar during their first week of school. The seminar focuses quite a bit on pledging and hazing. If you'd like to let both the definition and the College policy be known, why don't you simply read it out loud?"

Mark was silent for a moment. "Well, Your Honor, I don't have those materials with me."

"That's unfortunate, isn't it, Counsel? Maybe next time you'll come prepared."

Mark nodded and returned his attention to the witness. "John, have you ever been physically or mentally abused by anyone associated with Sigma?"

"No. Never."

"Really? No one's ever made you do push-ups?"

"No one but my football coach."

"No one's ever made you walk ten miles, in the pitch-black, with an empty keg strapped to your back?"

"No."

Mark pretended to be confused. "When I call the other fifteen surviving pledges, will they tell me the same thing?"

"Yes."

"You're reminded that you have signed the Honor Code contract—"

"Objection. Counsel is badgering the witness."

"Sustained. Mr. Jessy, if you have no more questions except those of the 'are you sure' variety, then I'll have to ask that you excuse the witness."

"Sorry," said Mark. He took a sip of water. "John, did you ever have to march naked across campus, singing Sigma songs, with hard-boiled eggs taped to your testicles?"

The only female juror let out a giggle. All eyes turned to her, and she put a hand over her mouth. "Sorry," she said.

"That's okay, Lillian," said the dean. He glared at Mark. "Was that a real question, or are you trying to turn this courtroom into the *Jerry Springer Show*?"

"It was a real question, Your Honor."

Schwitters stood up again. "Your Honor, it's clear that counsel has no pertinent questions to ask the witness. He's hoping that the mere *suggestion* of impropriety will somehow convince our esteemed jurors that Sigma has wronged in some way. I know it's early, but it's my recommendation that this case be thrown out of court."

"Wait a minute!" shouted Mark. "These are pertinent questions. I remind the court that I'm a former Sigma. These questions are based on my own pledging experiences."

"Mr. Jessy," said the dean, "whatever questionable activities you engaged in during your time at Sigma are not relevant here. You had your trial."

"Your Honor, I'm not referring to—"

The dean held up his hand. "Unless you have a question that can be supported by some sort of evidence, I'm going to have to ask you to excuse the witness."

Mark started to say something, but decided against it. "Fine. The witness is excused."

The dean turned to Andover, who was by now looking quite confused. "You're excused, Mr. Andover."

"If it please the court," said Schwitters, "defense would like to exercise its right to cross-examine the witness."

"I'll allow cross-examination."

"Thank you, Your Honor." Schwitters buttoned his jacket and walked toward Andover. "Mr. Andover, are you proud of your affiliation with Sigma?"

"Objection," Mark said. "Of course he's proud. He's still alive."

"Oh, come *on*!" moaned Schwitters.

"Mr. Jessy!" bellowed the dean. "If you don't watch your mouth, you'll be held in contempt!"

"Your Honor, the witness is a pledge who wants membership. But just because he's proud doesn't mean that Sigma didn't kill one of his fellow pledges. I'm sure the majority of Hitler's psychos were proud to be Nazis, but that doesn't mean they didn't commit gen—"

"*Objection!*" screamed Schwitters. "Your Honor, is counsel comparing my client with *Nazi Germany*?"

The dean took off his glasses and rubbed his eyes. "Sustained. First of all, Mr. Jessy, that may have been the worst analogy I've heard in twenty-five years in education. And second, I truly believe you misunderstand the point of calling witnesses. This is *your* witness! He's supposed to support *your* case! If he says he's proud of his affiliation with Sigma, then I'd say you called a lousy witness." The dean turned to Andover. "Please answer the question."

"I'm very proud of my affiliation with Sigma Delta Phi."

Schwitters nodded smugly. "What's this pride based on?"

"It's a brotherhood in every sense of the word. We respect each other, and value each other's opinion and well-being."

"Can you describe the reaction of the Sigma brothers following the tragic death of Chad Ewing."

"Certainly," said Andover. "The brothers were as devastated as the pledges. They planned the entire memorial service."

"And how did the brothers treat Chad's family?"

"Like they would treat their *own*."

Schwitters nodded and turned to the jury. "Now do these sound like the same bunch of thugs who supposedly forced Chad to consume shots of alcohol, as Mr. Jessy has claimed? I don't think so." He turned to the dean. "I have no more questions, Your Honor."

"Very well, the witness is excused. Thank you, Mr. Andover."

Andover left, pausing long enough to flash a touchdown grin in the direction of his Sigma cohorts.

"The prosecution may call its next witness."

Mark looked down at his notepad. "The College calls Tim Barringer."

Ten minutes later Barringer arrived. He, too, fit the physically impressive Sigma mold. While the dean conducted the swearing-in, Mark stood and walked toward the witness stand. When the dean was finished, he quickly attacked.

"Are you Timothy Barringer?"

"Yes."

"And currently a Sigma pledge?"

"Yes."

Mark nodded and began to pace slowly. "How's pledging been so far?"

"Just fine, thanks."

Mark looked at Barringer sympathetically. "Tim, I was a pledge, too. It's okay to admit that you aren't fond of being a pledge."

"Objection. The prosecution's personal recollections of pledging are irrelevant."

"Sustained."

Mark glanced at his notepad. "Tim, are you looking forward to initiation into the brotherhood?"

"I can't wait," Barringer answered enthusiastically.

"Oh? What's the big rush?"

"Well," said Barringer, as though the answer was obvious, "brotherhood's the ultimate goal."

"I see. And that wouldn't have anything to do with the fact that pledging *sucks,* would it?"

"Objection! Choice of words."

"Sustained. Please rephrase."

Mark nodded apologetically. "Tim, would you say that the pledge period has been especially taxing?"

"What do you mean?"

"I mean, wouldn't you say that pledging is a very difficult, time-consuming activity?"

"Objection. Leading the witness."

"Sustained."

Mark gave an exasperated sigh. "*Is* pledging time consuming?"

Barringer shrugged noncommittally. "I guess so."

"Yes or no?"

"Yes." He eyed the defense table nervously. "So are a lot of things."

"Like football?"

"Excuse me?"

"You do play football, don't you?"

"Yes, I do."

"Great," said Mark. "I'm an athlete, too."

"I know. You play lacrosse."

"And I consider it to be very time consuming. I mean, I have practice *every* day, and sometimes I'm gone for the *whole* weekend. I imagine football's the same way."

"Of course."

"At least as time consuming as pledging, am I right?"

"Definitely," agreed Barringer, "probably more."

Mark nodded, pausing to build the suspense. He put his notebook down on his table and strolled casually across the courtroom, his eyes focused on the ceiling to simulate deep thought.

"Tim, did you look forward to the end of the football season?"

"Pardon me?"

Mark focused on the witness. "I mean, during the season, were you eagerly anticipating the end of it? In other words, were you *glad* when the season was over?"

Barringer shook his head. "I love football. When the season ended, I was disappointed."

"Really? What was your record last year?"

"Objection! Where's counsel going with this?"

The dean nodded at Schwitters and looked Mark's way. "Mr. Jessy?"

"Your Honor, this will all make sense in just a moment. Please, let me finish."

The dean raised his eyebrows. "Okay, but hurry up with it."

"Thank you, Your Honor. Tim?"

"Our record was one and nine."

Mark feigned shock. "You mean, you won only *one game*?"

"Yeah," Barringer grunted defensively. "We had some bad breaks."

"I'll say. But still, I imagine it must be very difficult to endure a season like that. I mean, *one* and *nine* is pitiful!"

"Objection! Prosecution is insulting the witness."

"Sustained."

Mark nodded and held up his hand to the defense table, but couldn't help but love the indignant look on the face of A. J. Dominic, captain of the pitiful football team in question.

"Tim," he continued, "you mentioned that you didn't look forward to the end of the football season, because you love the game. Is that right?"

Barringer nodded. "No matter what our record was, I enjoyed the challenge."

"College sports are challenging, no doubt about that. And you like that part of football, don't you?"

"Yes."

"Then, I'm a little confused. I mean, I can certainly identify with your sentiments. I, too, feel that sports on the collegiate level are difficult and time consuming. But

I'm on a *winning* team, and that makes the whole thing very enjoyable."

"Objection!" shouted Schwitters. "Are we here to listen to counsel brag about his athletic exploits?"

"Sustained. Mr. Jessy, if you don't establish relevance with your next question, I'm going to excuse the witness. You're boring us."

Mark nodded and crossed his arms. "Tim, you've mentioned that football is time consuming, difficult, and challenging. On top of all this, as a team, you guys stink up the field, yet—"

"Objection!"

"Sustained."

"Sorry," allowed Mark. "As a team, you guys are less than good. Yet, you are sad when the season ends. On the other hand, pledging is also time consuming, difficult, and challenging. And you can't wait for it to be over. Why *is* that?"

The courtroom was silent. Mark stole a glance to his left and saw that the jurors were watching the witness closely.

Barringer shifted in his seat. "Football and pledging are different."

"How so? They sound the same to me."

"Well," said Barringer, "pledging is the means to an end. There's a greater goal to be achieved. We're trying to become brothers. When pledging is over, that means we're in."

"Okay," said Mark, "that's a good point. But, suppose you knew, *right now*, that you were going to get a post-season berth at the end of next football season. In other words, the regular season was going to be a 'means to an end.' Would you still look forward to the end of the regular season?"

"Well, no. I'd be excited, but I'd still enjoy the regular season."

"Let me get this straight. You can't wait for pledging to be over, yet you mourn the end of each football season. Both are time consuming, difficult, and challenging. What's the difference?"

Barringer shrugged. "Football's fun."

"Aha!" said Mark, pointing. "Football's *fun*! And pledging is not?"

Barringer looked uncomfortable. "Pledging's different."

Mark stole a glance at the defense table. Schwitters was conferring with Fairchild, while Dominic and Thresher listened tensely.

Mark returned his attention to the witness. "How is pledging so different?"

Barringer looked to the dean for help. When none came, he turned back to Mark. "It's, um, not a game. Football is."

"Do you go to fraternity parties?"

"Yes."

"Would you say that those are fun?"

"Sure. They're a blast."

"But they're not a game, like football, are they?"

Barringer hesitated. "No, but they're social."

"So," Mark reasoned, "for something to be fun, it has to be a game, or it has to be social?"

"Not necessarily."

"Let me put it this way, Tim. Is it safe to assume that pledging's neither a game nor is it social?"

Barringer shook his head quickly. "I didn't say that."

"Tim, is pledging humiliating?"

Barringer shifted anxiously. "No."

Mark looked at his notepad. "Tim, did the Sigma brothers ever make you wear a dress, to all meals, for a week?"

Barringer pulled at his tie. "No."

"Are you *sure*?"

"Objection."

"Sustained."

"Did the brothers ever make you rent a cow costume, stand at the milk dispenser, and moo while you handed out glasses of milk?"

A light chuckle from the jury.

"No," Barringer said, his jaw clenched.

"Tim," said Mark, raising his voice, "remember, you signed the Honor Code. Did the brothers ever make you shove a corn cob up your own ass?"

Gasps.

"*Objection!*"

The dean stood and hammered the lectern with his gavel. "That's it. You're in contempt!"

Mark made a face. "What are you going to do? Throw me in jail?"

Stark white with anger, the dean shook his head. "Unfortunately, I can't do that. But one more inappropriate question or comment and I'm throwing this case out of court."

"I'm just asking a few questions, Your Honor. Just being a lawyer."

"And in the process you're nauseating us. I hope

you're not planning on using shock value to win this case."

"As a matter of fact, Your Honor, I figured just the truth would do."

"Then stick to it, man!"

All heads turned toward the source of the angry shout. A. J. Dominic was standing, towering over the others in his bulk, giving Mark a look of pure murder. "You better watch your—"

"Objection!" Mark sang. "I'm being badgered."

The dean looked at Mark, then at Dominic. "Um, sustained. Please, Mr. Dominic. Try and keep your outbursts to a minimum."

Grudgingly, Dominic sank to his seat. Mark returned his attention to the witness.

"Tim, was Chad Ewing ever hazed?"

"No."

"Did the brothers ever make him spend one whole Saturday in the nude?"

"No."

Mark paused, looked down at the floor, and rocked on his heels. Then he regarded Barringer again and crossed his arms. "I have just one more question, Tim. Did the brothers force Chad Ewing to do shots of Jim Beam whiskey?"

Barringer opened his mouth to speak, but was overcome by a coughing spell. When he'd caught his breath he answered in a weak voice, "N-no. No, they didn't."

Mark shrugged evenly. "Funny. That's not what I heard. The witness is excused."

The dean raised his eyebrows and shook his head, as

though trying to clear water out of his ear. "Does the defense wish to cross-examine the witness?"

"Yes, Your Honor." Schwitters stood, buttoned his jacket, and strode toward the middle of the room. "Mr. Barringer, are you looking forward to this summer?"

"Excuse me?"

"Are you *looking forward* to the end of the semester? Are you *looking forward* to summer?"

Barringer eyed the defense table nervously. "Um, yes."

"Would you say that the course load here at Simsbury is *challenging*?"

"Yes."

"Would you say that you spend a good deal of time studying? In other words, would you say your studies are *time consuming*?"

"Yes."

"So, in summation, Tim, is it fair to conclude that you have found your brief academic career at Simsbury to be challenging and time consuming, and you can't wait for the semester to be over. Is this accurate?"

Barringer shrugged and glanced toward the jury. "Don't get me wrong, I enjoy—"

"Yes or no, Tim."

"Uh, yes, that's more or less true."

Schwitters nodded and began to pace slowly, as though he were weighing all the evidence. "It's funny, that sounds a lot like the way you described your feelings toward pledging." He paced a few steps more, then snapped his fingers, dashed over to the jury panel, and pointed his finger in the only female juror's face. "Ladies and Gentlemen of the jury, I hereby charge you with hazing!"

There was stunned silence, and Schwitters pressed the

attack. "How *dare* you approve the payroll for challenging professors! How *dare* you encourage the offering of time-consuming courses! I think that you must look at the evidence and conclude that each and every one of you is guilty of hazing Tim Barringer!"

Schwitters stared at each juror for a moment, then turned to the dean. "I have no more questions."

He returned to his seat and was met with handshakes and smiles.

Mark shook his head, thinking, *Simon Schwitters is very good at this.*

"Mr. Barringer, you may step down. Mr. Jessy, you may call your next witness."

Mark stood. "If it please the court, the prosecution is done for the day."

"So . . . you'd like to request a recess?"

"Sure. A recess."

The dean frowned. "That means you have only two days to call the rest of your witnesses. Let me remind you that the last day of the trial will be this Friday, regardless of how far down your list you've gotten."

"I'm aware of that, Your Honor."

"Okay, then. We'll recess until four o'clock tomorrow." He slammed his gavel once on his desk, and that was that.

Mark gathered his notebook and his jacket. On his way out he bumped into Dominic, who'd strategically positioned himself between Mark and the door.

"You're all done, pussy," Dominic hissed under his breath.

"Haven't even started, dickless," replied Mark.

He bounded down the steps of the Administration

Building and out onto the quad. He stopped at a campus phone, called Coach Capofina, and begged out of practice for academic reasons. Then, while the rhymes resumed their formulative place, he quickened his pace to a light jog toward the library.

7:12 P.M.

Late for his date with Linda, Templeton typed the e-mail quickly, and without sitting.

> *T-Bone. As I'm sure you've heard, today was another bloodbath. Spoke with two jurors, who "consider it an outrage," that Jessy's still at it. I told them he's a bad seed, with psychological issues.*
>
> *Anyway, thanks very much for the deposit. It has been my pleasure. Looking forward to getting together when this is all done, which should be tomorrow.*
>
> *Dinner on me.*

CHAPTER FIFTY-FIVE

The 200th Year
Wednesday, March 11

8:24 P.M.

It was dark, and maybe that's why no one noticed. Or maybe the Pledgemaster had gotten cocky and neglected to do a head count. Then again, it's been said that the human eye gets used to seeing things a certain way and will continue to see things that way even after the scenery has changed. Whatever the reason, the Triumvirate session had been almost completed before the brothers noticed that a pledge was missing.

The Leader stopped in mid-rhyme.

"Someone's missing," he said, and though none of the brothers or pledges present realized the immediate significance of this two-word utterance, it was the beginning of the first nonrhymed sequence of words in Sigma Triumvirate history.

The Leader craned his hooded head and searched the second row of pledges. The pledges in this row had fanned out, to make it appear as long as the first. They knew a pledge was missing, and how bad it would be if the brothers knew, too.

The Leader counted heads. "Fifteen. Who's missing?"

No response.

The Leader grabbed the Sword of Tradition from the Sergeant-at-Arms and slammed it down on the oak table.

"Who's missing?"

Some of the pledges looked at each other. Finally, a tremulous voice answered from the second row. "Pledge Turlington."

A pause. "Well, where is he?"

"We just don't know, sir."

The Sword thundered down once more, and the brothers began to hiss.

"You've been *ordered*," raged the Leader, "time and time again, not to appear before the brotherhood unless you are complete in number. Haven't you?"

"Yes, sir!"

"Then tonight you have failed! And you'll be suitably punished, as will pledge Turlington."

"Pledgemaster, take the pledges back down to the upstairs libes. Hold them there until we locate pledge Turlington. Keep them all night if you have to."

The Pledgemaster nodded. "Pledges, replace your fucking blindfolds."

8:42 P.M.

With the pledges secured, and the sophomores and juniors standing guard downstairs, the seniors began fuming in the Brotherhood Room.

"*Fuck!*" shouted Gamma. "That little *shit!*"

Kappa turned to Beta. "What do we do?"

Beta sat silently in the corner, a far-off look in his eyes. He just shook his head slightly and shrugged.

"We beat the shit out of him again," urged Delta. "We shove his tongue down his throat. We brand his right shoulder, and feed him the scabs from his left. That's what we do."

"We have to find him first, shithead."

"Hey, man, suck my dick!"

"Both of you, shut up," said Gamma. "First of all, we still have Silas, who can refute anything Turlington says. That's *assuming* Turlington plans on testifying against us, and *assuming* we don't find him, which we will, because this is Simsbury College, not New York City. Kappa, you go over to his room. See if he's stupid enough to be there. Upsilon, you check the library. Delta, you take the Cage. I'll go take a look at Jessy's apartment. I got a hunch that Turlington's there."

"What if he is?"

"I'll tear a new asshole in both of them. Then I'll come back here and tell pledge Drew Silas that he's my fucking hero."

8:50 P.M.

Turlington had agreed to stay in the quaint Freeport Hotel only if Mark picked up the tab. In possession of six hundred dollars he'd no longer be spending on South Padre Island, Mark had agreed to the terms and had even thrown in a pizza, on which he and Turlington now munched as the hour neared nine.

Mark finished his last slice, consulted Turlington's watch, and decided it was time to act. He stood, thanked Turlington for the risk he was running, and as he walked

toward the door instructed the freshman to latch and bolt
it behind him.

Stepping from the room, he turned to issue some final
warnings, but found Turlington standing in the doorway,
pizza crust in his hand, wearing an uncertain look on his
face and clearly having something more on his mind than
the night's perilous plan.

Something with roots nearly three weeks old.

"I almost had him," Turlington said.

Mark raised his eyebrows, not following.

"I almost had him," repeated the freshman.

Mark shook his head. "Who?"

"Chad. I almost had him. I saw him staggering around
by the balcony railing. I saw him, Mark. I saw the poetry
on his skin you asked me about. He . . . I knew he needed
help, but I didn't want to startle him, so I crept . . . when
I went to save him . . . I was still so wasted . . . my hands
touched his naked back." He looked down, tortured still
by this memory that would linger forever. "I . . . I just . . .
I just missed him."

He looked up at Mark, his eyes moist. "I just missed
him."

Mark nodded, and watched the freshman's face crum-
ple. He put his hand on Turlington's shoulder, gave him a
squeeze of support, then turned and walked down the
hallway.

9:31 P.M.

The brothers reconvened in the Brotherhood Room,
concluded that Turlington was still missing, traded theories and rage for a few minutes, then headed down to the
upstairs libes.

They rounded up the pledges, led them down to the barroom, and hazed the shit out of them.

10:05 P.M.

Standing stone-still in the rear parking lot, Mark stared up at Sigma and all its white monstrosity. Never had the house looked so large, or so alive. Tree branches and twined ivy beckoned like talon-clawed fingers. Darkened windows on white siding watched like the black eyes of a shark. Loose gutters and drainpipes rattled warnings, and wind-whistled alcoves shrieked bad intentions.

A new scream split the night, and he threw himself against the side of the house. A loud roar followed, and as the evil chill of the mansion's siding clutched at the nape of his neck, he realized what he'd heard was music.

Loud, violent music.

Heart hammering, he stepped away and looked down through the basement window. In the sickly orange-yellow light of the barroom, he watched Pete Thresher and Lou Janosco tower over a pledge, shouting the same old rhymes at the poor kid while he did push-ups. The pledge "*gave 'em heart and gave 'em twenty, then got up and drank aplenty,*" while Thresher and Janosco slapped his bare stomach as hard as they could. When the pledge had finished the beer, he dropped to the floor and resumed his calisthenics. Mark wished he had a camera.

He backed away from the basement window and looked up to one particular window on the third floor. Then he gave a final glance to College Street, where students streamed to and from the library, too caught up in academic deadlines and spring-break plans to bother looking westward for a wayward student dressed in black and about to break the law. Concluding the coast would never be more clear, the time never more right, he ducked low and skulked toward the fire escape.

He reached for the bottom rung, pulled himself up, then scaled all three flights, his steps rattling the black iron steps and railings. Halfway up he realized that, with his black attire, he stuck out like a moving pimple against the white, unblemished face of the house. The climb seemed to last an eternity.

At the top of the third flight, he rested on the grated platform; a quick breather before extreme danger. His target window was across the steeply inclined roof.

If he fell, he would die.

He hauled himself onto the roof's tar, then lay spread-eagled on the slant for a moment, gathering courage. He felt around with sweaty hands, discovering dark patches of ice. Standing would be foolish.

But absolutely necessary.

Just beyond his outstretched hands, protruding from an icy sheen, was an anchored piece of steel piping, and next to that was a brick chimney of sorts. Lunging forward, he grabbed the piping with his right hand and pulled toward the chimney, over the lip of which he draped his left arm. He hauled himself to a standing position and readied for the tricky part.

Between here and the window there would be nothing to cling to but luck.

He knew from experience—he'd spent many nights on the roof as a brother; it was considered a cool, brave place to hang—that the only way to get to the window he sought was to run, fast and without stopping. If he dragged too much he'd slide down the roof, and then he'd *really* be all done, and wouldn't it be a shame to outwit an assassin only to have gravity splat his slow ass all over asphalt. If he sprinted in a parabolic arc, however, he could make it.

He gripped the chimney tightly, his legs shaking, his knuckles cramped. Had he all night, he would have taken it. But he didn't, which meant there was only one way to do this.

Quickly.

He touched the beads once and got a good jump. He scratched and scampered his way toward the window, angling toward the roof peak, pinwheeling his arms for balance. He slipped twice, each time losing five feet in altitude, and one time almost losing it all. Ten feet from the window he dove, just barely managing to catch hold of the sill. His legs threatened to slide down the remainder of the roof, but his grip wouldn't let them. Panting, heart exploding, he closed his eyes and whispered thanks to his able body.

He hung there a moment to catch his breath. To his right was the spot where he, Ran, and Fairchild had sat sipping Brother Beam on his last night as a Sigma.

You guys promise we'll always be brothers?

Hell, yes!

Every Homecoming, we'll meet right here . . . This is our spot.

No, just your spot, thought the former brother who now hung from the windowsill like a goddamned outlaw. He dragged himself to his feet, keeping one hand on the sill to brace himself. With his free hand he opened the window. Poking his head inside, he scanned the third-floor hallway. Empty. Everyone was in the barroom, beating the piss out of the beloved pledges. He stepped lightly through the window, touched down silently on the hardwood, and crept down the hall to the Brotherhood Room.

Would it be open? It always used to be. Even though the brothers referred to the room as "The Most Sacred of Rooms, at the end of The Most Hallowed of Halls," the door was never locked. Despite the room's holiness, Mark guessed that even the self-centered Sigmas realized that no one else gave a rat's ass about all the flags, banners, books, and bullshit the room contained. It probably never occurred to them that someone would actually try to steal something.

Not their first mistake.

But perhaps their last.

He opened the door and stole through the utter darkness to the far side of the room, where he knew the Triumvirate Table stood, four legged, oak, and haughty. He crouched, reached beneath the table, and found the cardboard box. He worked a hand under one of the flaps, and when his hand closed around the cottony fabric, his entire body convulsed. He ripped the box open completely, and there they were.

He gathered the bundles, closed the box, and left the Brotherhood Room.

From here it would be easy. He walked down the hall to the third-floor fire exit, which was locked only from the outside. He opened the door like a civilized criminal, zipped his loot into his jacket, and fled down the stairs.

10:44 P.M.

Realizing that all the hazing in the world wasn't going to make Turlington reappear, the brothers finally released the rest of the pledges. Turlington was nowhere to be found, and now the brothers would have to assume the worst.

The seniors, the saviors, gathered in the Brotherhood Room.

"Well," said Theta, "he's gone. What do we do now?"

There was a hopeless silence.

"Good thing we branded him," said Beta.

"Oh, fuck off!" shouted Gamma. "We did what we had to do!"

"Alpha's gonna kill us."

Another silence. A couple of the brothers left the room, apparently having had enough.

"One thing's for sure," Delta said finally, "we need Drew Silas more than we've ever needed anyone in our lives."

CHAPTER FIFTY-SIX

The 200th Year
Wednesday, March 11

11:05 P.M.

Slightly drunk and heavily battered, pledge Drew Silas unlocked the door to his room, shuffled inside, and hoped his roommate was asleep. The cuts on his face still bled, the bruises had begun to color his shoulders, chest, and neck, and he had no energy to invent bullshit explanations. He flopped down on the couch and closed his eyes.

Turlington was gone. Of course, only Silas knew what that meant, for he was the only other nonbrother who knew what had caused Chad Ewing's great fall. He imagined the other pledges assumed the brothers were upset because Turlington's absence represented a breakdown in pledge solidarity, as well as lack of respect.

Not even close. Silas understood the truth. He knew that more than just Brother Beam had cascaded down three pledges' throats.

But he couldn't believe Turlington would be so stupid. He just couldn't believe it! Despite the abuse he himself

ROB KEAN

had taken, he'd do anything to honor the vows he'd pledged, anything to protect the brotherhood.

Anything at all.

He hoped the brothers knew that.

The phone rang, shattering the near-midnight silence. He was oh-so-close to letting it ring, for he was in no mood to talk. Then again, it occurred to him on the fourth ring that it *might* just be Turlington calling. If Turlington was foolish enough to betray Sigma, then maybe he'd be foolish enough to trust Silas. Silas would gently coax Turlington into confiding his whereabouts, then he'd quickly turn around and inform the brothers. The brothers would catch Turlington, and Silas would be the hero.

"Hello?"

"Pledge Silas?"

His heart sank. Why, oh why, had he answered the phone?

"Yes, this is Silas, sir."

You're a brave man, Silas, for answering the phone. We're not done with you yet. The Rock. Come alone.

CHAPTER FIFTY-SEVEN

The 200th Year
Wednesday, March 11

11:21 P.M.

Filled with a foreboding that only he and fifteen survivors understood, Silas crunched through the snow, across the darkened athletic fields, and toward the wooded area that lined the complex.

Toward the Rock.

He tried to imagine what the brothers were going to do to him, and why. He guessed they were in the mood to punish someone for Turlington's insubordination, and he was the logical choice. His best bet, he figured, would be to try and convince the brothers that he had no intention of betraying them. His lips were permanently sealed, and he would convey that between tongue-lashings or fist thrashings.

As he reached the first row of pine, darkness swallowed him, blotting out what dim, blanketing light the acres of treeless snow had provided. Unseen needles brushed against his face as he bobbed and wove his way through the skeleton of branches. Ice and twigs crackled like fire beneath him.

Upon reaching the first of two clearings, he broke into a chilly jog.

He could vividly recall the only other time he'd been summoned to the Rock. After making him climb the slippery face of the eight-foot boulder, they'd forced him to sing Sigma songs at the top while they pelted him with snowballs and ice chunks. Now, looking down at the ground passing beneath him, he noted it was good packing snow.

Reaching the second line of trees, he lowered his head and burrowed past the prickly twigs. Once in the second clearing, he looked up.

They were waiting for him.

In front of the Rock stood three figures dressed in black robes and black hoods.

The Triumvirate.

Swallowing dryly, he approached cautiously, his heart smashing against ribs that were already bruised.

The Triumvirate towered like dark, developing storm clouds, calm now, but poised to unleash unforgettable damage, the content of which was yet unknown. They seemed as one, their wind-driven robes intertwined and feeding blackly off one another. The two flanking the Leader held torches that added no warmth to the scene at all, serving only to make them loom larger, adding shadow upon shadow upon shadow.

It was, thought Silas, as duty dragged him haltingly forward, an awesome sight.

When he was within ten feet he knelt reverently, fixed his arms firmly against his sides, and waited for either instruction or infliction.

For a shrieking moment, the entire natural world rioted

as the wind and the trees and the snow whispered then
shouted then screamed complete chaos. The natural then
gave way to silence, then to unnatural rhyme.

On this night, Pledge Silas, the brothers look to you.
So remember your oaths, whatever you do.

Reach deep inside, and bring forth all your talents.
For two hundred years lie rich in the balance.

A wind gust punctuated the preamble, and punctured
Silas's face. Too afraid to turn from the icy explosion (for
it would certainly signify weakness), he endured it and
loathed the tears that bled from his eyes.

Turlington's gone, need not we say more.
But just to be thorough, here's the full-guided tour.

Understand, young pledge, as you kneel in the dark,
That Mark Jessy designs to make like a shark.

He's hooked a big fish, of Turlington name,
And now swims with teeth, seeking Sigma as game.

Need we be fearful? We think there is reason.
Especially with Turlington now poised for treason.

It could get really ugly, when Greg takes the stand.
So we must get crafty, and first play our hand.

Another gust electrified the trees. Falling pinecones
peppered the clearing.

And what is that hand, you no doubt are wondering.
You be that hand, all brothers are thundering.

You are the one who will lead us to light,
One half of the two who survived that bad night.

You remember that night, don't you, young pledge?
Surely its memory needs no deep dredge.

Surely it sits as a bad mindful fixture,
For Brother Beam and roofies are an unsettling mix-
ture.

It would be a real shame to go through that again.
It would be a real shame to put you back in pain's
pen.

Silence.

"Wouldn't it, Pledge Silas?" said the Leader. "Wouldn't it be a shame to have to meet the new-and-improved Brother Beam again?"

His tongue pinned by a distasteful memory, Silas could only manage a nod.

An understandable response, a reply that makes
sense.
So let's look to the future, to what happens hence.

We have spied a small opening, and so spying must
nab it.
The prosecutor, we believe, is a creature of habit.

He'll call alphabetically, note today's two star wit-
nesses.
Being creative, we guess, is not one of Mark's fit-
nesses.

Which bodes well for us, as T follows S,
You'll get your chance before Greg; that's our guess.

Silas nodded again, completely baffled by the direction
of this rhyme.

Here's what you'll do, when called to the stand.
You'll tell what you know, the truth is your hand.

Unleash that bad night. Lay it all on the line.
Let the jury peruse it, and that will be fine.

Bend the prelims a bit. Take away some facts gory.
And take away some other tidbits from the story.

Speak not of the rhymes, speak not of the race.
But speak of the rest with truth's grace on your face.

It will be unexpected, but oh so effective,
A forthcoming counterstrike, a shocking elective.

For within all that truth you'll do some small lying.
A fib that will finish off all future prying.

The source of your drugging, you'll say with your
tongue sly.
Was not current brothers, but some Sigma alumni.

Now Silas was beginning to see it, but he was not quite sure he believed it.

I can see in your eyes a look of confusion,
As what I've been saying makes clear its infusion.

You're wondering why you should opt to incriminate,
Especially before company that tends to discriminate.

Trust us, Pledge Silas, we know what we're doing.
We're masters of game, when a crisis is brewing.

This last rhyme drifted off, wind-dissipated, leaving poetic echoes in Silas's freezing head. Long echoes. Hushed echoes. Awkward echoes.

Still unclear echoes.

"Um, I—"

Quiet, Pledge Silas, you know the rule.
We brothers be teachers, and this be our school.

Which means you will hush till it's time to respond,
In a brave rhyming voice, of which we are fond.

I'm sure you have questions, how could you not?
Well, we have the answers for queries you've got.

No, they'll not punish us for alumni wrongdoing.
So there's no need for worry, no need for stewing.

The reasons for this are built into the charter.

A deed set in stone, unsmiling on barter.

The D-Squad has rule over only the students,
Jurisdiction beyond whom just wouldn't be prudent.

And since the alumni have received their diplomas,
Theirs is an air of nonstudent aromas.

What is this bylaw that will keep us alive?
Charter Article Nineteen, Section Four, Rule Five.

Silas nodded somewhat, as if to suggest he either understood, or had read the charter cover to cover. Neither was true.

The D-Squad brings trial against only the brothers,
Sophomore to senior. Forget all the others.

For there are no others, at least none that matter.
Despite what we've preached of the hierarchical
ladder.

Brothers live brief lives, four years and gone,
With no further care except who keeps the lawn.

Which is why we can do this, and get away with it,
too.
Which is why, on this night, we all look to you.

For five weeks (or was it six now?) Silas had questioned nothing, taking abuse as warranted and unwarranted, mindlessly listening and responding when asked and as taught. His obedience to date had been so regimented, so self-programmed, that he was shocked when his mouth opened in rebellion, and his voice now cried, "I don't get it!"

Silence.

Oh, you fool, he thought to himself, flinching. *You deserve everything coming to you.*

But no harm came.

Just more rhymes.

Aren't alumni true brothers? Is that what you're asking?
Aren't they one and the same, in matching light basking?

Let me ask you, Silas, that very same question.
You can answer it yourself, that's my suggestion.

Are alumni true brothers? What do you think?
Do they plan the parties? Do they drink the drink?

Do they run the fields, travel tight-knit to class?
Do they fight the fight? Do they kick weak ass?

Do they rhyme the rhymes, do the things we esteem?
Do they fuck the young pretty? Do they make the girls scream?

They do none of these things. Therein lies the answer.
Believe it right now, for doubt is a cancer.

*And since alumni aren't brothers, they cannot be
tried.*
And therefore, to their deeds, we cannot be tied.

Not directly, at least, and that's all that counts,
*In the courtroom where small-college evidence
mounts.*

Silas now felt the first rays of logic from this very impressive poem. The Leader, perhaps sensing this, began
to speak louder, squashing the few surviving bugs of uncertainty.

So you'll tell what you know, in moderate detail.
*But you'll throw a false bone, down a whole other
trail.*

It will ring so conclusive, when you tag the alumni,
*Such a soul-searching admission, from a gracious
young guy.*

And through it all Schwitters and Sigma will protest,
Object and cry foul, from their defense-table nest.

*And this shock will show that we had no real knowl-
edge*
*'Bout what happened to you three, at this liberal
arts college.*

But you just keep talking, through all the fake fuss.
Tell it all you will, tell it all you must.

For when it's all done, the guilt will be hung,
Round the necks of the elders, not the hearts of the
young.

The Turlington bomb won't by Jessy be dropped,
The dean will step in, and a plea will be copped.

He'll wrist-slap the brothers, dole some sort of pro-
bation.
And the alumni'll be banned from endowment dona-
tion.

And who fucking cares, 'cause we'll get the nod.
And we're already well-funded, with more money
than God.

The Leader stepped forward, separating himself from
his candle-bearing brothers.

It's time, Pledge Silas, to grab the world by the balls,
To keep Sigma tradition housed in hallowed Greek
halls.

It's time to get tricky, play the craftiest hand.
Be bold and creative, do you understand?

He stepped closer. "Do you, Pledge Silas? Do you understand? And are you ready, willing, and able to do the
things necessary to save this brotherhood?"

Doubt left Silas in a rush, for these were the words
he'd longed to hear through all the beatings and thrashings and general humiliations. It suddenly no longer

mattered that he didn't fully understand what he was being asked to do. All that mattered was that he was bowed before the Triumvirate, that they were giving orders, and that they were counting on him, so he stuck out his chest, and gushed the rhyme he could say in his sleep.

I'd no sooner stray, than burn deep in hell,
Say I with a bad-ass and brotherly yell.

The rhymes you command are mine to obey,
Weakness invites me, but I say no way!

Silence.
For a long time.
The Leader finally nodded and, stepping back, rejoined his brothers. "Good boy. We knew we could count on you. We are invincible, Pledge Silas, and we're going to prove it tomorrow."

Silas nodded with enthusiasm he hadn't felt since the night he first pledged.

Go back to your room, and get ready to lie.
Do a good job, or Sigma will die.

Silas scrambled to his feet, turned, and walked quickly from the Rock, not daring to look back. When he'd broken through to the first clearing, he quickened his pace to a jog, and when he'd reached the athletic fields again, he stopped and put his hands on his knees.
And vomited.
Through watery eyes, he turned and looked back at the

wooded area. Then, closing his eyes, he tilted his head back, processing what he had just been told.

They were counting on him.

They were counting on him to save the whole fucking brotherhood.

He opened his eyes and began walking again, in the direction of the campus his future brothers ruled. An immense feeling of pride lengthened him, grabbing his chin and his chest and pulling them forward.

The Sigma brothers needed him.

Finally.

He would not let them down.

11:51 P.M.

The Triumvirate waited in silence as stony as the Rock until they were sure Silas had gone home and would not be coming back. Finally, the Leader gave a nod, and all three simultaneously removed their black hoods.

Caitlin Kittiwake, an SWA member known for her height and the *Keep Your Laws off My Body* bumper sticker that blared from her backpack, stared in amazement at the Leader and said, "You barely even stuttered."

"Hey," said Marcia Heery, an equally long-limbed SWA member whose own backpack screamed, *Dead Men Don't Rape.* "That was fun," she said to the Leader. "Are we, like, *brothers* now?"

Mark Jessy dropped his hood and draped his arms around the necks of both women, both of whom had been ferociously offended when told that Sigma had fabricated an attempted rape charge, both of whom had been spittingly incensed that an SWA president herself had been duped during the setup, both of whom had agreed to team up with a victim of macho maneuvering and settle their own kind of score.

"How about sisters?" said Mark, as he broke into what felt like the most sincere smile of his life. "I've had enough brothers."

12:04 A.M.

The man with the broken nose and two black eyes had a score of his own to settle. He was lacing his boots when the phone rang, and he nearly ignored it, so lost was he in plans of vengeance. However, the incessant ring eventually prompted him to pick it up and grunt a distracted hello.

"It's me," said T-Bone, his tone darker than ever.

"I'm busy."

"You better be. Forget what I said this morning. I want that kid out of the picture."

"Oh, I'll take him out all right, but understand—this one's for me."

"It's also for five hundred grand, so don't fuck up."

The man stopped tying, set his hands on the bed, and steadied himself. "Half a million?"

"You heard me."

"Sounds like *someone's* scared."

T-Bone bit down on the next few words. "Just get the job done."

The killer stared at the wall a moment longer, then continued fiddling with his boot laces. "The cocky little fucker will be dead in an hour. Count on it."

CHAPTER FIFTY-EIGHT

The 200th Year
Thursday, March 12

1:14 A.M.

Mark awoke from his deep slumber with a start, his senses immediately on edge.

Something wasn't right.

And then, from the darkness at the foot of his mattress, he heard the growl rumbling from Casey's tiny, taut-muscled body, which until now had been draped noodlelike across his ankles. Having spent the last week being tied to a tree, fondled by the vet, and shuttled back and forth between her normal domain and the strange, frilly apartment of a woman who knew a lot about dogs but was also a stickler for rules and discipline, she'd learned in short time that this great, wide world wasn't always about curious smells, comfy laundry piles, and chewable furniture.

It was also about danger.

And so she'd learned how to growl.

Which was what told Mark that something was definitely not right.

And then he heard a second noise, coming from the kitchen.

A low, clicking noise that fit the blackness.

Click. Rattle-click. Rattle.

Fear arrowed through his body, and told him to wake up. *Now.*

Click. Rattle-rattle. Click.

His heart pounding wildly, Mark leaned all the way to the foot of his bed and peered through his open doorway. The kitchen was equally as dark as his bedroom, save for the bright, rectangular glare from the campus lights that gleamed through the glass door and reflected off the linoleum.

Outside, a stiff, sudden breeze blew, and the neighboring snow-covered tree branches groaned at the strain. A twig smacked against his window. He flinched and missed a heartbeat or two. Casey yelped, then settled into a growl that slowly dwindled.

And then all was quiet again.

For a moment.

Click. Rattle. Click-click.

His eyes slowly scanned the bedroom, then back out into the kitchen.

The white, rectangular reflection was now dark with two legs, a torso, and faintly moving arms.

A man.

Hunting him.

Mark crept from his mattress and armed himself with what had once been a lacrosse stick he would have liked to pass on to his *own* son. He clutched the jagged, home-made weapon close, and as Casey poised to pounce he slipped behind his open door and caressed his beads.

And waited.

Click. Click. Rattle.

He heard the doorknob turn, and the front door pop open with a sharp, sucking sound. A cold draft swirled through the bedroom, cocking Casey's head and rustling some loose papers on his desk like dead leaves.

Thock!

Thwack!

A high-pitched gasp and a muffled moan followed the two reports of violence. Then boot steps clomped back across the brief front porch, snow crunched, a car door slammed, an engine revved, tires spun wildly across snow, and ice chunks flew through the open kitchen door and skittered across the linoleum.

Mark emerged from his hiding spot and tiptoed slowly through the kitchen. Casey followed him, woofing at the departing ruckus. Looking through the open doorway, Mark watched the black BMW screech away from his apartment and down College Street.

He stood there a moment.

Then he turned his attention to the open doorway, where Casey was licking the frame just below the hinges. He approached hesitantly and knelt to investigate.

Then smiled.

Jutting from the door frame, embedded in the wood, was one of the six razor-sharp harpoon lilies his beloved uncle Kiko had given him as a going-away care package, the day Mark had left the deep woods and dangerous waters of Wellfleet for the exclusive purity of Simsbury. Skewered on the three-inch iron point, like so many tuna flanks had been at one time or another, was a piece of black denim.

And dripping from the spot where fabric met iron, was blood.

Sigma blood.

Overcome with victorious relief, Mark closed his eyes, shook his fist slowly, and whispered a stream of grateful incoherencies. For clearly, the booby trap had worked. The two lilies manning this particular door had been set up to fire from one side of the frame toward the other, and in the process take out whatever legs might enter the apartment and trip the monofilament fishing line stretched across the doorway. And since only one lily had made it all the way to the opposite side of the frame, Mark could draw a satisfied conclusion regarding the current location of the second lily.

He stood once more, and as the breeze tumbled through the open doorway he wondered, without the slightest ounce of pity, just how painful it would be to have a harpoon lily halfway through the knee.

"That one was for you, Kiko," he whispered into the night, as he sunk to the floor again and wrapped an arm around Casey. "That one was for you."

CHAPTER FIFTY-NINE

The 200th Year
Thursday, March 12

4:11 A.M.

The man with the broken nose, two black eyes, and a harpoon lily halfway through his knee decided now was as good a time as any to call. He'd be assured of reaching nothing more than an answering machine, which was a good thing, for the excruciating agony pulsing upward from his knee left him in no condition to argue, and the blood loss had weakened him to the point where insults might actually finish him off.

Besides, after three sleepless hours of cursing at the ceiling, he knew exactly what he wanted to say.

He picked up the phone and dialed.

"T-Bone," he said, when the beep cued him, "it's me. If you and your brothers want Mark Jessy dead, then be the men you say you are and try to kill him yourselves."

10:55 A.M.

His heart as heavy as it had been since the day his wife discovered a lump in her breast, Bill Turlington finished loading the rest of his son's things into his Cherokee, then slammed the gate down and joined his devastated son by the car door.

For a long moment, father and child stared in equal silence at snow that lacked its trademark luster.

"I'm sorry, Dad," Greg said finally, in a small voice. "I tried . . . to be as good as you. I really tried."

Fighting back tears, Bill Turlington pulled his firstborn to him, rubbed his back, and kissed his hair. "You're every bit as good, Greg," he said fiercely. "In fact, you're better than your old man will *ever* be, and I'm so damn proud of you." As he soothed, he turned and gave one last glance to the Simsbury College that had made him a hero, that had given him brothers, that had made him a man, and he felt his eyes grow dark. "It's *this* place that let me down." He shook his head with a mixture of anger and sadness. "This isn't the Simsbury College I remember."

He sniffed, then patted his son one last time. "Come on, kid. Let's go home."

11:22 A.M.

President Carlisle sat at his desk, surrounded by things he didn't know how to use. A computer with countless tiny buttons and a bizarre e-mail function. A fax machine that screamed while sending. Faceless, babbling voice mail. Creations that marked the first signs of the apocalypse.

It didn't bother him that he was a techno-illiterate, for he was too old and stubborn to care. Besides, he didn't need Internet access to know he was smart. A bachelor's from Simsbury itself, and both a masters and a Ph.D.

from Harvard—those sort of things weren't exactly given away.

At the same time, he wasn't blind to his deficiencies. He knew that the world had lapped him and that his time was nearly up. A disease, the name of which he sometimes couldn't remember, was slowly beating him. He no longer recalled professors' names or times of meetings. He was seventy-one, and he was tired. This would be his final year at Simsbury.

And he hoped he would die quickly after stepping down, because he knew it would break his heart to watch the inevitable crumbling of his beloved alma mater. The college would be taken over by manipulative bullies like Templeton who believed that they were bigger than education, and a generation of youths with no concept of honor.

His intercom beeped, and while he tried to figure out which machine the sound was coming from, it beeped again. He pressed several buttons, until he finally heard the patient breathing of his secretary.

"Yes?"

"You have a call on line two. A student named Shawn Jakes."

He frowned. "What's this about?"

"I don't know, but she says it's urgent."

"Oh. Well, in that case, put her through."

Line two began to flash, and he pressed the corresponding button.

"Miss Jones?"

"Jakes. Shawn Jakes."

"Yes, Miss Jakes, what can I do for you?"

"Well . . . you don't know me, I'm sure. I'm a senior, and until recently I was a member of the D-Squad."

"Oh?"

"That's right. Listen, about the Chad Ewing case . . . I think there's something you should know."

CHAPTER SIXTY

The 200th Year
Thursday, March 12

4:03 P.M.

"All rise!"

All rose.

"Call to order *Simsbury College v. Sigma Delta Phi*." As the jurors sat, the dean put on his glasses, moved from his bench, and looked sternly at Mark. "Mr. Jessy, before we begin today, I feel I must categorize your behavior yesterday as deplorable. You have insulted the jurors with your crass line of questioning."

"Your Honor," Mark replied calmly. "A student is dead. As unpleasant as my questions may be, I don't think they're *nearly* as unpleasant as Chad Ewing's fate. Do you?"

"Don't patronize me, young man."

"My apologies. May I call the next witness?"

The dean turned and addressed the court. "Ladies and Gentlemen, I can assure you of my dissatisfaction with the course of these proceedings. It's my inclination to throw this case—"

"*No!*" shouted Mark, "*Your Honor! Please!*"

The dean whirled and stared at Mark.

"Please," begged Mark, "allow me this one day. If by the end I haven't established a case, I'll gladly forfeit. I swear."

"Your Honor," said Schwitters, "I agree with you. This has been a complete waste of time for both the members of the court and our esteemed jurors, who've taken time out of their busy lives, only to be insulted again and again by sleazy innuendo—"

"Actually . . ."

All eyes turned toward the jury, searching for the source of this voice. Standing, Roosevelt Jefferson claimed responsibility.

"I'm not insulted at all," explained Jefferson. "In fact, I'm *quite* interested in this case. As far as I'm concerned, there's *nothing* in this world more important than finding out what happened to Chad Ewing. If it takes a little unpleasant dalliance to get there, so be it."

Most of the other jurors nodded in agreement, and Mark felt a smile play on the corners of his mouth.

"Besides," Jefferson added with a smile, "I'm retired. I don't have busy days."

The jurors chuckled, and the dean stood frozen. It was suddenly obvious that the jurors were also his bosses.

He swallowed hard and nodded. "Very well," he said quietly. "We'll continue." He scurried back to his lectern.

Feeling as if he had the entire courtroom in his pocket, Mark stood and for a long, daring moment stared at the defense. Only Schwitters responded, with the same look of scornful pity he'd shown for the past three days. The three Sigmas, on the other hand, sat slightly fidgety in their Sigma blazer best, their eyes darting from the jurors to Mark to the floor.

Greg Turlington was missing.

And they were scared.

Mark gulped the smile that wanted to break through and turned to the dean. "Your Honor," he began, "while I reserve the right to call pledges in the future, I'd like to switch gears for a moment. The College calls David Troy Fairchild to the stand."

Fairchild shot Mark a look of thin, exhausted surprise, and Schwitters leapt to his feet. "Objection! This witness is not on the list!"

The dean nodded quickly, nervously. "Mr. Jessy, you can't call people who aren't on the list."

"I know that, Your Honor, but I figured since he was here—"

"It doesn't work that way. We've got to go by the book."

Mark clasped his hands together. "Please . . . I lived with Mr. Fairchild for a year, and I consider him to be a close friend. It's surely not my intention to engage in hostile questioning."

The dean looked at Schwitters, who was looking at Fairchild, who was still looking at Mark. Forcing a smile, Sigma's president shrugged. "Sure. I'll take the stand."

Composed, Fairchild moved toward the witness chair. He stood stoically as the dean swore him in, then sat in the witness chair and threw a more natural, chipped-tooth smile Mark's way.

Mark returned the grin.

"Dave, are you the current Sigma president?"

"Yes, I am."

"You were Rush Chairman last year, were you not?"

"I was."

"And the year before that?"

"Treasurer."

"Well," Mark said appreciatively, "it seems that your fellow brothers have as high an opinion of you as I do."

"That's nice of you to say."

"My pleasure."

"Objection! Is counsel going to make a pass at my client?"

"Sustained. Can we stop with the mutual admiration society?"

"Sure," Mark said agreeably. He turned to the witness again. "Dave, does Sigma have an active alumni presence?"

Fairchild nodded. "Very active."

"Could you elaborate?"

"Sure. Aside from fiscal contributions, the alumni have a hand in almost every decision that's made concerning the brotherhood."

"That's impressive," commented Mark. "I know that in some fraternities the alumni are rather apathetic."

"True. Not ours, though."

"Do the alumni play a role in the pledge process?"

"Yes. They're very active in pledge orientation."

"Are they present at many of the orientation events?"

"We usually have some sort of alumni presence at all of our functions. As chaperones."

"Really. That must set a great example for the pledges. I mean, seeing former brothers regularly come back to the house must make the pledges want initiation *that much more*."

"I'm sure," said Fairchild. "But the alumni aren't *former* brothers. They're still considered *active* brothers."

"Oh. You mean . . . because you're a brother *now*, you'll *always be* a brother?"

"Always."

"Even when you're, like, eighty-eight years old?"

"Always."

"So, there's no difference between yourself and, say, a brother who graduated fifteen years ago? I mean, in terms of dedication to the brotherhood and stuff like that?"

"No difference whatsoever. Except I still have student loans to pay back."

The jurors chuckled knowingly, and Mark allowed a smile. "I'm soon to be familiar with that dilemma. But, getting back to the alumni, would you expect them to behave with the same integrity as yourself? And vice versa?"

"Of course."

"So, to sum it up, there's no real difference between the undergraduate brothers and the alumni, except for age?"

"Correct."

"Thank you. The witness is excused."

The dean looked at Schwitters. "Does the defense wish to cross-examine?"

On the verge of laughter, Schwitters stood and said, "No, Your Honor. That's okay. Counsel can stand up and make a fool of himself any time he wants."

"That's enough, Simon. The witness may step down."

Fairchild returned to his seat, and Mark took another

moment to study the defense. Schwitters, Dominic, and Thresher were smiling at one another and shaking their heads, obviously believing Mark's line of questioning was absurd and harmless. Dominic offered a thumbs-up smile to Fairchild, but the frat president would have none of it. He was staring at Mark, his expression pre-occupied.

Mark drained a glass of water, wiped his mouth, then turned to the dean.

"Your Honor, the College calls Sigma pledge Drew Silas to the stand."

Mark watched the victorious grins leave the faces of Dominic and Thresher. Only Schwitters, who didn't yet realize the importance of Drew Silas, continued smiling.

Mark sat on the edge of the prosecution table, skimmed his notes, and waited for Silas.

The freshman appeared within two minutes, pale and slender in comparison to the previous witnesses. His militant look of determination, however, belied his piti-ful appearance, and as he strode proudly past the de-fense table, he flashed its occupants a triumphant look. Fairchild nodded supportively at the freshman. Dominic flexed his traps, reminding Silas just whose team he was on and just how large his teammates were.

Silas took his oath, sat down, and eyed Mark with dis-dain.

Mark almost pitied the kid. *Almost.*

"Are you Drew Silas?"

"Yes."

"And are you a Sigma pledge?"

"I am a pledge at Sigma Delta Phi fraternity."

"Isn't that what I just asked you?"

Silas lifted his pointy chin and stuck out his bony chest. "I prefer to refer to the fraternity by its full, given name."

"Oh. Excuse me."

Silas said nothing.

"So," said Mark, "how have you enjoyed frat life so far?"

Again, Silas looked disapprovingly at Mark. "It's a *fraternity,* not a *frat.*"

"Is there a difference?"

"There sure is. Would you call your *country* a *cunt*?"

Mark stifled a laugh, then feigned horror, and watched while all four men at the defense table cradled their heads with embarrassed dismay.

"Um, Mr. Silas," said the dean, "this is no place for language like that."

"Sorry."

"The prosecution may proceed."

"Thank you, Your Honor. Drew, how have you enjoyed *fraternity* life so far?"

"I've liked it very much."

Mark examined his fingernails casually. "Looking forward to initiation?"

"Yes."

"Think you'll live that long?"

"*Objection!*"

"Sustained. Watch it, Counsel."

"Sorry." Mark glanced at the jurors, many of whom were frowning at him. He had overstepped his bounds. It was time to get on with it.

"Drew, do you remember the night of Saturday, February twenty-first?"

"Yes, I do."

"Could you describe to the court your experiences that night?"

"Certainly." Silas glanced toward the defense table and began to speak. "On the night in question . . ." He paused suddenly, for a stretch so agonizingly long that Mark could feel, literally *feel,* his whole life hanging in the balance.

Silence.

Silence.

A cough, from somewhere in the jury.

Silence.

And then Drew Silas continued.

"On the night in question, there was a house party at Sigma. All the pledges were there, and most of the brothers. We spent most of the night in the barroom, socializing with one another, and with other random students.

"Later during the night, I don't recall exactly when, I went up to the second floor to change the music. It was then that a bunch of hands grabbed me from behind, put a blindfold over my face, and carried me down the hallway—"

"Objection!" shouted Schwitters, rising to his feet, eyes wild with sudden panic.

"Uh, on what grounds, Mr. Schwitters?" asked the dean, whose face and tone were also strained by unease.

Schwitters looked down at the defendants for help. Fairchild, Dominic, and Thresher were staring at Silas, expressions of horror, complete and utter horror, stamped on their faces.

"Mr. Schwitters?"

"I . . . um . . . rescind the objection. I'll wait until cross-examination to completely discredit this testimony."

"Good idea," said Mark. He returned his attention to Silas, who was nodding knowingly in the direction of the three defendants. "You may continue, Drew."

"Okay. So, I was carried down the hallway to this room. They made me kneel on the ground, and then they handed me a double-shot glass. They told me to drink what was in it, so I did. Then they made me do three or four more."

"What was it?" asked Mark.

"Pardon me?"

"What kind of shots were they?"

"Oh. Whiskey. Jim Beam."

"Just whiskey? That doesn't sound so drastic to me."

Silas shook his head quickly. "As I was to discover later, the shots were laced with a drug."

"Objection!"

"What sort of drug?"

"Objection!"

"Shut up, Simon. What sort of drug, Drew? What sort of drug was the whiskey laced with?"

Silas's face grew full with a halting, should-I-do-this breath, then thinned with expulsion.

"Rohypnol," he said finally, in a voice so clear and audible that Mark wanted to close his eyes, smile, and throw his arms exultingly into the air. "I'm pretty sure it was Rohypnol."

Mark nodded, halting his questioning long enough for the ghastly murmurs resonating from the juror box to subside, long enough for he himself to take in an almost sexually satisfying view of the players around him. The dean, his hand lying limp next to his gavel, was staring at Silas like a condemned man. Dominic was a picture of hulking panic, hissing at Schwitters to "do something, man." Schwitters was shaking his head dumbly, gawking at a situation that all his precious international law classes had yet to teach him how to handle. Fairchild looked strangely sad, relieved, disappointed, and appreciative. Thresher looked ready to cry.

Mark turned back to Silas, then looked down at his notebook. "Rohypnol. Also known as 'roofie.' Commonly referred to these days as the 'Date Rape Drug.'" He looked up at Silas and squinted. "You're *pretty* sure it was Rohypnol?"

"I *know* it was," said the freshman, with such confidence that Mark would have hugged him had he been able. "Greg Turlington, another pledge, was in the room, too. They made him do the shots also, and he told me a couple of days later that it was Rohypnol. He described the symptoms to his professor, I guess. Look, I just want to say that—"

"Objection!" bellowed Schwitters. "In the absence of the professor and this Turlington fellow, I move to strike this testimony."

"Sustained. The jury is asked to disregard this last answer."

Mark turned to the jurors and watched all of them look strangely at the dean.

"Drew," said Mark, turning back to the witness. "Are you saying you weren't alone in the room?"

"No. Greg Turlington was there, and so was Chad Ewing. But, can I just tell you—"

"How do you know they were in the room? I mean, weren't you blindfolded?"

"Yes, I was. But after the other guys left the room, I took off my blindfold. Just me, Greg, and Chad were left."

"What happened next?"

"Huh? I don't know. I passed out in the upstairs hallway, I guess."

"And the next morning Chad was found dying in the living room?"

Silas closed his eyes and nodded sadly. "Yes. See, it was the alum—"

"Drew, how did you feel that morning?"

"What? Awful. Chad was a nice kid."

"I'm sure he was, Drew, but how did you feel *physically*?"

"Oh. Sick, I guess."

"Is it conceivable that had you woken up in the second-floor hallway, still drunk and blindfolded, you might have fallen—"

"Objection!" Schwitters's voice was high-pitched and desperate, a doomed dolphin cry.

"Sustained!"

Mark took a step back, finally ready to let Silas speak uninhibited. "Drew, *who* did that to you?" he asked, adding insulted rile to the atmosphere, for Silas's answering benefit. "*Who* made you drink drugged whiskey? Was it the brothers?" He threw an indignant glance toward the defense table, meeting Dominic's murderous stare with a judgmental one of his own.

Silas smiled reassuringly and shook his head. "*No!*" he nearly shouted. "That's what I've been trying to *tell* you!

It wasn't the *brothers*. It was the *alumni*!" He nodded emphatically and shot a winning look in the direction of the Sigmas.

Mark watched four jaws drop like stones.

"Oh, I see," he said slowly. "It was the *alumni*." He tried to look disappointed. "Are you *sure*?"

Silas nodded eagerly. "Yup. They were alumni, all right. I snuck a quick peak at them over my blindfold. They were older, and I recognized their faces from the photo composite next to the fire extinguisher on the second floor."

Mark scratched his head. "Wait a minute . . . are you saying that it was the alumni, and *not* the brothers, who murdered Chad?"

"Objection! We have not established that Chad Ewing was murdered."

Mark looked at Schwitters. "Oh, he's dead all right."

"You make it sound as though he was killed *on purpose*."

"It *is* starting to sound that way, isn't it?"

"Objection!" Schwitters's face was purple.

"Sustained!"

Mark turned to the dean. "On what grounds, Your Honor?"

The dean wiped his brow. "Just rephrase the question."

Mark raised his hand apologetically, then lowered it dramatically to his side. "Drew," he said, his tone slow and precise, "are you saying that it was the Sigma alumni who *drugged* Chad, thereby causing him to subsequently tumble over the balcony railing the next morning?"

"Objection!"

"Sustained."

Mark took a deep breath, his deepest breath in days, and repeated, with the same precision, the first half of his previous question. "Drew. Are you saying that it was the Sigma alumni who drugged Chad?"

"Yes." Turning rueful, he said, "I wasn't going to say anything, because I didn't want the brotherhood to be restricted from general endowment funds. But I no longer feel I can keep this a secret, especially since the brothers themselves have been wrongfully charged with the crime."

Mark nodded and began to pace again, his thoughtful focus directed toward the floor, as if the answer lay in the fibers of the Persian rug. He stole a glance at the jurors, all of whom were glowering harshly in the direction of the defense table.

He stopped suddenly, turning to face Drew Silas. "Drew, Dave Fairchild just testified that there's *no difference* between Sigma alumni and Sigma undergrads. Are you aware of that?"

At the onset of his O-mouthed confusion, Silas looked to Fairchild, whose dead stare was locked on the table. Dominic and Thresher, too, were gazing glaze-eyed, punch-drunk on disobedient words.

Mark watched Silas slowly realize, over the face-changing course of several seconds, what he'd done.

"No difference, whatsoever," repeated Mark. "Were you aware of that?"

"Wait a minute!" squealed Silas. "Did I say that—"

"I guess you *weren't* aware," said Mark simply. "Maybe next time you'll learn a little bit more about a *frat* before you join it. The witness is excused."

He turned and walked back to his table, sat down in his chair, and waited. He noticed the dean staring dumbstruck at him, and thought, *Happy job hunting, dickhead.*

Schwitters stood bravely amid the hush and tugged at his collar. "Your Honor, defense would like to cross-examine."

"I'll allow it," the dean said weakly.

Schwitters strode to the middle of the room and stood before Silas, who was continuing his visual plea with Fairchild, Dominic, and Thresher, a look of undivided panic on his face.

"Mr. Silas, did you actually *see* Chad drink the shots? I mean, you were blindfolded, right?"

Silas just stared at Schwitters, not sure what to do.

"Mr. Silas, how can you be sure that just because *you* drank the shots, Chad did as well—?"

Suddenly, Silas jumped to his feet and shouted, "I plead the fifth!" He vaulted from the witness chair and sprinted from the room. Fairchild took off after him, calling his name, begging him to stop. The jurors erupted into furious chatter. The dean pounded his desk so hard that the mallet flew from the handle. Schwitters, meanwhile, stomped around the room, flapping his arms and screeching, *"Mistrial! Mistrial!"*

Two jurors got down from their seats and approached the dean. The rest simmered into a whispering huddle.

Shooing the jurors back to their seats, the dean slammed his desk repeatedly with the palm of his hand. *"Order!"* he shouted. *"Order in the court!"*

Just then the door to the conference room flew open, and in like a navy-skirted lioness marched Shawn Jakes, carrying a cardboard box, followed by a giant, uniformed security guard and Jason Lyle, roommate of the late Chad Ewing. Gorgeous, dignified, and determined, Shawn led her comrades to where Mark sat stunned. She placed the box on the floor in front of the prosecution table, motioned for Jason to sit next to Mark, and turned to face the dean.

"Your Honor," she said with directed self-assurance, "the College calls security guard George Bianco to the stand."

The dean blinked, unable to comprehend the scene unfolding before him. He leaned forward and shook his head slightly. "I don't believe this."

"Neither do I!" raved Schwitters. "Your Honor, Miss Jakes is no longer the prosecutor in this case. She resigned!"

"I've reconsidered, Your Honor," said Shawn. "I'm asking to be reinstated."

The dean shook his head and latched on to Schwitters's point. "I'm sorry, Miss Jakes, you *did* resign. You can't just come and go as you please."

"I made a mistake. I'm sorry."

"Your apology is accepted, but we're doing things by the book here."

Shawn nodded understandingly. "The way I see it," she began, "we can either do things by the book, or we can do the right thing. I would hope that, as judge, you would opt for the latter."

"Miss Jakes, *I* present the options around here."

"So do I, Anson," said a new voice, and all eyes again turned toward the door. There stood Edison Carlisle, president of the college, looking taller than he'd looked in years, staring nobly and defiantly at the dean. "So let me present you with a couple. Either you let her speak, or you're fired!" The president finished with a nod that spoke volumes, strode across the room, and sat in a chair beside the jury.

"Your Honor," persisted Schwitters. "Your Honor, Mr. Bianco is not on the witness list. He can't be allowed to testify."

Shawn looked at Schwitters and sneered. "No, he's not on the list. He's on the stand, and I've got some questions for him, and you're going to listen, so sit down and shut up, you *little shit*!"

"Language, Miss Jakes," the dean muttered feebly.

"Kiss it," she said with a dismissive wave of her hand. Then she turned to the dean. "On second thought, please grant me a moment to confer with my fellow prosecutor."

The dean looked from Shawn, to Mark, to Carlisle, then back to Shawn. Defeated, he sank into his chair and nodded.

Turning, Shawn looked down at Mark and gave him a smile beyond the reach of description or duplication. She walked slowly toward him, then reached into the pocket of her white blouse and pulled out a single piece of notebook paper, which she unfolded and handed to her boyfriend.

"Read it," she whispered.

He stared at her a moment, then obeyed.

And as he did, as his eyes registered rephrased words from the last page of *Crime and Punishment,* one of the most unlikely relationships in the romantic annals of

Simsbury College came full circle and reached a new level.

Yes, her convictions can be yours now . . . Her feelings, her aspirations at least . . .

Mark read the message only once, for unnecessary repetition would have cheapened it. Then he looked up and smiled.

She let the moment linger another instant, then returned to the witness.

"Mr. Bianco, were you on duty the morning of Sunday, February twenty-second?"

"I-I," he stuttered.

"Take your time. There's no rush."

"Y-yes. I was on d-duty."

"Did you receive a call at roughly seven thirty that morning?"

"I d-did."

"What was the nature of that call?"

"Th-there was an accident at S-Sigma House."

"And so you hurried over to the scene?"

Bianco nodded eagerly. "Yeah. I was there even b-b-before the EMTs."

"And what did you see when you got there?"

"There was a k-kid on the l-living-room floor."

"Was it Chad Ewing?"

"Y-yes."

"Mr. Bianco, can you describe the initial condition of the body?"

"He w-wasn't breathing. He was b-bleeding. He was d-dying."

"Objection! He's a *security guard,* for Christ's sake, not a medical examiner."

"Sustained."

Shawn rephrased. "Mr. Bianco, what did Chad *look* like? Was there anything unusual about the body, other than the obvious physical injuries?"

"Yes."

"Such as?"

"He was n-naked."

"Anything else?"

"H-he had ink all over his b-bod-body. Head to t-toe."

"Had someone written all over him?"

"Objection! Prosecution is asking for conjecture."

"Sustained."

"Mr. Bianco, did it *look* as though someone had scribbled all over Chad?"

"N-no."

Shawn frowned. "It didn't?"

"No."

"What did it look like?"

"It . . . it wasn't scribble. It was p-poetry."

More murmurs from the jurors.

"Poetry? You mean, like . . . Some things are red, some things are blue, O. J. was guilty, and Sigma is too?"

"Objection!"

"Sustained. Shawn . . ."

Shawn waved off the dean. "Mr. Bianco, do you remember the subject matter of this poetry?"

Bianco shook his head, then nodded.

"What do you remember?"

Bianco kept nodding.

Shawn smiled patiently. "Mr. Bianco, what was the subject matter of the poetry?"

Bianco ceased nodding, then turned and stared down the defense table. "E-evil."

Shawn frowned, then turned, knelt, and rummaged through the cardboard box she'd brought with her. From the box she pulled a blue and white bandanna, which she held high in the air.

"Have you ever seen this kerchief, Mr. Bianco?"

"Y-yes."

"Where?"

"Until y-yesterday, it was in m-my office."

"Where was it before that?"

"I t-took it from the n-neck of Chad Ewing."

"When?"

"That m-morning."

"So he was written on and naked, with only this kerchief that could have been a blindfold around his neck?"

"Th-that's right. Of c-course, there was that p-pin."

Shawn reached into her pocket and pulled out a small object. "*This* pin?"

Mr. Bianco squinted at Shawn's extended hand and nodded. "Y-yes."

Shawn turned in a slow circle, displaying the pin for all to see. "This is a Sigma Delta Phi pledge pin. Where did you find this pin, Mr. Bianco?"

"It was s-stuck in Chad's ear."

"Like an earring?"

"Y-yes. L-like an earring. But Chad didn't have no p-p-pierced ear."

"How do you know?"

"Because there was t-too much b-blood. My niece wears earrings. She don't b-bleed like that, though."

"Thank you, Mr. Bianco. You've been very helpful. You may step down."

The dean looked to the defense table. "Does the defense wish to cross-examine?" His voice was nearly a whisper.

Schwitters deferred to Thresher and Dominic, and Dominic shook his head. Schwitters stood. "No, Your Honor."

While Bianco lumbered from the witness chair, the jurors whispered with barely contained outrage. Shawn turned to face the dean.

"Your Honor, the College calls Jason Lyle to the stand."

Schwitters opened his mouth to protest, but no words came out. He'd finally given up.

Small and fragile, Lyle took the stand. He sat in the witness chair and smiled nervously at Shawn.

"Mr. Lyle, what was your relation to Chad Ewing?"

"He was my roommate."

"What'd you think of him?"

"He was a nice kid. Really wanted to be popular."

"He told you that?"

"Not exactly. I could tell, though. That's why he joined Sigma."

"Objection," said Schwitters. "I don't know where counsel is going with this, but the witness can't *possibly* guess what Chad's motives were for joining a fraternity."

"Sustained."

Shawn paced across the floor. She stopped near the

jury and turned to face the witness. "How many nights a week was Chad occupied by pledge events?"

"Three or four."

"On these nights, did he tell you where he was going, and what he'd be doing?"

Jason shook his head. "No. He said he couldn't tell me. He said it was confidential."

"What was his mood before these events?"

"Objection."

"Sustained."

"Jason, did he *seem* edgy?"

"Yes."

"Tense?"

"Yes."

"Scared?"

"Yes."

Shawn paused, nodding at the ceiling. "Were you ever in your room when Chad returned from these events?"

"Usually."

"Was he ever visibly upset upon his return?"

"Always."

"Did he ever display any physical signs of abuse?"

Jason hesitated, warily eyeing the defense table. "Sometimes."

"Any examples?"

"One time," remembered Jason, "he came home with a bloody nose. Another time, he came home with his finger wrapped in a tee shirt."

"And why was this?"

Jason looked at the jury and swallowed hard. "His fingernail had been ripped off."

Gasps from the jurors. Shawn made a gruesome face as

she walked across the room and again reached into the cardboard box. This time she emerged with a white tee shirt and another bandanna. She shook the articles until they separated, and the jurors gasped again at what they saw.

Blood.

Lots and lots of blood.

Shawn held up the tee shirt. "Is this the shirt which was wrapped around Chad's finger?"

Jason squinted. "It could be."

Now Shawn shook the bandanna. "Did you ever see Chad with this bandanna?"

Jason nodded. "One night he took that with him when he left for Sigma. I assumed it was his blindfold, or something like that."

"Did he return with it?"

"Yes."

"And where was it?"

"Covering his nose."

"Why?"

"Because it was bleeding."

"Thank you, Mr. Lyle." Shawn turned to face the jury. "These items were mailed to me by Mrs. Carla Ewing, Chad's mother. Mr. Ewing found them under his son's bed."

"Objection," said Schwitters, standing. "How can we be sure about this? I mean, shouldn't Mr. and Mrs. Ewing be here to testify?"

President Carlisle stood and put his hands on his hips. "Young man, what is your name?"

Schwitters swallowed hard. "Simon Schwitters."

"Simon Schwitters," said Carlisle, "shame on you!"

Schwitters sat down quickly.

Shawn put the items back in the cardboard box and turned to face Jason one last time. "Jason, when was the last time you spoke to Mrs. Ewing?"

"Three nights ago. I spoke to her on the phone."

"And what did you tell her?"

Jason blinked. "I'm sorry?"

"Just before you hung up, what did you tell her?"

Jason shifted in his chair.

"Jason," Shawn said, her tone motherly. "You were crying over the phone, and before you hung up you said something to Mrs. Ewing. I have it written down here, in case you've forgotten."

Jason slouched in his seat, his face growing despondent. "I told her that I missed Chad."

"And?"

Deep breath. "I told her that I thought Sigma killed him."

And now the courtroom erupted. Schwitters was the first to his feet, but his frantic "Objections" were lost in the cyclone of chaos around him. Dominic charged the witness stand with one last linebacker's bull rush, his mitts curled in a gnarl meant exclusively for Jason, but before he could reach him he was clipped from behind by Bianco, who tossed the Sigma powerhouse right back over the defense table. Thresher weaseled his way to Shawn and hissed threats of unspeakable violation, but she got right in his face and returned each threat with an alley-cattish one of her own, and seemed ready to slam the Sigma against a wall when Mark arrived and did the honors for her. Meanwhile, Templeton and Carlisle pounded on tables with mallets and fists and begged for order, while the jurors looked on, aghast, as an all-out melee raged at the college they adored and revered and solicited money for.

And in the middle of it all sat the cardboard box containing the blood of Chad Ewing, who could now, finally, rest in peace.

For the second time in eighteen days, Madame Rumor butchered all other regularly scheduled campus songs into submission, and sang of a fall. She interrupted conversations, ripped books from hands, and pulled the plug on stereos. She showered in locker rooms, spooned with would-be nappers, and waited in dinner lines.

And all the while She sang.

Her many performances drew mixed reviews. Some clapped passionately and longed to hear more. Some booed bitterly and turned a deaf, disgusted ear. Some merely listened to every last strain, then shrugged and went about their business.

But one thing was for certain, the masses concluded.

Sigma Delta Phi was as dead as Chad Ewing.

It was only a matter of time.

CHAPTER SIXTY-ONE

The 200th Year
Thursday, March 12

7:42 P.M.

The victorious wave had carried Mark and Shawn to her apartment and ripped the clothes from their bodies— and they'd stayed that way until the rhythm of thrust and roll gave way finally to hunger of a more conventional kind. Somehow, they'd recovered the bare minimum of thongy, boxer-briefy articles that would make them presentable to the pizza delivery man, but no sooner had they tipped Monty's finest than a rogue swell knocked them to the floor again for one last stormy surge. Physically spent, they collapsed on the couch and turned their attention to the mushroom-and-black-olive pie, which was now gone, save for a few errant crusts hauled off by Casey.

Maybe later they'd talk. Maybe Mark would tell Shawn about the attempts on his life, and his new allies from the SWA, and how he'd rhymed the pretend rhymes of pretend brothers. Maybe he'd tell her how hard it had been to trust her unexplained absence, though now he was glad he had.

And maybe Shawn would tell him about the scare tactic that had come in the form of a muscle-bound break-in, and how it had worked, but only temporarily.

Or maybe they would say precious little.

Shawn hoisted a can of diet soda and finished it off. Then, licking her lips, she met his slow lean halfway and with a seductive smile said, "Kiss me, and I'll kiss you back."

7:51 P.M.

On any other evening, Templeton might have read T-Bone's failure to respond to any of his three voice mails or two e-mails as a symptom of a billionaire's busy day, or simple absence from home or office. However, this wasn't any other evening. Sigma was going down, and the whole world seemed to know it, which meant Templeton had good reason to be worried.

If not terrified.

He waited at his desk for another half hour, his eyes alternatingly fixed on a phone and a computer screen that screamed silence and blankness.

Then, giving up, he grabbed his jacket, turned off the lights, and left for the liquor store.

8:00 P.M.

Board members Davenport and Jefferson sat at the bar of their favorite Freeport restaurant, picking at their martinis and shrimp.

Jefferson took a sip and shook his head. "I don't believe what I saw today."

Davenport peeled a shrimp and eased it into his mouth.

"Neither do I, Rosie," he muttered between well-spaced chews. "Neither do I."

"You know what this means, don't you?"

"Of course I do. We're going to have to place Sigma on social probation."

Jefferson looked at Davenport. "Are you kidding me? We're going to have do more than *that*."

Davenport shook his head.

"Hank," Jefferson said, leaning closer to the chairman. "Like I said in that very first meeting with Templeton, we're going to have to shut them *down*. We're going to have to call the *police*. We have to let the authorities press *criminal charges*."

"No."

"What do you mean, *no*?"

"I mean, *no*, we're not going to shut them down, and, *no*, we're not going to let anyone press criminal charges."

Jefferson blinked. "Are you out of your mind? We don't have a choice."

Davenport breathed heavily and turned to his fellow Board member. "Okay, Rosie. Suppose we shut down Sigma. Where does that leave us? On the right side of morality? Sure. But is that warm, fuzzy feeling enough to outweigh the millions of dollars of annual endowment we'll lose to all those angry frat boys we're going to alienate? I say hell, no. Now let's suppose we call the goddamned police and tell 'em what we learned today. Where does *that* leave us? On the right side of the law? Sure again. But is that law-abiding feeling enough to outweigh the damaging effect of the probes and inquiries and criminal charges? Again, I say hell, no. Think of the *scandal*, Rosie. Think of the black mark next to *our* pristine name, and the sudden and sharp decline in quality applicants that will follow."

"For Christ's sake, Hank, we're not talking about money and reputation. We're practically talking about *murder.*"

"No. We're talking about a *mistake.* We're talking about an *error in judgment.*"

"Murder," repeated Jefferson.

"Jesus, Rosie, stop saying that word."

"Murder, Hank, and we'll never get away with sweeping it under the rug. Do you honestly believe the media won't have a field day with this?"

Davenport slammed his glass on the bar and grabbed Jefferson's shoulder. "Stop being such a petty nigger, Rosie!" he whispered venomously. "Yes, Sigma snubbed you because of your skin color, but that was over forty years ago. Forty years! Give it up!"

Jefferson stared at Davenport, then looked down.

Davenport took a deep breath. "Look, I'm sorry. But listen to me. Sigma had its trial. And they *will* be punished. I cannot, however, authorize the death sentence for that fraternity, just as I cannot allow the police or FBI to turn this into a circus. I mean, we don't even have any names of individuals responsible. What are the *police* going to do, arrest an entire fraternity?" He moved his hand from Jefferson's shoulder to his forearm. "I've got funds to protect. I've got rankings to protect. I've got connections to protect, and I'll do that very thing. And if you think I'm going to let some politically correct D-Squad or Ackerly Task Force or some small-town police department pressure *me* into making a decision about the future of the college *I've* been entrusted to run, then you're out of your goddamned mind. We *will* get away with it, Rosie. I can promise you that."

There was a rich silence.

Finally, Davenport motioned for service. "Bartender, another round for me and my friend."

8:34 P.M.

Sigma House towered dark and desolate, livened only by the candlelit window that glowed three stories high, watching over the inimical world like the singular eye of an injured beast.

But in the neck and the belly, silence.

For two hundred years the hardwood gut of the house had resonated the marching sounds of mindful men on the muscular move. The loud sound of loyalty. The soft sound of severity. Rhymed orders had rolled through the house like matching silver coins on a preordained, piggy-banked path, enriching every great gear on the way, forti-fying the fraternity, layer upon layer upon layer. On this night, however, nearly seventy-three thousand nights after the very first night of the brotherhood, stillness ruled the walls that had once ruled all, for a nearly incon-ceivable message had roared from the halls of the D-Squad and across the fraternity.

For the first time ever, Sigma had lost.

And since it was assumed that all those associated would be punished, the evacuation had been swift. The pledges had been the first to go. Those with remaining nerve had come en masse, handed over their pins and books to the Pledgemaster, and fled for telephones. Fif-teen former pledges now hid terrified and sickly thankful, waiting for parents to come get them. One former pledge already sat safely at home, crying tears from a bottomless well.

The next to leave had been the sophomores, who really had nothing but dues and brief memories invested in the brotherhood. They'd packed quietly, subtly, then scampered like rats for the safety of the independent dorms. Each knew at least one buddy he could crash with. All knew they were now marked men, their faces, if found, targets for fists of the older brothers who hadn't yet jumped ship. It would be a long time before they could look in the mirror and like what they saw.

Most of the juniors had stuck around, perhaps because they had more collective soul sunk in the brotherhood, perhaps because they were most familiar with the intestinal fortitude of the seniors, who'd proved themselves a gritty, resourceful, perhaps unbeatable bunch. If anyone could get the brotherhood out of this mess, it was Dominic and company. Four of the juniors, however, had signed an official statement, predated March 6, stating that they had suddenly become aware of wrongdoing within the fraternity and that they were effectively dropping out. These juniors had left Simsbury forever, their now-dead hearts set on state schools, where they could mill about with the general masses and try to forget what it had been like to be a brother, and what duties being a brother had once entailed.

The unthinkable had happened.

Brothers had actually put *themselves* before the brotherhood.

Brothers had actually dropped out of Sigma Delta Phi.

Lots of them.

The beast was dying.

Or maybe not.

All the die-hards now gathered in the Brotherhood Room. The mood was tense, angry, and confused; no one was quite sure what had gone wrong, how Mark Jessy had been able to turn two of their own against them and how Shawn Jakes had found witnesses in a world where no witnesses had the balls to exist. All the uncertainty, however, drifted like murky pond water beneath the fiery ice of resolve.

Where there was a will, there was a way.

The band of remaining brothers seated on the floor of the Brotherhood Room provided the will.

Now they just had to find the way.

And Alpha was here to show it to them.

He'd roared in like a fierce storm from Boston, and his shocking arrival had filled the bulk of the remaining twenty-one brothers with a mixed sense of terror and awe. A brave few had offered him handshakes, others had obliged him with unsolicited promises to die and kill for the brotherhood. Most, however, had simply watched the man move about the house like an imperial lord, his frame tall, hard, and void of complacence, his ebony eyes blazing pure confidence. And so watching, the undergrads had fed off his obvious power. Just the mere sight of this omnipotent man who represented the omnipotent many . . . well, it was enough to inspire feelings of omnipotence.

And now, as they stared up at him from their places on the Brotherhood Room floor, even the most lead-laden brothers felt buoyed by hope.

Surely, Alpha could rescue the brotherhood.

Couldn't he?

Of course he could.
With a little help from his brothers.
He began to rhyme.

Who'll stand tall and admit to the sin?
Who'll take the rap, so Sigma might win?

Who'll say he did it and did it alone?
Who'll say he was wrong and now must atone?

Who'll be a man and shoulder the blame?
Who'll take himself out of this back-and-forth
game?

Who'll stand up tomorrow and say he's a killer?
Who'll forever be viewed as a fine Sigma pillar?

The end of Alpha's poem left a hush heavier than the combined mass of all in the Brotherhood Room. Not that the rhymes were over, of course. Far from it. They still bellowed singsong echoes in minds, and their underlying order thundered through the twenty-one brothers seated on the floor.

But outside the minds, silence loomed huge.

It was the most awful of quiets, perhaps even more so than the horrible stillness that had hovered before them and above the smashed body of Chad Ewing. For this silence teamed terror and death (yes, there was a sense of death in the air tonight) with two new and pathetic sensations, one of which they'd been taught was truly unacceptable, one of which was completely alien to them.

Cowardice.

And shame.

Both sensations, of course, could be buried with a single movement. All *one* brother had to do was find his brave feet, stand like a man, and take Alpha's command. It should have been easy. Hadn't they each—some within the hour—vowed to *die* and to *kill* for the brotherhood? And hadn't they meant it? What was being asked of them now paled in comparison to some of the oaths they'd sworn. It would be so easy to obey Alpha and all the brothers he represented, but yet so difficult, because although he hadn't asked for the ultimate, the ramifications of obeying this particular order would still be enormous.

So not a muscle moved.

And not a sound was made.

And so Alpha waited for one brother to be a hero.

Agonized minutes passed. Eyes met with each other briefly, with those of the man above, but mostly with the floor. Fingers fidgeted beneath sitting thighs. Toes curled tensely within sneakers and hiking boots. Hearts pounded beneath down-low chests that had been built with iron. Ears tried to ignore the ancestral demands and outraged stirrings of corner ghosts.

And then one man stood.

All heads turned.

Brother Mu stood as tall as he ever had, his cluttersome midsection sucked mightily upward by lungs filled with the manliest air. His boyish shock of brown hair hung slightly listing above matching eyes that could sometimes smile on their own.

"I'll do it," said Mu.

Alpha nodded, and his black eyes caught fire.

Mu, it's of you I'm a brotherly fan.
Walk tall with good reason, for tonight you're a
man.

A new hush fell over the room, a hush admiring and
grateful. The other twenty were off the hook, in love with
Mu and his pending do, but off the hook. They nodded,
sat straighter, and without airing publicly how disgusted
they were with each of their cowardly selves, approved of
the situation.

"No!"

Now heads snapped in the other direction, and startled
eyes fell on Beta, who stood drawn and jaded (what was
up with him, anyway?) with his back to a bannerless wall.

"Don't do it, Mu," he begged lowly. "Don't do it,
man."

"I want to, Beta."

Beta moved forward, away from the wall, through the
maze of stunned, sitting brothers, toward his friend. He
stood in front of Mu, no less tall, no less passionate,
though his fever was perhaps a desperate one. He shook
his head but kept his eyes locked on Ran's.

"Don't you do it."

Mu tilted his head slightly backward, and the banner's
shadow overcame half his face. "I want to," he insisted.

Beta regarded this response for a moment, then
stepped forward, grabbed his friend and brother by the
collar, and pressed him against a two-century wall.

"You listen to me, you dumb fuck! Think about what
you're agreeing to! Think about it!"

Mu kept his pinned gaze unwavering, and he managed

to say, "I've already thought about it. I know what I'm doing, and I'm ready to do it."

Beta shook Mu once and released him, then took a step back and turned to the rest of the brotherhood. "Brothers," he said, his voice pleading now, "there has to be a better way. There has to be!"

"No," said Alpha, his voice calm but rhymeless; he hadn't foreseen such dissension. "There's no other way."

Now Beta stepped across his brothers in the direction of Alpha, stopping inches from the older man. "This is just a frat," he spat. "Just a goddamned *frat*!" He thumbed over his shoulder, motioning to Mu. "You're messing with this kid's *life*!" He turned for a moment, letting his outraged expression fall on each of the seated brothers (*this was unbelievable!*), then returned his attention to Alpha. "He'll get kicked out of school. He might even go to jail!"

Alpha closed his eyes and shook his head. "He won't go to jail."

"How the hell do you know?"

"Because we own this town, as we own this school, as we own this country," Alpha replied, his voice beginning to rise at this unspeakable treason. "If I say he won't go to jail, then he won't go to jail. And it won't matter if he gets kicked out of school." He peered past Beta at Mu. "Because I'm offering him immediate employment with my company. Seventy-five thousand dollars a year to start, with benefits."

Beta stared at Alpha, then turned once again to Mu.

"I don't care if I get kicked out of school, Beta," said Mu. "I have the least to lose, anyway. My grades suck, and I hate my major. The only thing I care about here is Sigma."

"That's the fire," said a voice on the floor.

"You're the man, Mu," said another.

Beta looked downward, then up again. "Mu, that's not the point. It doesn't matter what your grades are. All you need is that piece of paper that says you graduated from Simsbury. No one—*no one*—will ever be able to take that away from you." He shook his head. "If you do this now, you'll never get it. Not from here, not from *anywhere.*"

"Diploma or no diploma," countered Alpha, "he'll be a millionaire by the age of thirty if he plays by the rules."

Beta turned on Alpha. "You're a psychopath, you know that? I don't know how the hell you sleep at night, but if being a brother means being like you, then I'd rather be dead."

Setting his jaw, Alpha said, "You stink of weakness, Beta." Then, shifting to gain full view of Mu, he began to rhyme again.

My loyal young brother, stay the set course.
Rise one level higher in our brotherly force.

It takes a real man to do what you're doing,
But real men are needed when full wars are brewing.

The brothers embrace you, all over this land.
Embrace them right back, is my final command.

Embody the essence of sacrificial behavior.
Be our Jesus Christ. Be our lifelong savior.

And when it's all done, when the war is well won,
You'll forever be known as our most sacred son.

"Amen," said a voice from the floor. "A-fucking-men."

Silence ensued, a soundless stretch that opened itself to a thousand possibilities. Any or all of the brothers could have stood at any moment and, with safety in voices numbered, convinced Mu not to do what he seemed willing to do. Any or all could have said they themselves would *never* sacrifice their futures (let alone their lives, for God's sake; that particular oath they'd sworn suddenly seemed so ridiculous and out of the question) for this fraternal cause. And Mu could have backed out on his own, without anyone's approval save his own. For that matter, Alpha himself could have relented, could have accepted defeat for the first time in his life, could have let his dear brotherhood go, could have returned to Boston and continued living high on life's hog.

But he was unwilling to back down.

And so was brother Mu.

And so were the seated brothers.

And so it was that Beta broke the silence.

He sprang across an unseen line into the world of fraternal treason, smacking his fist against Alpha's face. The force of the punch threw Alpha against the wall, but the billionaire bounced back in his imperial way.

He calmly reached out, wrapped his hand around Beta's throat, and began to squeeze.

For a scratching, clawing moment, twenty watched in frozen horror as one leader choked another.

Then they jumped in.

Gamma was the first to his feet, and only by knocking Beta backward was he able to pry Alpha's fingers from the superstar's windpipe. Kappa and Delta jumped on Beta and pinned his breathless body to the far wall, while Gamma and Epsilon somehow wrestled Alpha to the floor.

Order, by its current definition, was quickly restored. Alpha was escorted to his car, where he issued final orders before heading for his hotel. Beta was brought down to one of the deserted bedrooms, where two seniors helped him catch his breath, and six others watched in silence.

Once the gasping stopped, the crying commenced, and through soft, distant weeps Beta whispered his wish to be alone with Mu.

All but Mu left and joined the juniors in the barroom, where they'd drink the last of the stale beer, try to deal with what had just happened, and steel themselves for one last day of battle.

Only Gamma was missing. He had some unfinished business to take care of, and it wasn't in Sigma House.

He moved like a focused freight train across campus, hungry for vengeance.

10:03 P.M.

. . . You stupid, selfish bitch!

The hateful words had flown at her so fast, and with such naked fury, that Jocelyn Patricola was almost done with her when-we-get-to-Aruba-I'll-make-you-forget-all-about-what's-going-on speech when the true malice of Pete's interruption registered. Stopping short, she yanked the phone away from her face as if it were a scalding iron, blinked at it, then held it to her head again.

"I . . ." she stammered, then trailed off, too verbally stricken to continue.

"That's right, *you!*" hissed Pete. "It's all about *you*, isn't it. My two-hundred-year-old fraternity's in trouble, and all *you* can think about is how you're gonna spend the next two weeks. You make me *sick*."

"Pete . . ."

"I'll tell you how you're gonna spend your next two weeks. You're gonna go home to Framingham, sit on your bed, and think about how your big fucking mouth started all this."

"We . . . leave tomorrow, Pete," argued Jocelyn weakly.

"Oh no we don't. Thanks to you, I'll be in court."

"I . . . already bought the plane tickets. They're nonrefundable."

"Then maybe next time you'll think twice about yapping to a bitch like Shawn."

Jocelyn opened her mouth, then clamped it shut, then blew a crop of bangs from her eyes and licked dryness from her lips. "You can stay here if you want," she said shakily, but with a trace of involuntary rebellion. "I'm getting on that plane."

"Bullshit you are!"

"Bullshit I'm *not!*"

A long, heavy silence followed this, the first-ever act of true defiance shown by Jocelyn Patricola toward Pete Thresher.

"You go," Pete said finally, "and we're done."

Done. *Done.* The word's blunt mass struck Jocelyn

right where it hurt most, in the part of her soul that normally couldn't bear the thought of being alone. Yet the sting faded almost instantly, like the intense hairy prickle after a ratty Band-Aid is torn from new skin. The prospect of loneliness suddenly ached far less than the bruises that had accompanied companionship, and though the root of this lightning flash was unknown to Jocelyn, she took to its warmth.

"Then I guess we're done," she said easily, softly, and with a dignity that both surprised and impressed her.

"*Cunt!*" screamed Pete, and the sound of a slamming phone exploded in Jocelyn's ear.

She gave the receiver a vexed look before placing it carefully on its cradle.

Then she put away all dignity.

And began to laugh.

Christ, did she laugh! She cackled and giggled and gave her hardest-body-on-the-beach abs and her liberated soul the very best brand of workout. She roared and punched her thigh, then dropped to the floor and rolled around and happily kicked her stocking feet through the thin ice she'd walked on since Pete Thresher stomped into her life.

She allowed her fit of silliness to dwindle at its own free pace.

Then she sat up, sighed, and reached for her boots.

10:16 P.M.

Shawn had finally insisted that the fabulously fulfilling yet academically unproductive tide of sex yield to clothing, so she could study for her last exam before spring break. Mark had dressed and whistled for Casey, but she'd fallen asleep with one uneaten crust in Shawn's laundry basket, and they'd both decided the scene was too cute to disturb. He'd kissed his puppy, kissed his girlfriend, and left to do some studying of his own.

The air outside was unseasonable, measuring about forty degrees on the skin-felt thermometer that northern students had grown accustomed to dressing by. Mark cut across the lacrosse field, taking his time, pausing to do whatever in this postgame peace he pleased. He threw snowballs for distance at nothing and skipped melting ice chunks across puddle ponds. He whistled a movie tune and blew breath smoke. He walked intentionally through wetness and quacked like a duck.

It wasn't until he was within twenty yards of his apartment that he saw the figure sitting alone on his back porch, his features masked by darkness.

Whoever he was didn't appear to be hiding, however.

He simply appeared to be waiting.

"Hello?" called Mark. "Who's there?"

"Keep coming," said a low, familiar voice. "I'm waiting for you."

Dominic.

"A. J.," said Mark. "What are you doing here?"

"I've come to play," Dominic said as he laughed lightly, but left whatever humor he found in the comment behind as he began to slowly circle Mark. The linebacker wore blue jeans and a ripped sweatshirt and looked like a giant. Misty dew crystallized his short hair and lashes, and his mouth fired cloudy bursts of menace. If the Sigma enforcer had indeed come to play, Mark had a bad feeling about the game he had in mind.

Dominic eyed him disdainfully as he circled. "You tricked us."

Mark turned with him, tracking his progress, careful not to turn his back. "I don't want to fight you, A. J."

Dominic nodded, then yanked each of his sleeves higher over rising slopes of muscle. "I know. You'd rather creep around like Tonto and trick our pledges into fucking us over." He took a step closer, then continued his orbit. "See, I don't mind conceding a round like *that* to a sneaky little Indian like you, just as long as you play one round *my* way." Dominic stopped circling and smiled. "Man to man. This way, no matter what happens tomorrow in that bullshit trial, I'll always know I got the best of you when it counted. And you'll always know that I'm the better man."

Mark swallowed hard, took off his jacket, and dropped it to the ground.

The mocking smile left Dominic's face. "I'm gonna dance on your face, Indian boy. And when I'm done with you, I'm gonna go find your father."

"You dance on my face, and I'll bite your feet off," said Mark, rolling up the sleeves to one of Shawn's flannels and briefly touching the beads as he began to circle as well. "But if you do find my father, tell him his son broke two noses this week." He spat sideways. "One of them yours."

Dominic cocked an immense fist and charged, firing a devastating punch that exploded against Mark's jaw and knocked him to the ground. Thrown by the momentum of his punch, Dominic toppled over him, and both fighters landed in a deep puddle of slush.

Mark staggered to his feet and cleared his eyes in time

to catch the Sigma running straight at him. He ducked, lowered his shoulder, and drove it into Dominic's stomach, lifting the larger man off the ground. For one brief moment they both hung frozen in place, the only movement coming from Dominic's churning legs.

Then they crashed to the ooze below.

The force of the fall expelled the wind from Mark's body, paralyzing his lungs, convincing him he would never breathe again. Taking advantage, Dominic pinned him to the ground, his trunklike legs squeezing Mark's hips like a vise, his fists slamming repeatedly against Mark's head.

Mark lashed out with his own fists, finding nothing but air. He absorbed ten, twelve, fourteen hammers to the face, each one flashing like a skull strobe. He tasted blood all over his tongue and throat, and with each blow he was filled with the increasing sensation that this wasn't just a fight for pride but yet another in a weeklong series of fights for his life.

He groped desperately with hands he couldn't see to steer, feeling for Dominic's face. He finally found its flesh, and as he continued to take punishment he dug thumbs into the linebacker's exposed eyes. The beating stopped suddenly as Dominic screamed.

Mark dug his thumbs deeper into the softness, until finally he felt the warmth of blood running down his knuckles and forearms. It was now Dominic's turn to be desperate, and he clawed at Mark's arms feverishly, trying to free himself. Sensing an opportunity, Mark let go with his right hand and guided it down his torso, to the heavy spot where Dominic's crotch straddled his stomach.

He wrapped his hand around the only soft part of Dominic's body.

And squeezed with everything he had.

A new, more gruesome scream split the night, one that doubled in pitch when Mark's right hand was joined by his left.

Mouth wide with holler, eyes red with blood, Dominic fumbled frantically for mercy. Now on the hunt once more, Mark removed his right hand from Dominic's crushed manhood, balled it into a fist, and unleashed a punch that splinted shock tremors the length of his own arm.

And broke Dominic's nose.

The linebacker fell to one side with a moan.

Mark labored to his feet, groggy from the pounding he'd taken, and aimed his swollen vision at the scene below him. The ground was pink with the snow-sweet blood of two, and in the middle of the gore lay Dominic, one hand clutching his crotch, one hand covering his nose.

A beaten boy from a beaten brotherhood.

"No matter what," managed Mark through knuckle-knocked lips, "I'm the better man."

Overcome, he dropped to one knee.

He was aware of footsteps, lots of them, approaching from the rear, and he heard several voices. Then he was tackled to the snow. He was too tired to fight back, so he just lay there, his face immersed in a hypothermic puddle, the icy water soothing his battered face. If all the Sigmas had come to finish him off, he'd let them, just so long as they realized it had taken all of them to do it.

He was pulled to his feet and found himself staring

dumbly into the wide eyes of Matt Moriarty, his next-door neighbor.

"Jesus, Mark!" gasped Moriarty, "Are you okay?"

Mark nodded once and winced as he did. "I think so," he mumbled, then collapsed in Moriarty's arms.

CHAPTER SIXTY-TWO

The 200th Year
Friday, March 13

The dawn's early light caught the first of the money machines, this one a German jobber with Jersey plates that power-everythinged its way from the horizonal interstate and roared on four arrogant liters through town before coming to a stop in Sigma's parking lot. The next one, a custom-designed SUV that mocked everything else with four wheels, rolled in five minutes later, right about the time two private jets angled, from somewhere south and west of dominance, toward the tree line that separated Georgeville and five other pissant towns from Portland's airport. By 7:00 A.M., the number of vehicles surrounding Sigma had increased threefold in number and tenfold in worth. By 9:00 A.M., the exterior property was as packed with chrome and tint and leather as it ever would be.

But though these engines brought together the nation's most fraternal and powerful *family,* these were not family cars. They exuded no warmth.

Rather, they exuded wealth.

Wealth that many brothers would kill and die for.

9:13 A.M.

For the sake of long lost, happier times, they had spent the night in the room they'd shared as sophomores. They had talked night into morning, reliving the golden way things had once been, back before a best buddy's setup, back before drugs and death dragged their beloved brotherhood from the sky. They had laughed a little and cried a lot, and when the sun had come up, they'd gone out onto the roof to appreciate the view one last time.

Now they dressed in silence.

David Troy Fairchild finished dressing before Michael Kent Robinson, and he smiled as he watched his friend struggle with his tie. He'd never seen Ran in a suit, and under any other circumstance this would have been a very funny moment. Fairchild walked over to his troubled friend, pushed fumbling fingers out of the way, and said, "Here, let me do it." He redid the knot, tucking it sleekly beneath Ran's chin. Then he patted him lightly on the cheek. "All set."

Ran turned to the mirror and examined his reflection. "I look ridiculous, don't I."

Fairchild shook his head and smiled. "You look fine."

Ran chuckled an ironic note or two. "I guess I better get used to outfits like this. I'm going to the big city. Gonna be a businessman."

"And you're going to be great at it."

Ran turned to face him. "You think?"

"I *know.*"

Ran picked up a comb and worked it through his hair. "Maybe someday you'll play for the Bruins," he said hopefully, "and then we can live together in Boston. That would be cool, huh?"

Fairchild bit his lip, nodded, and said, "That would be cool." Then he looked away.

"Dave," said Ran. "Dave, look at me."

Fairchild sighed heavily and looked at him.

"Dave," said Ran, thumbing his barrel chest. "This is *my* chance to be a hero. My only chance ever, probably, until I have kids or something. Please . . . let me have this moment."

Fairchild regarded him intensely, then gave a single nod.

Ran smiled. "Besides," he added, "in ten years, none of this will matter anyway. We'll all be successful and happy, and we'll still have a place to reunite every spring. Right up there." He pointed toward the ceiling, and the roof that lay beyond it. "*This* is where we all learned to love each other. *This* is where we'll keep on doing it."

Fairchild shook his head with wonder that hurt. "I'm really going to miss you."

They exchanged a long look, and as they did, a thousand magic and tragic memories ran the baselines between them, too many to recall within one last, longing connection.

Pulling away, Ran glanced at his watch.

It was almost time.

For both of them.

"Ready?"

Fairchild shook his head and looked at the floor. "I have to call Hughes quickly, so you go without me. I'll be over soon."

Ran shrugged. "Okay. Hey, by the way, where am I going?"

"Administration Building. Third-floor conference

room. Check and see if A. J. and Pete are in the kitchen. You guys can go over together."

"Oh. Okay. Well, wish me luck."

Fairchild hesitated a moment, then reached out and placed his hand on Ran's heart and Ran's on his. "Good luck, Michael Robinson. We'll always be brothers."

As Ran walked solemnly out of the room and down the hallway, Fairchild gave a silent salute to his brave friend, and whispered a final good-bye.

Then he went back inside the room, took out a single piece of paper and a pen, and wrote two simple words.

On the roof where brothers Beta and Mu had watched the sunrise, the ghosts of Sigma Delta Phi gathered with two centuries of luggage, and began waving their arms, like stranded victims of catastrophe in need of rescue.

They saw what was coming.

And they were getting out before all hell broke loose.

CHAPTER SIXTY-THREE

The 200th Year
Friday, March 13

9:31 A.M.

The tarp of morning that had covered the campus luffed away, though it left behind an eerie still of grayness that muffled bird chirps and boy-girl chatter. Mark moved about sorely and self-consciously, expecting his battered face to draw looks and murmurs. Most campus folk, however, gave him nothing more than a second passing glance, their minds more focused on life at the edge of spring break.

He was grateful for the apparent anonymity as he stepped tired but wired through the doors of the Student Center and down the stairs to the mailroom. He kept his eyes on the skid-proof steps as he descended, each step jarring a multitude of aches.

He found nothing in his box, but something behind him as he turned.

There, within arm's reach, stood the short SWA general who heretofore had led Marcia Heery and Caitlin Kittiwake in a quad crusade against Mark and his equally offensive macho ilk. Her lips were slightly parted, perhaps yearning to form words, but her eyes sat soft atop a scowl-free expression. Her posture, though still blanketed with the baggy wear of woman-roar, suggested no militancy.

Mark exchanged an inquisitive look with the woman, wondering what was up.

What was up was *respect*.

The general nodded first and hesitantly, as if responding unsurely to a tricky, long-considered question, then bobbed with authority and grinned.

Mark met her nod and returned the smile with one of his own.

The general abruptly peeled off like a plane in formation, her battle done.

Turning, Mark headed for his own.

9:39 A.M.

While the money machines sparkled outside, Sigmas of every age and one common tax bracket gathered in the living and dining rooms of the house they had once and still called home, and exchanged the secret handshake they couldn't possibly forget.

And when all were ready for battle, they filed out the hallowed doors, a force in formation, a militia on the move.

Apparently, the game wasn't over yet.

Not by a long shot.

9:44 A.M.

Having ruined his right on Dominic's face, Mark knocked on Shawn's door with his left and braced for a predictable sequence of events. First, she would gasp and put her hand over her mouth. Then she would ask what happened. Finally, upon learning the truth, she'd lecture him on the immature and destructive evils of fighting, and wonder out loud what had happened to the newly mature boyfriend she thought he'd become.

The door swung open and there she stood, looking like the six-figure model she could have been.

Until the state of Mark's face registered.

Then she gasped and put her hand over her mouth. "Jesus, Mark! What *happened*?"

"A. J. Dominic."

"Oh," she said, her voice returning to normal. "I hope you kicked his ass."

Mark swallowed his shock and stepped inside her apartment. "Let's just say that I did better than I look."

"Hmmm. That's not saying much." She kissed him lightly on the cheek, and he winced. "Oh, you big baby!" she sang. "I'm almost ready. Let me just grab my coat." She bustled down the hallway to her bedroom, and Mark stepped into the bathroom to cringe at his badly stomped face. "By the way," she called, "I ran into Jessica while I was walking the dog. She said she was sticking around until tomorrow, so I let her have Casey for the day. I figured we'd both be tied up for a while."

"Oh. Whatever, that's fine."

She appeared behind him and made a face at the damaged mug that looked at her from the mirror. "Boy, did any of his punches *miss*?" she said, and tousled his hair. "C'mon slugger, we're going to be late."

9:51 A.M.

Two doors on opposite ends of the Administration Building opened simultaneously, and in stepped two men who shared nothing but disdain for each other. Dean of the college Anson J. Templeton and president of the college Edison T. Carlisle exchanged a lengthy, distasteful stare, then started down the long hall toward each other.

Had it been a western movie, they would have spat tobacco all the way, their hateful gazes never wavering, and twenty feet from the other they would have drawn guns pistol-quick and proven who was the faster man.

But this being Simsbury College, tweed-blazered Templeton hopped in a vacant elevator, while three-pieced Carlisle headed for the stairs.

Their duel would be settled elsewhere.

9:55 A.M.

Mark had assumed his previous night's donnybrook with Dominic had marked the end of his altercations with Sigma. He'd dodged blades and brothers for close to a week now and, having remained alive, felt fairly secure. He'd won the sick game and had expected Sigma to finally roll over and submit. This hope was dashed, though, when upon arriving with Shawn in the lobby of the Administration Building, he discovered a mob scene.

Blue-blazered, eagle-emblazoned Sigmas of every generation and every distinguished appearance lined the chairs and couches and walls of the lobby. It was a tableau of wealth. Even Mark, who'd grown up in a homemade, often heatless shack, could sense the dollars these men represented. A bit intimidated, Mark reached beneath the knot of his tie to touch his beads.

They hate me, he thought, and though the notion shouldn't have surprised him, he halted in his tracks just the same, stopped momentarily by the sheer force of their loathing. But as he scanned the spiteful eyes of his former brothers, of the men who'd set him up on rape charges and even tried to murder him, the faint fear wrought by such power and money vanished. Suddenly, he saw the billionaire brothers of Sigma for what they really were.

Boys.

And he felt pity, slight but surprising. But then he saw a second sight that stopped him cold, a face of arrogance and eyes of blackness, identical to those that had stared at him from a team photo in the Cage.

Terrence Bonnell.

"T-Bone."

Locking eyes with the man behind his rape setup and God knew what else, Mark felt his entire body both tighten and ignite; he'd dreamed of such a confrontation. Mark, on the winning side, with an audience. T-Bone, on the losing side, in full view of the undergrads who took his orders and the alumni who helped dictate them. He had his opponent right where he wanted him; it was an empty-net opportunity in front of a large, hostile crowd.

But before he could start in on the prick, he felt a soft, strong tug on his jacket sleeve, and he heard the sweet, stubborn voice that always knew right from wrong.

"Come on, Mark," Shawn said as she inched toward the stairs. "Let's go."

He gave a final glance T-Bone's way, then followed his girlfriend.

"Run along, Jessy," T-Bone said.

Breathing deep through clenched teeth, Mark stopped and turned. "T-Bone?"

T-Bone smirked and crossed his arms.

"Just walk away, Mark," said Shawn.

T-Bone snickered. "So long, Tonto. Your squaw is calling you. Careful not to let *her* get shot."

Mark looked at Shawn, visually pleading for permission to be a man, to tear T-Bone apart in front of everyone who mattered, to *really* settle the score in a *colossal* way. She returned his visual beg with a trusting nod; it was up to him to decide just what it meant to be a man in this situation. Mark stared at her a moment longer, then set his jaw and turned to T-Bone again.

"I win, T-Bone," he said with simple softness. "I win."

T-Bone made a wicked face. "Like hell you do. You're Indian trash, like your father. In the real world, you don't even matter."

Mark smiled and shrugged. "Maybe not, T-Bone. Maybe not. But right now, in *this* world, I'm *all* that matters." He paused, cocking his head. "And as the only one who matters, you know what I want you to do?" He moved a step closer and leaned to within inches of the despicable face. "Wave a white flag, to borrow a phrase from my ancestors. Wave it *high,* for the whole world to see."

He turned in a slow circle and saw once again that every Sigma eye in the tomblike lobby was on him. Sigma mouths hung open, Sigma heads shook, Sigma lips curled, but every Sigma eye looked his way.

Mark smiled a final time, turned, and walked away. He met Shawn halfway up the first flight of stairs, and they walked the rest of the way together.

10:03 A.M.

Roy and Carla Ewing, and their daughter, Julie, marched through the wintry graveyard, their heads bowed to the whipping wind. Each carried a rose and, with it, more memories than could be counted.

They slowed as they neared Chad's grave, and stopped before their booted toes could reach the earth that was, in its freshly turned state, still so soft. Not that the forgiving soil guarding their son and brother was the only reminder to how recent his passing had been. The stone slab, shiny and smooth, was so painfully new. The flowers, bright and breeze-fluttery, still held much of their original color. The whole deathly rig was so untrodden and polished that it screamed to them that they should still be screaming.

The Ewings stood screamless for a minute or two, watching the grave and beyond.

One by one, each stepped forward, and placed a fresh rose neatly before the headstone.

Then they hugged.

And walked away together.

10:08 A.M.

The crowd in the Administration Building lobby had thinned and spread, but a few alums remained stuck to their wall posts, eyes fixed on the floor. Jack Dunn, in particular, hadn't moved a muscle since watching Mark Jessy and that gorgeous blonde disappear up the stairs. He was troubled, so troubled that he didn't notice the tall figure's approach until he felt a strong hand on his shoulder.

"Suck it up, Jack," said T-Bone.

Dunn looked up at him, then shook his head.

"Don't give me that," shot T-Bone, and then he moved a step closer. "In *ten minutes,* Sigma will be exonerated. And when the smoke clears, this brotherhood will still be the tightest, richest, most powerful fraternity in the country." He reached out with his pitching hand and pressed it to Brother Dunn's heart. "Winning. *That's* our tradition."

Dunn returned the stare for a long moment, then placed his own, suddenly believing hand on T-Bone's heart, and whispered, "Long live the brothers of Sigma Delta Phi."

Meanwhile, on the other side of the lobby, two white-haired Sigma alums one year from their sixtieth college reunion leaned on hand-carved canes and took in the sights and sounds of modern-day Simsbury, and modern-day Sigma.

"I came here," said one to other, his chin high, "out of loyalty. I came because I owe a great deal of my success to Sigma. I came because I took certain oaths long ago, and I will honor those oaths until I die."

He moved forward and rested his free hand atop the hand of his friend, his classmate, his brother. "But I look around, and all I see are fat wallets and indignant expressions. And I ask myself, whatever happened to *our* tradition?

"Whatever happened to *honor?*"

10:12 A.M.

The first thing Mark noticed upon taking his seat in the conference room was that Dominic looked worse than he did. Huge reddish black moons encircled each eye, pressing the peak of his nose misshapenly higher. But it was more than just the pickled state of Dominic's face that gave wordless proof of his defeat. It was his posture. The gargantuan block of limbs and landscape sat hunched, his enormous back overtaking his sunken front. His eyes, normally crystalline, now were painted gray ovals on bloodshot paper.

Dominic was a beaten man, inside and out.

Lifting his head, he peered lifelessly Mark's way. Then, after a locked spell, he twitched his mouth and nodded nearly invisibly. A grudging gesture of respect? Mark didn't know what to make of it, so he volleyed the motion graciously.

Thresher, of course, looked like a prick, but a *defeated* prick. His barbed face angled downward, as if rapt on something floorbound, and it struck Mark that Thresher would rather die than look him in the eye, which was too bad, because Mark had been looking forward to giving him a glare.

Next to Thresher perched Ran Robinson, looking like a little boy in a big-boy setting, and it was a moment before Mark was able to pinpoint the incorrectness of the scene and ask himself the question that essentially asked itself.

Where was Dave Fairchild?

The dean rose, requested all others to do the same, and tapped his gavel. "Call to order *Simsbury College v. Sigma Delta Phi.*" He sat, put on his glasses, and glanced nervously at President Carlisle, who was seated a body-length from the jury. "Is the prosecution prepared to make a closing statement?"

"Yes, Your Honor," said Shawn. "We are."

Mark stood and walked to the center of the room, then turned to the jury. Ignoring the flinching responses to his mangled face, he cleared his throat and spoke.

"Ladies and Gentlemen of the jury, I'd first like to thank you for your time and patience. I realize this was frustrating to watch at times, as I'm an admitted amateur when it comes to trial law.

"In fact," Mark added lightly, "I'm now convinced that law school is not an option for me."

Polite laughter.

"I do hope, however, that we've been able to prove what we set out to prove: that Sigma Delta Phi is responsible for the death of Chad Ewing. Accordingly, I hope you'll find the defendant guilty as charged. While such a verdict won't bring back the deceased, it might bring a feeling of justice and closure to this terrible chapter in Simsbury's history. Thank you."

He returned to his seat.

Schwitters stood and moved to the center of the room.

"Ladies and Gentlemen of the jury, I, too, appreciate your efforts this week, and on behalf of my client I'd like to thank you."

He turned to the defense table and motioned with his hand.

Ran stood up.

Schwitters turned to the dean. "Your Honor, Sigma brother Michael Robinson has something he'd like to say." He sat down at the table, closed his briefcase, and folded his hands in front of him.

Ran unfolded a piece of notebook paper with trembling fingers.

Mark and Shawn leaned forward in their seats.

The jurors did too.

Then, with a shaky voice, Sigma's nicest senior began to read. "My name is Michael Robinson, and I have a confession to make. I didn't come forward before, because I was afraid, and I was hoping the whole thing would blow over. However, it's become clear to me that too many innocent people will pay for this tragedy, which is why I must stand before you and admit the following." He looked up and at the jury with apologetic eyes. "I alone am the reason you're here. I alone am the one who should pay the price."

A low, confused murmur rippled through the room.

Shawn turned to Mark, a baffled look on her face, and whispered, "What is he *doing*?"

A knot forming in the pit of his stomach, Mark shook his head and looked to the Sigma side of the room. Dominic and Thresher were holding hands above the table, their eyes closed to the self-sacrifice.

"On the night of Saturday, February twenty-first," continued Ran, "I—"

Suddenly, the door to the conference room burst open, and in ran J. C. Miller, his face wet and wild. He stopped next to the dean, and for a moment did nothing but suck deep breaths over an unstable jaw.

"A. J. . . ." he gasped, "Pete . . . Ran . . . Mark . . . come quick . . ." He slammed his eyes shut, bent at the waist, put his hands on his knees, and panted.

"What?!" demanded Dominic, rising to his feet.

"It's . . . it's Fairchild."

And then came the wail of approaching sirens.

CHAPTER SIXTY-FOUR

The 200th Year
Friday, March 13

10:27 A.M.

Mark would eventually forget the frantic sprint from the Administration Building to the Sigma lawn. And he'd never realize the ironic significance of his racing bruise-for-bruise with Dominic, though he'd vaguely recall how they simultaneously arrived on the scene as the ambulance bounced up and over the lawn's lip. But he'd always remember the image of Sigma's front door bursting open like a sniper's gunshot, and Mike Scully staggering through, his face twisted into something vicious, followed by Neil Birmingham and Kevin Daly, each of whom bore half the weight of Dave Fairchild's lifeless body.

The sight grabbed Mark by the beads and snapped his neck backward, as if one more step would send him hurtling back down a deep, bottomless crevasse he'd spent most of his life climbing out of. Dominic, however, thundered past, to where the body was just now being laid on the snow.

The lawn filled with the speed of a sinking hull, as Sigma House continued to bleed brothers and alumni from its hallowed doors, while court members and class-goers clotted several yards from the grisly nucleus and began gasping whatever gibberish rolled across their tongues.

For a moment, Mark just stood there, unblinking, un-moving, unbreathing, as his eyes struggled to explain the picture to his brain.

Then he advanced toward his dead friend.

He knelt, placed one hand on Dominic's wide, heaving back and the other on Fairchild's drawn, motionless chest. Both eyes, however, he fixed on the closed lids, as-phyxiated cheeks, and slightly parted lips, each of which he half expected, at any moment, to break brightly into a chipped-tooth grin for the humble benefit of a crowd who'd once again gathered to cheer and love him.

But deep down, Mark knew this swollen face of bluish clay would be Fairchild's eternal mask.

The thick noose around his neck had seen to that.

Mark whipped his head away as if he'd been bashed in the face and for an instant saw nothing but haze. Soon enough, however, he focused on the predator that he'd apparently never fully dodged, that he'd never truly been distant from, that had escaped his mind's darkest pen.

But this time, the animal wasn't his alone to live with and fear.

No, it belonged to everyone now, having struck first on a sleepy secret Sunday, tunneled beneath the Madame-shadowed snow for nineteen days, and finally reared its fanged head and strangled a hero.

Mark turned numbly to the gathering of shocked,

flinching onlookers and watched the ivied world of Simsbury look death in the eye.

The crowd of students, faculty, and alumni parted as the cops and EMTs pushed their way through, followed closely by a crew of TV reporters and cameramen. Mark took a moment to despise their arrival, then turned back to his friend's corpse, cradled and rocked by Dominic, who in the span of minutes had been reduced from the most physically destructive student on campus to the most emotionally destroyed, one too blind with tears to realize the futility of his whispered pleas to hang in there, buddy . . . don't you dare die on me now . . . hang in there . . .

Then, all at once, Dominic seemed to sense it was over. The liberal arts student who'd once proudly blown an Arab to four different directions hung his head and began to sob.

And as he did, a folded piece of paper slipped from his grasp.

Mark watched the scrap settle, then reached out and picked it up from the slush. He ran a finger across the damp pulp, over the ragged ridge of a frayed square of masking tape, and as it occurred to him that the scrap itself had been stuck to Fairchild's body, he simultaneously realized that the scrap's two written words had heretofore been stuck to Fairchild's conscience.

Forgive me.

Slowly, he looked up from Fairchild's last act of leadership and locked eyes with Shawn, her cheeks wet with grief.

And together, they exchanged the unspoken question.

What have we done . . . ?

Meanwhile, thirty yards south of tragedy and two stories closer to heaven, the room Dave Fairchild, Ran Robinson, and Mark Jessy had shared as sophomores was nearly silent. The only movement was from the severed length of rope that swayed like a ceaseless pendulum from the ceiling fan, a reminder to those who'd sponsored and witnessed the unraveling of a hero that Fairchild had died because, for the first time in his life, he'd failed to live up to his own lofty expectations.

And because he no longer lived for that which he'd once been willing to give his life to save.

11:09 A.M.

At precisely nine minutes past eleven she was born again, a swaddling bundle of poundless, ounceless grief immaculately conceived by the sexless, loveless fornication of eighty-eight stunned witnesses and one dead hero. She choked and whimpered and gasped for breath, then stole it from helpful lungs that couldn't bear death's brunt alone and simply had to share. So nurtured, she rose to feet that needed neither breeze nor backpack on this day where sadness had a name, a face, and a motion of its own.

So risen, the Madame began to walk across campus.

And as She did, she wept her latest tale.

Dave Fairchild was dead.

CHAPTER SIXTY-FIVE

The 200th Year
Friday, March 13

7:11 P.M.

Each of the twelve alums had been forced to do the unthinkable and break into the quarantined house they'd vowed to die and kill for. Each had performed the task silently, and at a strategically inconspicuous interval, but with fists clenched like vises and blood boiling in and out of hearts that thumped a brotherly tune. Each had ascended two flights of unlit night and turned passionately leftward on floor number three. Each had floated like a ghost of fleshy dimension down the most hallowed of halls to the most sacred of rooms.

Each had been Beta in his day, just as each would perhaps have his turn as Alpha.

Each had a personal worth of at least eight figures, and in some cases ten.

Each had murder or some other felonious tit to thank for his bountiful tat.

Each was ready to commit one more crime, at least.

All were seated in the Brotherhood Room.

The initial minutes of discussion had been explosively unorganized. Irrational threats had been randomly hissed, then retracted. Insane suggestions had been thrown out, then struck down. Personal business interests had been championed, then ridiculed. In essence, words had been flung with no sense of the oneness and order that had defined the first one hundred ninety-nine years and two hundred four days of the most exclusive, powerful fraternity the nation had ever known.

And then quiet had been demanded, and Greek names, preceded by the letter *Nu,* had been handed out like vaccines.

To all but one alum.

He already had a name.

"You know," said Nu Delta finally. "The kid had potential. He had *earning power.*"

"He also had a weakness," pointed out Nu Theta. Then he turned to his left. "Didn't you tell me he tried to block Operation Blue Eagle?"

Nu Kappa motioned toward the figure sitting in the shade of the largest banner. "Ask the man."

All heads turned toward the man, who offered a single dark nod from the shadows.

And nothing more.

"Sounds to me like he never should've been Beta in the first place."

"We had no control over that," said Nu Rho. "The undergrads looked up to him, and they voted for him."

"Wouldn't you have?"

"Not with the future of the brotherhood at stake. The kid was too . . . *nice.*"

"Says the man who always lobbies Democrats."

A short chuckle ensued, lightening the mood.

For a moment.

"I don't see what's so funny here. We've got another weakness to eliminate."

"First we've got a weakness to *find*. The bastard's disappeared."

"Please. This campus is the size of a postage stamp."

"Fine. *You* go find him. I'm flying back to Philly to close a deal."

There was a long, rich silence.

"I thought we were going to wait until after graduation," said Nu Gamma finally.

"And risk him yapping from now till then? Think again, bean counter. The house may be lost, but I'm sure as hell—"

"For *now*. The house is only lost for *now*."

"For now," agreed Nu Omega. "But I'm sure as hell not going to risk going to jail over this thing." He leaned forward. "Besides, this whole disaster is *his* fault. The Board could've hired any of a hundred more qualified applicants, but we made sure they picked *him,* because research said he'd do for us what Ackerly wouldn't." He threw up his arms and scowled. "And this is how he thanks us? By letting Mark Jessy bring down two centuries of tradition and threaten our way of life?" He leaned farther forward and clenched a fist. "I'm telling you, he has to *pay*."

Another silence, richer than the one before.

And then the man in the shadows stood, moved to the center of the room, and said, "He will."

Twenty-two eyes grew wide, then narrowed with understanding.

"I thought your man quit."

"He did quit. Idiot got beat, *three times,* by a fucking twenty-two-year-old."

"And now he's running around with all our secrets. I never did like the thought of an outsider doing our dirty—"

"Oh, and who was gonna do it? Hughes? Edelstein? All those two know how to shoot is a round of golf. And what about you? Gonna *investment-bank* our obstacles to death? Trust me, the guy's got no conscience. Besides, he'll be the first one sentenced if he talks."

"Fuck this. We're sitting here analyzing the traits of people who aren't around anymore, and meanwhile we've got a weakness to—"

"Yeah, we know," said Nu Kappa. *"We've got a weakness to eliminate.* You like saying that, don't you. Makes you feel like the Godfather."

"Fuck you, asshole. Go build a boat or something."

"Like the tankers I sell you at a discount? Don't get condescending with me, because I can easily take those contracts and—"

"Enough," said the man who'd emerged from the shadows. "We do have a weakness to eliminate, and it will be done."

"How? If you're thinking of doing him the way we did Ackerly, I should probably mention that I forgot to bring my skis."

"Good god," said Nu Epsilon. "That's all we need. The irony of another task force named for someone we . . ." He shook his head and looked up at the man who led them. "Okay, how will it be done?"

"Violently. And with outside help."

"From whom?"

"The individual I mentioned in that e-mail, the day we found out who was getting tenure."

For a moment, eleven tycoons searched memories. Then Nu Delta looked up and cried, "The *woman!*"

"The *unemployed* woman. I slipped her that mean old tenure committee's list, and showed her how she's going to be job hunting as of graduation day. Then I slipped her a little financial security."

"I don't buy it. All she lost was tenure. What makes—"

"No. She lost a game. She thought Templeton would help her get tenure. Turns out he couldn't. And now we're going to pay her a million dollars to get revenge."

"I still don't buy it," said Nu Rho.

"You already did."

"Is a million enough?" asked Nu Gamma.

"Plenty. She's a *teacher.*"

"But will she *kill* someone?" asked Nu Theta.

All twenty-two eyes met briefly, then drifted expectantly upward and watched the man from the shadows reach out and wrap his hand lovingly around the Sword of Tradition's ancient handle.

All twenty-two ears waited for Alpha to respond.

And when he did, the deadliest hush of all descended on the Brotherhood Room, one sparked by a glint of surprise but sustained by the steel of resolve, as heavy and hard as a two-century blade.

10:44 P.M.

Naked, drunk, and on the run, Templeton took three deep breaths, then closed his eyes and settled back into the three puffy pillows stacked against the queen-sized headboard in the westernmost room of Georgeville's easternmost bed-and-breakfast. He inhaled once more, exhaled in shifts, and wiggled toward the middle of the bed. He swirled his glass of mostly cubes and wished he had another pint. He trembled and watched the door with needy intent.

He waited for Linda.

He wished she were already here. He wished she were curled up catlike beside him, or even *on* him. He wished they were dreaming the tandem dreams of southbound air travel, two hours into the first leg of the most timely Jamaica vacation ever booked. In fact, he wished he were anywhere other than here, but she'd freaked after Fairchild's suicide (he was her favorite student) and careened off into the midday mist. Templeton might have followed and consoled her had he not been completely consumed by fear for his *own* life.

So instead he'd fled to his own corner of the world.

And hid.

She'd buzzed his cell phone just before five. She assured him she was still going to Jamaica with him, but was way too upset right now to fly, so could they maybe shack up for the night and fly out in the morning? She'd even offered to make the arrangements, something she never did. She called him back with an inn name and a room number. She told him to expect her around ten.

So she was now almost an hour late, which on any other night might have annoyed him. On this night, however, with Sigma's ship sunk, and its captain probably deeming him both the responsible party and the holder of information that might screw all the others on board, Templeton was just thankful she was coming.

He'd forgive any degree of tardiness. He'd let her fuck him, and even welcome the physical punishment that often accompanied such an allowance. He'd wait for the sun to announce USAir's next scheduled flight to Jamaica.

And then he'd run like the wind.

By noon, he'd have transferred all his Grand Cayman Fidelity funds to an unknown account and destroyed all incriminating records. Then he'd sit somewhat rich and barely clean in a hot tub, and figure out where to go from there.

He drained the last of his drink, sucked on a cube, and waited.

And waited.

And waited.

His bladder finally diverted his attention from the latched door, and he rose with a tangy shiver from the bed. He tiptoed to the bathroom and tensed as the cold shock of tile chilled the soles of his feet. He danced before the toilet and shuddered, and for one last peaceful moment he eyed his thin self in the mirror and managed a smile.

Everything is going to be—

The knock at the door interrupted positive thought, then accelerated it. Linda was here. Relief flooding all but his already-flooded-but-willing-to-wait bladder, he breezed from the spiced bathroom, scampered across the romantic carpeting, and unlatched the rose-petaled door.

For a long moment, he seesawed between bewildering confusion and utter paralysis.

He wanted to see Linda, holding luggage.

But instead he saw T-Bone, holding a sword.

Recognition lifted the shackles from his limbs, and he was overcome by several different urges, each requiring frantic animation. But each fantastic vision was systematically crushed beneath the actual one that stood three feet away, six inches taller, fifty pounds heavier, and armed with something steel and massive.

So this was it. His biggest fear was about to be realized, in a manner that would certainly be excruciating, at least for a moment. Yet strangely, he felt at ease, as if uncertainty itself had been the most gut-wrenching aspect of the dangerous game. He felt no further compulsion to fight back, nor would he beg for mercy. Instead, his one and only notion was to go with dignity.

So he took three steps back and allowed T-Bone to enter.

Anson J. Templeton stood there, locking eyes with arrogance and stone-cold evil. He opened his mouth to speak, then closed it. He swayed a bit, then steadied himself. He blinked a few times, but never lost contact with the eyes that had come to watch him die.

Then he took a deep breath, nodded once, and closed his eyes.

In the instant that death swung his way, a thousand abbreviated thoughts ripped through his mind, most centering on a surprising regret for the way he'd chastised his parents' moneyless but loving marriage, the way he'd abused a basically good woman like Judith, and the way he'd sold his soul to the biggest group of brotherly assholes the world would ever know. But, like the fantastic visions that had preceded them, each reflection was squashed, this time beneath a simple, three-word thought

that summed up the life he'd lived, and the death he was
about to die.

Checkmate.

I lose.

And then his skull caved in.

11:00 P.M.

As a distant clock chimed a lusty toast to eleven brothers fleeing south by west, the twelfth stared down at his
first checkless, wireless murder and smiled faintly on behalf of nine hundred and eighty-six fraternal others
whose way of life would now be ensured. He laid the
sword on the ground, gathered Templeton's despicably
insignificant corpse in his arms, and shoveled him face-
down onto the bed. Then he backed away and took a deep
breath.

For a long time T-Bone stood there, looking down at
the bony white ass of the naked fool predominantly responsible for Sigma's temporary fall.

Then he pulled the gravy baster from his jacket pocket.

He stared at it, and dreaded what he was about to do.
Not that he was afraid. It was more a matter of distaste.

But absolutely necessary.

He lifted the baster to eye level, shook it lightly, and
watched the semen within swirl against plastic. He
gripped it tightly and turned the point toward its target.
He inhaled hatred through his nose, and exhaled hesitation. He closed his eyes, clenched his teeth, and recalled
the words that had challenged his manhood, the words
that had eaten at him since yesterday morning.

*. . . be the men you say you are and try to kill him your-
selves . . .*

Then he opened his eyes suddenly, raised the baster high overhead, and plunged it deep into the bony white ass.

11:41 P.M.

Cumberland County's newest millionaire sat behind the wheel of her Civic and trembled violently. She'd twice now failed to complete the first simple step of her escape plan; instead of jetting toward the airport, she'd been seized by debilitating anxiety attacks, each of which had run her off the road before second gear had even kicked in. Her second failed attempt had left her propped against a snowy embankment on Georgeville's most rural road, and it was there she now sat.

Trembling.

Violently.

Her regret was colossal, a hundred times more so than the anger that had put her in this unfathomable situation. She'd accepted a million dollars to put Anson in some sort of "isolated, reachable position." *She'd accepted a million dollars to be perhaps an accomplice to murder!* The admission was enough to yank her jaw chestward, shake her head dumbly, and ball her manicured hands into claws. It was all she could do to keep from turning these talons on her own stupid flesh.

She shook her head one last time, then closed her eyes, settled deeply against imitation leather, and took long, deep breaths.

Eventually she opened her eyes.

And tried again.

This time she made it to third gear with only an occasional skeletal shudder, and as the early spring breeze blew the sweat and the self-loathing and the random tear or two from her face, she was buoyed by the conservative conviction that she was going to get out of here and that eventually she would forgive the minor role she had played in the inevitable murder of a rather nasty man.

She paralleled the quarter mile that called itself Simsbury, but never glanced its way. Which was probably a good thing for her state of mind, for the campus loomed as tall, dark, and deadly as the man who had made her both rich and guilty.

Finally finding fourth gear, Cumberland County's newest millionaire rolled up the window, stepped on the gas, and headed for Portland.

CHAPTER SIXTY-SIX

Saturday, May 30

11:32 A.M.

For the third straight year, Graduation Day had dawned gorgeous and pledged to stay that way. The air crackled crisp, the sky beamed sunny, and a light breeze toyed with treetops and three hundred and forty-three tassels. Friends and family agreed that the day was perfect, fittingly so.

The Alumni Parade had ended moments before, with the annual reading from the oldest living alum, a man whose years numbered one hundred and six. The uniformed members of the Old Guard now stood solemnly behind President Edison T. Carlisle, who was beginning to read the names of the graduates.

"Tonya Abbot . . ."

The majority of students were ridiculously hungover. Some hadn't even slept. Still, they'd all managed to line up, alphabetically, in their caps and gowns by 9:00 A.M. The processional had been a sweaty, shaky nightmare, but now the graduates were seated mercifully in their metal folding chairs, in twelve long rows, facing the steps of the Hendrigan Art Museum. Four years of all-night cram sessions, six-inch stacks of index cards, and thirty-two-page term papers had culminated in one final task, which required them merely to stay awake until their names were called, at which point the next wild rumpus would start.

In the sixth row, cap pulled low over his eyes, candidate for Bachelor of Arts degree Mark Morningstar Jessy sat with his head cocked and tilted slightly upward, a mannerism no doubt learned from his six-month-old puppy. His hands were folded. His knee bounced impatiently, waiting for the official end to a liberal arts education.

"Demetrius Brown . . . Susan Browning . . ."

Mark turned in his seat and scanned the crowd of sunglassed onlookers, searching for Kiko. He hoped his uncle had made it to the ceremony. Kiko had called the night before, asking for—of all things—directions to Georgeville. As a graduation present to his nephew, he'd not only learned to drive, but even traded a fistful of dollars for a fifth-hand truck whose maiden voyage would carry him to Simsbury College, so that the first-ever college graduation of a Jessy would be properly commemorated.

Mark didn't see him in the crowd, but that didn't alarm him, because the only crowds Kiko felt comfortable around were those of fish. He was probably hanging out behind a tree somewhere, watching from a distance. Mark turned back around and lent as much interest as he could to the ceremony.

"Monica Canavan . . ."

The proceedings were dragging, but he knew it could

have been worse. He could have been hungover. Then again, it was impossible to be hungover without having partied, and it was hard to party by oneself.

He was alone a lot these days.

"Petra Dennison . . ."

Of course, he was alone by choice; he no longer had the heart for companionship. That he had stuck it out *this* long was a miracle in and of itself.

"Joohi Joshi . . ."

He'd gone home for spring break after Fairchild's death, determined never to return. However, after a miserable week of floating on his surfboard in near-freezing water, he'd realized he had no choice. He *had* to go back; without a college diploma he'd end up hauling nets for the rest of his life. He returned to Simsbury at the conclusion of break, but not before divorcing himself emotionally from everything that had to do with the college.

"Carolyn Egan . . . Jeanette Estridge . . ."

Upon returning, of course, he found the campus in even greater upheaval than when he'd left. The dean had been murdered. Sodomized and beaten to death with a heavy, blunt object. An all-out murder investigation had been launched, initiated by Georgeville's police chief and eventually presided over by the FBI, who had apparently decided enough was enough, and sent some agents to the campus to stem the bleeding.

"Tamara Gregory, summa cum laude . . ."

One of the Feds, in fact, had tried to question Mark, noting that he and the dean had spent quite a bit of time together in the weeks before Templeton's death, and maybe he could help shed some light on the dean's comings and goings, perhaps his state of mind? And did Mark

know anything about an armed man posing as a U.S. marshal to bona fide marshals on the night of March 10? And
did Mark know of any possible connection between these
two events?

Mark had looked the guy right in the eye and told him,
for the record, to fuck off.

"Brenda Gullickson . . ."

A full-scale investigation had turned up nothing (as the
press had so lewdly reported, the extraction of semen
from Templeton's rectum had failed to turn up a legiti-
mate suspect, other than a half-blind sculptor who sponsored his peaceful dream through regular deposits to area
sperm banks), save for the possibility that Health professor Linda Regis's sudden disappearance (missing since at
least the Friday before spring break) might be linked to
Templeton's death. An international manhunt had begun
for Regis, and she'd remained at large through April. She
had even been featured on *America's Most Wanted*.

"Luanne Harris, cum laude . . ."

During the first week in May, the top half of Linda
Regis's stabbed and strangled body had gotten snarled in
the hand lines of a Jamaican fisherman. Her remains had
been examined, her last days pored over, and investigators had surmised, through vague discussions with
Regis's friends and family, that she must have been killed
by the guy she'd been seeing, a guy whom no one had
met, whose name no one knew, with whom Linda had apparently up and run off to Jamaica. A new search had
begun for *her* killer. Both her death and Templeton's, it
was eventually concluded, had been the unrelated results
of secret affairs with violent lovers.

"Jill Herrick, cum laude . . ."

Amid these made-for-TV murders, the deaths of Chad Ewing and Dave Fairchild had been relatively forgotten by the stunned majority of the student body.

Madame Rumor had nothing on the national media.

"Micheline Hollander, magna cum laude . . ."

At the height of all the fuss and speculation, the Sigma Delta Phi fraternity house had been quietly shut down, per unanimous vote of the Board of Directors, who had somehow found time to vote between the many memorial services. Scattering the brothers like dandelion fuzz to independent dorms, the college had seized control of Sigma's physical premises, and the Board had made immediate plans to convert the tainted mansion into a more noble structure.

"Brendan Hunter . . ."

Mark had heard whispers, just the other day, in fact, that Sigma was still conducting brotherhood activities "underground." He barely had an ear for such murmurs, however. He just didn't care anymore.

About anything.

"Lynnette Ibernesser . . ."

Despite the rampant morbidity with which spring break had begun, only two students had failed to return to Simsbury after the two-week spell: Michael "Ran" Robinson and Anthony James Dominic. Both, it was widely held, had snapped after Fairchild's death. Ran, it was rumored, had taken up landscaping with his brother in Maryland. Dominic, presumably, had returned full-time to the Marines.

"Karen Innis . . ."

Elliot Segal had told Mark that the whole sordid mess had dealt a heavy blow to the college's funding as well as its prestige. Of the five hundred and fifty students who'd been accepted to Simsbury for the upcoming year, only one hundred and thirty-six had sent in their housing deposits. The Admissions Department was now considering admitting *all* high school seniors who'd been wait-listed, as well as a handful who'd been previously rejected.

"Curtis Jackey, magna cum laude . . ."

Mark had rejoined the lacrosse team immediately after spring break and had broken the college scoring record during the first quarter of a meaningless game against Boston College. The team had finished nine and five, a couple of wins away from NCAA tournament consideration.

"Shawn Jakes, summa cum laude . . ."

The sound of the most beautiful name in the world grabbed Mark by the chin and snapped his face and attention toward the Hendrigan steps. He watched with mixed emotions as Shawn strode to the podium to accept her diploma, her gilded hair wisping around her cap. She smiled brightly as she shook President Carlisle's hand, and Mark noted with all-over dryness that she was looking well.

Their relationship had ended, for all intents and purposes, the moment Fairchild's dead body was laid in the snow. The feelings had still been there, and still were—perhaps more than ever in physical absence. However, together they'd done something unforgivable; or at least *he* had.

He had used the law to kill.

And Shawn had helped.

And so he had ignored her many attempts to see him, then her countless phone calls. Finally, their relationship had been reduced to strained, passing "hellos" on the quad.

His gut told him he'd someday look back and kick his own ass for willingly punting away what might have been the love of his life. But these days, without a life he felt like claiming, it seemed pointless to try to keep love in it.

And so, finally, the four-year journey was coming to an end. Looking around now, he retrospectively viewed Simsbury College not as he had once thought he would. Not as a haven for the liberal and artsy. Not as an arena in which to display skills. Not as a place to find friendship and family and love. But a realm of deception, where money begat money, and realism—rather than idealism—ruled. He was moments from graduating, and he knew he wouldn't shed a single tear of nostalgia, not ever! He wouldn't throw his cap, nor would he stick around to mug for random, phony photos.

Rather, he'd grab that piece of sheepskin and head for a better world.

"Mark Jessy . . ."

He worked his way toward the podium, ignoring the smattering of golf claps that greeted the announcement of his name. He shook hands with Carlisle, and as he accepted his diploma he made brief eye contact with the president, who offered him a boyish smile and wink. Mark managed a slight mouth twitch, gripped the diploma tightly, and returned to his seat.

When Carlisle had finished reading off the names, he issued a final thank-you to the graduating seniors. This would be his final graduation, he announced, and he would always hold a special place in his heart for this particular class.

A blessing was blurted, and then the ceremony was over. Caps soared, cameras blazed, champagne bottles exploded, and students mauled each other.

Mark made a quick exit. He ducked through the celebration, disregarding the foreign sounds of family, searching for the man with the five-bill pickup truck that would haul his ass home.

Scanning the crowd, his gaze settled on an attractive woman who stood alone beside one of the many quad statues, one hand on her hip, the other shielding her eyes from the sun. There was something familiar about her, and he slowed his walk as he blocked out the periphery and focused on her. His first assumption was that she was a professor he'd never had, but had seen from time to time on this too-small campus. But then he reasoned that a professor, on graduation day, would be surrounded by grateful pupils and parents. And the slower he walked, and the more he stared, the more he realized that the pretty eyes beneath the hand shield were staring right back, oblivious to the other three hundred and forty-three graduates. This woman was *connecting* with him, and he was strangely drawn to her.

"Hello, Mark," she said, when he'd closed to within a communicable distance.

"Hi," he replied.

She switched the positioning of her hands and shifted her weight to her other foot. "You don't remember me, do you."

"Uh . . . I . . ."

"It's okay. We never met. Not in person, anyway. You may have seen me once, right here, on a gray day, but there's no way we could have spoken. I was busy learning how to grieve." A shadow of sadness came across her face, then perished in the daylight. "We *have* spoken on the phone, though. Do you recognize my voice?"

Mark opened his mouth, then closed it. He shook his head.

"I'm Carla Ewing. Chad's mother."

Mark felt a stone drop from his throat to his gut, and he swallowed away the sediments. "Oh. Hi."

"Hi."

"Hi."

She removed her hand from her face, squinted at him, and let loose a soft chuckle that trailed off quickly and left her shaking her head. She stared at the ground a moment, then looked up at him. "How are you?"

The automatic response of "Good, how are you" came to his lips, but he bit back this reply and shrugged honestly. "I don't know."

Carla nodded, but said nothing.

"How are *you*?" asked Mark.

The hand returned to her eyes, as if shielding her from the question, from her forthcoming answer, from life in general. "Well," she said honestly, "I know it sounds trite, but a part of me has died, and it's never coming back."

Now it was Mark's turn to give a wordless nod.

Twisting at the pelvis, she looked about the campus that had claimed her only son. She seemed to be damning, with her eyes, the quarter mile that called itself Simsbury, while at the same time forgiving it. Watching her, Mark decided he'd never before seen such an expression so open to interpretation.

"I told myself," she said as she turned back to him, "that I'd *never* come back here. I mean, what's really here for me? Nothing. Just reminders of the phone call, the day, the week, the month that changed my family's life forever." Her face contorted into something singularly ugly. "I *hated* Simsbury, Mark. I hated it with every ounce of my being."

She stared, for a long moment, into the space between them. And as she did, the hate left her face, slowly but steadily. By the time she spoke again, her expression was bright, animated. "But then I remembered . . . that for a short, sweet time, Chad loved this place. I heard it in his voice during our weekly, Sunday-night phone conversations. I saw his smile through the phone, as he told me about *this* party, and *that* girl, and *this* professor, and *that* class. In the end, his passion for Simsbury led him to darken the wrong doorstep, but I can't fault the first five glorious months for what happened in his last few weeks."

She shrugged carelessly. "And that's why I'm here." She spun in a small, tight circle, her eyes on the tops of the building and the steeples and the pines. "I'm here to walk the walkways and lean against the trees. I'm here to sit on the quad and chew blades of grass. I'm here to imagine *this* party, and *that* girl, and *this* professor, and *that* class."

She threw up her arms and let out a soft cry that hinted of both torture and liberation. "I'm here to be with Chad."

Listening to her, watching her stand there, an almost giddy look on her face, Mark was overwhelmed with the sudden urge to hug her. He refrained, however, because he'd known her for about two minutes. Besides, he'd divorced himself emotionally from everything that had to do with Simsbury. He would keep his hugs to himself.

"I'm also here to thank you," she said.

He stared at her a moment, then shook his head. "There's no—"

"Please," she begged, putting up both hands in front of her. "Let me say this." She sniffed, rubbed her nose, and looked down. "You . . . fought your best friends for the honor of a boy you'd never met, and for that you've earned my admiration." She looked up again. "You're a hero, Mark."

Am I? he thought. *Is that what I did?*

"Mark," Carla said softly, as if reading his mind. "You're twenty-two years old. You have a lifetime to live with severity. Go be young and cool and irrationally passionate." She leaned closer and tried to smile. "Go have some fun."

He opened his mouth, then closed it.

He nodded.

She met his nod and matched it, as if approving the completion of one-half of her mission, and telling herself it was okay to continue, to move on to the informal investigation and discovery of the quarter mile her son had loved until it began killing him. She turned and began to walk away, but as she did, Mark felt a sudden loss, as if he, a motherless son, had missed the opportunity to make his *own* connection with this sonless mother. He started after her, then checked himself, and shouted, "Carla!"

She stopped and turned, and once again threw that hand-shield above the eyes she may have passed down to a child she outlived. She looked at him curiously, expectantly, patiently. She waited for the connection.

"He's not alone up there, you know," Mark said. "He's not alone."

Slowly, very slowly, a genuine smile came across her face, and Mark couldn't help but reflect a painful grin of his own. She nodded one last time, then turned and began making her way toward the quad, toward the many walkways and trees and blades of grass, toward discovery of the quarter mile that called itself Simsbury, all of it and more lit by golden sunlight shining through a slit in heaven.

He found Kiko in the shade of an enormous tree.

"Hey, you made it."

"Of course." Kiko beamed. "Have I ever let you down?"

Mark shook his head. "No," he said honestly. "Thanks for coming."

Kiko gave a dismissive wave of his hand. "East winds these days, anyway. Nothing but dogfish around."

Knowing this was Kiko's best attempt at sentimentality, Mark smiled. "Ready?"

Kiko shielded his eyes from the sun that wasn't hitting him. "Are you?"

Mark glanced back quickly at the celebratory scene on the quad, and caught a brief glimpse of his classmates lining up for pictures, chugging champagne, and opening cards from grandparents.

Turning back to Kiko, he bit his lip and nodded. "Let's get out of here."

As they strolled back to his apartment, they talked about simple things. Cod fish and catch limits. Ripped nets and the rising price of diesel fuel. The words were unsophisticated and familiar, having nothing at all to do with the lump in Mark's throat.

When he saw Kiko's truck he whistled. "Gee, that's a real beauty. What color would you say it is?"

"It's green today, because I washed it. Usually it's more of a brown."

"Interesting."

He loaded the truck quickly; he'd packed all his things the night before, and now merely had to shuttle it from apartment to flatbed. He had neither the time nor the heart to drag out his departure, and within thirty minutes the apartment was empty, except for school-issued furniture and the heavy, stale smell of dog damage and beer.

He loaded Casey into the cab, then closed it securely behind her swinging tail, wiped his hands, and walked around the front of the truck to the passenger side.

Kiko was waiting for him. "All set?"

Mark gave a crude glance back at the apartment. "I think so. Key's under the doormat, dog's in the truck. Ready to roll."

Kiko leaned against the passenger door and crossed his arms.

"What's up, man? Getting cold feet? I'll drive if you want."

His uncle just stared at him, an odd expression on his face.

"What is it?"

Kiko hesitated a moment longer, then reached into his back pocket and pulled out a small, balsa wood package. He turned it over in his hand once, then handed it to Mark.

"For me? Aw, Kiko. You being here was enough."

"I know."

"Well, then you shouldn't have."

"I didn't."

Mark frowned. "Who . . . ?"

But even as he asked half the question, he knew the full answer. And for a moment he felt naked, ashamed that after all he'd been through over twenty-two years and three weeks, after holding up pretty well during his intense exchange with Carla Ewing, that a simple surprise could so easily crush his new fuck-the-world facade. He fought weakness for an instant longer, then slumped against the rusted rump of the truck. Closing his eyes, and tilting his head toward the one ray of breeze-blown sunlight that had penetrated the pines, he surrendered to the small package he held like a child's pinkie in his hand.

The package, he knew, was from his father.

He sucked in a gulp of Maine and opened the box.

Beneath the balsa's upper lid, on a pygmy maple leaf, lay a chiseled Mohawk arrowhead, as brown as the box that bore it. Attached to the arrowhead, snaking beneath the leaf, was a tarnished gold chain. Mark worked his trembling fingers into the box, pulled free the necklace, and raised it slowly to eye level. He watched the arrowhead spin randomly for a spell, then returned the necklace to the box, and slipped the box into his pocket.

Then, casually sniffing something away, he lifted his eyes toward the distant sounds of graduation and leaned back against the truck.

"He wanted to be here," said Kiko. "But with everything that's happened . . . with the FBI and all . . . it's just not a safe time—"

"I know," Mark said, returning his focus to the ground. Then he shifted his attention to something distant, on a horizon he couldn't fathom reaching. "Is he still living up north?"

Kiko shuffled over to the truck and joined Mark in his lean. "Yep," he answered in a voice that still couldn't help sounding sad.

"Where."

"Outside Longlac. North of Superior."

Mark nodded, then toed the ground with feigned interest. "What . . . what does he know about . . . me . . . ?"

Silence answered, long and suspenseful, and for a moment Mark thought there'd be no response. He was beginning to wonder why, when Kiko placed a gnarled grip around his wrist and bobbed headlong into view, his eyes, perhaps for the first time ever, looking right into Mark's.

"He knows his son's a hero," he said. Then, leaning forward, he whispered, "And it makes him proud."

Mark shrugged.

"He loves you, Mark. They *both* do."

Mark nodded, then quickly looked away, in time to spy an obese squirrel lumbering toward a garbage bag beside the door to his apartment. "Well," he said lightly with a single handclap. "I'm ready when you are."

He climbed in the passenger seat and threw an arm around Casey, who was engaged in a tugfest with the strawberry air-freshener that dangled from the cracked rearview mirror. He gently worked the cardboard from her fangs and told her they were going home.

Kiko settled into the driver's seat with a sigh and a cheerful "Okay," and on the third try he managed to start the engine.

The truck lurched and wheezed into motion.

As it rumbled down College Street, Mark grudgingly looked to his port side and took in one last eyeful of Simsbury College, the quarter mile where he'd laughed but mostly cried, won but mostly lost.

He shook his head and looked away.

Then he closed his eyes to hide the tears and whispered good-bye.

CHAPTER SIXTY-SEVEN

Friday, October 9

5:04 P.M.

For a pristine and glorious moment, the majestic bluff overlooking Longnook Beach in Truro towered in rare, undisturbed beauty against an imperial Cape Cod sky.

And then the dog appeared.

She was, by beauty's standards, no less gorgeous in her own right, her coat as gold and wispy white as the dune that embraced her. Her tail, once a vibrating little mood nub, now swept side to side with queenly feathers. Her neck, once a tawny thread, now sported a royal mane that covered the rope burns inflicted during the only bad week of her life.

Her name was Casey.

And she was a beach dog now.

She barked once at the joy of it all, then tore down the cliff, to where the ocean shook the earth.

And then her master took her place.

He was considerably less regal looking. His dark hair drooped a tad long. His grisly work clothes bore the spatters and smears of barbed gills and wayward chum. His eyes were the vacant color of shallow water.

A repaired necklace of beads gripped his throat like a noose, one degree tighter than the arrowhead that hid from a retreating autumn sun in the shade of a heartless chest.

Beneath one arm he carried a surfboard.

For he had a decision to make.

The shed of fishing togs left him wetsuited, and submission to downward, duneward gravity left him at the cooler edge of deep-blue violence. He paused a moment to fasten a Velcro leash to his ankle and inhale a deep breath of papery air ever curling at the edges. Then he plunged into the surf and began to paddle.

He duckdived all oncoming rollers and scaled all peaking breakers until he reached an offshore position where deep-bottomed swells merely eased him rhythmically to heights and troughs. Turning, he paralleled the shore, and almost managed October's first empty smile at the shoreward sight of Casey, her beachlong shadow ten times larger and fiercer than she, engaged in a bark-infested game of tag with thundering waves. Then he shivered away the paltry grin and sat up.

And with his feet dipping into the Atlantic, the sinking sun dimming his world of sapphire to one of indigo, Mark Jessy reached into the pocket of his wetsuit and pulled out a coin, which he looked at for a long time before flipping it into the night.

But he never caught it, and never checked its landing. Instead, he watched it slip splashlessly and decisively into a strip of watery brine lit only by a harvest moon.

And wished for strength.

CHAPTER SIXTY-EIGHT

Saturday, October 10

9:04 A.M.

Route 6 westbound was deserted; it was Saturday, and all traffic was on-Cape. A low, milky fog—not unlike the mist that had ruled the morning of his *first* voyage to Simsbury, four years ago—loitered thickly on the side of the road, clinging desperately to trees as sunshine and wind tried to fry it. The easterly breeze made Mark feel better about blowing off work that day. Wind from the east, fishing the least. There'd be no tuna on this day.

As he drove north toward Georgeville, the leaves reddened and the sun broke through, and the hum of the truck's toy engine grew hypnotic. The highway became an expected path as the road signs and Yankee landmarks evolved into walking memories, ankle-deep in dead leaves, just dying to go for a long-awaited ride.

He tightened his grip on the wheel and gritted his teeth as the memories poked their poetic heads through the cab window and whispered with crackly smirks for him to keep his eyes on the road, but to give their poisonous rhymes just due.

Let us inside your poor tortured head.
Let us gambol about, and dance with the dead.

Let us pound on the spot where once beat a heart.
Let us bridge the black space where now and then part.

Let us tickle your skin and swim through your ears.
Let us highlight the past and show you four years.

We dine on the bodies that now lie in dirt.
We pledge to be painful, so get ready to hurt.

And so he let them in, and began to see, and hear, and feel.

He saw a first day's fog settle like hopeful dew on imported beer bottles and wondered if things might have been different had their eventual emptiness led him somewhere other than to great, white, intoxicating power.

He saw a gang of his athletic type walk tall and wreak havoc, and heard their pledge to die and kill, and wondered how he ever could have called those men brothers.

He saw regret through rooftop tears, felt the flank of two best friends, heard their promises, and wondered how a moment of such bonded sincerity had contained so many hollow vows.

He saw a familiar floor smash a naked stranger to pieces, heard the secret reasons why, felt the rush of a deadly game, and wondered who still mourned the slaughter of a kid named Chad Ewing, and why.

He saw the arms of blameful players lay a great lifeless leader on the snow, heard the gasps of ivied horror, felt the guilt he'd lived with every second since, and wondered if the world would ever again see a man so blessed in life die so senseless a death.

He saw something spectacular, beautiful, and real swallow the moonlit space between him and a seaside angel, heard her sweet change of tune over oceanic thunder, felt kissed lips kiss softly back, and wondered if the angel saw, heard, and felt it, too, when the sun set over the nightly water of her new battlefield.

He saw.

He heard.

He felt.

He . . . wondered.

But mostly he hurt, as the memories had promised he would.

2:42 P.M.

The sudden loom of the Simsbury College gates knocked his breath away.

And stopped the truck cold.

For a moment he idled . . . locked eyes with cast-iron power . . . clenched his jaw and tried to imitate the intimidating sneer of the black iron bars. For a moment he actually considered turning around and heading back to Wellfleet.

But the moment, like everything else he knew, eventually died.

And so he touched the beads, pressed his foot to the accelerator, and passed beneath the archway of the gates.

It was then that his heart exploded to life.

For Simsbury was equally alive with the countless colors of college, its buildings and towers, adorned with fresh vines of trademark ivy, stretching as royally as any golden dune into a sky splashed with New England brilliance. Leaves of passionate fire swirled from thinning tree limbs to the incandescent green below and gathered at the feet of sustained prestige. Baggy denim strolled amid tailored khaki, and a healthy autumn puff parted the seas of unbuttoned fashion statements and tossed cardinal ties over shoulders. Faces grooved happily to varying depths of age, as cheeks pulled lips into smiles, and thrown-back heads roared laughter at a lemon sun and rainless wisps of cloud. Arms carried books and bags, and every so often wrapped themselves around a friend, long lost or just seen. Hands clasped and pointed to buddies and caught the occasional Frisbee. A massive banner, suspended above College Street from cooperative pines, read, "Welcome to Homecoming."

Simsbury was so incredibly alive.

It had survived.

And was calling for Mark Jessy to do the same.

He nodded at the possibility as he parked next to a randomly mingling horde of students and alums gathered on the steps of the Student Center.

Then he got out of the truck, and began to walk.

Football was his first giddy thought. There had to be a football game under way. He angled his stroll toward Emmett Lee Stadium, but made sure to take his time.

He passed his freshman dorm and recalled his first-night background swap with Elliot Segal, who was now getting rich at a company named after a stern bear. He passed the Environmental Studies Building and re-called all those hungover mornings when not even un-derwater footage of mating nurse sharks had been enough to keep him awake. He passed the brand-new Linda Regis Memorial Statue, "Dedicated by the Sims-bury Women's Association to Worldwide Awareness of the Plight of Domestic Violence Victims," and recalled a teacher who'd seemed far too vibrant to be a murder victim.

He passed many places.

And recalled their legacies.

Sure enough, the pine-needled parking lot of Emmett Lee Stadium was mobbed with tailgaters. Students chat-ted up alums, husbands kissed wives and asked where the kids were, and the men of the Old Guard regaled each other with blatant exaggerations about the way things used to be. Beer made love to blood, and gave birth to conversation that didn't seem to care that the home team was getting crushed. Little children threw hot dogs at one another beneath the breezy shade of trees and tripped over the excessive length of the sacred red-and-white football jerseys mommy and daddy had just bought for them at the campus bookstore.

Mark managed October's first genuine smile, then ducked inside and watched the game's final two quarters. Predictably, the homecoming game was one-sided, but still well attended, as graduates from seven different decades drank outside and yucked it up. How many times had Mark and his nonfootball buddies gotten blitzed in

the north end zone, telling harmless lies and pointing out
the girls they'd tried to romance the night before? Too
many to remember, but he would try.

The masses began filing out with thirty-three seconds
to go, right after Middlebury hung points fifty-two
through fifty-eight on the scoreboard donated by an alum
who'd certainly envisioned his alma mater posting more
than a mere fifteen points against such a tally; not even
warm sunshine and cold beer could prolong this party. No
matter, for the good times would be taken elsewhere,
probably to Theta Kappa Rho, the first name in fun now
that Sigma was gone.

Mark guessed he'd end up at TKR, but wasn't yet
ready to commit to a nightlong scene. He was still consumed by the sights, sounds, and sensations of this square
mile he'd purged from his mind, so he circled the campus
slowly, like a retired soldier revisiting the scene of some
great battle, stopping here and there, checking things out.
And as he walked, he saw, heard, and felt the simple com-
plexities of a pain-free world he remembered better than
he'd previously thought.

A poetic world of . . . wonder.

Students cuddling in twos, and huddling in fours,
Kissing and hugging and damning all wars.

Anthology sonnets and speaker-cast songs,
The world's wrinkle-free future sorting rights from
the wrongs.

Hand slaps and hacky-sacks, and meetings on
mountain bike,

*And who does that fox sitting alone by the fountain
like.*

*Jocks wearing sandals, hippies with charge cards,
Guys statured like jockeys, and girls built like nose-
guards.*

*Clusters and pine trees and wind gusts and beer,
Walkways and chitchat and nothing to fear.*

*Laughter and smiles, don't be set in your ways,
For these are the good times, these are the days.*

In the midst of investigation and rediscovery, Mark
was suddenly compelled to do something young and cool
and irrationally passionate, as he'd once been urged to do
by the lively mother of a dead boy. Turning, he jogged to
the Student Center, bounded up the steps, and disappeared inside.

Five minutes later, he emerged, holding a small white
bag.

He stopped on the top step and once again looked out
across this beautiful world, the running, walking, and sitting forms that defined it losing definition to the sinking
sun.

He cut diagonally across the quad, toward the library
and the small crowd that clotted around a thin young tree,
bowed but stubbornly unbroken in the late-afternoon
breeze.

He slowed as he approached.

On the ground, set in wood chips covering the roots,
was a plaque:

This tree is dedicated to the memory of David Troy Fairchild, who every day gave his all in the pursuit of academic, athletic, and social excellence, and did so with a touch of class. We miss you. Love, your family and friends.

Reaching out with a hand that couldn't resist, he ran fingers across the young wooden skin, and as he did he noticed the letters carved halfway up the slender trunk.

"We love you, Beta."

Forgive me.

Mark turned from the tree.

And began to run.

He curled around the last turn in the winding, branching path that connected the ivy-veined dorms and buildings to each other, bounded across College Street, and looked up.

And there it was.

The former Sigma Delta Phi fraternity house still sprawled mightily against the dimming sky, its sheer mass shadowing the impeccable landscape of the largest nonquad lawn on campus. The house had survived wars, fires, sanctions, and death. It was timeless in its magnificence, built by men who took pride in their craft, and thus built to last.

There was something different, though. It wasn't just the new gray paint job or the noticeable absence of the Greek letters that had once hung proudly from the balcony. And it wasn't the young, sprouting tree (Chad Ewing, could it be that we also remember *you*?), or the nonathletic aristocrats who lingered like grandparents of kinder, gentler boys on the lawn.

The simple truth was that the house no longer looked powerful.

It merely looked big.

And that was all.

Walking closer, Mark spotted a placard on the front porch.

Welcome Alumni. Come inside and see the newest addition to our campus, the Anson J. Templeton Memorial Gay and Lesbian Studies Building.

I'll be damned, thought Mark.

He shoved his hands into his pockets and walked slowly across the lawn, looking up and remembering a house that had once fulfilled his dream of family, but that had ultimately threatened to kill him.

Now this big, brotherless house was simply a part of his past.

On the roof, a flash of brown against a pumpkin sky caught his eye. Brown hair. A head. And Mark knew exactly whose, for he was suddenly remembering, in the form of drunken, sophomore words, that this was Homecoming, and the roof was their spot, and they'd party like rock stars, and they'd remember it all.

One by one, the memories released their own private poisons, and the death, guilt, and pain floated away like balloons from a nine-year-old child, over and above the lawn and the trees and the alternative music and the polite talk of income. Now free and dovelike, the memories whispered from high into Mark's ear again, in a three-dimensional, motherly, fatherly, best-friendly voice he'd miss only if he forgot, and betray only if he gave up.

Our son and my friend, no sin to forgive.
Not now, never was, so walk tall and live.

He opened the small white bag, pulled out the post-card, and stared at its polish. The Simsbury steeple, spearing a sky of limitless potential, its face frozen in a single chronological moment, as if waiting for someone to catch up with it.

Mark nodded one last time at the photo, then began catching up.

He reached back into the bag, pulled out a pen and turned the postcard over. Then he knelt to the lawn, and using his thigh for support, he addressed eight simple words to a seaside angel.

I miss you . . . do you miss me back?

Finished, he jogged across the lawn to a mailbox that waited to accumulate and send. He pulled the singular stamp out of the small white bag and applied it to the postcard. Then he dropped his message into the box, took a deep breath, and turned back to the roof.

He broke into a trot.

On Monday, he'd embrace the future. Maybe he'd buy a suit and a power tie and apply for a job. Or maybe he'd fill out those grad school applications and delay his permanent entrance to the real world a few more years.

Or maybe he'd hitch a ride to Cazenovia and kiss a grave that kissed back every day, in every unseen way.

Or maybe he'd tell Kiko how much he wanted to see his father.

Or maybe he'd engage the federal government in one last battle, and race both the U.S. Postal Service and his postcard to the Chesapeake Bay, where he'd tell Shawn Cara Jakes how much he loved her, now, more than ever.

But that would be Monday. Right now, there was still a little Saturday sunlight left, and Monday looked to be about four years away.

Besides, someone was waiting for him.

He jogged around to the rear of the house, grabbed the bottom rung of the fire escape, and with muscles that could still fire a lacrosse ball at blinding speeds, he pulled himself up. He ascended the stairs two at a time, as he'd done before as both hero and outlaw. This time he was neither, just a man who'd come to dance with some ghosts and to finish with a step that would leave his booted kicks rooted in the land of the living.

Reaching the top step, he peered expectantly across the roof.

Ran Robinson sat alone near the old Brotherhood Room window, leaning back on his elbows, holding a beer in his hand.

The two friends exchanged a smile that transcended earthly meaning.

"You remembered."

"I'll never forget."

Mark hoisted himself up on the roof, danced nimbly across the slanted, tricky part, and sat down next to his friend.

And together, they looked out across the campus, drank some beer, and remembered it all.

EPILOGUE

The 201st Year
Saturday, October 10

6:07 P.M.

In the woods surrounding the athletic fields, the joyous sounds of Homecoming faded to a distant, irrelevant murmur. The Maine sky had turned classically purple, cold, forbidding, and beautiful, and a crisp, north breeze warned of winter's proximity.

The wind died suddenly, and near stillness settled on the dark green and purple. Water creatures whisked weightlessly across rain puddles. A night bird called out once.

And then, under the weight of heavy feet, the wooded area came to life. Dried twigs snapped, dead leaves crackled, and prickly-pined branches were shoved aside.

There were twelve of them.

They came from all directions, but shared similar black attire, senior status, and a common disdain for the college administration.

Though they traveled individually, they were accompanied by ghosts.

They hadn't yet convened formally. Instead, they'd communicated through secret, encrypted e-mails, Finally, after nearly six months of planning, they'd been ordered to convene.

So they glanced at one another proudly and silently, as they followed orders and moved toward the Rock.

Where their Leader was waiting.

He was finally satisfied that no federal probe related to last spring's string of tragedies would lead to him, nor to the hundreds of others who made annual fortunes off their brotherly relationship with one another. He wore the sacred black robe, of course, and he held the lantern and Sword, and he was glad that the Feds had stopped their investigation where they had.

Just short of the depth where life after death would have been impossible.

The wind had begun to freshen again, and it tossed the looseness of his robe randomly. The lantern threw his shadow on the dead ground, making him appear larger than he was.

The newcomers gathered around the Leader and knelt reverently to the ground. Twenty-four dedicated eyes watched him and waited.

For a moment, all was powerfully silent.

Then the Leader raised the Sword high overhead, and slammed it down on the Rock.

And the poetry began anew.

Rob Kean attended Bowdoin College in Maine and now lives in Boston. THE PLEDGE is his first novel.